THE CURSE SERVANT

A Division of **Whampa, LLC**
P.O. Box 2160
Reston, VA 20195
Tel/Fax: 800-998-2509
http://curiosityquills.com

© 2015 **J.P. Sloan**
http://jp-sloan.com

Cover Art by **Conzpiracy Digital Arts**
http://www.conzpiracy.co.uk

All rights reserved, including the right to reproduce this book or portions thereof in any form whatsoever. For information about Subsidiary Rights, Bulk Purchases, Live Events, or any other questions - please contact Curiosity Quills Press at info@curiosityquills.com, or visit http://curiosityquills.com

ISBN 978-1-62007-822-8 (ebook)
ISBN 978-1-62007-823-5 (paperback)
ISBN 978-1-62007-824-2 (hardcover)

This book is dedicated to the memory of my mother.

From the tragedy of passing blossoms the promise of new life.

So may it be.

TABLE OF CONTENTS

Chapter One	6
Chapter Two	13
Chapter Three	21
Chapter Four	29
Chapter Five	34
Chapter Six	39
Chapter Seven	53
Chapter Eight	58
Chapter Nine	65
Chapter Ten	75
Chapter Eleven	79
Chapter Twelve	86
Chapter Thirteen	98
Chapter Fourteen	106
Chapter Fifteen	111
Chapter Sixteen	125
Chapter Seventeen	131
Chapter Eighteen	138
Chapter Nineteen	147
Chapter Twenty	162
Chapter Twenty-One	169

Chapter Twenty-Two	175
Chapter Twenty-Three	180
Chapter Twenty-Four	187
Chapter Twenty-Five	200
Chapter Twenty-Six	209
Chapter Twenty-Seven	215
Chapter Twenty-Eight	220
Chapter Twenty-Nine	225
Chapter Thirty	232
Chapter Thirty-One	240
Chapter Thirty-Two	246
Chapter Thirty-Three	254
Chapter Thirty-Four	261
Chapter Thirty-Five	269
Chapter Thirty-Six	276
Chapter Thirty-Seven	286
Chapter Thirty-Eight	292
Chapter Thirty-Nine	298
Acknowledgments	302
About the Author	303
More Books from **Curiosity Quills Press**	305

CHAPTER ONE

I knew this wasn't going to be the typical meeting with Julian Bright when, instead of the usual political organ-grinders at the campaign headquarters, I found a soccer mom duct taped to a chair, foaming at the mouth. Her grunting and growling echoed off the bare sheetrock walls of Julian's office, vacant except for the three of us.

I peeked through the blinds covering the locked storefront to make sure none of volunteers were back from the morning rounds. Satisfied we were alone, I turned to Julian.

He waved his arm at the woman in a lazy circle. "So, this is why I called."

"Who is she?"

"Her name is Amy Mancuso. You know her?"

I shook my head.

"She's a volunteer. Her team was working Cold Spring by Loyola when she started swearing and spitting at the residents. By the time her team captain called me, she'd kicked someone's dog. Terrier, I think. Or one of those purse dogs."

I winced. "Remind me not to hand out yard signs for you. Jesus."

"It's not like we do background checks on volunteers. I figured she probably missed some meds or something."

"But you called me instead of the paramedics."

"Right."

"Why?" I asked as I took a step toward her.

Amy's grunting halted as she straightened in her chair. Her head swiveled slowly in my direction, and her eyes sent the creeping chills up my neck.

With a nerve-rattling tone she growled, "Is that Dorian Lake I smell?"

I'd never enjoyed the sound of my own name less.

Julian turned a shoulder to me and whispered, "That's why."

"Gotcha."

I slowly approached Amy, pulling my pendulum from my jacket pocket in a slow, non-threatening motion. Last thing I needed at that moment was to send a crazy person into a panic. I assumed she was crazy. My pendulum would determine whether she was unnaturally energized or the usual cat-shaving flavor of lunatic.

Her eyes were dilated; her mouth twisted into the most unsettling smile one could imagine on the face of an otherwise average woman.

"Have we met?"

"Poor little Dorian lost his soul."

Okay, this was probably a legitimate problem.

I dangled the pendulum in front of Amy. The little nugget of copper spun from the end of its chain in a perfectly Newtonian fashion. Nothing pulled it contrary to the laws of Nature. I couldn't even feel a tug on the chain.

She continued, "Lost his soul, he lost his soul. Dropped it down a rabbit hole."

"I suppose you think you're being clever?"

"Is he doomed or is he dead? Will he damn your soul instead?"

This conversation had lost all of its charm.

"Who am I talking to?"

She sucked in a huge gulp of air and craned her neck at a painful angle toward the ceiling. A sick squealing noise leaked from her lips as her arms trembled. When she finally released her breath and sank back down into her chair, she simply chuckled.

"We're going to find it, you know. And when we do, we're going to eat it."

I leaned in as close as I dared and whispered, "If you think I'm afraid of you, then you need to know something. I'm not impressed."

"It won't be long now."

"Did someone send you, or is this just a courtesy call?"

She smirked. "We're going to enjoy this."

I was knitting together a clever response when a loud rip of tape crackled through the room. Her hand slammed up underneath my jaw, fingers clamping around my throat. My head filled with blood, and I tried to cough through the gag reflex. The harder I beat on her hand to let go, the wider that creepy smile got.

I was close to blacking out when her palm arched away from my windpipe long enough for me to catch a breath. Her lips pulled back into a thin grimace as her body quaked. I jerked away from her grip, scrambling backward on my hands and feet.

Amy groaned and slumped forward, unconscious. I followed a pair of wires from Amy's back all the way to the Taser gun in Julian's hand.

I rubbed my throat and stood up as he pulled the prongs from Amy's blouse.

"You carry that thing all the time?" I coughed.

"I'm running a campaign in Baltimore City. What do you think?"

"Don't carry anything more lethal than that, do you?"

"Not today."

After catching my breath, I plucked my pendulum off the floor and gave Amy another once-over. "Well, for what it's worth, I don't think she's crazy."

"Is that good news?"

"I think something was trying to make contact."

"With you?"

I nodded. "Yeah. To gloat."

"This business about your soul—"

"Forget about it."

Julian knelt down and checked her breathing. "So, is this over?"

"How am I supposed to know? Not really my scope of practice."

"Well, we have to do something."

"I guess we should just wait and see if she comes to." I snickered. "Interesting."

"What is?"

"I don't think I've ever once run into a legit demon possession before."

"Demon, huh?"

"Well, you can call it a demon. It's as close as our culture comes to describing it."

"What would you call it, then?"

Hell, Julian knew enough about my peculiar vocation. He was ready for this. "The Dark Choir."

"Charming."

"It's what my old mentor used to call the old beings. Older than God, or what we call God."

Julian wrapped the wires of his Taser around its barrel and sighed as he looked down at Amy. "How do we fix this?"

It was a good question, and one I didn't have an answer to. "Holy water and a cross?"

"Well, I can't keep her here."

Amy seemed to be breathing normally. Her breaths weren't as ragged, wheezy, or filled with Hell as they were before Julian shocked the crap out of her.

"Let's give her a minute," I offered. "If she doesn't come out of it, we'll take her to the hospital."

"I'm going to need a story, then. Maybe she had a seizure?"

I leaned against a nearby desk, massaging my throat. "We can't have a normal week for once, can we?"

"Well, it is only Thursday."

"We have plenty of time to screw this up even worse, I guess."

"So, Dorian."

Here it came. I stuffed my hands in my pockets and braced for it. "Yeah?"

"Monday."

"I know."

Julian arched a brow. "Where were you?"

"Philadelphia."

"That's funny because our meeting was supposed to be in Baltimore."

"Look, I got caught up with some research, then I-95 traffic got me."

Julian stepped to the front of the office and peeked through the side of the blinds. "And your phone died, I guess? Because you didn't call."

"It was, like, eleven at night before I realized I boned it. I'm sorry."

I could tell Julian was trying to force a smile, but was failing miserably.

"Dorian, you know I try to work around your schedule. And it was easier before I brought you on salary." He took a long breath. "It's not the first meeting you've missed, either."

"I know."

"You're late. You're distracted. You're pissing off the staff."

"They deserve it."

He paused, then shrugged. "Well, no argument there. But this isn't the best time for you to start checking out on me, Dorian."

"I'll make it up to you."

"This thing with your soul. Is that what's going on with you?"

I snapped, "I said not to worry about that, and I meant it."

Julian blinked and nodded.

I had a good thing going with Julian before I screwed it up. I crafted charms for the Mayor of Baltimore, and Julian paid for it out of his own pocket. Not usually in the Deputy Mayor's job description, but Julian believed in Mayor Sullivan the way most people believed in God. I liked Julian. He was always straight with me, and he always delivered, and he knew just enough about the hermetic arts to keep up in conversation. He had even convinced me to show him a few basics, but he proved unable even to execute the Lesser Banishing Cross, the first, most basic of exercises to clear a space of unwanted energies. The Banishing Cross anchored the practitioner in hermetic space through powerful thought bonds, often invoked as compass "quarters," while filling the area with the individual's personal charge. Julian couldn't find a powerful enough image to connect with, and thus his energy only gushed around him like an unmanned fire hose. I figured his industry was better served in politics.

Then he got the idea of putting me on salary, which would have saved him money and given me some kind of regular income. At the time, it was a clear win-win. But Julian was right; I had been distracted lately. Ever since my botched attempt at outsmarting a weasel soul-monger, my soul had been floating in the dusty crawlspace between the hereafter and the here-and-now. I had to locate it and find a way to shove it back into my meat sack before something else found a use for it. The prospect of serving an eternity at the vicious whim of the Dark Choir was something of a focus-breaker.

Not that Julian fully understood what I was doing on my own time. I'd made an effort to segregate my business with Julian from the Craft. We'd made an arrangement, and I wasn't holding up my end. I was the dick, here.

Amy coughed in her chair. Her feet jerked a little, and she released a pitiful moan.

Julian and I circled her, waiting to see who had the lights on.

"What—happened?"

Julian laid a hand on her shoulder. "You had an attack. You're safe."

Amy opened her eyes and glanced up at Julian. "What?"

"Some kind of fit. A seizure."

She dropped her head slowly and pawed with her free hand at the tape binding her wrist to the chair. Her eyebrows screwed together. "What the hell is going on?"

I nodded to Julian. "I think she's okay now."

He picked at the tape and unwrapped it from her skin. She winced and looked away, her gaze settling on me.

"Do I know you?" she muttered.

"No."

"I think I know you."

"Probably just from the seizure."

She squinted at me as Julian moved to free her other arm. "No. I feel like I know you. Like, I feel some kind of memory."

"A good one, I hope."

"No. Hate. I feel like I should hate you."

It was probably a leftover from her possession, but there was no way I was going to even try to explain that to her.

"I have one of those faces people like to punch."

"I'm sorry. I don't know what's going on. Who are you people? Why am I—"

Julian interrupted with one final tug of the tape, "My name is Julian Bright, Miss Mancuso. You had an episode while canvassing for the Mayor's campaign."

"Yeah, I remember that."

"Well, you got violent and assaulted someone's dog."

"Oh, God."

"Your team captain brought you back here, and you went into a seizure."

"Where is he?"

"Hmm? Oh. I sent him home. I didn't want him… I wanted to spare you the embarrassment."

Amy looked back and forth from me to Julian, her face stiff and guarded.

"I don't feel so good."

"Come on," he said, offering her a hand. "I'll take you to the hospital."

He helped her to her feet, and as they moved to the front door, she kept an eye on me. By the time Julian had unlocked the door and escorted her to the passenger side of his car, she was avoiding my face altogether.

Julian closed the car door and trotted around to the driver side, giving me a pointed look.

"We need to finish this conversation."

I nodded. "Druid Hill, tomorrow night?"

His eyes narrowed. "Let's make it Gordon's, Monday morning."

I shrugged, but it bothered me that Julian wasn't coming to the Club anymore. I met him at the Druid Hill Club, after all. He was one of the last regulars before it nearly went under. Thankfully the Club was on the rebound, thanks in no small part, I liked to imagine, to my renewed patronage. I knew the real reasons were far more complex than that, but the narcissist in me enjoyed co-opting reality from time-to-time.

I watched Julian pull out of his parking space when I heard an engine start. A dark blue Chrysler was parked just across the grassy divide between the campaign office and the chain restaurant next door. The side window rolled up before I could spot the driver. Julian was out onto the main road before the Chrysler jerked out of its parking space and whipped around the rear of the restaurant.

Lovely.

I had grown more or less accustomed to the continuous feeling of the shadows staring down the back of my head. Ever since I'd lost my soul, I'd been plagued with the hungry interest the Dark Choir held for me. But the ephemeral nature of those nagging, little shadows and imp-like phantoms amounted to little more than the panic one feels after waking from a nightmare. They came rapidly and faded. Mystery sedans watching me from across parking lots, however? Not so ephemeral.

My phone rang and broke me out of my cold sweat. It was Edgar Swain, probably the only real friend I had in the world.

"Dorian, you in the city?"

"Close enough. What's up?"

"Got lunch plans?"

I checked my watch. How was it almost noon already? "Not really. Where are you?"

"The Market. I got someone I want you to meet."

Edgar was remarkably well-connected. He was one of the most reliable suppliers of hermetic materials and reagents in the Mid-Atlantic. He was what people in my circle called a Collector, a practitioner who acquired and occasionally re-sold objects of esoteric value. This private collection of Edgar's was rife with cursed objects and other items his wife would rather see dumped into the Chesapeake. That collection also earned him the notice of the Presidium, unfortunately. And that had become something of a cornerstone for our friendship. We were two sorry bastards small enough to operate directly under the Presidium's nose, gambling with their mercurial sense of what is and isn't permissible. It was the business plan of Damocles, but at least we didn't have any competition.

"Sounds good. I'll be there in forty."

CHAPTER TWO

Lexington Market was essentially the nerve center of what locals called "real Baltimore." It had operated continually since just after the founding of the nation, and was about as far from the whitewashed tourist mecca of the Inner Harbor as one could imagine. It was cramped, unsanitary, and reeked of fish. But on a busy day, it thundered with conversation and the odd jazz trio huddled in front of one of the grocery stalls.

I'd made it a point to meet with Edgar every time he managed a trip to Baltimore. Edgar kept poking his nose around the Market, looking for some side-obscured stall with an old school Collector who had managed to avoid the Presidium's all-encompassing attentions. Before 1812, when the Presidium effectively seized power in D.C., Lexington Market was the port-of-call for the European cabals trafficking in any kind of worthwhile hermetic interest. It had been Collector Heaven.

I found Edgar standing in front of his favorite falafel cart. He sported one of his obnoxious floral print shirts. His head bobbed in conversation with a short man wearing a threadbare plaid blazer. The man was mostly bald with the remnants of a ginger mane mixing with silver ringing his ears. His face was wrinkled, his cheeks stubbled in white and red whiskers.

"Dorian, man!" Edgar bellowed as he spotted me. He handed me a foil-wrapped falafel. I never had the heart to tell him I despised the dreck that stall called food. He was such a fan.

"You really shouldn't have," I mumbled as I nodded to Edgar's friend. "Hello."

Edgar announced, "Dorian, I want you to meet Del Carmody."

Carmody squinted up at me and thrust out a hand.

"Dorian Lake? A pleasure, sir." His spoke with a peppery British accent lurking beneath a husky tobacco-ravaged throat warble. "Gone these years, and never met you face-to-face."

"Hi."

"So, you're Emil Desiderio's magnum opus?"

Christ. I always loathed when complete strangers recognized me as a student of Emil Desiderio. It rarely went well for me. Either they fell on the roster of Emil's enemies and counted me an enemy by association, or they were old industry pals of Emil and blamed me for being the reason he effectively dropped off the face of the Earth. At the end of his life, I was Emil's only friend. Admittedly, not a good one.

"You knew Emil?" I tried to keep my tone friendly.

"I did. Complete nipple, that one."

"I'm sorry?"

"Head completely up his arse. Loved him for it, but he was utterly clueless."

"He was pretty focused. I'll give you that."

"Focused? Christ. He was living in fuckin' fairyland. No idea where he was or what he was doing, but the bastard could hex the shit out of a cat's arsehole if he thought it wasn't translating Greek properly. Brilliant suffering bloke."

"You'll probably be disappointed to hear he lost his love for hating things late in life."

"Oh, I know it. Thanks in no small part to yourself, I assume?"

"I have no idea how to answer that."

"Well, I do. And he did. And you are, so pleasure to meet you, mate."

I shook Carmody's hand with a grin. "So what's the business of the day? Are you a Collector, too?"

Edgar sniffled over a bite of falafel. "No, man. Del's pretty much an anything anywhere man. Been in the business a long time."

Del added with a wiggle of his red-and-white brow, "I know where the bodies are buried, one could say."

"Netherwork?" I asked.

"On occasion, though lately there's more money to be had in information. Which brings me to the point of our present acquaintanceship." He spoke the word like a child trying on his father's clothes.

Edgar nudged my arm. "You're gonna love this."

"I'm listening."

Carmody drew me in closer with a jerk of his head. "I hear you have a minor soul problem, vis a vis, it's backstroking somewhere in the Nether."

"You heard that, have you?"

"I hear things, Mister Lake. That's what keeps me in business these days. It's what keeps me alive, and more importantly, drinking. Yeah, I heard all about your little skirmish with Osterhaus. So has any pisser with half an ear to the bedrock."

"What's your point?"

"I know someone."

"You know someone."

Carmody pulled a manila envelope from his jacket and dangled it by his ear. "That's what I said. I know someone with some experience in these matters. Experience you may well find useful."

I gave Edgar a look. He was stuffing the last of the falafel into his face, his eyes steady on Carmody.

"That sounds almost improbably useful to me."

"Probability has nothin' to do with it, mate. It's supply-side hermetics. I got the source, and I just found a buyer."

"What's the price?"

"Not so much a price as a favor."

"You want me to curse someone, don't you?"

His face curled into an amused sneer. "Do I look like Aleister Fucking Crowley to you? Do I look like a tourist? If I wanted to curse a poor bastard, I'd have his balls in a steaming cup of how-do-you-do in time for my afternoon shit. And don't you dare look down on me, mate. I was laying out virgins with your dearly departed mentor while your parents were sniffing mainlines during the Reagan years. So when a person like myself has something you need... not want, need... consider paying him the common fucking courtesy of not rushing to judgment. Right?"

I was liking Carmody less and less by the second, but he had an envelope I desperately needed. It was time to tuck it in.

"I apologize. Didn't mean to—"

"Oh, unclench your arsehole. I was just takin' the piss. Here."

He shoved the envelope into my chest. I took it cautiously, waiting for the inevitable condition to fall onto my head.

"So, no favor then?"

"Well, yeah. Thought I'd be friendly is all. My favor's this. Emil had a book. An old hand-written text from Macedonia, circa 1650's. It's of, how should we say, extraordinary personal value to me."

"Is this the kind of book Emil would keep under lock and key, by any chance?"

"Precisely that kind of book."

I shoved the envelope back at Carmody. He caught it before it fell to the ground.

"Not interested."

"You can't be serious?"

"Look, Carmody—"

"Call me Del."

"Del? I've gone through tremendous personal pains to keep Emil's library out of anyone's hands but my own." I gave Edgar a sidelong glance. "No offense."

Edgar shrugged.

Carmody rubbed the back of his head. "Look. I understand these books are valuable."

"They're dangerous. They're living, breathing little pissed off things. Keeping them locked up behind wards upon wards is about the only responsible thing I do with my life. So, sorry. No deal."

"Would it suit you to know this particular book isn't expressly evil? It represents only the most innocuous of bastardy."

"It's still Netherwork."

"This isn't Lesser Banishing Crosses, I'll grant you. But it's not brain-rape, either."

"I'm not selling."

Carmody glared at me for a tense moment before his eyes eased over to Edgar.

"You were right about this one."

Edgar chuckled, "Told you, man."

"Listen, Lake," Carmody pressed. "I get the sense you're digging your heels out of turn. Consider what I'm offering here. And if it matters, go and find that book and decide for yourself whether it's worth passing up this information."

"I'd love to take you at your word, Carmody. But that hasn't exactly played out in my favor in recent memory."

Carmody grinned and held out envelope. "Here, then. As collateral."

I stared at the envelope. This was bold.

"Just take the fucking thing, would you? Swain vouches for you, and that's good enough for me."

Obligations were always dicey in the esoteric world. I hated owing anyone anything. On the other hand, I really needed that info.

I took the envelope with a quiet exhale.

Carmody circled his finger over the envelope. "Got all the vitals inside. Her name is Quinn Gillette. Lives in Portland. She's thoroughly versed in soul magics. And, what's more important, managed to lose part of her soul and find it again."

Interesting.

"Do tell?"

"Right. Stupid doughnut was making servitors, and lost one. Can you fathom that? Lost a fucking servitor. Bleeder walked off on her."

"Servitor?" Edgar asked with a squint.

"A cognizant thoughtform," I explained. "Usually powered by soul magic, or worse." I turned to Carmody. "How'd she find it?"

Carmody shrugged. "Well, that's worth a phone call, I'd imagine. Meanwhile you see if you can scare up that book for me." He fished a business card from his blazer. It was a blank white card with a phone number scribbled in ink. "Give me a jingle when you decide you're comfortable releasing it into the world."

I pocketed his card and nodded. "I'll do that."

"And that, gents, is all the time I have for socializing today. Edgar? Always a dreadful pleasure."

Edgar wiped his hand on his pants then shook Carmody's.

"And Mister Lake? I dare say Emil would be very proud of you."

"I can't imagine how that could ever be the case."

"Yeah. Me neither. Just putting some lipstick on the pig, so to speak. It's been a gas, gents."

Carmody tipped a couple fingers to his brow and trotted off, slipping between two large women with brown bags.

Edgar nudged my arm. "Falafel's getting cold, man. Doesn't taste right when it's cold."

I tucked the manila envelope under my arm and took a slow, careful bite of my falafel.

Horrid.

"Mmm."

Edgar's grin broke into toothy mischief.

I shook my head. "You know I hate these things?"

"Yeah."

"Then why do you keep buying them for me?"

"I don't know. Keeps you humble."

I tossed the falafel into a nearby trashcan. "You're a dick. You know that, right?"

"But I'm a dick who gets you envelopes."

I nodded. "That was sweet of you. I'm afraid we're going to have to hug."

He shoulder-checked me as we moved back out to Paca Street. "We still on for Saturday?"

"Are you kidding?" I sputtered. "Wren wouldn't let me cancel if an asteroid hit Camden Yards."

It was no joke. Edgar's wife was five-foot-even of psychopathic Orioles fan. And as my house was reasonable walking distance from the Yards, and I didn't mind babysitting their kids while they indulged in an afternoon of beer and baseball, my usefulness to Wren rivaled indoor plumbing.

Edgar gave me quick looks as we weaved through the midday lunch pedestrians.

"What?" I asked.

"You know what you should do? You should invite Ches over."

Christ God Almighty.

"No."

"No?"

"The opposite of yes."

"Why not, man?"

"It would be weird."

"How would it be weird? You just say, 'Good Morning, Ches. My usual coffee flip-o-chino, and oh by the way, I'm having a thing at my house on Saturday, would you like to come?' See? You talk. She listens. Things happen."

"She says no."

"You don't know that."

"Bad thing is that's the not the worst thing that could happen."

"What's the worst thing?"

"She says yes."

Edgar released his chuckle-sigh that usually meant he was annoyed. It was as close as Edgar got to anger, and I learned to respect it.

"It's been a month, Dorian. You mention her at least once every time we get together."

"For the record, you mentioned her this time."

"Don't you think it's about time to put your quarters on the table?"

"What's the rush?"

"What are you afraid of?"

I stopped on the street corner and turned to face Edgar full-on. "Remember how my last relationship went down? Right? The last thing I need in my life is another…"

"Another what?"

I couldn't find a way to say it without sounding like a complete tool. So I said nothing.

Edgar shook his head. "You're going to stop blaming yourself one of these days, right?"

"I know, I know. Carmen was using me."

"There you go."

"But that's my point. You've seen my house. It's not like I hide my profession in there. If I invite Ches over, she's going to look around, and she's going to pick up a thing or two. Oh, what's this? A darquelle? It's shiny. What does it do, again?"

"Most people don't even believe in magic, Dorian. You're making up reasons not to ask her."

"What if she does?"

"That's not it, man. What you're really worried about is what if she says yes? What if she likes you?"

"I'm not afraid of asking her out on a date. Just not to my house."

"You really think Ches is going to turn into another Carmen?"

"Let's just say I'm not desperate enough to find out."

Edgar squinted at me, and I felt like a toddler.

"This isn't your typical Goetic nut-knockery, Dorian. It's dating."

"I'd prefer the nut-knockery. At least it makes sense. There are rules. You do this, you get that. Relationships? It's just so pointlessly complicated."

Edgar laughed. "You're the only person I know who thinks Goetia is less complicated than asking a girl out."

"You don't know many Goetics, do you?"

I never faulted Edgar for trying to convert me into the Way of the One True Relationship. It worked for him, and when most guys recognize a successful formula they try to apply it to everyone else. I wasn't necessarily opposed to the concept of a relationship, either. I just couldn't see how I could keep my personal life and my hermetic life separate.

I was most certainly uninterested in blending them, especially after Carmen. That particular mistake cost me my soul. With any luck at all, however, Quinn Gillette would give me the first real lead on how to get it back.

Chapter Three

When I returned to my two-story brick row house on Amity Street, I headed down the steel-door-secured stairway leading to my basement work space. Moving my hermetic operations into my basement had proven to be a tremendous time-saver. Instead of humping it out to that old mini-storage in Catonsville, all I had to do when I punched the clock was take a flight of stairs and get to work. The downside, necessarily, was that I was effectively shitting where I ate. Esoterically speaking, this wasn't the safest choice. Energies can be subtle, and they build up when one isn't looking. Too much lingering focus, and a practitioner could find himself living with a giant hole in his wards, or worse.

Not to mention Emil's Library. I had inherited my mentor's collection of Netherwork texts shortly after his untimely demise. That wasn't the kind of memory I wanted to conjure up in my living space, so I did my best to ignore them. But, as Carmody reminded me that morning, those books were in demand.

And they were dangerous.

I still kept them in their dark-stained walnut cabinet, now locked away in my basement instead of a cage. I felt their energy as I pulled open the double-doors. A spiral-bound notebook swung on a nail driven into one of the doors. This was as close to an index as Emil had ever managed, and it was a glorious mess of vague descriptions, sidebar notes, and seeming non-sequiturs that made finding an individual book in this cabinet a very specific kind of pain in my ass. Most of the texts were thin bundles of hand-copied verbiage without spines or even cover pages. It could take hours just to figure out if one of the books listed in Emil's notebook was even in the cabinet. After wading through the index, I managed to find an entry that credited an Ottoman-era Bulgarian Gnostic with what Emil had described as "primer curses".

Now all I had to do was find the damn thing. But I was already exhausted, and my patience with the hunt had lost all of its charm. I closed up the cabinet and decided to leave that chore for another day. I turned and took a seat at my work table, instead, to review Carmody's end of the bargain.

I opened Carmody's envelope and slid out a couple sheets of paper. The information was hand-typed on an old-school typewriter; the letters were embossed into the paper. Carmody was definitely a throw-back. His information was concise. A name: Quinn Gillette. A phone number. A post office box in Portland, Oregon. The second sheet was a paragraph that basically summed up what Carmody had already told me.

Gillette specialized in soul magic. There was no information about her training or affiliations. I was aware the West Coast was far more permissive than the East, the Presidium's sphere of control still being roughly geographical. The practitioners in the West enjoyed a more liberal environment to ply their trade. I had managed to keep my practice clean, and until recently avoided unwanted attention from the Presidium. Practitioners less interested in playing Russian roulette with the Presidium tended to hang their shingles elsewhere. Thus, I cornered a bit of the market. That was the plan, anyway.

Gillette, it seemed, had seen fit to create a servitor, or a cognizant thoughtform. Thoughtforms were generally short-lived and limited in their abilities. The more intense the focus and intent, the stronger the thoughtform. But nothing so intangibly rendered could last for very long. Gillette's solution? Soul magic. She had shaved off a shard of her own soul in order to power her servitor. It was old, dark magic. Netherwork. The kind of thing the Presidium black-bagged people for.

Fortunately for Gillette, the Presidium didn't have the resources to police every slice of Netherwork in the Pacific Northwest. Unfortunately for Gillette, her servitor developed a will of its own and went AWOL. This was where her entire misadventure became relevant to my particular predicament. She managed to locate that little shard of soul and incorporate it back into her own. As a man on the hunt for his own soul, I was keenly interested in how she accomplished this feat.

I stepped upstairs to make the phone call. The combination of underground walls and hermetic wards made phone reception next to impossible in my work space. The phone rang four times until it rolled to one of those generic "'insert number here' is not available" voice mail prompts. That was disappointing. I still had no read on her age or personality, so I had no idea how to address her. When the time came to leave a message, I had to think fast.

"Quinn Gillette? My name is Dorian Lake. I was given your name…" I thought twice about implicating Carmody. Volunteering his identity would have been a professional discourtesy. "…regarding soul magic. I have some questions I'd like to ask you when you get a moment." I left her my number, keeping it brief.

And I was left with the rest of my day.

I made a call to order some sandwiches for Saturday, and when I hung up, my phone rang immediately. Oregon area code.

"Hello?"

A smoke-scratched voice answered, "You're Dorian Lake?"

"Gillette?"

"What do you want?"

Charming.

"Yes. If you have some time, I'd like to discuss some matters of a hermetic nature with you."

"I have no idea what you're talking about."

"I'm sorry?"

"You have the wrong person. Goodbye."

"You're not a practitioner?"

"I don't even know what that means."

"Oh. I apologize. I was lead to believe—"

"And if I were, I wouldn't discuss such matters on the phone."

Ah.

"Then… if one were to put down such questions in writing and mail them to Post Office Box 1563, Portland, Oregon?"

After a long silence, she replied, "Because matters of a delicate subject are better put in an easily intercepted envelope?" She sighed loudly into her phone. "I'm between projects right now. If you're in the area on Monday, I'll be available for about an hour at midday."

"I'm afraid I'm nowhere near the area. I'm in Baltimore."

"Then best of luck."

"Wait! I mean, Monday? You can meet face-to-face, is what you're saying?"

"Twelve to one. I'm having lunch at the Green Tree on Columbia. That's west side. Be there or don't, your call."

She hung up.

The entire conversation was unnervingly familiar. Her palpable sense of suspicion, her churlish brevity. It was like talking to Emil.

Two things were clear to me by the time I returned to my work space. The first being that Gillette had made some powerful enemies in her lifetime. Her encompassing paranoia was obviously defensive. She had learned hard lessons in her years of Netherwork, and probably had become increasingly defensive as time progressed.

And the second? I was going to have to book a flight to Portland if I wanted any useful information from Gillette. Last minute plane tickets weren't cheap, and my bank account wasn't as flush as I liked. I had traded the feast-or-famine income of a private hex peddler to the steady-yet-meager income from Julian. It kept the coffee flowing in the mornings, but unexpected expenses weren't as easy to absorb as they once were.

Carmody must have known how uncooperative Gillette would be. Collateral, indeed.

Once again, I was faced with an open day. It was a little late to go to the café. I suspected Ches would still be working, but it would be busy with the lunch rush soon enough, and she wouldn't be able to chat. By the time I envisioned Edgar sitting on my shoulder with a pitchfork urging me to go anyway, I resolved to find some work.

I pulled up my Hit List for the week, the list of business contacts from voice mail and email which I had to pore through every Monday. Here it was Friday, and I had yet to touch it. One benefit to working on salary for Julian was that I could be more discerning in whom I took on for hexes and charms. After weeding out the bitter divorcees and jilted cheaters, I landed on the name Ari Leibnitz. I gave Mr. Leibnitz a call and made a lunch date.

I drove past the café on my way into downtown, and spotted Ches hauling out a serving tray of salads into the outdoor seating. Her curly chestnut hair was pinned up over her ears, and spilled down the back of her head. That was all I really caught before I had to slam on the brakes to keep from bumping into the Cadillac in front of me. I was immeasurably grateful Edgar wasn't there to see that.

The food carts down Baltimore Avenue were belching out the savory fumes of barbeque and Thai and whatever else the brilliant bastards inside those trucks were concocting. Men and women in business suits spilled out of the skyscrapers, rushing into vicious lines for their thirty minute fix, each peeling away with a take-out box of pure guilt and eyeing one another in their secret pact of culinary misgiving. Ari Leibnitz found me as I took a place in the barbeque line. He was a portly fellow, about five-five, with very thick glasses and about the most laughable comb-over I'd seen since London.

"Mister Lake?"

"The one and only. Mr. Leibnitz, I presume?"

He nodded bashfully.

"How did you spot me?" I asked, more than half-interested as I hadn't described myself to him.

"We've met. I didn't say anything on the phone, but we spoke once at an event. In March?"

I vaguely remembered attending a fund-raiser in March for Sullivan to placate Julian. But I was reasonably certain he wasn't high enough on anyone's food chain to merit notice from the Presidium.

"I see. So you need a hex?"

Leibnitz ducked his head and looked side-to-side. "Should we…?"

"Don't sweat it, Mr. Leibnitz. We're not selling state secrets, here." He stood stiffly next to me as I advanced in line. "Lunch is on me. You like pulled pork?"

He gave me an uncomfortable look, and I took the hint. Stepping out of line, I ushered him aside to a shaded ledge of a concrete planter well away from the lunch rush.

"Listen, you need to understand a few things," I began as he dusted off the concrete and took a seat beside me. "What I do is perfectly legal. Most people don't even believe in what I do. Ask the average pencil-pusher in one of these buildings, and they'd tell you you're throwing your money down a rat hole. Snake oil, they'd say. There's no such thing as magic."

"But is there?"

"That's the question, isn't it? You obviously believe in magic. Enough to call me, at least."

"I talked to someone. They mentioned your name."

"Sounds about right. I don't advertise. Everything I do is on referral. Who dropped my name, if you don't mind me asking?"

"I… wouldn't be comfortable with that."

"Fair enough. But you're nervous, and I wanted you to know there's nothing illegal or even unethical in the services I offer."

"How can you say that?"

"Hmm?"

"You hex people."

"Right. I don't suppose you're fully aware of what, exactly, a hex is?"

"A curse?"

"Wrong. That's something totally different. Curses are damage. Pure and simple, they're hatred turned into lasting, permanent damage. And they're powered by dark forces. A hex, on the other hand, is an engineered consequence. You may or may not believe in karma, but I power all of my workings on it. See, I believe there's a Cosmos, and maybe not so much an intelligence, but a sheer force of Nature that governs it. A set of principles. A person lives a life that's selfless and beneficial to the Cosmos, that person gains upon himself a certain… let's call it gravity. A person goes the other way? Let's just say the Cosmos has something in store for that person. So what I do is tap into karmic gravity. If someone does you wrong, I coax the Cosmos into delivering their karma ahead of schedule."

"Do you sell curses as well?"

I squinted. "No."

That was technically accurate. I had never actually sold a Nether Curse. In fact, I had only ever fired one curse in my entire life, and I was damn lucky the Presidium hadn't dropped my body into the Chesapeake Bay for it.

"How do we proceed with this hex, then?" he asked.

"Right. Well, there are ways of doing this. A hex is a consequence. He does A, then B happens in response. And there's an exit strategy. When this person decides to stop hurting you, the hex goes away. It's clean. It's fair. It's legal. And you're not compelled to believe me at all. All you have to do is pay the fee. I do the rest."

Leibnitz released a tense breath and rubbed the folds on the back of his neck.

"That's actually a relief."

"So who's the particular thorn in your side?"

"His name is Jacobs." He left it at that.

"And?"

"He just made partner."

"Lawyer?"

He looked up at the skyscraper behind us. A large bronze plaque spelled "Grey & Lisle" just above the rows of glass doors at street level. I had heard the name before, mostly on sponsor banners at local events. They were one of the big tower firms on the East Coast, but beyond that I knew very little.

"And you were in line to be partner?"

"Oh no. No, I'm just… no."

"Okay?"

"I'm a certified accountant. And as such, I was made privy to certain inaccuracies."

"Inaccuracies? I'm thinking in the whirlwind world of accounting and corporate law those aren't exactly business builders?"

"You'd be surprised. No, these were internal errors. Only, they weren't errors. They were quite intentional, and my purpose is to report these."

"To Mr. Jacobs?"

"No. To the senior partners. It was Jacobs who created the parallel ledger."

"Okay, you lost me."

He waved his hands in front of his face. "Don't worry about the details. If you don't need them, you won't want them."

"Fair enough."

"The point is he defended himself, and won."

"You lost your job?"

"Heavens no. But he made partner shortly after."

"And?"

"And that's it."

Holy crap, this guy was actually gunning for justice. "You just want it brought to light?"

"He's a bad man, Mister Lake. Just trust me. He shouldn't win. He just shouldn't win."

I gave Leibnitz a long look and felt humble. "Sounds like we can do business, Ari."

"Good. What's your price?"

"Five thousand."

"Done. What do you need?"

"Well, I need a piece of Jacobs." He blanched a little. "Don't worry. I mean a piece of his energy. His person. Hair is good. Blood is better." I didn't mention that my typical marital infidelity clients tended to provide semen.

"I think I can do that."

"Great. Call me when you have whatever you have, and I'll arrange a pickup. Something like this can be a one-day turnaround."

Leibnitz seemed almost excited by the time we parted company. The meeting was good for me. I had grown considerably more jaded within my own practice in the past six months. I'd almost forgotten there were people out there who needed real help. And even then, this particular accountant wasn't looking for help or revenge as much as a real sense of justice. It felt like a good hot shower.

Chapter Four

Usually my morning safari for presentable clothes off the floor of my bedroom put me in a rock-chewing mood by the time coffee became reality. Perhaps it was that emotional deliverance, that shining ray of celestial caffeine brought to me each morning at the café that painted Francesca as my saving angel? More likely I was succumbing to my life-long habit of prescribing ideals to otherwise mortal women, but it usually felt somewhat religious.

This morning, however, I wasn't in a foul mood. I wasn't even brooding. The sky was clear. The chill of morning air had yet to melt under the heat of the Mid-Atlantic summer sun, and Ches had her hair up in a ponytail again.

I was still flying a bit from my meeting with Leibnitz the day before. This was more than simple comfort with my practice. This felt righteous. I had a solid lead on finding a way to reacquire my soul, at least as solid as I had seen in the past half-year. Not to mention the party on Saturday. Aside from the ever-present sense of impending doom that usually haunted the periphery of my consciousness, it was a pretty good morning.

Ches eyed me from inside the café as I took my usual seat out underneath the canvas awning, tipping my feet up on the black wrought-iron balusters separating the eating area from the sidewalk. She emerged from the café with my usual, a large cup of Americano with a tiny pot of half-and-half. She shook her head with a grin.

"You look chipper this morning," she chimed as she set my coffee down on the iron table.

"I had a good week."

She sighed and leaned against the aluminum pole holding up this side of the awning. "I'm jealous."

"Problems?"

"My brother."

"Again?"

"Yeah. I know, I know. He's going to lose his kids if he doesn't do something."

About a week ago, Ches started opening up details of her family life when it was just me and her in the mornings. Her life was like a primer in vetting hexcraft customers. I had almost a dozen ways mapped out in my head to keep her brother from losing his kids in the divorce. But I wasn't going to bring it up at the café. It was my Holy of Holies, and I wasn't going to drag the Life inside.

"But that's him, right? I mean, you're doing okay."

She shrugged. "I suppose. Fall semester is going to make my budget suck out loud. Not looking forward to that."

"Cutting your hours?"

"Still working mornings, though," she muttered, her eyebrow lifting ever so slightly.

My heart slapped a quick beat against my sternum. I knew that comment was directed at me. She was dropping hints lately that she could be interested in something beyond our usual morning coffee small talk. I was getting really bad at pretending not to notice.

It could have been the coffee, which was extra strong that morning. It could have been the sunshine, or my unusual optimism of the moment. Hell, it could have been some kind of alignment of Venus and Jupiter. Whatever it was, I started talking without thinking.

"I'm having a party Saturday after the game. Some friends of mine are coming over. I'm going to cook something I'll pretend is a family recipe, and they're going to pretend they like it."

She grinned. "You have friends?"

"Baffling as it may sound. So, anyway, here's the part where I stumble over myself trying to invite you to come over while looking cool and disaffected."

"Disaffected?"

"You know. Aloof? Manly?"

"I don't think that's what disaffected means."

"Oh?"

"I think it means pissed off and dissatisfied."

"Ah. Not exactly what I was going for."

She crossed her arms and shot me a sharp grin. "How about smarmy and disingenuous? Because you pretty much got that nailed."

"You coming or not?"

"Yes. Yes, I am."

"Well, you could have just said so." I took a long sip of coffee and wondered what was wrong with me. "If I could possibly be more awkward, you'll let me know. Right?"

"What time?"

"Oh, any time." Ugh. Any time? "I mean, I'll be home all day, but everyone else will be coming over after the game. It's kind of hard to tell when baseball games end, from what I gather."

"Okay. Well, I'm just going to go with six o'clock. That work?"

"Sure."

"And home is?"

"Hmm?"

She snickered. "Your address?"

I sat for an uncomfortable moment, my jaw unwilling to move. I had avoided this particular collision of my professional and private lives to date. It took effort to will the words into sound.

"Ten twenty-four Amity Street. It's just around the corner."

Someone inside the café barked at her, and she pulled herself away from the pole with a sniffle.

"It's a date."

Ches stepped inside, leaving my bewildered face mug-deep in coffee. It was. It was totally a date. How did this even happen?

I mumbled, "Fine, Edgar. We'll play it your way," before unfolding the paper and trying to ground myself again.

A brown envelope slipped out onto my lap. I jostled my coffee, managing not to spill it all over my khakis. The envelope had no address. It was blank, light, simply bound by one of those string-and-wheel gizmos that were all the rage with the Baby Boomers. I felt the envelope for any strange lumps or devices, and once I was satisfied the only danger its contents posed were in the form of paper, I unwound the string and opened it.

Within the envelope I found five glossy photos of Julian and myself guiding a disheveled and panicky Amy Mancuso to his car.

What was this, a warning? I remembered the blue Chrysler that sped away from the adjoining parking lot. It must have been a private investigator, possibly one of Sooner's political gravediggers. The election season was just gaining real speed. The yard signs and billboards were already up. The first of the television ads would be airing soon. And as much as Sooner liked to bill himself as a responsible alternative to Sullivan, a man free of political entrenchment… he was, in truth, the puppet of Joey McHenry.

I had dealt with McHenry once before, and I was very certain he didn't relish that particular experience. Nevertheless, he was an industry magnate. I was a hermetic practitioner. In any fair scheme of things, our two worlds shouldn't have ever intersected. But they had. They intersected in the person of Julian Bright.

I thumbed through the photos, trying to keep them well hidden in my lap. They were clear. Our faces were clear, at any rate. As was Ms. Mancuso's expression of fear and confusion. If these photos were removed from any sensible context, they could prove devastating to Sullivan's reelection campaign. Questions would be asked, and we didn't have any real answers. Sullivan would have to ask Julian who I was. I had met the Mayor once before, but I was positive he wouldn't remember me. For all he knew, I was a grass-roots organizer, whatever that meant. Being a devout Catholic, Sullivan wouldn't hear "hex crafter" and "payroll" in the same sentence with any kind of joy. Julian would have to come clean, and it would cost him his job. It would be embarrassing for me, but nothing I couldn't overcome. No, this wasn't meant for me. This was meant for Julian.

So why was it slipped into my morning paper?

"Can I bring anything?"

I sucked in a breath and slid the sports section over the envelope as Ches rounded my shoulder.

"I'm good," I replied waving my coffee in front of my face.

"No, I mean your party. Do you want me to bring anything?"

"Nah. I've got it covered. Family recipe, remember?"

She put a hand on my shoulder and stood there, looking at it. It was the first time she had ever actually touched me.

"I'll have you know I'm completely rearranging my social calendar for this, so your family recipe had better be dynamite."

"You have a social calendar?"

"Yeah. It's a Post-it on my fridge that says 'Get a Life.'"

I tried to laugh, but my mind was on the photos in my lap.

And I was having such a good morning.

CHAPTER FIVE

I tried to call Julian when I got home, but his voice mail announced he had taken a day trip to North Carolina with the Mayor. I left a simple "It's Dorian; call me" message and leaned back in my chair at the roll top desk overlooking Amity. I had to make a decision, and quickly. Less for Julian's benefit, but more for the virtue that I was letting politics derail my search for my soul.

Or was it the other way around?

I knew how Julian would answer that question. I needed to reevaluate my priorities. The steady income was nice. Unspeakably nice. I had taken care of substantial unfinished business in my personal and professional life thanks to Julian's monthly checks. I'd cleared my debts. I'd installed the steel door to my basement. I'd even managed to fully update the rental properties that had gone neglected for far too long. My tenants seemed happy, especially Abraham Carter, my superintendent. When old Abe stopped showing up at my stoop with his hat in his hand about some damned busted air unit or a leaking gutter, I knew I had finally achieved the level of passably acceptable landlord.

But the constant demand for my attention was draining. I had a soul to find, damn it. And when I managed to carve out some time to look for it, I received an earful of shit from Julian about it. I really wanted to like Julian, and the money was making that harder and harder every week.

Just as I was about to give up and pour myself some wine, my phone rang. Private number.

"Hello?"

A deep, resonant man's voice stated, "You received my photos."

Aha. "I did."

"Good."

"I take it you're my friend in the blue Chrysler?" I knew a power play when I felt it. I tried to knock this fellow off his stride before he got too much momentum.

"What? No."

Oh well. It was worth a shot. "What do you want from me? These photos don't mean anything."

"To you, maybe. To the Deputy Mayor? The Mayor? I think you know what these photos could do if they go to press."

"I do."

The man sighed. "Which is why I sent them to you instead."

"Come again?"

"I want to meet. In public."

I wasn't sure if I was quite ready for a Deep Throat scenario with a man I didn't know, but ignoring this was clearly a more dangerous option. "Where and when?"

"Inner harbor, by the aquarium. In a half-hour?"

I quipped, "Well, I'll have to cancel my tea with the Daughters of the Revolution."

"I'm trying to help you, Dorian."

I took a seat at my kitchen table. "Do I know you?"

"Just meet me."

"How will I recognize you?"

"I'll recognize you."

He hung up.

The Inner Harbor was close enough to walk, and it was a nice enough day. Finding parking would have been a bigger time sink than hoofing it the twenty-some-odd blocks into downtown, so I just grabbed my sunglasses and got to walking.

I made the Inner Harbor in twenty-five minutes, and found a planter next to the stanchions marking the ticket line for the aquarium. A middle-aged, black man in blue shirt-sleeves approached me, his eyes moving everywhere as he walked. He seemed vaguely familiar, the fact of which granted me a modicum of relief.

"Dorian. We meet again."

He held out his hand, and I shook it briskly.

"Yeah. See, thing is—"

"You don't remember me. That's okay. It's been a long time."

I had this trouble with clients now and then. They'd remember me, but I would lose their name in the sea of faces I'd done business with over the years. Considering the circumstances, I put a bit more effort in remembering this one.

"I want to say… Cedric?"

"Cecil."

He pronounced it SESS-ul, without a hint of pretentiousness. And it started to click. He had been a client of mine, one of my early clients back when I had just returned to the States from England. I remembered his was a basic vindictive ex-wife taking him to the cleaners scenario. She had more karma coming to her than the person who invented telemarketing. The job was cake.

"Right. Cecil Rawls?"

He nodded and urged me away from the planter with his elbow. "Let's keep moving."

"How are things? I mean, aside from taking surreptitious photos of my clients."

"I didn't take the photos, Dorian. They were given to me to publish."

"Small relief, I suppose." I stiffened my spine. "Wait, did you say publish?"

"I work for The Sun. I'm the Editorial Assistant for the Baltimore City government reporter."

"Look at you!"

"These were dropped onto my desk by an individual I won't admit to knowing personally, nor am I willing to discuss his identity."

"Understood."

"I recognized your face. And knowing what I know about who gave me these photos to pass along, I knew they needed to land in the right hands."

"Thanks for that. Seriously. That was pretty incredible of you."

"Well, don't thank me yet. We both know the odds that those photos exist on a hard drive somewhere."

"I suppose you're right. So, not to sound like a colossal dick here, but what was the point then?"

He sighed and turned us toward a brick walkway leading to the piers of sailboats stretching out into the harbor alongside a series of chain restaurants.

"You work for the Mayor."

"Not exactly."

"Still, you're clearly involved with the Deputy Mayor here. Everyone in the city desk knows Julian Bright is a play-maker. These photos? It's just a political gadget play. The whole point is to catch the other side off-guard, put them on the defense, and start pushing for yards while they burn one news cycle after another trying to craft a statement."

"You didn't play football in college by any chance, did you?"

"You get these into Bright's hands, and he'll position the Mayor such that he won't lose ground. Better yet, he could parlay this into a win. If they're ready for it. Do you see what I'm saying? It won't matter who has these photos."

I had to give Cecil credit. The man was deeply immersed in the political world, and it showed. Unfortunately for Cecil, he wasn't fully aware of the peculiar dynamic between Julian and Sullivan. Namely, Sullivan would can his ass in a heartbeat if he admitted hiring a person in my line of work.

"What if it's more complicated than that? What if there is no way to parlay this into a win?"

Cecil shrugged. "You have skills, Dorian. I've seen them. I've benefitted from them. As has the Mayor if I may be so bold. His approvals are sky high. They were, anyway, before Sooner got in the game. I know a man like you could change the rules if he needed to."

He was right. I had been changing the rules. In fact, I had more skills than when I first decided to hang my shingle in Baltimore. Netherwork wasn't a real option for me. But if I wanted it to be an option, I had Emil's Library. And the Presidium knew that, which was why I really, really had to watch my ass.

"I'll be sure this gets into Julian's hands, Cecil."

He lingered for a moment, still scanning the brick walkway in front and behind us.

"Is there something else?"

"Everyone knows Sooner is bankrolled by Joey McHenry."

"Right."

"I wanted to bring you here today for a reason." He stepped ahead a few paces and held out his hand over the water. Across the inlet stood a series of glass and sandstone-painted concrete condominiums towering over the adjacent buildings. "Harborside Towers, courtesy of McHenry Construction."

"Yeah?"

"I grew up in Federal Hill, Dorian. Just behind those towers. I went to school in an old, decaying building just across the water, there. Least it was before it was leveled to build these monstrosities. Before they leveled the house I grew up in. Or the corner bar where my father met my mother. Or the grocery store where he was gunned down." He sighed. "A lifetime of memories, Dorian. A legacy. All torn down to let rich people move in and the poor people move out."

I looked up at the condos. I had always admired them. They looked clean. Glass, concrete, stucco, palm trees out front. Iron bars painted beige, separating the driveway from Key Parkway and the rest of Federal Hill. It was as far from the red brick row houses of Baltimore as any man could conceive. I had never really thought about it, but to anyone who had grown up here, those towers had to look alien.

"This is personal, huh?"

"When McHenry says he wants to clean up Baltimore, I want you to set aside the rhetoric and the money. I want you to hear what he's really saying. What is he really trying to clear out? Who is he clearing out?"

Cecil gave me a lot to think about. I wasn't sure why he was pitching this all to me at that moment, but it was pretty compelling.

"Well, you don't have to convince me not to vote for Sooner."

His shoulders wilted a little. "I'm just trying to broaden your vision."

"And I appreciate it. Really."

Cecil held out his hand once more. "It was good seeing you again."

"You too. Everything work out for you since last time?"

"Oh yes. Remarried. Three kids. All girls."

"Wow."

"I love my work. I'm living. And I don't know how much of this would have been possible without you."

"What can I say? You get what you pay for."

He chuckled and gave my shoulder a tap with his knuckles before stepping quickly back up the brick steps to the street.

Cecil Rawls, editorial assistant to some asshole at The Sun. Married with three daughters. And a dozen years after hiring some jerk selling him a hex against his ex-wife, he's in a position to change city politics. Hopefully for the better.

Hopefully for the better? That had been my professional credo since Emil died. It wasn't every day I was given concrete evidence that I was changing people for the better. Yeah. It was a good day.

Chapter Six

The next morning I still hadn't reached Julian on his phone. I left a series of "it's Dorian; seriously, call me" messages and decided to focus on the more terrifying part of my weekend. The date. Well, it was kind of a date. It was her and I and the entire Swain clan, and we were all going to be in my house.

That was the scariest part. Ches was going to be in my house.

By the time Edgar and Wren dropped off their kids before heading over to the Yards, I had retrieved the sandwiches from the corner deli, removed as much of the esoteric bric-a-brac as I could from the first floor, and started working on Aunt Viv's cassoulet.

The Swain kids settled into the house without much fuss. The younger, Edgar Swain Jr., gave me a seven-year-old bro hug before hunkering down on my couch with some kind of electronic distraction machine. Elle, his thirteen-year-old sister, stayed at my elbow as I started layering the beans and spinach in a casserole dish. Her mouth kept moving. I mean, it never stopped. It was clear she was trying to impress me. She had been nursing a minor crush on me for a year, now. I honestly had no idea how to deal with that beyond putting her to work cutting onions.

She stood behind the island in my kitchen, chopping a yellow onion with the delicacy of a Visigoth.

"My Mom's going to murder you."

"Why, this time?"

"I'm not supposed to use knives."

"Still got ten fingers?"

"Yeah."

"Keep up the good work."

Elle waved her knife at the countertop. "What is this, anyway?"

"It's an onion."

"No, the food. What are we making?"

"It's a cassoulet. French dish."

"Where did you learn to cook?"

"I didn't. I mostly just burn things, then order pizza."

She snickered awkwardly. "Do I have to eat it?"

"You saw the sandwiches, right?"

"They have mayo."

"So?"

"I hate mayo. So does Eddie."

"I didn't know that. Maybe you can scrape it off or something?"

"Dad says it'll give Eddie the running shits."

I winced at that.

"Elle? You better watch your mouth. Okay?" I didn't get a response, so I turned to face her. "Elle?"

She finally looked up at me, her cheeks flushed.

"I'm serious. You can't go full S-Word when your parents aren't around."

She nodded dourly.

"I know I'm not your parent, but they kind of trust me not to screw you up too much when they leave you alone with me. I take that seriously. Crap, I keep a box of Captain Crunch around this place just for you."

"I get it," she mumbled.

"Good." I returned to my beans and reached for the cumin. "These running shits kick in immediately, or what? Because I'll need to make a run for toilet paper."

She snickered again.

I had barely put the cassoulet in the oven when my doorbell rang. It was too early for the game to let out, and the Swains mostly just barged in. It had to be Ches. Checking the clock, I noticed she was a full hour early.

I brushed Elle off by the couch and went for the door. Ches stood on my stoop in a blue and yellow sundress, her hands behind her back. Most of her hair was pulled back into a charmingly sloppy bun, a few ringlets of light brown spilling over her eyebrow.

"You found me," I muttered.

Ches reached from behind her back and produced a bottle of wine.

"I don't even know if you drink wine," she offered, "but I know I do. So, I figured…"

"Thank you. Looks great. Come on in."

She stepped into my foyer, her eyes taking in my personal space as I took the bottle from her.

"I'll, uh, get this chilling."

"Oh, I love these old houses. I love the way they smell. Kind of like—oh. Hello."

I had just reached the kitchen when I realized what had happened.

"I didn't know you had kids, Dorian."

I slipped the wine bottle into my fridge and hustled back to the front room. Before I could say anything, Elle rushed across the rug and threw her arms around me.

"Daddy!"

"Uh, no."

"I love you, Daddy!"

"They're not mine," I yelled over Elle.

Ches lifted a brow and grinned as Elle crossed her arms.

"How can you say that?"

I elbow checked Elle into the couch as I stepped past her. "You are such a brat. Their parents are at the game."

Eddie added without looking up from his electronics, "They're getting drunk."

"They're not getting—well, your mother, maybe."

Ches covered her mouth to conceal a chuckle.

"Welcome to Casa du Lac," I announced with wide arms.

"Maison," she whispered.

"Hmm?"

"It's maison, in French. Casa is Spanish."

I nodded and shrugged.

Elle beamed at Ches with unhealthy interest, so I tried to break her stare.

"She's correcting my Esperanto now. You're seeing this, right?"

Elle smirked at me and replied, "You're not my real father."

I ushered Ches further into the front room with a quick wave. "As the wine chills, can I offer you anything? I can make a vodka martini, I think, if you don't mind skipping the vermouth."

"That'll work."

I managed to keep an eye on Elle from the sideboard as I dropped a couple ice cubes into straight vodka. Ches leaned against the arm of my chair, looking over the books stacked along the bookcase. I did a quick mental check to be sure I had removed anything specifically occult. Sometimes I forgot what was and wasn't forbidden knowledge, so it wasn't a given.

I gave Ches her drink. It wasn't much, but the crystal martini glass came from Italy and the vodka was top shelf. The only cheap thing in my house was my hospitality. She took a long sip and closed her eyes for a moment, and I tried not to stare.

Elle asked, "So, are you his girlfriend or what?"

Ches's eyes shot open, and she gulped hard at the vodka. After she cleared her throat, she waved her hand dismissively. "I'm his barista."

"What's a barista?" Eddie asked from the couch across the room.

Ches leaned forward and replied, "It's kind of like a secret agent."

Eddie's eyes moved slowly from his device to her.

Elle huffed, "No. She makes coffee."

"Secret agents make coffee?" he whispered.

My legs buzzed with restlessness, and I nodded to the back of the house. "So, want the nickel tour?"

She nodded and stood up, cradling her martini between her fingers.

Elle hopped up as well. "I think you need a chaperone."

"I think you need to find something on TV," I retorted.

She glowered at me as I offered Ches my hand, leading her to the hallway.

"So, this is the rest of the house."

Ches paused, then snickered. "This is it?"

"Well, there's upstairs. But that's just my bedroom, and I didn't want to come off like a complete sexual predator."

"I appreciate that."

"Mostly I just needed to get away from Princess Tongue in there."

"She's adorable. Reminds me a lot of me when I was her age."

"No kidding?"

"Well, yeah. I had three older brothers, and I had to yell at the top of my lungs if anyone was going to hear me. Learned how to throw a football, all of that."

"You like football?"

"Yep. Go Dolphins."

Sports. Great.

She gave me a sidelong glance and dropped her chin. "You're not a big sports fan, are you?"

"I never really understood sports. If I'm going to pour that much sweat, blood, and money into something, I'm going to need something better than a trophy to show for it."

"The trophy isn't the point, though."

"What is?"

"It's the experience. Deciding to make that moment life-or-death. It's a lot like religion."

"I never understood that, either."

She laughed.

"What?"

"I don't know. It's usually the other way around. I mention football and guys I date end up going on for hours. And I lose interest."

For whatever reason, I didn't really care for the way she said "guys I date" in the present tense.

"Maybe we should move on to cars or politics, then?"

"Yeah, that Audi outside?"

"Right?"

"Yours?"

"Sometimes I think I belong to the car."

"See, now we're getting somewhere."

So, she liked sports and cars. Never in a hundred years would I have assumed I would end up on a date with a woman like this.

I leaned against the steel door leading to my basement. The cold of the metal seeped through my shirt, just reminding me it was there, not three feet from Ches.

"I need to check on dinner," I stated, brushing past Ches toward the kitchen.

"Smells homey. What is it?"

"A dish my Aunt used to make in her restaurant. It's a cassoulet."

"A what with the what?"

"White beans, some duck and pork, onion and carrots. I wasn't bullshitting you about the family recipe. Aunt Viv ran a restaurant on Long Island for most of my life. I picked up a dish or two when I moved in with her after…"

Her eyes wrinkled a little, and I regretted mentioning Aunt Viv. Time to change the subject.

"Uh... let's check that oven."

I made a big fuss over opening the oven door and checking on the dish in order to compose myself. I didn't want to look like one of those needy guys who has to have everything approved by his... whatever Ches was. Besides, based on the look that crossed her face when the aroma from the cooked spinach filled the kitchen, I had a feeling Ches was going to opt for the sandwiches.

I spotted Elle peeking around the corner at us.

"Out of whiskey, Elle?"

"What?"

"You finished your straight Glenny?"

Elle cocked her head at me histrionically and made a gagging noise.

Ches leaned in and said, "You two act like brother and sister."

I shrugged. "I suppose so. Never had a sister, so I wouldn't know."

"Brothers?"

I shook my head.

"So, what about your parents? Are they local?"

I bent down and checked the oven again. "We're from New York."

"The city or the state?"

"City. People from upstate say 'New York State.' The rest of us just say New York."

"What do they do?"

"My father was an investment banker. My mom wrote freelance for a few local magazines."

"Are they retired?"

This was getting painful. "They've passed away."

"Oh." She held a hand up to her eyebrow and scowled at the floor. "I'm sorry. I keep thinking you're my age."

"I'm not so old. It happened during my senior year. It was a long time ago. How's that wine looking?" I swept across the kitchen to open the fridge, thankful for the blast of cold air on my face. I pulled her wine out and searched for the corkscrew I never seemed to put back in the same place twice. "So, what about you? Dolphins fan. You're from Florida?"

"Jacksonville, yeah. Undergrad at Miami, applied to University of Maryland and fast forward to tonight."

I started chuckling as I tried to pull the cork out of the bottle.

"What?"

"Sorry, it's just… my last girlfriend was from Miami."

"Ah. Well, I hope you don't hold that against me."

"Nah, I think you're safe. Unless you're a high-priced call girl who lies about getting pregnant to screw over her boyfriends." I grabbed the corkscrew tight.

Why did I say that out loud? Stupid. So, so stupid.

I ventured a slow peek in her direction. She was half turned, focusing on her martini glass.

"Sorry. I guess I'm a little bitter."

"No, that's not… You're fine."

I picked up the bottle to try and fish out the uncooperative cork, which only managed to break in half in the neck of the bottle. I slammed the bottle down and stepped out of the kitchen door into the side alley. It had to look so childish, but I needed a moment.

Big, fat fucking mouth. What were the odds I could pull something out of this debacle? I took a few slow breaths and looked up at the sky just beyond the glass high-rise tower behind my house. The smell of the beans in my kitchen blended with some meat one of my neighbors was grilling down the street. I could hear a city bus squealing its brakes over on the MLK. Some kids screamed bloody murder about something unimportant a block over.

This was my house. I had invited her here, but it was still my turf. I didn't have to feel like a whipping boy. I had no reason to be defensive. Right. I just got careless.

Not that any of that mattered to Ches, who was either already out the front door, or at best standing awkwardly in my kitchen wondering what kind of man-child storms out of the room because he can't open a wine bottle.

"Got it," a voice drifted over my shoulder.

I turned to find Ches holding out a goblet of pale wine for me.

I took the glass and exhaled. "Thanks."

"No problem. Those corks can be tricky. It was probably a cheap cork, anyway. In fact, I don't think I'll ever buy that wine again."

I smiled and took a sip. It was exquisite.

"No, you should definitely keep buying this. Very nice."

We rejoined the kids in the front room, and I let Elle take a turn at abusing Ches for a while before Edgar and Wren hopped up my stoop and stormed into the front door.

I stood to greet them, bracing for Wren's inevitable bear hug. It came as expected, a little lower than I was prepared for perhaps.

"Back early?" I gasped.

Edgar bobbed his head back and forth. "They were getting slaughtered. I got bored."

Wren sighed, sending beer breath wafting across my face. "I didn't want to go, but he reminded me that you were in charge of the kids, and I figured 'Hell, they're either bleeding to death or summoning a demon.' So we came back."

I squinted at Edgar, who squinted back.

That was when Wren finally noticed Ches.

"Oh, holy shit. Did I just say that? Who are you?"

I jumped between Wren and Ches, trying to back the conversation up twenty seconds. "Wren and Edgar Swain, I want you to meet Francesca… uh—"

"Baker," she finished, holding out her hand. "Call me Ches."

Edgar shook her hand as did Wren though she spent more time giving me the "atta boy" stare.

Ches waved her wine glass at Elle and Eddie. "I've been chatting with your kids. They're adorable."

"Now I know she's a fake," Wren quipped.

I blurted, "Wine?" as I grabbed Wren by the arm. "You need wine to dilute that beer."

"Uh, sure."

I dragged Wren into the kitchen and paused by the island. She stood there rubbing her neck.

"Dorian? You're being weird."

"I need you to calm down."

"Don't get me wrong, you were all dominant and that was kind of hot, but Edgar's got a way bigger—"

"Please don't be so, what? You. Don't be so you right now, okay?"

"What are you talking about?"

I stepped forward and lowered my voice, fully aware of how sound travels in my own home. "Look, she's about half a screw up away from walking out already."

"So? If she can't take you the way you are, then she can fuck off."

"Wren. I don't want her to fuck off."

"Oh. Oh!" Her eyes went wide. "Holy crap, you like her?"

"What do you think this is?"

Wren put a hand over her mouth. "Dorian, God. You gotta warn me when you spring a girlfriend on me. You know how I am on Orioles days." She slapped my arm. "Why didn't you tell me?"

"Hey, this was Edgar's idea. I figured you were in on it."

She reached for the corner of the island, steadying herself on her feet. "I'll take that up with him later. So, have you screwed up in front of her, yet?"

"Maybe. I name dropped Carmen. Also, she likes sports. I mean, what am I supposed to do with that?"

"I like sports."

"Yeah, but you're creepy."

She smacked me again. "Okay, now that I'm on board, I have to make sure you don't screw this up. What did you tell her?"

"I told her about my parents. Also, what Carmen did for a living."

"Jesus, Dorian. You didn't." She snickered, then stared. "What does she do?"

"Hmm? Oh, she works at the café down the street."

Wren sneered. "Dorian, I realize there's this special bond between a man and the person who brings him coffee. Just try not to confuse it with romance. 'Kay?"

"I'm nothing but confused at this point."

"Does she know what you do for a living?"

"No."

Wren cocked her hip. "Why not?"

"You know why."

"Because you're an asshole?"

I wound around her to turn off the oven. "Because my line of work doesn't really mix with romance. You know this."

"Edgar and I do fine."

"That's because you're Wiccan. You're kind of playing for the same team. You were ready for this."

"What about her?" she asked, fiddling with the chef's knife on my cutting board.

"Trust me. She's not in the Life."

Wren gave me a squint before draining her glass. "You know this because you asked her?"

"I can tell. I think that's why I like her."

"But you don't trust her."

"I trusted Carmen. Showed her the Life. See where that got me?"

Wren frowned, then looked back into the front room. After a short moment, she beckoned me with a tilt of her head. As I sidled up next to her, she pointed into the room. Edgar sat next to Eddie, equally immersed in whatever game Eddie had been playing. Ches and Elle sat in chairs, both of them with feet tucked under their legs, animated in their conversation.

"She's passing Elle's test, you know," Wren whispered. "Elle doesn't like people. She likes you, unfortunately. And it looks like your Ches is doing pretty damn good." She walked me back into the kitchen.

I took a deep breath and stretched my neck. Wren was nothing if not grounding for me.

"I take it back, Wren. I'm totally glad you're you right now."

She gave me a hug and snatched the bottle of wine. "Dorian? Serious talk, though?"

"What?"

"Are you just looking for fun with her? Or do you want something long-term?"

"I have no idea, Wren. It's way too early for that."

"Have you seen anyone since Carmen?"

"What does that have to do with anything?"

"Sure you're not scared? Scared of her? I think she's getting to you, and I'd hate for this to be a time delay rebound." She put a hand on my shoulder and squeezed hard. "Want some advice?"

"Not really."

"Too bad, because this is important. I want you to promise me you're going to let her be Francesca Baker."

"Huh?"

"Let her be who she is. Because she isn't Carmen."

"I know that."

"Do you? Don't assume she's going to have some agenda. Don't assume she's going to screw you over. Just because Carmen did, doesn't mean you get to hold that grudge over Ches. I'm serious. If it's going to work, you'll have to wipe the slate clean."

She was right. My whole snit over the wine bottle was about Carmen. Ches handled it better than I'd deserved.

"I promise."

She shoved the bottle into my hand. "Good. Now pour some wine and quit being a tool."

After that point, the party went smoothly. Everyone talked, and no one was awkward. Everyone pretty much avoided the cassoulet. I ate those leftovers for a solid week.

By the time the sun set, the Swains had to return to Frederick. Ches and Elle exchanged some kind of secret handshake before the Swains stepped out into the street. Edgar, who had refrained from commenting on my getting the nerve to ask Ches over all evening, gave me a solid, meaningful nod on his way out.

Then I was left with that awkward moment when Ches and I had to figure out if she was going to leave or stay.

We lingered in the foyer for a moment, each of us clutching onto our wine glasses for dear life. Finally, I decided to say something.

"How do you feel? I mean—"

"Too tipsy to drive, if that's what you mean."

"Ah."

"But I took the bus."

"Oh."

"We need music."

"That… I can do that."

I wrestled with my digital music remote for far longer than was warranted as Ches wandered around the house looking over my wall art and gewgaws. By the time I landed on a smooth jazz station and dialed the music down to a conversational level, she had wandered into the hallway. I found her looking over a photo of my parents hanging on the wall just across from my steel door.

"They were so young," she mumbled.

"Yeah."

"Was it an accident?"

"Mom was. A truck T-boned her taxi. She held on for about an hour before the internal bleeding…"

"What about your father? He wasn't in the cab?"

"No. That's—"

"I'm sorry. I shouldn't be asking this. I blame the wine."

I gripped my glass, my fingers tapping like mad against the stem. "He shot himself. In our home office. Something he had done at work caused a lot of people to lose a lot of money."

"Jesus."

"That was a week before Mom's crash."

"One week? You were all alone. You've been alone that long?"

"Oh, I had people. Aunt Viv." And Emil… but I wasn't going to get into that.

Ches looked up into my eyes, balancing the wine glass delicately in her fingertips.

My heart raced. It wasn't the wine. It wasn't her Florida sunshine wholesome vibe. It wasn't that candy-scent perfume she was wearing.

I was afraid this was all going to be just casual to her. I was suddenly terrified this was all we were going to be.

She cocked her head as her eyes traced the shape of my steel door.

"That's a hell of a door. You have a panic room or something?"

My pulse kicked up a notch. "No. That's just my basement."

"Is that where you hide the bodies?" she asked with a wink.

"What, you didn't see the fifty gallon barrels in the alley?"

She lifted her hands. "Sorry again. I'm just being a nosey bitch tonight."

I took a deep breath and examined her face. Sure, she was a little tipsy. Very much outside of her comfort zone. But she was keeping up with me, every bob and weave. She wasn't letting me back down or pull away.

I repeated Wren's advice a few times in my head. She wasn't Carmen. She wasn't Carmen.

"Tell you what. Want to see what's down there?"

She released an "Ooo," as her eyebrows popped up.

"Nothing spectacular. It's not even locked."

I only locked the door when I left the house, but that wasn't important at the moment. I pulled the lever and eased the door open. Reaching inside, I flipped on the light switch and started down the stairs. She followed me into the finished space of my basement. My octagonal worktable, my shelves of reagents.

Emil's Library.

I positioned myself so she wouldn't accidentally run into it, touch it, or really even look at it too long. She walked a slow circle around the table, pausing at the jars of myrrh, frankincense, dragonsblood, amber, dried scorpions, and all kinds of goods I had been buying from Edgar over the years.

"See? No bodies."

"No," she whispered. "This is way creepier." She tapped on the jar of scorpions. "Cozy."

"Yeah, it's kind of cramped. Thought it'd be bigger when I moved in, but you work with what you got."

"What do you do down here?"

"Truth?"

She nodded.

I answered, "Magic."

"Magic?"

"Hermetic workings. Charms and hexes. That's my business, by the way. I sell charms—"

"—and hexes. Got it."

She turned to my table and ran her fingers over the carved inscriptions in its surface.

"What is this, Greek?"

"Good eye."

"I took a couple years of Greek as an undergrad. What does it say?"

"It's an incantation. A line from Pythagoras of Samos. It says 'Above the cloud with its shadow is the star with its light.' It's a declaration of cosmic dichotomy. One of the fundamentals of classical hermetic... what?"

She grinned at me and shook her head. "I've just never met anyone like you before." She leaned back, her eyes dancing with something new. There was an interest there I hadn't seen before.

This was going very well.

Ultimately, she sobered up and fatigue set in. I offered to drive her home, but we both recognized I wasn't in a position to sit behind the wheel. Instead I escorted her to the bus stop and waited with her. She gave me a peck on the cheek when we saw the bus round the corner of Fayette.

"Say, what are you doing next Saturday?" I blurted before the air brakes squealed.

"Nothing special. What you got?"

"I'm a member of a club up by Druid Hill. I'd like to take you. It's my home away from home."

She rolled her chin a little before nodding. "Sounds fun. What kind of music do they play?"

"Not that kind of club."

"So, what's the dress code?"

The bus doors opened, and the driver looked like she didn't have much patience for long goodbyes.

"Evening gown too much to ask?"

She winced a little, then shook her head. "I'll find something," she added before squeezing my hand and stepping into the bus.

I took a long, slow stroll back to the house. It wasn't until I was at the stoop that I realized I had left my phone on my desk. It was ringing.

I rushed to unlock the door, and managed to catch it before it rolled to voice mail.

Private number.

"Hello?"

Cecil Rawls' voice vibrated through the phone, "Dorian? Have you spoken to Bright yet?"

"No, can't reach him. He's out of town."

"You may have less time than we thought."

I dropped into my chair. "What happened?"

"Copies of the photos landed at the Charm City Spectator. It's a short run rag out of Canton, but people are already talking about it."

"Fuck. Okay. I'll try again."

"I'm taking a risk, here."

I took a deep breath and nodded. "I recognize that, Cecil. Thank you."

"I'm saying this is it. This is as far as I can go with this. You won't hear from me again."

Before I could say "Understood," he hung up.

So much for my weekend.

CHAPTER SEVEN

"Hello?"

"It's Julian."

I checked the clock radio by my bed. Six in the morning. What a bastard.

"Yeah. You back yet?"

"We're driving in this morning. I have six voicemails demanding I call you, so I'm thinking this is important?"

"Yep. Campaign-ending important."

"It's always when I leave town."

"I'll keep my day open for you."

"I can't get into this right this very second, but what's the five-word version?"

"Uh… Amy Mancuso. Me. You. Photos."

After a long pause he replied, "We're in Philly now. I'll call you in four hours."

"Roger."

My Sunday got busy, all of a sudden. I pulled myself out of bed and slushed through the laundry on the floor on my way to making breakfast. Ches never worked Sunday mornings, so instead of hiking over to the café, I warmed up some cassoulet and made my way down to the basement. I rifled through Emil's library for that stupid Macedonian-Bulgarian-Ottoman text for Carmody. Dealing with those tomes was never easy. The energies bound within and around those books were almost blindingly distracting. The old stories of books driving men insane were based on the hornet's nest of infernal intent that swarmed around such texts. And it wasn't even intentional. The knowledge contained within was simply that potent.

I paused when I stumbled across a text written by Asok the Sharqui in the late seventeenth century. Emil had jotted down the words *thoughtforms, darql craft, servitors, soul traps* in the margin. This was the book I needed to bone up on before I made my meeting with Gillette. I plunged headlong into the Indian heretic's treatise on soul manipulation, not knowing precisely what to expect. The man had been a cultural Muslim during the Moghul Empire, but claimed a Rajput ancestry. The blend of political and religious conflict during his lifetime had driven him outside of the more conventional pursuits of near-Eastern mysticism, pushing him into what could only be described as "utterly sinister" practices, even by modern standards. His ultimate goal of slicing his soul into representations of traditional deities was interrupted by an ill-timed wave of plague, taking his life and those of his followers. Though not before the last managed to put to parchment his theories, means, and observations in his attempts. The document fell into the hands of Muslim landlords a century later, and ultimately rested in the hands of a Vatican emissary just prior to the First World War. Said emissary, regrettably, contracted a rapidly progressing case of tuberculosis during his voyage from Tyre to Italy. The ship made it to Rome intact. The text landed in the hands of whoever taught Emil his craft.

I recognized Emil's handwriting on every other page, his translation of the original. The translation was colored predictably with his resentment of Eurocentric colonial ideals. After three hours of plodding through Emil's butchering of Urdu, I surrendered and returned upstairs to check my phone.

I had a voicemail from Leibnitz. He had acquired the necessary reagent from his target, and wanted to hand it over as soon as was humanly possible. I figured a man of his focus and seemingly sparing constitution deserved as much quick attention as I could afford. I showered, dressed, and made my way to the street in front of Grey & Lisle.

He looked like hell. His eyes were sunken, his face more pallid than last I saw him, and his shirt looked like he slept in it last night. Maybe he was working off an all-nighter, maybe he'd hit the sauce last night. Either way, he wasn't the ray of sunshine I quite frankly needed at that moment.

Leibnitz shoved a black plastic bag into my hand and turned to walk off.

"You okay?" I asked.

He spun a circle of steps without stopping and returned to my side. "You should be able to work with this."

"Good. But, are you okay?"

"No."

"What's going on?"

He looked up into my eyes with an expression of nauseating dread. "I got what you needed. I don't want to talk about it."

Leibnitz turned to retreat once again.

"Ari? This isn't witchcraft. This is karmically clean."

He paused as his eyes worked lines on the pavement alongside his shoes.

"Just take him down, Mister Lake," he muttered before finally retreating into the lobby of his building.

My hex would be karmically clean. Sure. I could vouch for that. But as I jostled the plastic bag in my hand, I wondered if Leibnitz was clean any longer.

When I returned to my house, I went straight to work. I had ideas of how to deal with the target, Jacobs. It had been a long time since I had a hex I could spin which didn't involve lovers, sex, or children. I had a particularly tangled hex already spelled out in my head that involved sleep deprivation and impotence. Two effects on one hex would require a strong linkage.

As I opened the plastic bag, I realized I had all the linkage I needed. A bloodied cotton handkerchief fell from the bag and onto my table. I paused for a moment, recognizing the look of terror filling Leibnitz's eyeballs. What had he done?

There was probably no way to ever really know. It would be unprofessional to ask. I never had before. I just couldn't imagine a mouse like Ari Leibnitz drawing blood from a man. Not on purpose, at any rate.

I grabbed a pair of yellow rubber cleaning gloves from the trunk under my worktable, and scooped the handkerchief into my tiny iron cauldron. It was technically a novelty iron pot I purchased at one of those interstate restaurant gift shops filled with what everyone pretends is genuine old timey crap. I had been using a stainless steel fondue pot for a while, but cast iron packs so much more wallop. I doused the handkerchief with a solution of distilled water, iron shavings, and some dried Chinese wolfberries to tone the blood energy. I let that sit to render while I scraped a fresh parchment and prepared some ink.

Spreading the parchment flat out on the worktable, I found the center of the leaf and began plotting the points for a spiral of golden rectangles with Emil's old calipers. I double-checked the ratios and put quill ink to parchment, scribing the sacred geometry. Then, with my mainline of chakras in the correct balance, I began the scripture. For this hex I chose Ionic Greek, notorious for its efficacy in sex magic. Endowing each sigil and word with intent and fate-twisting energy, I spiraled the text of the hex. Its effects, its purpose, its condition for termination. In this case, I made two conditions to balance the two effects. The hex would lift if Jacobs made a public confession of wrongdoing, or if he was otherwise removed from his ill-gained privilege. Until that time, the bed would be a place of frustration and failure for him, in regards both to sleep and sex.

As the ink dried, I removed the handkerchief from the cauldron and set it over a cup of sterno to heat. The tonic steamed as the blood congealed. When the linkage achieved the correct consistency, I fished out my athame from the tool box and dipped it into the cauldron. I traced the Sigil of Sabi'un in Jacobs' blood over the hex and folded it neatly into a golden rectangle before burning it with the sterno flame.

The hex was cast.

I had barely cleaned up and bleached my equipment before my phone rang. It was Julian.

"You're back?"

"I only have a few minutes."

"Where can you meet?"

"Better meet me here. Out front."

"Where's here?"

"City Hall."

Fuck me. "Alright. I'm ten minutes away."

I had to take the Audi into the city, and parked in the fire lane across the street from City Hall. I had a feeling Julian could fix that ticket if a zealous flatfoot decided to drop the axe on me.

I waited by the front steps, Rawls' envelope of photos tucked under my arm. Julian finally emerged from the building, stepping quickly.

"Are those the photos?" he asked in a low voice before I was quite able to hear it.

"Yeah. Someone inside The Sun dropped these off for us yesterday. Thought he had an exclusive on these pics, but he was wrong."

"Who else has these?"

"Charm City Spectator."

Julian winced, then nodded. "Okay, I can work with this. Mancuso isn't a strong witness, and she has some history."

"Julian?"

"Hmm?"

"She shouldn't suffer because of us."

He blinked twice and squinted. "I don't intend to do her harm if that's your meaning."

"I don't want her in play at all. She was the victim, here."

"Dorian?" He waved the envelope in front of his face. "She's already in play. We didn't start this, but by God, I'm not going to let Sullivan tank to save face for a heroin user."

"She's on heroin?"

He nodded.

"How do you know that?"

"I didn't spend the last two decades of my life studying dead languages and mysticism, Dorian, but I did learn a thing or two about politics. I'll pull together a counter for this, hopefully before The Charm City Spectator even goes to print."

He cradled the envelope under his shoulder and turned back for the entrance.

"You're welcome," I called out.

Julian paused and turned to me slowly, his brow lifted. After giving me a tired look, he took a deep breath and nodded. "Thank you."

I watched Julian slip back into the pool of city politics without so much as a ripple, and wondered what had become of our friendly repartee? He wasn't the young lion I had met at the Druid Hill Club nine months ago. He had been so impressed by me, so eager to do business. I even gave him some basic lessons on the hermetic arts as he had always fostered an interest. They never came to much, unfortunately. Julian simply didn't have the time or the available space in his gray matter for the Craft.

But things were tense, now. He wasn't my buddy. He was my employer, and with the mayoral campaign about to hit the public, he had precious little interest in kissing my ass anymore. I shuffled back to my car, perhaps a little pensive. I missed those nights at the Club sipping wine with Julian, talking about unimportant matters. But things had changed. Those moments of homecoming were little more than echoes now, bouncing off the marble halls into which he had retreated.

It was Sunday afternoon. The day had been a bag of pissed off cats, and I wasn't feeling particularly good about myself at that moment. The Club was precisely what I needed.

Chapter Eight

The arboreal drive to the Druid Hill Club was densely canopied, the last dying rays of sunset unable to penetrate the Live Oak leaves along the gravel lane. I had to grip my steering wheel whenever I drove through dark streets or tunnels. Too many shadows. For whatever reason the shadows enjoyed taunting me when I visited the Club. Perhaps they knew this was where I found my center, refilled what vital essence the week had worn away.

Perhaps they knew I would die there some day.

That's all they really wanted. My life. A man without a soul was a man doomed, and the moment of my death would bring them like sharks in a frenzy.

Ramon took my car keys as I pulled up to the porte cochere. I struck up a conversation with Ramon whenever I could. He had an intimate understanding of the interiors of the club members' cars, and a sharp eye for incriminating miscellanea found therein. He fed me dirt from the parking lot, and I fed him dirt from inside the club. He only recently stopped changing my radio to the one and only salsa station in Baltimore.

I stepped inside the double oak doors and paused in front of Kim, the Coatroom Dominatrix. She pretended not to notice me for a few seconds before finally giving me a cock of her brow.

"Card?"

I had it ready in my front pocket, and slid it casually across the coatroom counter. She picked it up and pressed it against her lips, leaving huge lipstick marks on the laminate. With a wink, she slid it back to me.

"I suppose I'll let you in."

"Don't think I'm not grateful. How's the room?"

"Sunday. Business, y'know?"

"Hey, you seen Julian Bright around much lately?"

She shook her head.

"Okay."

"Listen, Dorian. I have another sit next Wednesday. Property managers from Columbia. You have those photos yet?"

"Shit. Forgot."

"Think you can take care of that by tomorrow night, and email them to me?"

"I'll do it."

Kim had started up her own interior design business a few months ago in an attempt to escape the Club, and I'd hired her to take a crack at my upstairs. I owed her photos, but my mind had been everywhere but décor.

She snapped her fingers at me. "You on another planet or something?"

"Sorry. I've been… well, I'm sort of seeing someone."

She blinked furiously and took half a step back. "You're kidding."

"No. Actually not kidding about that."

"Jesus, Dorian!"

"Right?"

"Is she… does she work here?"

I deserved that. "No. She's not in the trade. But, I might bring her here next weekend. You can meet her."

Her face stumbled through shades of shock and mirth. "You're seriously bringing her here? You sure about that?"

"Yeah, why not?"

She shook her head before tapping the front of my suit with the back of her hand. "Better go see Ben before he hears you flirting with me."

I moved on down the hallway and into the main room. Clutches of settees, couches, and wingbacks speckled the enormous space, separated by columns and potted palms. The crowd tonight was definitely the shirtsleeve set. Sundays were typically "business over drinks" night at Druid Hill. The working girls didn't push as hard, and those that did tended to sit on armchairs most of the night. Sunlight still spilled through the last of the French doors lining the exterior wall, sending orange hues slicing through the palm leaves. The stripes of sunset light bounced off the back bar mirror as Big Ben Setleigh poured a martini for a man easily in his eighties.

"Ben?" I called once the octogenarian had returned to his embarrassingly young escort. "I think I'm going to have to find a new entrance to this joint."

"Kim giving you shit?" he asked, his broad face glistening with more sweat than was called for.

"Yes, and you should have her fired immediately."

"I have a feeling I'd be doing her a favor. So what's your pour tonight, Dorian?"

"Let's start with an Argentine malbec and see where it goes?"

He nodded and reached for the lattice wine rack behind him.

"Still got your Glenny if the mood strikes."

"I'm good."

"The whole point to owning an expensive Scotch whiskey is to drink it from time-to-time, you know?"

"Just wine."

He pulled the cork and poured me a glass. "So, a man in my position comes to notice a thing or two when he's doing little else but pouring drinks and listening to worthless assholes like you complain all night."

"Do tell?"

"And a man like me would notice that you haven't been patronizing our club to its fullest potential."

"I've been busy."

"How are you and Bright doing lately?"

"Again, busy."

He lifted a brow, and I wilted.

"It's been better."

"Honeymoon's over, huh?"

"We went straight to our bitter golden years, but thanks for asking." I added after taking a sip, "No, it's just we both have eyes on our own specific prizes."

"What, you got a new job?"

"Not that kind of prize."

Ben pulled a stool from under the bar and settled his girth upon it. "I knew it!"

"Jesus."

"Who's the lucky girl?"

"Lucky isn't the first word that comes to mind."

"Shut up. Name."

"Francesca."

"Local girl?"

"Not really. She's in college."

His brow lifted.

"What?" I spat.

"Nothing. You're, what? Thirty-five?"

"How do you know my age?"

Ben gave me a smug, tight-lipped grin.

I shrugged. "The age difference isn't that significant. I mean, it won't be when we're both in our forties. At least, when she's in her forties."

"Going to bring her here?"

"Saturday night."

"Wow. Must be serious."

"It really isn't."

"You're bringing her to this place, Dorian. That's like bringing her to meet your parents, and you know it."

I leaned back on the bar stool and took another long quaff of wine. Ben gave me a warm, knowing smile and withdrew to attend to another customer. I watched him work for a while. He was terrifyingly out of shape. He was the kind of man you could imagine dining on two slices of bread soaked in bacon grease every night with a pack of cigarettes and a nightcap. He always listened to me, and he never withdrew his approval from me. Even during all the unpleasantness with Carmen.

But I hadn't realized how much I cared what he thought about me until I had someone for him to meet.

I retired to the room for a bit of brain-numbing conversation with the others. I stumbled into a deep, emotional argument over the proposed gas tax, and managed to stay far from mayoral topics. Though I could tell from keeping my ear pressed to the ground why Julian had been avoiding the Club. This had become Sooner's audience in a big way. Happily I wasn't publically linked to Sullivan. Hopefully it would remain that way.

After draining my wine glass, I wandered back to the bar to get my own refill. The girls were giving me a wide berth, and for good reason. Their new house mother had warned them about what had happened between Carmen and me. It seemed I was on a blacklist among the working girls in the Club, and it suited me fine. That particular service of the club hadn't been sitting well with me for a while now.

I stepped past the dark side of the room before the single lamp lit inside registered in my brain. A chill trickled down my neck as I stopped mid-stride. Backing up a couple steps, I spotted a familiar figure seated in one of the wingbacks, smoke from his cigar wreathing his head.

It was the man I called Mr. Brown. I'd had run-ins with agents of the Presidium in the past, but Mr. Brown was the only bona fide Presidium member to date who had spoken with me in person.

If he was here to see me, I couldn't ignore him. I set the wine glass down on a planter and ventured inside the dim room.

"Have a seat, Mister Lake."

I complied, trying not to give Brown any reason to take offense.

"How have you been?" I asked, dutifully weeding out any trace of sarcasm as I took a seat across him.

"You've kept us busy as of late, Mister Lake."

"Have I?" A little sarcasm may have crept into that one.

He stared at me from beneath those snow white eyebrows, a sneer creeping onto the mouth buried inside his ivory beard.

"The Baltimore mayoral campaigns don't garner much attention inside the Capitol Beltway, which is good news for you."

"Then this is a social visit?"

"As I've said before, there are associates within our organization which feel you represent a real opportunity to forward our mission. There are others, however, who consider you to be reckless in the extreme. Stubborn. Arrogant. And dangerously uninformed."

"I cancelled my subscription to Newsweek." Okay, I couldn't fight the sarcasm anymore. He was starting to piss me off.

Mr. Brown's eyes bored holes through my head, and I shifted in my seat.

"Also, callously flippant."

"Sorry."

"Until recently your affairs haven't compelled us to take action. Hence our relatively benign conversation. The regrettable fact is this all could have been avoided."

"What could have been avoided?"

"Oh, where to begin? You've insinuated yourself into the election of a major public figure. You've met in broad daylight with the Deputy Mayor on more than one occasion to discuss sensitive esoteric matters. Trading with inconsequential corporate accountants is one thing, but a man who is viewed as holding the political marionette strings for a major U.S. city is quite another. And when faced with a genuine metaphysical crisis, rather than coming to us, you've resorted to your own paltry miseducation and fly-by-wire hermetic gimmickry. On what level did you feel we were ever going to ignore this?"

My blood pressure raquetballed from vessel-bursting anger to piss-my-pants fainting levels.

"The Presidium is getting involved?"

"More accurately, we've already involved ourselves and the matter is dealt with. The Sun and The Charm City Spectator threatened to expose hermetic activity close to a seat of political power. We simply can't let that happen." Brown cocked his head. "This can't be news to you."

My stomach dropped to my knees.

He took a long puff on his cigar. "Dangerously uninformed seems a bit on-the-nose."

My brain rewound the conversation a few seconds as I rose to my feet. I inched back into the main room as Brown looked on.

"Mister Lake? This could have gone differently. Please try to remember that in the coming weeks."

I withdrew into the room and hustled over to the bar. I gripped the bar rail as I scanned the television hanging in the corner. All I could see were cars festooned in corporate logos taking several hundred left turns. Ben wandered over to me and coughed discretely into his sleeve.

"Another?"

"Can I get the news?"

"It won't be on for another hour-some. What's up?"

"Don't know. Just expecting bad news, I suppose."

I waited at the bar for that hour-some, not speaking a word to anyone. By the time I realized what Brown was going on about, the room was largely empty.

There was a massive pileup on the Jones Falls Expressway. It was a tragedy. An entire family had been killed when their car spun out from road debris. They speculated it was gravel from a poorly secured dump truck. A man, his wife, and two young daughters were killed upon impacting an overpass support column.

Cecil Rawls deserved better than that. His children sure as shit deserved better. Whatever poor bastard at The Charm City Spectator that probably met with a sudden, tragic demise did, too.

In one of those moments I generally regret later, I marched back to the side room. Brown was gone.

I stared into the shadows, and spotted something flickering just beneath the wingbacks. Something small, withdrawing its impish legs before I could quite see it directly. The entire room seemed to crawl with malevolence. The shadows twitched like a fly-covered horse. They were getting restless.

Things could have gone differently, Brown had said. It could have been an Audi wrapped around that support column.

But still... two little girls.

As I drove home with remarkable vigilance, I put a great deal of thought into my current vocational situation. Politics simply wasn't agreeing with me. It certainly didn't agree with Cecil. I couldn't withdraw myself from Julian's employ without a great deal of crow-eating and self-debasement. But wouldn't that have been preferable to seeing more innocent people eliminated for the sake of hermetic expediency?

As I turned off the freeway into downtown, I spotted the tops of Harborside Towers and remembered what Cecil had told me. This wasn't simple politics. This was a quiet takeover of a city. I was certain Cecil would have done everything he could to protect his family from the inherent dangers he must have sensed lay in his line of work. And yet he persisted. Now that he was gone, I had a choice to make. I could let Brown muscle me out of the campaign, or I could try to honor Cecil's memory by continuing his work.

Perhaps I was simply being too sloppy? I had been too distracted with finding my soul. I let myself get photographed. I wandered up to the front of City Hall with damning photographs in a conspicuous envelope. This was as much my fault as anyone's.

I had to focus.

I had to get my soul back.

Happily, I was hours away from catching a flight to Oregon, and with any luck at all, I'd finally have a means to find it.

Chapter Nine

I was musing on what reason the city of Portland, Oregon, decided to put a mountain at the end of their airport runway as our plane touched down. I had visited the Pacific Northwest only one time before, some six years ago when I helped Edgar negotiate a purchase of a Han Dynasty altarpiece. I remembered it had never stopped raining the entire time I was there. It was that constant, drizzly misting rain that drove me to the end of my ragged nerves. As we sidled up to the concourse, I was relieved to find endless sunlight bathing the city of Portland.

I secured a cab ride across the Willamette and into the downtown Westside. As the cab crossed one of the dozen-odd bridges spanning the river, my phone rang.

It was Julian.

"Hey, Julian."

"Dorian."

"This whole thing with the photos has been taken care of."

"How do you mean?"

"Trust me, and I mean you really have to accept this when I say it... you don't want to know."

"Granted." After a long pause, he continued, "So, I'm here at Gordon's."

"Having a late lunch?"

"Where are you?"

I blinked away the question. "Oregon."

"The state?"

"Yeah, that one."

"That's funny because it's kind of hard to make a meeting here at

Gordon's when you're in the state of Oregon."

Shit.

"Right. That… that was today."

"I know we had a lot of back-and-forth in the last couple days, Dorian, but I had some people I wanted you to meet."

"Sorry, Julian. I… shit. Yeah, that's on me."

"This would almost be funny if this wasn't basically our standard operating procedure at this point."

I rammed my head into the cab's upholstery a couple times. "I didn't—I just forgot. I'm not blowing you off."

"And I had people here for an hour and a half."

"How many ways can I apologize here?"

He went silent for a while.

"Julian?"

"I'm not saying this whole arrangement was a mistake, yet."

"Okay?"

"But you're not giving me a lot of reasons to think otherwise."

I balled a fist trying to figure out how to save face without losing patience here. "I know it."

"Is this about finding your soul, or whatever you're doing?"

I didn't want to confirm nor deny. So I just shut my mouth.

"Dorian, I need you with me, or I need to get you out of my peripheral vision. You're distracting me more than you're helping me."

"Someone died yesterday, Julian."

"What?"

"A whole family. A couple and their two kids. It looked like an accident, but I know it wasn't. It was damage control. Our damage. You and me."

"The photos?"

"That's just part of it. I want to help you, but you need to take a moment and get some perspective. You're focused on the mayor race. That's great. I'm on board. There's some specific bastardy McHenry is whipping out of his pants right now that I wouldn't mind shoving back up his ass. But there are people in higher places than City Hall who have me under a really big microscope. Now, I'm going to say 'I'm sorry' exactly one more time for missing this meeting. And then, you know what? I'm going to see you again this week. Hell, I'll pound some yard signs into the ground if you want. And if you feel like we can't continue this arrangement, no hard feelings. But right now, right this very minute, I just have bigger problems."

Julian simmered on that for a good while, but I didn't give him anything else.

"How does your Thursday look?"

"I have a meeting with Julian Bright, but after that…"

"Alright, smartass. Gordon's. Nine a.m.?"

"I'll be there."

"You promise this time?"

"Barring an act of God or people in scary high places, yes."

I hung up in time for the cab to roll onto Columbia Street. A row of trees lined the one-way two-lane cutting through the middle of Westside Portland. I oriented myself as I stepped out onto the brisk bustle of morning pedestrians. I spotted a canvas awning sporting the words, *Green Tree,* in what could be generously described as twig-letters. My watch read eleven-fifty. I was early, but only just.

A young man skateboarded directly in front of me as I tried to cross with the light, and nearly knocked me over. No one seemed to notice or care. In Baltimore, that kid probably wouldn't have made it a half-block without something unnatural in his thorax. Taking a moment, I continued across the street and on to the Green Tree.

The old birch door creaked as I opened it, and one pathetic brass bell jingled as I stepped inside. Warped hardwood slats groaned as I took the first few steps, their surfaces worn from years of snow-tread and street salt. The room swam with the scents of cedar and old books. The walls of the narrow retail slot were lined with bookcases. Near the front all I could find were dog-eared paperbacks, mostly recent. But as I ventured deeper toward a clutch of wrought-iron tables and a coffee bar, I spotted more and more leather bound spines peeking at me through the dim halogen lights.

I ordered an Americano and took a seat at the rear-most table, watching the front of the room. There was only the one goateed barista working, and an elderly man near the front windows, his face buried in a faded paperback. I sipped the coffee as quickly as the heat would allow. Something about the claustrophobia of this joint made me edgy. The cedar was fairly strong, perhaps more than the bookcases merited, even if they were hewn from solid cedar planks. No, this was an essential oil, probably burning in a censer somewhere behind the coffee bar.

And as cedar was a powerful warding reagent, I made sure to keep my energy wound tight around my mainline.

At ten after noon, the door opened with its creek and jingle, and a woman stepped inside. She was tall, remarkably so. Her broad shoulders were draped with a dark trench coat. The coat was clearly more of a fashion statement in the middle of summer, but somehow it seemed to work for her. The rest of her clothes were tidy, but bland. The sides of her head were shaved bald, with the middle swath of close-clipped copper-red hair settling into a rat tail. Her nose and eyebrow were pierced, and her ears sported a half-dozen shiny dark stones. Probably hematite.

But it was her eyes that put the hook in me. They were clear blue, and burned with a kind of nameless anger that I had come to recognize in the few people Emil called "friend." Despite her youth, this woman was clearly Old School, and I wished I was more prepared for her.

She stopped directly in front of my table. I stood out of a sense of respect and etiquette, but couldn't find anything intelligent to say.

She reached into her coat and pulled out an e-reader, setting it onto my table without ceremony. The barista steamed some milk without order.

Finally, as she pulled a chair to take a seat, and I found myself following suit, she spoke.

"So, you're Lake?"

"Quinn Gillette?"

She cocked her head in a half-shrug and reached for her reader. She clicked it blandly, eyes moving in sharp jerks. The barista brought her coffee and withdrew without a word. I sat in silence, watching her sip and read, never once looking up at me or further acknowledging my presence.

It was horribly awkward.

"Ms. Gillette, I wanted to speak to you about, well, sensitive matters. Matters relating to our chosen Craft."

She cleared her throat and clicked her reader.

"Soul magic, to be specific."

"So you said."

"I'm lead to believe you're practiced in creating servitors."

Her eyes finally lifted to meet mine. "That a fact?"

"And that you powered these servitors with shards of your own soul."

She returned her attention to her reader. "Not an unusual practice."

"Unusual in my particular corner of the nation."

"Where did you say you were from?"

"Baltimore."

Her eyes lifted again, this time in genuine surprise. My phone call had made precisely zero impact on her.

"You live in the lap of the Presidium, you dolt. Of course you're not going to practice soul magic."

"I realize that."

"Then what are you talking to me for?"

"I have a problem."

The door creaked open, and Gillette jerked around in her seat. A trio of college age women whispered with each other and started scanning the book racks. Gillette exhaled and turned back to me.

"I don't want to know about your problems, Mister Lake."

This conversation was getting tiresome. "Well, you know what? You gave me little option but to fly out here on a short notice, so maybe you could spare me fifteen God damn minutes of your attention?"

She glared at me for a long moment before laying her reader down gently on the table. She cradled her mug and repositioned herself to face me full-on.

"Didn't mean to get your tampon in a twist," she grunted before taking a long sip of coffee. "Go ahead. Bore me."

"As I said, I have a particular problem. I signed my soul into a contract with a soul monger."

"Stupid."

"I had reasons."

"Your reasons were stupid."

"Anyway, before I could buy it back, he destroyed the contract."

"How do you know he destroyed it?"

"He burned it in front of me. Out of spite."

Gillette smirked. "Sounds like a real son of a bitch."

"I've known more than a few. So, here I am. My soul's been released into the ether, and I'm starting to see things. Moving shadows. Things haunting me in the corner of my vision. Same thing happened to my mentor, just before the shadows tore him limb from literal limb."

"Was that recent? I hadn't heard about that."

"No. It was more than a decade ago." I didn't want to drop Emil's name in front of this woman. There was a better than average chance she had heard about Emil at some point. "But the point is you lost a part of your soul once. And you found it again. At least that's what I hear."

The door creek-jingled again. Gillette turned to watch as the college girls exited in a fit of conversation.

"So you think you can apply my method to finding your soul? That's what this is about?"

"That's right."

"Well, you would be correct."

I sat stunned for a moment. The confirmation came so quickly and matter-of-factly that I almost missed it.

"I would?"

"The laws of conservation are still in play at the interstitial plane."

"Interstitial?"

"The void where ancient malevolence, daydreams and nightmares, and yes even misplaced souls abide. Your soul should be intact as long as it hasn't been re-captured or consumed by something on the other side."

"Funny you should mention that."

"I figured as much." She set down her now empty coffee cup and leaned back in her chair. "So what are you proposing?"

"I'm sorry?"

"I know what you want. You want my method. My notes, perhaps. A deeply personal, but still not entirely un-embarrassing view into my struggles with soul magic. What are you offering in exchange?"

I wilted in my chair. For whatever reason, I hadn't thought to prepare to negotiate. I was expecting a more or less cooperative conversation. Instead, I was met with this mercenary frontier mentality, and I really should have known better.

"I'm a hex and charm crafter by trade."

She snickered and shook her head. "Fuck me. You're really going to try and impress me with charms and hexes? If I need to make a pretzel out of my own karma, I'm qualified to do it myself. So thank you, but what else you got?"

I balked. The cedar fumes were getting to me. Either that, or I was so close to a real way to find my soul that I was getting desperate. I didn't want to beg.

"What did you have in mind?"

She shook her finger at me. "You're presenting yourself as weak. Bad idea. It would have been wiser to start with Curses, but if you want to bury your lead—"

"Curses?"

"You are a Curse Merchant, aren't you?"

"I—"

"You took out Osterhaus with a simple and particularly nasty curse. A sly bit of Netherwork that pancaked him in so many tons of iron and cement. Not entirely uncalled for, considering he torched your soul contract, but still."

"I never told you his name."

"Who, Osterhaus?"

"That's right. How do you know about—"

"Just like you never mentioned Emil Desiderio by name. Or the fact that you lived with him in London for the better part of ten years? Or the fact that Del Carmody skittered all the way to Baltimore with my name in a hot little envelope ready to drop into your hands without so much as a dislocated pinky?"

My stomach was in free-fall, so keeping my mouth shut seemed to be the best choice at the moment.

She continued, "I understand the Presidium has you East Coast practitioners thumbscrewed and pissing your pants, but out here on the West Coast we actually do our homework."

"Just wanted to watch me wiggle on the hook?"

"Welcome to real life. You want my method? Tough shit. I'm not inclined to share knowledge with a shit-kicker like you. But I need a curse, so I'm willing to do the work for you."

"A curse?"

"That's what I said."

"What else can we work out?"

"You're pretty squeamish for a man who's killed with magic."

"That's mostly why I'm squeamish."

"Well, that's my price. I want you to curse a man. Not a hex, not some clever-shit way to needle my mark into wishing he was a better man. I want him to meet his end. I want it done quickly, and I want it clean. You do that, and I'll find your soul for you. Hell, I'll even put it back in your body."

This sounded too familiar.

"What, you're trying to teach me a lesson or something? I've been around that particular racetrack already."

"I honestly don't care what you know or feel or think, Lake. This man has been a pain in my ass for far too long, and I am beyond whatever point of compassion I pretend to have with the people who don't actively screw me."

"Who's your mark?"

"Del Carmody."

Of course. "He's a handful, I'll grant you, but—"

"He's made a career out of poaching and selling grimoires and personal dealings among the West Coast practitioners. He knows we're all ready to shove a pentacle up his ass sideways, so he took precautions."

"Why would he give me your name, then? He'd have to know I'd contact you. Doesn't really follow."

"It does if you're the kind of man who will side with someone out of a misplaced sense of Judeo-Christian morality. Are you?"

"I'm not a murderer, if that's what you're asking."

"Alright. If labels are important to you, then fine. You're not a murderer. But you are a Netherworker. Like it or don't. You've tainted your soul with infernal magic." She leaned forward slowly. "Only, you haven't, have you?"

"Sorry?"

"Your soul? Was it on your person when you cursed Osterhaus?"

"No."

Gillette grinned. It was unnerving as hell.

"You're in a unique position, Lake. Your soul is elsewhere. What your body does until you locate it? Well, one doesn't often get the opportunity to indulge in Netherwork without consequences."

"There really has to be another way. I can get money together."

"Carmody came to you. Specifically you. He's slippery, and the one thing I want is for him to know he failed. That means you have to do it."

"I'm not sure if I can even find Carmody."

She leaned back and checked the door again. "That's your problem."

"Gillette. This is my soul we're talking about here. I don't mean for you to go fetch it for me. All I'm looking for is information."

"I know."

"Is this really necessary?"

The door opened with its creak and jingle. Gillette didn't bother to turn and look, but I did. A long-haired young man stepped inside carrying a skateboard. I recognized him. It was the kid who nearly ran me over on the street.

There are moments when you realize that shit's about to go down, and you're utterly powerless to stop it. I was getting really damn tired of those moments.

The skateboarder lingered across the shop from the elderly man still thumbing through his paperback. He was my life vest. As long as he was here, I suspected they wouldn't jump me.

"Friend of yours?" I whispered.

"No, and neither is grandpa."

The skateboarder cracked his knuckles.

The old man looked up just in time to see him hoist his skateboard into the air and swing it in a swift, savage arc into his face. His nose crunched and a spray of blood misted the nearby bookshelves. His body tumbled backward in her chair as the skateboarder pulled a silver blade from his baggy shorts. Two stabs and he was done.

The barista sighed and swept around his bar with a handful of towels.

"Dammit, Gillette," he grumbled as he moved to mop up the pool of blood forming on the hardwood.

The skateboarder dead bolted the front door and twisted the front blinds closed.

I clenched my jaw and finally released the breath I hadn't realized I was holding, glancing over to Gillette who hadn't looked away from me once.

"Christ," I spat.

"You're never going to be rid of them," she stated matter-of-factly.

"Who?"

The skateboarder approached with something in his hand. He dropped it onto the table directly in front of Gillette, who poked at it with a folded napkin. It was a charm on a gold chain. The Eye of Providence.

"He was Presidium?" I muttered, rubbing my eyes.

"They're willing to follow you all the way to Portland. Imagine how far up your asshole they've already crawled when you're in Baltimore."

"You had to kill him?"

"The Presidium doesn't have the muscle to police us out here. They want you to think so, but they don't. And we've been enjoying a kind of

Cold War since the late 1860's. Things were actually fairly quiet for the last couple decades. Then you show up."

"You can't blame me for this."

She folded the charm into her napkin and pocketed it. "I wanted to you to see how things are, Lake. How they really are, in a world that isn't insulated and artificial. This is what we live. This is how we survive. When people like you and Carmody run and hide under the Presidium's skirt, it doesn't exactly impress us."

"I'm not going to curse Carmody, Gillette."

She blinked rapidly, then sighed. "So, if that's a deal-breaker for you, and it looks like it is, then I guess we're done here."

I stood up. The skateboarder didn't flinch. Nothing about me seemed to register as a threat to him or Gillette. I hadn't felt that small in a long time.

Gillette shrugged and picked up her reader again.

By the time I reached the front door, the barista had expended all of his towels, and the blood was still spreading. He gave me a miserable look before returning to the back for more. The skateboarder trotted up beside me and unbolted the door.

Gillette called over her shoulder, "When the shadows start coming for you, you have my number. Try not to hold out too long."

I stepped out into the fresh air of the street. The door closed and bolted behind me. The tiny bookstore seemed to simply melt into the other innocuous stoops along Columbia Street.

So there it was. I had come to the brink of finding my soul, and all I had to do was one more curse. One curse without consequence, without damning my soul. If Gillette were to be believed, it seemed that Carmody had made this bed.

As I called a cab, I had serious doubts that I would be the one to lay him in it.

Chapter Ten

I spent most of the week thinking about Carmody, despite my best efforts otherwise. My brain continued to wander down the path of justification Gillette had provided for me. I had no soul at the moment. Whatever my body did while it was away was effectively karma-free. Or was it? There was no guarantee the Cosmos didn't hold my chips regardless of my soul's disposition, and what few texts in Emil's Library dedicated to soul magic offered me little clarity on the subject.

But even if I could curse a man with impunity, would I? Had Carmody actually deserved it? Did that even matter at this point? I had certainly appointed myself judge, jury, and executioner for Osterhaus. Why would this circumstance be any different? Granted it would be a moot decision unless I could acquire a piece of Carmody. Until that point, I had little to act upon. Still, the struggle proved to be an ongoing distraction.

The next day, I delivered a few gallons of interior latex paint for my property manager, Abraham Carter, when I passed a new sign staked up by the corner of Fayette and Carrollton. *Another urban revitalization project from McHenry Construction.* The sign displayed a series of modern mixed use structures resembling glass and steel townhomes. There were restaurants and a large fountain surrounded by cobblestones. The words *The Manor at Carrollton* swished across the top of the sign in labored cursive.

I found Abe sitting on his porch, staring across the street blandly. He hopped to his feet when I pulled up to my rental properties, and he made it to the Audi before I could even try to carry the paint up to his porch for him.

"Afternoon, Mr. Lake," he whistled through his false teeth. "Mighty nice of you to bring me this paint."

"Don't sweat it."

It was a poor choice of words. The sun was high and oppressive, and Abe's skin glistened with countless bubbles of sweat breaking into one another.

He hobbled up the front walk to his porch and sat the gallons of paint on the old boards.

"You want some lemonade?"

"Nah."

"Aw, come on now. It's hotter'n shit out here today."

He was right. Also, he made monster lemonade.

We took a seat on his porch rockers and sipped as we rocked. There was a bizarre calm to the moment, and I realized how a man like Abe could live his entire life without a plan. All he had to do was sit and drink lemonade. A clutch of shirtless men huddled on a stoop across the street. Every now and then they would shoot us a dirty look, and one of them even circled my car.

"They out of work," Abe commented without really looking at me.

"Not surprised."

"Nothin' better to do but sweat and talk, I suppose."

I spotted Lakeisha, Abe's next-door neighbor and one of my more vocal tenants, dancing up the street to something on her ear buds. She paused long enough to spot my car, and then me sitting on Abe's porch.

"Hey, what's up D-Lake?"

"Just catching up on all of the nothing I was planning to do this week."

"Hey," she shouted as she turned up Abe's walk. "You gonna sell or what?"

"Sell what?"

"Yeah."

"Huh?"

"You gonna sell?" she spat with a kick of her hip.

"What am I selling, Lakeisha?"

"Our homes. You ain't selling them, are you?"

I blinked and shook my head. "Wasn't planning on it."

I caught a glimpse of Abe releasing a held breath beside me.

"That's good 'cause I was gonna come slash your tires or something if you did."

"Oh, thanks."

"But you ain't, so we're all good."

The Dumont brothers, the tenants living next to Lakeisha, poked their heads out from their tiny fenced yard.

"Hey, Lakeisha," Tyrel bellowed. "That Lake over there?"

"Yeah, hon!"

The two men trotted around the hurricane fencing and up Abe's front walk, and I suddenly had an impromptu tenant meeting on my hands. Tyrel and Jamal Dumont were huge men. I was pretty sure they lifted weights, but I had never really had more than three sentences' worth of conversation with them.

Tyrel threw his massive hands on his hips. "Yo, Lake. What's this shit about selling these houses?"

"Where the hell is this coming from? Who said I was going to sell?"

Abe shifted in his rocker as he set down his glass. "Men came from the big retail project, knockin' on doors. One of them left this." He pulled a folded envelope from his shirt pocket.

I thumbed it open and gave it a quick read.

McHenry Construction letterhead.

"Why did they give this to you? This was supposed to get mailed to me directly. They shouldn't be bothering you with this."

I realized my tone was a touch stronger than I had intended. Both Abe and Lakeisha looked away as the Dumonts bristled.

"Sorry," I muttered. "Guess Joey McHenry's too cheap to bother with fucking stamps." I looked over to Abe. "Why didn't you call me about this?"

"Figured they called you already."

"They hadn't. First I'm hearing about it."

Lakeisha squirmed a little. "So, you still not selling, right?"

"No. I'm not selling the properties. Especially to this dick-whistle." I finished my lemonade quickly and stood up. The Dumonts didn't seem inclined to move out of the way. "Seriously, guys. I intend on being your shitty landlord for another ten years, minimum."

Tyrel gave me the tiniest of grins and stepped aside.

As I approached my car, the crew from across the street stood up together and started moving toward it. I fished my keys out of my pants quickly, but there wasn't enough time to keep this from turning into a scene. The first shirtless gentleman stood in front of my car, setting his foot onto the front bumper.

I shrugged at them. "Guys, really?"

"Nice car," his friend offered.

"Thanks. I'm going now."

"Sure about that?"

I never carried weapons. I didn't believe in them. My personal wardings were generally enough to scoop my ass out of danger when I needed them. Though I had to admit in a situation like this one, gnostic hermeticism wasn't as useful as a bodyguard.

"Look, I own these properties across the street. I'm just meeting with my tenants."

"Oh, we know who you are, Money." He smirked at the others. "See, if we owned shit like that, we figured we'd have plenty carrying-around cash, know what I'm saying?"

Fuck. This was going to turn into a mugging right in front of my tenants. Not what I needed.

A voice boomed from the front of the hurricane fence. "Yo, what's up?"

The thugs turned to find Tyrel and Jamal trotting up to my car. They gathered back into a line as the Dumonts eased up next to me.

"Problem here, Mister Lake?" Tyrel declared.

"No. Just chatting with your neighbors, T."

The second thug clicked his teeth and postured. "Best step away."

Jamal lifted his t-shirt to reveal a handgun tucked into his shorts.

The thugs backed away several steps.

I took advantage of the pause to jump into the Audi, but not before mouthing a "thank you" to Tyrel and Jamal. I watched as the clutch of thugs moved back across the street in my rearview mirror.

On the way around the block to my house, I wondered if McHenry even knew who all of the property owners were. Perhaps one of his employees had a list of names. It was possible he had no idea I was in his way.

And oh sweet Jesus, was I about to be a pain in his ass!

CHAPTER ELEVEN

Ches and I played a fun game of "pretend we totally don't have a date on Saturday night" each morning at the café. The game usually involved her bringing out my order with a bouncier smirk than normal, and me basically being awkward yet charming. I was a natural at that. Things felt right with Ches all week, which actually had me worried. I wasn't used to feeling normal, and this new emotion was as alien as it was opiate.

But before I could enjoy my weekend, I had to survive Julian's make-up meeting with the election staff. He held the meeting at Gordon's, as usual. The restaurant basically kept the back room open for Julian unless they had a bar mitzvah or a graduation. That steak restaurant, two blocks from the Inner Harbor, had become the unofficial campaign headquarters for Mayor Sullivan.

That week Sooner began his media blitz, painting the television with his "The Sooner The Better" ads attacking Sullivan's record as a liberal. Though in reality the two candidates stood on the same platform: clean up Baltimore. The fundamental difference came in the execution. Sullivan wanted to raise taxes on corporations to better fund the police and public services. Sooner wanted to relax the taxes on business and remove other obstacles to business growth in order to court major corporations to relocate headquarters to Baltimore. The money would mean jobs, which meant more income revenue, property sales, and a whole new demographic. Of course the obstacles to business growth were protecting both the poor residents of Baltimore and the health of the Chesapeake Bay, but that didn't seem to matter to Sooner or McHenry.

Julian's clutch of "territory managers" were in rare form, each grilling one another over which high school they attended, and God help you if you weren't originally from Baltimore. I lingered in the back corner, nursing a nagging headache, trying not to involve myself in the actual workings of the campaign. I wasn't entirely sure why Julian insisted I attend this meeting. He sure as hell wasn't paying me to knock on doors or run phone banks.

One particularly amphibian-looking territory manager croaked out his dismay at the Sooner ad blitz. "So when are we going to talk about the TV spots?"

Julian pursed his lips and leaned back in his chair. "We're waiting for polling."

"We have six spots already in the can, Julian," another advisor outlined. "We have Sooner on his flip-flop with the bailout funds, the parochial shutdown. If we wait too long, the midterm ads are going to start driving up the buys. What's Sully waiting for?"

Julian's face twisted in ambivalence. "I don't think he's ready to open Pandora's Box just yet."

"The box is open, Julian. What the hell?" the toad-faced advisor croaked.

"We don't know if Sooner's forward push is gaining any traction," Julian explained. "If he's spinning his wheels, it's better we let him dig himself deeper and deeper. And if I can labor the off-roading metaphor any further, someone please tell me."

"Has anyone bothered to connect the dots between McHenry and Sooner?" I asked. "Because Joe Q. Public might be interested."

The entire table fell silent and turned to me. Especially Julian. In fact, I regretted saying anything at all. Wasn't I supposed to be avoiding active politics?

The toad nodded. "One spot. But…"

"But what?" Julian grumbled.

"We're afraid it'll alienate the chamber. Developers. Small businesses, large businesses, retail."

"I get the picture," Julian mumbled, turning away.

The toad continued, "Sully carried a lot of business interests last election. Frankly, they won him the election. His record isn't bad for a Democrat, either. He's perceived as pro-business."

I shook my head and retorted, "Sooner is in McHenry's pocket. You're not going to lose the business vote with a TV commercial because you've already lost the business vote. McHenry is one of them. Hell, he's their crown prince, and everyone knows Sooner would be his mouthpiece in city hall."

"That's not how we understand the public perception," the advisor muttered before shaking his head at me and turning to Julian. "Who is this guy, anyway?"

Julian smirked. "Dorian Lake."

"And?"

"Grass roots coordination in West Baltimore."

The toad chuckled. "You're kidding."

Julian leaned into the table and held up a hand to silence him. "The point, Dorian, is that we need to know if unzipping our fly with McHenry will actually mean anything in the voting booth."

"It will," I spat.

"I suppose you have polling on that?" the toad jibed with more than a little smugness.

"When's the last time you really talked to someone in Federal Hill about Harborside Towers? Or people two blocks from where I live about this 'Manor at Carrollton.' I'm sure there's more."

The toad snickered and looked at the others for backup. "Is this guy serious? Sir, no one opposes inner city redevelopment."

"You think so?"

"Replacing abandoned structures that have become a den of drugs and crime with clean, green spaces and attractive mixed use developments? Where can I sign up because that's exactly what Sully did for the Inner Harbor."

Julian shot me a look. He didn't look pissed. He was waiting to see my response. Fuck. I was participating in active politics.

"You want to know something about the Inner Harbor? Ask someone who lives west of the MLK expressway. Seriously. It's like someone painted an actual line down the middle of the boulevard that says 'holy shit, you better be white and rich before you cross the street or you're going to get arrested.' You really want more of those lines painted through the city? Because if you're comfortable with that, I'm working on the wrong campaign."

He gave me a face-punchingly condescending grin. "If you think we're ignoring race in this campaign—"

"I'm not saying that."

"Because Sooner polls very well in West Baltimore, thanks to connections with Chief Bettis and the Food Service Workers. But I suppose you already know this?"

I held my tongue. This wasn't a bluff I was prepared for.

The toad leaned back in his chair with several tons of smugness. "Can we finally talk about the TV spots?"

The meeting continued for another half-hour before someone found another tape to play. I turned to Julian and gave him a quick finger-salute before stealing out the back of the room as the lights dimmed. Julian let me get all the way to the street before he caught up with me. He snatched my elbow and eased me to the side of Gordon's, his face tight with anxiety.

"Dorian? Are you still with me?"

I guided us off the street and into a storefront, weaving between nearby racks of power suits. "You think I'm not?"

"I needed you to meet these guys."

"Thanks for that. Can't say I'm a better person for it."

"Good," he chirped.

"Huh?"

"Between you and me? I hate these guys. They're small-minded misanthropes with Poli Sci degrees. I wanted you to see what Sullivan is working with."

"Why? What does it matter?"

"Because you're not just a hired gun, Dorian. You actually give a shit, God help us."

"I haven't been delivering lately."

"I noticed."

"Thing is, with karma, you're dealing with a limited resource pool."

He furrowed his brow. "I thought you said a person can't run out of good karma?"

"Well, that's true to a point. But every charm I make for Sullivan changes his disposition with the Cosmos. It weakens him, in the long term. Honest truth, I'm not sure how much good I am to you anymore."

He shoved his hands in his pockets and examined the rack of jackets for a moment, nodding slowly. "Are you resigning, here?"

I gave Julian a long examination. "You know those properties I rent out down the street?"

"I remember."

"Guess who needs to buy them to flesh out his new mixed use parcel?"

"McHenry?"

"I don't think he even knows yet."

His eyes were alive again "Oh, that is just absolutely perfect."

"I wasn't just blowing smoke in there, Julian. My renters? They're terrified of McHenry. Cecil Rawls? He was, too."

Julian blinked away the mention of Cecil's name as if I had smacked him in the face with a rotting halibut.

"So, if Sullivan wants to lose this election, the best thing he can do is to forget how many registered voters in Baltimore live below the poverty line."

"He knows."

"Does he?"

"That's why we haven't gone negative. We don't have to. McHenry thinks he can buy an election. And yes, he's very rich and bordering on organized crime... but politically he's a novice." Julian held out his hand. "So, maybe stick around a little longer? I know McHenry's got some karma coming."

I smiled and shook Julian's hand. "Sure I can't convince you to come back to the Club. I may or may not be bringing a real date Saturday night."

"And when you say 'real date' you're talking about...?"

"I don't know. The fact that I felt like calling her 'real' probably says more than anything."

Julian laughed. "Sorry. The Club is *terra non grata* until the election. Besides, it smells old."

"Okay." I turned back front of the store and scanned the street for onlookers.

"I'll call you?" Julian asked as I nodded him to take an exit.

"Do it."

I left Julian feeling like we were on the same team again, and that was enough to carry me into the evening.

That night as I reached for the latest acquisition from the corner wine boutique, I paused. One of my crystal lowballs was sitting in the corner of my sideboard. I crouched down and looked behind the sliding door to the liquor bottles. A bottle of Talisker sat right in front. It was a decent Scotch, eighteen years. I never got around to drinking it after I bought the scandalously expensive Glenrothes I kept under lock and key at the Club. Then after the debacle with Carmen, I'd switched to red wines. My tastes had shifted. Maybe it was the loss of my soul. Maybe it was some psychological coping mechanism.

I poured myself two neat fingers of the Talisker and stood by the front windows overlooking Amity as I inhaled the heady fumes. The smoky peat aroma filled my sinuses, jerking me back to a time when life was far bleaker, but far less complicated. Sipping that whiskey by the front windows stirred up a familiar feeling, if not specific emotions; that old paranoia that used to drive me into a bottle of single malt every night crept up my neck. I toyed with those old emotions with an enjoyable kind of detachment. I didn't hate my life at the moment. All of the hidden rivalries and unfinished business had been either dealt with or at least aired out. I had a best friend whom I wasn't neglecting. I had a girlfriend. Kind of. She felt like one. At the very least I had a date, a real date with real nerves and actual saccharin butterflies doing rainbow swirl loops in my gut.

I was even getting the old Julian back.

By the time I noticed the shadowy figure standing across the street from my house, I nearly dismissed it as a phantasm from my past. But it stayed there even after I noticed it. I froze and slowly lowered my glass. It didn't react. It just stood there, its hands in what were probably pockets, though I couldn't make out any actual features on its silhouette.

I ducked to the side of the window and tried to center myself. The shadows came and went these days, usually just before I got into a near-miss on the freeway, or something otherwise horrible threatened my life. They swarmed around me, flicking in and out of my periphery like tiny buzzards waiting to pick my corpse clean. Only I knew they weren't going to wait for me to die. They didn't wait for Emil. They took him apart, limb by limb, and left him bleeding to death on his bed.

When I mustered the courage to double-check the window, I found it was still there just across the street, staring. It was bigger than the usual shadow, the typical imps that dart in and out of tree limbs and in between cars. This looked like a human. Despite the only street light on the short block of Amity between my house and Fayette, I couldn't make out a face.

I reached for the wall above my mantle, and the silver blade mounted there. My darquelle. It was a gift from Edgar, a blade charged with murdered blood, capable of cutting through both flesh and spiritual substrate. In this case, the blade had once belonged to Robert of Argyle, also known as Robert the Heretic. According to Edgar, this particular darquelle had shed the blood of Christian zealots in the Highlands during Cromwell's occupation. The darquelle was the chosen tool of trade for Netherworkers around the world, and at that moment, it was my best weapon against whatever the hell was eye-fucking me through my front window.

I pulled the darquelle from its iron mounting hooks and rushed for the front door. This thing was going to see me coming and know I wasn't afraid of it. When I opened my front door, however, I found nothing. It was gone.

I stood like an idiot grimacing at the street for a while. The thing had been there. I could still smell it. A musky animal scent lingered in the humid summer night air, and either the thing was six feet of monster, or a pack of alley dogs had just sprayed down my stoop. Either was likely at that point.

I stepped back inside, locked my door, shuttered my windows, finished my whiskey, and then went to bed. It took forever to actually fall asleep, not so much for the dark faceless creature haunting the street corner, but for the plans I had the following night.

Seriously.

Saccharin butterflies. Rainbow loops.

Chapter Twelve

The last time I put that much effort and angst into what I wore to the Druid Hill Club was the night I applied for membership. I had settled on my fourth shirt choice and my second pair of trousers. Ultimately it was pink silk with charcoal, respectively, though I opted out of the vest. The doorbell rang, and I stumbled down the stairs, suddenly worried about the volume of cologne with which I had anointed myself.

When I opened the door, I found Ches standing in a bronze and black gown, holding a black sequined clutch. Her hair was done up in ringlets. I had no idea her hair could even do that. What was most striking was the makeup on her eyes. Until that moment, I hadn't really put together the fact that she never wore makeup at work. Now here she was, her eyes darkened, deep, pulled up into a feline kind of sexy.

I actually stammered.

"Come… come in."

She tucked a stray ringlet behind her ear and grinned, bobbing her head in what I assumed was satisfaction.

"You look nice," she said, hovering in the foyer.

"I clean up okay. But you? You're like a goddess. And that's not a line. Coming from a guy in my trade, that actually means something."

"Thanks."

"I'd offer a shot of something to pre-game, but…"

She held up a hand. "I'm a serious light-weight."

"I seem to recall a bottle of wine that begs to differ."

She squirmed. "Well, I'm not really. I was just being polite. Didn't want to scare you off."

"Who would that scare off?"

"Guys get scared off."

I arched my brow at her. "By women who can drink?"

"Most guys confuse liver damage with penis length."

"Well, I don't mean to brag, but my liver's basically a shriveled handful of anger at this point."

She gave me a jab with her elbow as I escorted her to the car. I even held the door open. I wasn't following any prescribed set of motions; it actually felt sexy doing it. The sky was still fairly bright with the high summer sun by the time we exited the Jones Falls and wound our way up the arboreal drive to the Club. Ches leaned forward in her seat as the old white-bricked manse slipped into view.

"Looks old," she whispered.

"Wait until you see the inside."

"What is it, a country club or something?"

"A gentleman's club."

"You mean a strip club." Her voice snarled, and her eyes shot sideways at me in an expression that all but stated she was not okay with that.

"No, nothing like that. Kind of better, kind of worse. It's a social club dating back to Reconstruction. You have to know someone to get an invitation to join."

"Who did you know?"

"I did a job for a guy. He was so impressed with the product he ponied me up for the owners. Been a regular ever since."

"What do you like about it?" she asked. "The secrecy?"

"My dad belonged to a club. He went every Saturday night. I always figured… never mind."

"Is this place Men Only?"

I cringed. "Yeah. Male members only. We can bring guests, obviously."

She lifted an eyebrow. "Uh huh."

I pulled up to the porte cochere, handed Ramon my keys, and had joined Ches at the front door by the time the car disappeared around the corner. She stood still, gripping her handbag.

"You okay?" I asked.

"Your ex. She worked here, didn't she? You said she was a high-priced call girl. They have girls who work here, don't they?"

I stiffened and simply nodded.

She sucked in a breath. "And you thought this would be a good idea?"

"It's weird, isn't it?"

"You brought me on our first official date to a bordello where you met your ex-girlfriend. Why would that be weird?"

"It's weird. I shouldn't have—"

She lifted a hand. "Stop. This place is obviously important to you, and you wanted to share that with me. But you have to know this place is all kinds of wrong?"

I balled fists in my pockets. Not because I was mad at Ches, but because she was right, and I was being so completely stupid. "We don't have to go in."

She examined the doors, the concrete, my shoes, then finally took a long breath. "Well, at this point, I have to return this dress to the rental tomorrow, so I might as well get some use out of it. Besides, maybe I'll luck out and find an old acquaintance to tell me a crushingly embarrassing story about you."

"Yeah. That's pretty much a given."

I offered my elbow, and as she laced her arm through it, we advanced through the doors.

"You can rent gowns?"

"You can rent a tux, can't you?"

"Yeah, but I didn't know it worked for dresses, too."

We paused at the coat room, and I found Kim standing stiff at the counter.

"Dorian Lake, plus one."

"Hey Dorian," she replied in a quiet voice.

"Kim, this is Francesca Baker."

Ches smiled broadly and offered a hand. Kim stared at it for a split-second longer than was comfortable before giving it a quick, polite grip.

"How's the room tonight?" I asked.

Kim leaned forward, her eyes low. "Listen, Dorian… there's a thing."

"What kind of thing?"

"I need you to show me your ID."

My stomach tightened. I enjoyed this shtick with Kim, but in front of Ches, it felt awkward. I fished out my wallet and offered my laminated card for her inspection as usual.

What wasn't usual was the way Kim turned into the coatroom and pulled a phone from the wall.

Ches leaned into me. "Everything's okay, right?"

"I think so." That was a lie.

Kim cradled the phone and kept my card. "Just a minute, please."

"Kim? What's up? Is this about the photos?"

Ches whispered, "Photos?"

"Interior décor. Nothing creepy."

"Just a minute, please," Kim repeated, turning away from me. I could already see the guilt building up in her eyes.

"Something's wrong," I muttered.

After an uncomfortable thirty seconds, I heard a door open and spotted Giancarlo the manager swooping down the entry hall with two security goons on his sides. I had only ever seen the security goons once before, when one of the girls was getting thrown around by a client. Said client left with a broken jaw and a ruined social life after that. I was hoping for neither at the moment.

"Giancarlo? What's going on?"

His imposing frame stopped in front of me, his hands shoved into his pockets. Giancarlo was a beast of a man, but he was always fair and decent. I figured something had to be significantly wrong for him to block me this far forward.

"See, Dorian," he mumbled, "I gotta turn you out."

"What?"

He looked down at his shoes, then stepped to the coatroom. Kim held out my card as he snatched it.

"Membership's revoked. Look, I'm real sorry about this."

Giancarlo pulled his other hand from his pocket and produced a tiny pair of scissors. Without looking me in the face, he snipped my card in half and handed the pieces to one of the goons.

I looked over to Ches who was turning red and tucking her head to the side.

My blood pressure rose, but I knew getting smart wasn't going to make this go away.

"Can I have a word?" I whispered, gesturing away from Ches.

Giancarlo gave her a look, then nodded. We withdrew to a potted palm near the entry doors, and I tried to whisper loud enough to be heard only by Giancarlo.

"What's this about? I mean, I've caused my share of scenes in there, but you didn't bounce me once for that."

"Not once?"

"Okay, maybe that time with the Swedes. But I've been a saint lately."

"Yeah, you're a stand-up guy, Dorian. Which is why this sucks for me as much as you. But this comes from the owners, so there's nothing I can do about it. You know how this goes."

"The owners?" That son of a bitch. "McHenry, right?"

"I cannot comment on the identities of the owners."

"Right." I nodded toward Ches. "Timing really sucks. I mean, of all nights to do this to me, this was the absolute worst."

Giancarlo pulled in a breath to ramp out another genuine, but fruitless apology, but I turned on my heel and approached Ches.

"I'm really embarrassed by this," I said in as even a tone as I could muster. "We're going to have to go."

Ches looked over at the others then back to me. Her eyes were wide, focused, soft.

I led her back out the double-doors. The Audi was already waiting for me. Ramon had to know this would be a short visit. Who wasn't in on this? I thought about Big Ben behind the bar. I tried to catch a glimpse of the side windows in case he was watching, but the Club was made to be seen, not seen into.

I shoulder-checked Ramon away from Ches' door and closed it behind her. And without so much as a look behind me in the rearview mirror, I pulled back down the gravel drive.

Ches didn't say anything for a long time, letting me stew in my own juices. And stew I did! This was personal. It was a warning shot from McHenry, a petulant act of a man-child. Still, Julian had seen this coming, or at least had a sense of where the winds were blowing. He stopped going to the Club a while back, probably because he knew McHenry was one of the owners. Hell, I played to that fact the first time I actually met McHenry. And now he had just taken the Club away from me. He had no way of knowing how personal that would have been. And if he did know, then he would regret this.

I exited the freeway, and Ches finally spoke up.

"Sorry."

I shook my head, and gave her a smile with as much dignity as I could muster. "No, I'm sorry. This is all just some stupid misunderstanding."

She put a hand on mine as I gripped the gear stick. Her face seemed contemplative. I was on the verge of squirming when she replied, "I don't think so. I think that guy was just being rude."

"Who, Giancarlo? Nah. He's actually a pretty good guy. He had orders. It's... complicated."

"Well, you're better off. You might not realize it yet, but you are."

She was looking at me again, but this time I didn't feel like squirming. "You hungry?"

"Starving."

"I don't know where we can get a table last minute Saturday night, though."

"I do," she chimed.

She gave me directions to what I assumed would be her apartment. Instead, she led me to the other side of Baltimore to a charming blue-painted brick face restaurant called the Blue Moon Café. I wound around an alarmingly narrow lot until I found a not-so-legal parking space between an SUV and some utility meters.

We managed to get seated in a booth, and as we settled, we received more than our fair share of stares from the other patrons. Few people wear evening gowns to diners unless they're specifically looking for attention. In Baltimore, that wasn't necessarily out of the question, so we shrugged off the tourists and ordered some oysters and beer.

By the third oyster, the conversation finally returned to the events of the evening.

Ches forked some horseradish on top of an oyster and asked, "So, want to talk about it? The Club, I mean. You said it was complicated."

I looked over the iced platter of shellfish and thought about it. I really didn't want to discuss it, but I also didn't want to kill conversation. It would have been rude.

She waved me off with an empty half-shell. "Sorry. I'm being nosy again. It's not really my business." She took a drink of beer, her eyes moving up to the ceiling. "Of course, you did invite me, and I rented a dress, so it kind of is my business."

"One of the owners has it out for me."

"Why?"

"Oh, plenty of reasons. I'm mostly just surprised it took him this long to cut me off."

"What did you do?" She was leaning forward in her seat, grinning.

I leaned back in the booth and took a deep breath. "He's Joey McHenry."

She stared blankly at me, and finally shook her head slowly.

"He's an industry giant in the city. Drive past most of the construction sites downtown, you'll see McHenry Construction signs."

"Okay. I didn't have that place figured as a small-potatoes kind of joint."

"Right. Well, there's this election going on."

"For what?"

I took a moment before responding. "Mayor?"

"Really?"

"Yep."

"Don't we vote for everyone in two years?"

"No, it falls on the midterms. Do you not have television?"

"No."

"No shit?"

She waved her fork at me. "When I'm not working or pissing away an evening with a dapper smartass, I'm usually studying."

"What are you studying, by the way? I never asked."

She lingered over her glass, her eyes tracing lines in mid-air. "Psychology. Social decision and organizational science, specifically."

"Sounds heady."

She shrugged.

"You seem unimpressed with your own career path."

"Nah. I just don't like talking about it."

"Why not?"

She sighed. "Guys are threatened by psychology dates. You study enough behavioral sciences, you learn how people lie, and your bullshit detector gets pretty strong. When the guy knows this, he starts clamming up, closing off. Thinks everything I do is an experiment and won't let me just be who I am."

"Sounds like you're talking about someone in particular."

A rare scowl crept into her lips, and she looked down at the table.

"Now I'm being the nosy one."

She shook her head. "So anyway, don't sidetrack. McHenry. Election. And?"

"If you like, I can draw up some flashcards."

"I miss all of the drama from Florida. Family, extended family, friends, friends-of-friends. I left it all down there, and now it's just me and my job and school. I have a distinct lack of he-said-she-said in my life. You're all I got."

I spent an hour walking her through the talking points of the Sooner-McHenry intrigue and how I managed to insinuate myself in the election against my better judgment. When most of the dinner crowd had come and gone, we decided to take a stroll to walk off the alcohol. The air was thick and humid, and most of her hair had fallen. She finally pulled out a few pins and tossed it in her fingers, returning it to the more familiar look.

"Still," she said as we crossed a street, "you talked that place up like it was your personal sandbox. That's gotta sting."

"It does, but I'll be okay."

"You're playing this kind of cool, is all."

"How so?"

"I mean, I know you're not trying to impress me or anything. So you're probably the suffer-in-silence martyr type."

"God help me."

"Your friends, the Swains? Don't they snap you out of it when you get like this?"

"Yeah. When I see them."

"So, I'm doing it now. I want you to say something." She stopped on the sidewalk and pulled my elbow until I faced her. "Okay? Repeat after me."

"Shoot."

"Fuck," she intoned.

I repeated, "Fuck."

"That club."

I chuckled. "Fuck that club."

"See? Don't you feel better?"

I actually did. "Ches, you're impossibly amazing, you know that?"

"I totally do."

"So, I've wanted to kiss you for a long time now. And here we are, standing in the middle of Fell's Point, and I'm trying to figure a good way to bring that up."

She screwed her brow together. "Oh my God, you're actually asking permission to kiss me?"

"I figured the worst case scenario would—"

She gripped the back of my neck and pulled my head down to hers. The kiss was slow, and anything but delicate. She moved her lips in a constant writhe, her tongue taking furtive caresses of my mouth. It was the kind of kiss that made me breathe heavy. I ran my fingers up into her hair, pulling them down her back as those curls smoothed out over the skin exposed by the gown.

She pulled away and ran a slow thumb around my mouth, wiping away her lipstick.

"For future reference, never ask a girl permission for a kiss." She turned and continued down the sidewalk. "Unless you actually don't have permission, in which case you're just a skeev."

I watched her swagger up the pavement, and hopped forward to catch up with her.

"How is a guy supposed to know the difference?"

"Knowing is the entire point."

"Isn't that a little unfair?"

"Suck it up, magic man."

I reached out for her elbow this time, and pulled her in for a follow-up kiss. This time she stayed with me for even longer. Her tongue went deeper, and my hand fell lower down her back. When we were done, I ran my fingers over her hair, straightening the bits I'd tussled.

"That more like it?"

She smiled and nodded. "Quick learner."

"Want to come back to my place tonight?"

She stared into my eyes, streetlights casting a bright spark in hers. She looked down and gave me a chummy pat on the chest. "Ease up there."

"Just seemed like the whole 'go for broke' angle was working out pretty good for me."

She gave me a coy smile, and we looped a street corner before she finally broke the silence. "Can I ask you a direct question?"

"Sure, but only if I can ask one back."

"Deal."

"Your question?"

"Your ex-girlfriend. The one who was working, or whatever you call it, at that club. Were you her, what do you call it? Client? John? You know, before you were dating?"

I took several steps down the walk before I answered. "Yes."

"So you're into prostitutes?"

"That's not how I'd describe myself."

"But you patronized a club that kept hookers on staff. And, well, you patronized the hookers."

"That was before."

"Before her?"

"Yes."

"So she scared you off of prostitutes? That's a done deal?"

"Oh God, yes. Look, I'll be straight with you. I was a patron of that Club for years in the fullest sense of that word. And I never really thought about it, the girls I mean. I didn't have anyone, and it was easy to ignore everything else. You know, inside that place the rules feel different."

"What were you ignoring?"

"My life, I guess. I just wanted to feel like I belonged to something secret and special. Something that kind of proved I had made it."

"Like your Dad?"

I tucked my chin and walked in silence.

A dog gave us a snarling what-for from behind a gate as we passed his alley. Ches pushed into me, nearly knocking me into the street.

"You okay?" I asked, steadying her with my hands.

"Yeah," she muttered. "Just not a dog person."

"Don't like dogs?"

"They don't like me, is more like it." She pulled me back onto the sidewalk as she gave the dog the finger. With a cleansing breath, she proclaimed, "You never told me what happened with this Carmen. What changed?"

"I got stupid."

She smirked at me. "Could you be more specific?"

"I got possessive and made a scene. Almost got her fired. Things got ugly, and I stayed away from the Club for a couple years. She held a grudge and took it out on me."

"What, did she slash your tires or something?"

I stifled a grimace. "Not exactly." I turned a slow circle to face her. "Anyways, you are totally cheating, you know?"

"What?"

"You were supposed to ask me one question. Wasn't that our deal?"

She looked up at me and cocked her head. "Alright. Your go. What's your question?"

"Do you believe in what I do?"

"You mean magic?"

"I prefer not to call it that. But sure. Do you believe I actually manipulate the energies of the Cosmos? Or do you think I'm some wingnut with a Lovecraft obsession?"

She snickered. "I, uh… I like that you believe in it."

"So that's a no?"

She nodded furtively. "I'm a skeptic at heart. But I like that you believe in magic. And you're not some wingnut. You're finding a way to make a living doing something you believe in. Kind of pisses me off just thinking about how lucky you are." We continued a while in silence until she added, "So, educate me. What is there to magic that isn't, you know, rabbits in hats and men in fabulous sequined plunging necklines?"

It was a heavy question. I swallowed my nerves down hard.

"The idea is that there are mechanics to the Cosmos which we understand, like gravity and inertia. Then there are mechanics that are less obvious. Rules that we intentionally ignore because we don't want to understand them as human beings."

"Such as?"

"Affinities. Correspondences. There's a reason people believe in astrology."

"Beyond the fact that they want to believe?"

"Well, take scrying for example. It's a way of connecting a tool, such as a pendulum or a gazing stone, and stitching it to the energy of someone or something that's distant. It's not hocus-pocus. It's the affinity of energies."

"Sounds Eastern."

"Energy can be tangible, which is why the first step is learning how to ground and center. You have to keep your personal energy tight around your body, or it can reach out and affect the world in ways you don't intend. The first thing any practitioner learns is how to identify his own energy. Then you can use it to purify a space, such as the Banishing Cross… and I've lost you."

"No, it sounds very… yes. Yes, you lost me."

"That's alright. Thanks for listening."

Something caught my attention in my periphery. Something dark and small skittered from the eaves of the bar fronts along the street. I paused mid-stride, trying not to crane my neck in its direction. It wouldn't have done any good. I never caught a full glimpse of the moving shadows. They only ever just swarmed around the edges of my notice.

"What's up?" she asked.

"Nothing."

I hooked us across the street to make a return trip to our car. The conversation and the increased activity of the teeming shades had sobered me plenty. They only ever got this active when something big was about to happen, usually something that put my life in jeopardy. I offered to drop her off at her home, but she insisted I return her to the bus stop near my house. It felt needlessly dodgy, but I was really only just getting to know Ches, and as I waited on the side of Amity waiting for a city bus to pick her up, I had to follow Wren's advice and remind myself that she wasn't Carmen. She was a brilliant, young woman who was being careful with a man who thought he was a wizard.

CHAPTER THIRTEEN

I planned to spend Sunday largely indoors, away from moving vehicles, falling anvils, and steak knives. But then I got a call from Edgar.

"Dorian? You busy today?"

"Remarkably not busy. What's up?"

"You remember that guy I introduced you to, Del Carmody?"

Oh, how could I possibly forget him? He was my ticket for getting my soul back.

"I do."

"He called me last night, said he has something new for you. If you're interested?"

I wasn't sure how long I actually hung onto that question from Edgar's point of view, but to me it was an eternity.

"Yeah. Sounds good."

"Cool, man. He's in York today, said to meet him in Penn Common by the monument at noon."

"New York?"

"Pennsylvania."

Damn. I nearly had an excuse to travel back to New York. "What the hell is in York, Pennsylvania?"

"How should I know? That's just what he said."

"Gotcha. Thanks, Edgar. You coming with?"

"Nah," he sighed. "Elle's under the weather. I'm watching her while Wren takes Eddie to soccer."

"Jesus, Edgar. She's an actual soccer mom now?"

"Don't hammer that too hard, man. She'll run you over in her Jeep."

I knew she would, too. "At least it's not a minivan. Give the kids a hug, or I don't know. Give them a wet willie and tell them it's from Dorian."

I had plans now. Plans well north of Baltimore. That was a lot of freeway miles on a day when the shadows seemed to think they had a good crack at my carcass. Add to this particular gumbo of certain doom the fact that I was meeting with a man who had antagonized the entirety of the West Coast hermetic establishment to the point that they contracted a standing curse on his head, and I wasn't particularly excited to make the trip.

But I didn't have much choice, nor did I have a lot of time. I rushed down to the workroom and opened up the dark-stained wood cabinet containing Emil's Library. I had limited time to find that Macedonian text. I eventually found it, a clutch of hand-sketches and some pretty basic curses written in a mélange of Greek and Bulgarian. They were quick and lethal. "Tidy" was how Emil would have described them. Simple death, no histrionics. Short period until the effect.

Just what Gillette would have wanted.

I took notes.

The biggest trick to such a direct lethal curse was the requirement for "vital essence." I tended to impose this requirement on my own clients, even for simple hexes and charms. The reason was simple enough... economy. The closer you came to including the actual cosmic imprint of the target, the less work you have to perform. It could be substituted, circumvented, or even blatantly overlooked, but the laws of magic required a substitute. I had learned in my years of hermetic craft workings that skin and hair offered a reasonable alternative for real blood. The worst curses, however, were satisfied with no substitutes.

Which meant if I was going to curse Del Carmody to death, I needed his blood.

I returned the curse manual to the cabinet and leaned against it, thinking through my situation. If I found a way to extract a drop of blood from Carmody, I could murder him magically, and in doing so regain my soul. With any luck at all, my soul wouldn't notice such a black mark chalked up against me karmically. Two, if one counted Osterhaus.

On the other hand, how could I extract Carmody's blood without his noticing? Curses are powerful workings, but they aren't foolproof. Were I to simply walk up to Carmody, prick him with a blood meter and walk away, he would know what would be coming. I was certain a man in his line of work would recognize such an overt move from a known Curse Merchant, and take steps to shield himself. Hell, the man had managed to dodge Gillette and her compatriots for who knew how long, what chance did I have of landing a curse on that slippery son of a bitch?

After copying my notes, I tucked the Macedonian text under my arm and locked the Library cabinet. This was a first. I had never parted with one of Emil's books in the years since his death. The moving shadows were reminder enough that I had little time to secure my soul before they tore me limb-from-limb as they had Emil. I shook my head as I realized I was putting serious thought into cursing a man with a spell from the very book I was giving him. It was a dick move, but it was my best chance at dodging my fate. I would have to be an idiot not to try.

I looked up the directions to York and where to park, and set out on my journey into Pennsylvania. The sky was covered in a leaden blanket of low-altitude clouds, which didn't help the heat one bit. I managed to get lost in the maze of one-way streets, and finally spotted the monument from between two buildings. After securing a questionably legal spot to park on the street, I clutched the Macedonian text and jogged two blocks to the park of Penn Common.

I was ten minutes late, but Carmody was still there, spread out on a black wrought-iron bench at the base of the pillared monument. I stood almost directly over him before he noticed me.

"Oy, Dorian Lake, my new best friend!" He pulled himself upright and reached up to shake my hand. "How's the Life treating you?"

I shook his hand, bracing myself as he used me to pull himself to his feet. "Well enough." I released his hand, thinking more about how much pressure would be required to break his skin. My eyes made tiny motions around the park searching for rough concrete edges or exposed nails as he swept beside me, urging me to walk down a sidewalk.

"Cherry little snatch of papers you're sporting there."

"You're lucky I found this. Got sandwiched inside another book."

"It'll do nicely." He held out his hand, and with a great deal of internal debate, I set the text into his palm.

Carmody thumbed it over and nodded.

"So, you give Gillette a jingle?"

"I did."

"And how'd you come off, then?"

"She wasn't as helpful as I had hoped."

He clicked his tongue and shrugged. "Well, that was a possibility, I'm afraid. Self-important little bint, that one. Sorry about that, mate. Wish I could've helped."

"We're still in-process. I think she just has to get a fuzzy feeling about me before she'll help me."

Carmody looked up to a nearby tree and whistled at a robin.

There was a moment when his head was cocked up at the bird that I considered "tripping" into him, knocking him forward in hopes he'd bloody a hand or a knee. The moment passed as he spun on his heel and flashed me a sharp smile.

"So. Curse is it, then?"

"I'm sorry?"

"Gillette wants you to cram a curse directly up my asshole, or the orifice of your choosing, depending on how bleeding magnanimous she's feeling today."

I froze, trying to feel my way through this turn in conversation.

"Don't worry, mate. I'm not offended. In fact, it's all part of my clever plan."

"So there's a reason you broomed me right into Gillette's tender graces, after all?"

"Figured you'd be curious about that. Gillette, as you may well know, has a raging hunger for my imminent demise."

"I got that."

"To date, ineffectively. Not for a lack of trying, mind you. I've had to skirt that bitch for years. It's to the point of obsession with her. Mind you, she's a capable practitioner. Vicious. Brilliant. Her sense of fashion leaves a bit to be desired—"

"There's a plan, you said?"

Carmody's grin thinned. "I heard about you last year when I relocated underneath the petticoats of the Presidium. Gillette's a handful, but no one questions she's the Queen of Hell in the Northwest. I figure the best place to hide is the one place she's too afraid to lay tread. Wasn't long before I ran into an old client of yours. Some musk ox of a businessman in Jersey, said you dealt in karma. Knew how to push buttons, make things happen ahead of schedule." He stepped forward to lower his voice. "Precisely the kind of service I require."

"So why didn't you just make an appointment?"

"See, I knew you were the squeamish type. Trust me, I was gobsmacked when I heard about you and Osterhaus, that pointless fuck. Almost thought twice about approaching you. Then I met Edgar Swain. He swears on you like the bleeding Gospel of Christ. Still, I knew I couldn't sic you on Gillette without warning. And she'd see through you if you tried to wing it. No offense, but you have a shit poker face, mate."

"So you gambled on my integrity?"

"Integrity, cowardice, I don't know what you'd call it. Whatever drives you to insane limits in order to avoid getting your hands dirty."

"Hell of gamble, Carmody. I thought hard about it."

"How hard, if you don't mind my asking?"

"Let's just say I'm a drop of blood short of getting my soul back."

His smile thinned to the point of grimace. "That a fact?"

"This honesty thing is contagious."

"Well, allow me to complicate the situation then." Carmody reached into his pocket, and for a split second, I considered jumping for the bushes. He produced a small vial from his pocket and held it up to the gray light of the overcast day. The vial contained a dark red liquid. "See this?"

"I see it."

"You know what this is, then?"

"Is it Gillette's?"

"No, I wasn't born that lucky. It's mine."

"Your blood? You carry around a vial of your own blood? Not exactly playing it safe."

"Well, I don't carry it around all the fuckin' time, you git. Just today. Just for you."

I blinked several times before words came to me. "You're giving me your own blood?"

"I figure if you're at all capable, you'll be able to drop the Sword of Fuckin' Damocles directly on my head." He stepped forward and held it out.

I took a step back. "Horseshit. What is this?"

"Swear to whatever God you believe in, I'm telling the truth. It's my blood, and there's no trick."

"Why would you do this?"

"Because it's the only way a person like you will ever trust a person like me."

He took another step forward and pushed it into my hand.

My fingers wrapped around the vial, and he gave me space.

I held up the blood, inspecting it like a jeweler with a fist-sized hunk of diamond.

"So, now you can curse me, Lake. There's absolutely nothing stopping you."

"Except…"

"Except what?"

"I haven't decided if I'm going to do it or not."

He held up a finger and waved it at me. "It's your one chance to lay your mittens on your soul. You play Gillette's little magical hitman, I go tits up and floating in the Bay, and you're back in control of your own fate."

Carmody stared at me from under his hat.

I brandished the vial. "You don't think I'll do it?"

"I think you're not ready to murder someone. And I think beneath this finely crafted veneer of sarcasm is a genuinely decent man who still thinks the good guys ought to beat the bad guys when the show's over and the credits roll. I think Gillette has given you nothing but ultimatums, knowing her. I've given you nothing but the one way to really screw me. So, now… who do you trust?"

Who did I trust? It was a fine question. As idiotic a bluff as it was, it was still a move. I had to see where he was taking this.

"I suppose we'll both put a little faith in my integrity," I said as I pocketed the vial.

"You'll help me out with Gillette, then?"

"I'll be honest, Carmody. I tend to use vital essence even for my hexcraft."

"Bit of an overkill, isn't it?"

"I have a barn of satisfied customers who say it's not."

"Fair enough. But if you're planning on lifting some piece of Gillette off her person, I have to level with you, mate. You're not going to limp away from that."

"Then there's that whole issue of her knowing how to get my soul out of spiritual hock."

"There's got to be others."

"Maybe, but how long do I have to look for them?"

"So, give me time then. Remember, I walked away from the Life to pursue a career in information brokerage. I have sources. I'm the fucking Google of North American witchcraft."

"I don't think I can afford your rates, Carmody. No offense."

"Don't think of it like that. This is us trying to help one another. You hex Gillette for me, and I find you another stud to ride onto the track." He stared at me with sharp eyes over his stubble-strewn grin. "You have my blood, in any case. Consider it your insurance."

"I'll think about it." I turned to walk back to my car.

"Oh yes, lovely," he called out. "You think about it then. While you are, chew a little on this. I have information for you right here, right now. Information about your little political entanglements."

"Good for you," I answered without stopping.

I was nearly back to the statue when Carmody trotted up behind me. "Your little friend, McHenry? He knows you're on Sullivan's unofficial payroll."

"No shit."

"So you know that. What you don't know is that he's called in a specialist to deal with you."

I stopped. "What kind of specialist?"

"Our kind, if you take my meaning."

"McHenry's called in his own hermeticist?"

"Right."

"I suppose Sooner could stand a charm or two." I looked over at Carmody. "Who is it?"

"No clue. This is scuttlebutt. Prime grade scuttlebutt, but it's secondhand, nonetheless."

"So it's a big, fat maybe?"

"It's the truth. I can tell the difference in these things."

I studied Carmody's face. There was no way to tell if he was being forthcoming, or if he was leading me on. I had to make a judgment call.

"I'll look into what kind of hex I can cast from a continent away, without any of Gillette's vital essence. It'll take some time. These things don't really work that well from a distance."

He cracked a yellow-toothed grin. "Brilliant."

"Meantime, you go do your thing. If you find someone who can find my soul, then I'll have a hex ready to go."

He thrust out a hand. I shook it without mirth, though he did more than enough shaking for the two of us.

"My new best friend! I told you, didn't I?"

"Yeah. Well, see you."

I strode back down the sidewalk and exited the park. A wind picked up over York and rustled the treetops. Something darted through the alley across the street from my parking space, and I tried not to give it the courtesy of looking. They were still active. Maybe it was Carmody they were hungry for? It would have been a nice thought to cling to as I drove back across the Mason-Dixon line, but I knew it was sterile optimism.

Still, I had a new resource working for me. I didn't trust him, but he was naïve enough to think he could dupe me into thinking that blood was his. That meant for all of his snooping skill, he was a novice at the actual Craft. If I couldn't trust him, at least I could trust his ignorance.

It had been a dizzying weekend. With any luck at all, the coming week would bring me good news.

Chapter Fourteen

Monday morning was gray and blustery. It was likely to be a stormy afternoon. At least I would get my morning coffee fix before the rain hit. I bustled down the block for the café and stepped under the outside awning, choosing a table closer to the building wall in case the rain decided to get an early start. Ches spotted me from inside and popped out with my usual, a nervous grin on her face.

"Good morning, Mister Lake," she declared as she set the mug in front of me.

"Miss Baker."

She leaned against the brick, crossing her arms. "Do anything interesting this weekend?"

"Nah," I retorted after sipping the coffee. "Stayed inside, polished my silver. Oh, I did go on a date."

"And how did it go?"

I gave her a grin. "Outstanding."

Her lips pulled into a tight grin as her eyes dropped a little. Her mind seemed elsewhere. I was about to ask her what was up, when she stepped back inside. The owner haunted the window, staring a hole through me. He had noticed how chatty I had become with Ches, and I suspected my continued presence at this café would become difficult for her. I had only met him once or twice before, and only in passing. I didn't even know his name.

I let him stare as I nosed over the morning's Sun. There was considerably less campaign coverage than usual, thanks to a barge leak on the Mississippi. A good gust of wind blew the corner of my paper, folding it over in my view. Just beyond the paper, standing across the street, I spotted a man lingering as if waiting for a bus. But there was no bus stop there. The stop was halfway up the block, just around the corner from my house. He wasn't holding a bag or a briefcase. He was just standing there.

Looking at me.

He wore a dark coat and a short-brimmed hat. A bit warm for the season. I lowered the paper and returned his glare. He seemed normal enough, but his features were difficult to commit to memory. I was fairly certain he wasn't an acquaintance or client of mine.

We continued our eye lock for about a minute before he finally turned and stepped back up the street. He was certainly no shadow, no scampering imp hungry for the remains of my soul. He was real, at least real-seeming. It was the way he stared at me that truly put me off my feed. He was studious, full of gravity, and completely unimpressed that I had spotted him. And in a second, he was gone.

I wondered if I hadn't found McHenry's charm crafter? Or, more accurately, I wondered if he hadn't found me? As I ruminated on the matter, a sense of dread crept up my sleeves. I couldn't remember his face at all. I had no idea which direction he had gone. It had to be the effect of a glammer, a charm that altered appearance. Obfuscation glammers were very basic charms. A decent one could even make a person impossible to spot in a crowd.

Or at night.

"You okay?" Ches asked from behind my shoulder, nearly causing me to jump out of my skin.

"Huh? Oh, yeah. Fine."

"Look like you've seen a ghost."

"What does that look like, exactly? People always say that. If I saw a ghost, would I suddenly have white hair, bloodshot eyes?"

Ches's face fell, and she withdrew a step. "You just look freaked out, is all I meant."

"Sorry. I didn't mean to snap."

She cocked her head at me. "You didn't snap."

"Yeah, I did. I'm just a little weirded out. There was a guy..." I paused as Ches took a slow blink, her face growing pale. "Forget me, are you okay?"

Ches covered her forehead with her hand and leaned against the wall. "Uh, yeah. I mean no. Just feel off, all of a sudden."

I stood up and guided her to a chair. "Here. Sit. Need some water?"

"No, I'm really fine."

She really wasn't.

I looked up for the owner, but he was finally tending to some other business inside the café.

"Think you're coming down with something?" I offered, taking a seat beside her.

She shook her head slowly, her hair falling down the sides of her face.

A low chuckle bubbled up from her throat.

"Down? Down we go, Dorian Lake."

The hair on my neck stood on end. Ches's voice had adopted a hard, shaky tone.

She pulled her head up slowly. Her eyes were twisted into a menacing sneer. "Down the rabbit hole."

"No!"

She burst into a wicked cackle, her fingers snarling into claws on her chair's armrests. "Down, down falls Dorian Lake. Into the pit where all souls wait. Watch it boil and watch it bake."

I thrust a finger into her face. "You get out of her!"

"Watch him cheat you out of your fate!"

I slammed my hand onto the table. "You get out of her NOW!"

Ches lunged at me, knocking me over in my chair. Coffee splashed across both of us as we tumbled backward, rolling on the tile as the mug smashed into pieces. She leveraged herself on top of me, wrapping her fingers around my throat. Her mouth had contorted back into an animalistic grimace.

I gasped against her grip, kicking my legs against the nearby furniture to get the owner's attention.

Ches's chuckles turned into growls, and her grip redoubled. I coughed and gagged, blood pooling up in my head.

I managed to get a hand under her throat and pressed up against her windpipe. My thumb slipped into the notch between her clavicles, and she gagged. Her gripped loosened enough for me to twist my head. I sucked in a breath and brought my knee up against her ribs hard. She pitched off to the side, tumbling into more chairs.

I pulled myself to my side, gasping for air as she flailed her arms and legs. Her body skittered across the tiles until she hit the back iron banister separating the café seating from the alley behind the building. Her head struck the iron with a loud clang, and her eyes fluttered for a second. Her growls turned into gasps.

I managed to pull myself to my feet and cautiously approached her. With one last spasm, her arms fell still. Too still. I crouched down in front of her to check for breathing when I heard a loud booming voice behind me.

"Hey! Get away from her!"

I turned to find the owner stepping out of the café. He was holding an umbrella like a club.

I held up my hands. "Easy. I'm checking if she's breathing."

"Step away," he grunted, barreling toward me. I hopped to the side as he dropped down beside her. Ches was already moving her arm, lifting her hand to rub her head.

"What?" she whispered.

The owner moved to help her, but managed only to grab her shoulders. "Are you hurt? What did he do?"

Her eyes moved lazily from side to side until she managed to open them fully. When they centered on me, she pursed her lips.

"Oh," she gasped. "What did... what happened?"

I tried to step closer, but he jabbed the point of his umbrella at me. "You stay back!"

"I didn't attack her."

She shook her head. "No. I didn't mean to."

The owner moved his head slowly to her. "Baker? What's going on?"

She looked over miserably to her boss. I realized this was about to be a bad conversation for her.

"I didn't—"

I interrupted, "She didn't attack me. She spilled the coffee, and I over-reacted. I'm sorry."

"You over-reacted?" he sputtered. "What, did you hit her?"

"I didn't hit her."

"Dorian," she mumbled with panicked eyes.

I held up a hand to her. "Sorry. Things haven't been the same since I got back from Afghanistan."

The owner was on his feet, moving step-by-step into my space. "You expect me to believe you were in the service? What branch?"

I spotted a tattoo of an eagle and an anchor peeking out from under his sleeve. Fuck.

"No, I was visiting an uncle."

"Ches, did this man hit you?"

She huddled her knees up to her chest, tears falling.

I braced myself. I would have to sell this if Ches was going to keep her job. "It was an accident. I just get a little keyed up."

Two hands grabbed my shirt before I saw them move. He didn't hit me, or really shove me. It was more like he lifted me by my shirt and physically carried me to the street. With a sharp toss, he hurled me out from underneath the awning. I barely landed on the sidewalk without rolling into the street.

He glared down at me with bloodshot eyes and pointed a meaty finger at me. "You get out of here, and you don't ever come back. You read me? I'll call the cops on you the next time I see you."

I looked up at him, then over to Ches, who was still balled up behind the tables. I nodded and pulled myself to my feet, turning my back to the café for the last time.

It was only a block and a half to my house, but the walk took forever.

The Dark Choir had just crossed a line. This wasn't simple goading. This was intensely personal. It was an attack.

And they had violated Ches to do it.

I needed my soul back, and soon. Until then, it was going to be total war.

CHAPTER FIFTEEN

I tried to call Ches several times that day, but she never answered. I couldn't blame her. I had survived many trials in my years and experienced varied and sundry torments, but I couldn't claim to have ever been possessed by a malevolent entity from beyond the Veil. The experience must have been traumatic. If I was Ches, I wouldn't have answered my calls, either.

Especially since I was the one they were after.

My nerves were too shocked to think clearly. I thought about driving to the Club, when I remembered that was no longer an option. Instead, I spent an hour looking out my front window, searching for that shadow man who seemed to be haunting me. He didn't make an appearance, however, and ultimately I withdrew into my workroom basement to try to calm my brain inside of my triple wardings. The respite did some good. When I closed my eyes, I stopped seeing Ches' terrified face huddled down by the café railing. Instead I listened to the words.

Down the rabbit hole.

It was obviously the same entity that had taken a grip of Amy Mancuso. It was mocking me. Taunting me about my soul. And it attacked me both times. I compared the two women. What reason did it have to possess the both of them? I could understand Ches. She was close to me. It was as direct a slap as one could muster.

But Mancuso? She was a former addict, which could have left a permanent crack in her psychic shielding. Addicts and the insane tended to be open to attack from the other side. Was there something in Ches' past that left a similar crack? All I knew about her was that she was from

Florida, had a bunch of brothers, and that she was studying Psychology. Perhaps it was that study that had opened her up to invasion? The acceptance of unusual phenomenon?

No, she wasn't a believer. The greatest shielding any non-practitioner could construct was disbelief. Skeptics, objectivists, atheists, they were all nearly impossible nuts to crack for the Dark Choir. Perhaps it was natural selection that was breeding generation upon generation of skeptics and nonbelievers? A kind of hermetic evolution that was making Humankind stronger?

I fell asleep leaning against the Library cabinet. I had horrible dreams that night. Horrible dreams.

I awoke to the sound of my phone ringing upstairs. I made a habit of leaving it there, due to the poor reception that my wardings afforded in that basement. I made it to my phone almost in time. Just a second after they had hung up. I checked the call log.

Edgar.

He had called three times already.

I dialed him back immediately, clearing my throat as I tried to balance the phone on my shoulder while pouring myself some orange juice.

"Dorian?" Edgar answered.

When someone knows a person as well as I knew Edgar, one develops an automatic sense of that person's mental state within the space of a single word. I could feel Edgar's exhaustion pouring through my phone.

"Hey, Edgar. You okay?"

"You busy right now?" he whispered.

"You woke me up, actually. Jesus, yesterday went down in the Annals of Clusterfuckery, even for a Monday. I'm okay, though. I mean, I'm intact—"

"Dorian? I need your help."

I froze. Never once in the history of our friendship had Edgar ever asked me for help. I hadn't realized it until that moment.

"I'll be there in a half-hour."

"Thanks."

I was prepared for a day of Dorian-centered brooding and scheming. I wasn't prepared for a genuine problem. Not that my problems weren't genuine, but this was Edgar.

I skipped a probably advisable shower, choosing only to change shirts and run my head under the sink faucet. When I had finally put myself together, I still looked like shit. But my appearance didn't matter. I had to move.

I made it to the sleepy colonial town of Frederick in almost exactly thirty minutes, which implied a casual disregard for several speed limits. I parked behind Swain's Antiques and Novelties, and trotted to the storefront. Edgar was waiting for me at the glass shop doors, holding one open for me. He held a finger up to his mouth.

As I stepped inside the darkened shop, I whispered, "What's wrong?"

"Come up stairs."

I followed Edgar through the antiques shop and up the spiral stairs to their living space, a modest loft that had housed a couple generations of the Swain family. Toys were strewn across the shag carpeting in the living room. The kitchen was a wreck. Nothing out of the ordinary.

I didn't see Elle or little Eddie. Or Wren for that matter.

"Edgar? I'm starting to freak out, here."

He pulled me to the kitchen and leaned against the counter. His eyes were moving behind his spectacles, and he kept rubbing his fingers together. I had never seen him this preoccupied in my life.

"Something happened," he muttered. "I wanted you to check it out. Get your opinion."

These were carefully chosen words. His usual perma-baked drawl was crisper than usual.

"Sure," I said. "Anything."

"So, it's Elle."

"What happened to Elle?"

He shifted back and forth on his feet. "She's sick."

"Yeah, you told me that."

"No, man. Something's wrong with her."

My heart fell heavy. "You took her to the doctor?"

"Of course. What do you think? We took her to the doctor."

I held up my hands. He was testy, which only made me more nervous. "Okay. And they said?"

"It's complicated."

"So complicate me."

"I want you to see her first. You know, before I tell you."

"Elle's here?"

He nodded.

"Edgar? Where's Wren and Eddie?"

He sucked in a breath. "Wren's getting medicine. She took Eddie with her."

"Is she contagious?"

"You'll understand when you see her."

I looked past Edgar's shoulder at the hallway leading to the three bedrooms at the rear of the loft space. Edgar didn't have any lights on. The morning was gray, thanks to the still overcast sky, and the whole building was full of shadows.

I nodded toward the bedrooms, and Edgar turned aside, gesturing me on. Elle's bedroom was the second door on the left. The door was ajar, but almost no light escaped the room. I took a breath and eased it open.

Elle sat in her desk chair in the center of her room. She faced the doorway as if waiting for me, or Edgar, or whoever stepped through. She still wore her nightclothes, though they looked wet and splotched with unnamable fluids.

Then the smell hit me.

I tried not to gag, but it took work. Once I got a grip over myself, I took a step inside Elle's room. She was hunched forward, her hair covering her face.

"Hey, kid," I whispered. "I hear you're feeling rough."

Her hair swayed as she swiveled her head in my direction.

A weak voice answered, "Hey, Dorian."

"What's up, kiddo? Stomach bug?"

"No."

I took another step inside and sat on the corner of her desk. "I know. Bet it's mono. I caught mono in high school. Day after Gretchen Wilkins came down with it. You, uh… you doing anything to catch mono for?"

"It's not mono."

"Okay."

I watched her for a moment.

She turned her head away from me again.

"Your dad asked me to look in on you."

"Not surprised."

"Yeah? Why is that?"

"He trusts you."

"Uh… okay. I'm here to help."

"I know."

"So, tell me where it hurts."

Her head slowly moved back to me, still hung low, her hair draping the sides of her face.

"Inside."

"Can you be more specific?"

"Dorian?"

"Yeah?"

"Are you going to marry Ches?"

Probably the last question in the world I was expecting. "Why are you asking me that?"

"Don't you love me?"

My pulse quickened. She was being way too deliberate. "Elle? You're starting to give me the heebs in a big way, here."

"Do you love her?" she repeated, yet slower.

"I like her. Right now, I think that's all I'm going to cop to."

"You shouldn't."

"Shouldn't what, like her?"

"Love her." Her words dripped with displeasure.

"No offense, Elle, but shouldn't I be the one who makes that call?"

"I know something you don't, Dorian. Something about Ches."

The dark feeling vined its way into my brain. "What, Elle? What do you know about Ches?"

Elle jerked up from her chair, her hair flying up into the air, falling against her shoulders. Her eyes glared at me with grotesque, otherworldly intensity.

"I know what her insides feel like, you pathetic piece of shit!"

She fell back into the chair which had risen with her body. It was then that I realized she had been tied down to it.

I stumbled back for the door. Turning around, I looked for Edgar in the hallway, but he wasn't there.

By the time I caught my breath, I stole another glance at Elle. Her eyes were wide, round, boring holes through me. She was grinning at me. It was a sickening expression, at once mocking and vicious.

A horrible noise bubbled up into her throat, after which a thin stream of yellow fluid spilled from the corner of her mouth. She spat it onto the floor in front of me and snickered. "But you don't know what her insides feel like, do you? Not so much as a finger in her pussy. Shameful, Dorian."

"What... are you?"

Her grin widened, revealing both sets of canines. "I am the snake at the bottom of the rabbit hole. I am the ageless, the ever-dark. I'm the enemy of souls. And I'm going to find yours, Dorian Lake."

I balled fists, trying not to scream at whatever this thing was inside Elle's body. I shoved my hand into my pocket and pulled out a pendulum.

"Think so?"

"It is inevitable."

I continued as I paced around the chair, dangling the pendulum outside of Elle's field of vision. "And that's how you find my soul? Spending all your time trolling me from a thirteen-year-old's body? If you're trying to impress me, you need to stop because you're embarrassing yourself."

"You would know, wouldn't you? Embarrassing yourself in front of your fresh new lay? Fran-CHES-ca?"

That name. The way she said it. My stomach churned.

"She thinks you're a fraud, you know."

"I've been called worse."

"But that's your secret, isn't it? She's right about you. You're a fraud, Dorian Lake. There's no such thing as karma, and you know it. No justice. No Cosmic mind. There is only life, death, suffering, and Us."

The pendulum didn't tug or pull. There were no outside forces interacting with Elle. This was all inside. "Are you done with this girl, yet? You're starting to bore me."

"What if I like it in here? Will that break your heart? She's awful young for you."

"Suits me just fine. The longer you're inside her, the less time you're out there scraping the nether for my soul."

"Nothing will stop that."

"I have to say, though. You're giving me a hell of an ego stroke here. One man is worth all of this trouble? One soul out of millions, and you're going through all this trouble just to goad me."

Elle leaned back in her chair, rocking it back onto its hind legs. She lifted one foot, then another, balancing on the chair legs with uncanny poise. She chanted something incoherent. I had studied several dead and secret languages in my years. That wasn't any of the languages I recognized.

She finally fell forward, her head flying forward, her jaws snapping at me like a wild dog.

I backed away a step, moving toward the door. I heard voices down the hall. Wren was back.

"Well, don't get comfortable," I said. "You've pissed me off, now. And what's worse, you pissed off a woman who's not just a Wiccan, and a mother. She's scary on a good day. Fuck with her daughter, and she's going to shove a smudge so far up your ass, you'll be blowing smoke until the Second Coming."

Elle's face twisted into a sick grin. "Stop it. You're turning me on."

I turned away from her and took several breaths before stepping into the hallway. In my moment gathering myself, I heard Wren's voice rise to that special pitch she hits when she's truly, inexorably angry.

"Then what is he doing here?" I heard her bark in the kitchen.

Edgar mumbled something in response.

Before he received another lash from Wren's tongue, I decided to step back into the living room and make my presence known.

Wren spotted me from over Edgar's shoulder. Her cheeks were flushed and her eyes were still sharp with emotion. But as I gave her a slow nod, she grinned and stepped around Edgar to give me a quick side-hug.

"Hey, Dorian."

"Wren? You okay?"

She sighed and put a hand on her forehead. "I will be when Elle gets better."

"I want to help."

"Thanks. I wish you could."

Edgar gave me a guarded look from behind Wren.

"Give me a shot, maybe?" I prodded.

"Unless you have a license to practice psychiatry, I don't think you're going to have a lot of luck."

I shook my head. "Wren, you know what this is, right?"

She sighed and closed her eyes for a long moment. "I do, actually. And before you say anything, please fight your natural reflex to spout off your credentials, and listen. This is medical. Not magical."

I couldn't believe what I was hearing. Wren was generally the first to reach for the salt in a given situation of a bizarre nature. Yet with her own child she seemed to be leaning toward the Mainstream.

"What do you think is wrong, Wren?"

"I love you, Dorian. Really. But sometimes a cigar is just a cigar."

I lifted an eyebrow at Edgar. He tucked his head down into his chest.

"Look, Edgar. You called me. I'm just trying to help."

Wren peered over at Edgar.

Edgar looked up from his folded arms and shrugged. "I wanted to give him a shot, Wren."

"Again, what do you think is happening, here?" I asked her.

"Elle's just sick."

"Elle isn't sick, Wren. Something is being done to her."

"Next thing you'll say is this is somehow your fault?" She gave me a tired smirk.

"Well, not entirely."

She shook her head. "Trust me. This has nothing to do with you."

"Then why was she waiting for me? Why was she cocked and loaded with some frankly toe-curling salt when I walked into her room? There's a presence inside her, taking her over."

"That's not what's happening."

I threw my hands up and took a few steps. "How can you be so cavalier about this?"

Wren's face flushed as she slowly stated, "Because this has happened before."

Edgar rubbed the back of his head as he turned into the kitchen.

I blinked a few times and reached behind me for the side of their coach. "Elle's done this before?"

"Not Elle. This is new for her."

"To you?"

"Not me. Lilah."

"Who's Lilah?"

"My sister." She turned and brushed past Edgar, opening the fridge and pulling out a bottle of screw-top wine. "It happened when I was nine, I think. Maybe ten. That was a weird summer." She dropped into a seat at the kitchen table and took a slug straight from the bottle. "Lilah was going to be a freshman. On her way to high school. Worked up about it, too. Scared of boys, scared of girls, scared of teachers. She stopped sleeping. After the Fourth of July when we came back from the beach, she started shouting in her bed at night. Wet the bed. 'Night terrors' was what the doctor called it, but something had him worried. Mom, too."

I pulled a chair and took a seat across from Wren as she stared at the bottle.

"They gave her pills that put her to sleep, but that only made things worse. Lilah would start blaming me for wounds on her body. Tiny cuts. Said I was trying to steal her skin. Then she started seeing things when she was awake. Faces, she called them. Horrible, evil faces with sharp teeth. She'd be normal. We'd be having a regular conversation then she'd just get quiet and all the blood would drain out of her face. She'd get wide-eyed, and she'd stare into a corner. I mean the look on her face. It was terrifying. She'd shriek and shriek, trying to beat away the monsters. Said they were hurting her. One time, she caught me with her nails when I was trying to calm her down. Put three good red gashes across my neck. That's when they took her to the hospital."

I rubbed my face and took a moment. "What happened to her there?"

"The diagnosis was schizophrenia. They put her on drugs, but they only worked to a point, and we didn't have good insurance. She had to miss the first two months of high school, then another month. Our parents ended up putting her in a home out in the mountains. Same home Aunt Marla got sent to."

"Aunt Marla?"

"Same thing happened to her."

"So this is genetic?"

Wren nodded. "Edgar knows. He knows all about it. Which was why I didn't want him calling you in. I didn't want to get you in a tear and not be able to do anything."

I leaned back in my chair, trying to find a place to look.

Edgar cleared his throat. "I called Dorian because Elle was asking for him."

"Of course she did. She worships Dorian."

I squirmed in my seat.

Edgar continued, "And I wanted to at least get his take on it before you called Doctor Shenkar."

"He wasn't at the office."

Edgar jerked off his glasses and turned to Wren. "You went to his office? Wren, I thought we were going to talk about this."

She gave him a patient look from the business end of her wine bottle. "I've lived through this before, Edgar. And this time, it's my baby girl in there. Let me handle this, okay?"

"Still, Wren. You gotta talk to me."

"Doesn't matter, anyway. The office said he won't be in until Monday."

I leaned forward, spreading my hands out on the table. "Okay, so, I'm going to go ahead and just jump into the middle of all this. Wren?" I took as disarming a tone as I could muster. "I appreciate what you've been through with your sister, and I know you're Elle's mother. You need to do what you feel is necessary to help her. But, I also think you'd want all of the available facts before you make a decision. So, I have something to add."

She nodded.

"This thing with Elle? It's the third time in the last couple weeks I've seen it. Three different women. They were all the same voice, the same phraseology, same purpose. The first was a campaign volunteer up in Baltimore. She went berserk. I was called in to check it out. This woman was a complete stranger, okay? But the thing inside her knew me by name. Knew about my soul."

Wren blinked.

"Right. She taunted me about losing my soul, then jumped me. The presence left her, and that was the end."

Edgar asked, "Who was the second?"

I swallowed hard. "Ches."

"No shit? When?"

"Yesterday. At coffee. We were just doing our thing when some switch flipped, and she attacked me. It was over as soon as it began. But both times they were taunting me about my soul. Wren? I never told Ches about Osterhaus and the soul contract. How would she know?"

Wren set down the wine bottle. "What about Elle?"

"She not only hammered me about my soul, she knew about what happened to Ches. How would she know about that? She's been sick here at home for a few days, right? That's unnatural knowledge."

Wren looked up at Edgar then back at me. "Fuck me."

"Something on the other side is trying to get my goad, and it's pulling some nasty tricks to do it."

"So what you're saying is this thing is getting at you through my daughter?"

I sucked in a breath, and nodded. "Which is why I want to help her. I'm not trying to tell you what to do. I'm just trying to make sure we're treating the correct problem here. Before your doctor doses Elle up on anti-psychotics, will you give me a chance to try to work this out my way?"

Wren lingered at the sink, staring down at the dishes piled up inside. She turned to Edgar who was hovering behind me.

"I made an appointment for Monday morning with Doctor Shenkar. Way I see it, we can do it your way, and if we can't fix her, then we'll do it Dr. Shenkar's way. Sound fair to you?"

I nodded to Wren. "Sounds fair. This may not last long, anyway. If the other two women were any indication, this is more like a hit-and-run."

"I hope you're right," Edgar muttered as we all turned back to the dark hallway leading to Elle's room.

"Where's Eddie?"

"Dropped him off at his friend's house," Wren replied.

"How's he taking this?"

"He hasn't seen anything bad. Well, nothing worse than Elle gets naturally. He doesn't really know."

"Good. With luck, he won't have to."

I stepped back down the hall to Elle's room and, with a nod to the Swains, nudged her door open again.

Elle and the chair she was tied to were now on top of her bed. She sat staring wide-eyed at the door, her mouth still drawn back in that marionette grin.

"Back for more, Lake?" she chimed.

Wren bristled at my arm, but I held up my hand.

"I was just wondering how long this was going to take. I was going to bake brownies later, and you're kind of screwing up my schedule."

Wren leaned into me. I gave Wren a side-eye and a quick squeeze of her hand to reassure her I wasn't about to completely fuck this up. But I had to play this cool to try to unseat this creature's confidence. In my limited dealings with the Dark Choir in the past, their ultimate weakness was their utter disregard for humanity. This thing had me in its crosshairs, but it sure as shit didn't know what I was capable of.

"I know you want me out of this girl," Elle growled. "It turns your stomach looking at her like this. You're wondering if she can hear you. If she knows what's happening."

I wanted to puke. Every part of me wanted Elle to be asleep, dreaming somewhere. I didn't want her to see what was happening.

It cackled and tossed its head forward. Elle and the chair tumbled down toward the floor. I dove out to try and catch her. I succeeded only partially, managing to crack my knuckles on the floor underneath one of the chair legs. Elle's head would have struck hardwood if Edgar hadn't base-slid beneath her. I had never seen him move that quickly before.

Elle coughed and groaned, shaking her head. Edgar reached out and smoothed her soiled hair away from her face. She peered up at us with a frightened glance.

"Dad?"

Wren gasped, "Elle?"

"Mommy?"

Wren collapsed around me, reaching over my shoulders to cradle her face. I stiffened and tried to separate her arms.

"Wait," I whispered.

Elle's brow drew together and tears welled in her eyes. "Dorian? Why?"

"Hey, little sis."

"Why are you doing this to me?"

"What?"

She twisted her arms against the jute bindings holding her to her desk chair and started panting. "Stop it! Stop! Daddy?"

Edgar reached for the rope. I laid a heavy hand on his.

"Daddy, he tried to touch me."

My stomach twisted. "Stop this."

"I trusted you, Dorian. Why did you touch me there?"

Wren eased away from me, but I kept my eyes locked onto Elle's.

"They're not going to buy that crap. They know me too well."

Elle looked over to Edgar, tears cascading down her cheeks.

Edgar pulled his arm back and rolled to a seated position. I heard Wren stand up behind me, clearing her throat.

The room was filled with silence as Elle looked back and forth between her parents, then finally back at me. The sharp smirk returned to her eyes and she chuckled.

"You caught me. I was just having some fun."

Before I could respond, Wren brushed past me with enough force to knock me onto my side. She gripped her daughter's shoulders and shoved her back to the bed.

Wren's voice was low, clear, and terrifying. "You wipe that grin off your face. This is my daughter you're fucking with! Do you think there's anything I wouldn't do to rip you out of her body? Because there's nothing… NOTHING… I wouldn't do." She tossed a thumb toward me over her shoulder. "He's off the leash, now. You better pray he's quick."

Elle's smirk melted.

Edgar reached between the two of them and unwound Wren's fingers from Elle's night shirt.

Wren stood up and stormed out of the room. Edgar stood up, but stayed with me.

"Well, now you've done it," I said to the thing behind Elle's eyes.

"You're getting nowhere with this. You had your fun. Now it's time to move on."

"It eats you alive, doesn't it?" Elle rasped. "Seeing her like this? No, I think I'll stay for a while."

"Why bother?"

"Because it brings you suffering. Why would I ever deprive myself of that?"

I stood up and motioned for Edgar to help me pick her up. We settled her in the middle of the room and stepped outside.

Before I could close the door, she added, "Time's running out for you. The shadows are coming. Tick tock."

I gave it one last look before Edgar and I withdrew back into the living room.

Edgar muttered, "What is this thing?"

"This thing is a little bastard, that's what."

"Got a plan here, man?"

"This isn't exactly my field of expertise."

"Got anyone you can call?"

"You're the one with the Hermetic Rolodex from Hell. Got a priest or someone you trust?"

Wren barked from the kitchen, "No priests."

"Why?"

"Just no priests."

"I get that you're not exactly playing for their team, Wren. And from the sound of this thing, it's not dressing itself in a demon's clothes. I think it's a little older than the Church. But still, they have had success in the past with dis-possessing people."

Edgar leaned in to me. "Dis-possessing?"

"Evicting? I don't know, just trying really hard not to actually say exorcism."

Wren stepped out from the kitchen with a pharmacy bag. "Okay. If you can find a priest who will deign to step into a witch's house to exorcise her unbaptized child, then go right ahead."

"Well, first, thanks. Second, you're not technically a witch."

"I know that, Dorian."

"Yeah, I know you know. I'm just trying here."

She reached out and put a hand on my shoulder. Her eyes were tired and hardened, but they managed to thank me without making Wren say it out loud.

"I'll get to work finding that priest."

Edgar added, "What about Emil's Library? Anything in there that could help?"

"Very likely. Just have to drive back to the city and dig in." I turned to Wren. "What are you going to do with Elle in the meantime?"

She lifted the pharmacy bag and shook it.

"I got something to help," she replied.

"Aspenwood?"

"Sedatives."

"No offense, but how do you plan on getting her to keep pills down."

"They're suppositories."

"Oh. Ick. Yeah, well I'm definitely leaving before that happens."

Edgar walked me to the front door and gave me a quick, tight hug before I exited.

"Don't worry. I'm going to sort this out."

CHAPTER SIXTEEN

The drive back to Baltimore took longer than it ever had before. I never relished diving into Emil's books. They held knowledge that was palpably corrupting. Energy from malicious intent emanated from the very pages, some of which were of questionable materials. I debated as I exited the freeway how I was going to find a priest. I had no contacts within Christendom, a shortcoming I had never really noticed before. My work so seldom interlaced with the Church. This was going to be a learning experience for me.

When I returned home, I laid my phone on the kitchen table and descended immediately to the workroom. I opened up the dark wood cabinet containing Emil's Library and snatched his handwritten index from the nail. When it came to Demonology, there were plenty of books to choose from. Emil took a fancy to late Renaissance Demonology when we were in London. I kept skimming, however. This thing inside Elle might not be a demon, per se, and all of the information Emil had spirited from the Vatican's secret knowledge wouldn't amount to a handful of dog crap.

I grabbed two Goetic texts and a journal from a spiritualist contemporary of Harry Houdini who had cataloged his encounters with séance charlatans whom he couldn't debunk. The thing about entities such as these was that they may not necessarily know their own limitations. Just like people, they have a limited perspective on the Cosmos. Most of the entities that self-identify as "demons" only believe they are. Thus they carry all of the religious baggage that goes with it. Some entities, however, are older than the Church, and as such have never accepted the rules and limitations organized religion has deemed fit to saddle them with. And even worse, some of the very old entities remember a time before Humanity.

I had a sneaking suspicion I was dealing with one of those.

It wasn't likely a priest's exorcism would do much good against such a creature, so I resorted to something older, namely King Solomon and Hermes Trismegistus. Between the Clavicula Solomona and the Hermetic Texts, I might have found some footing to unhinge this unsavory little fucker from Elle's body. After three full hours of study, I had come to the conclusion I needed to identify the nature of the being first. It was paramount. There was no Step Two until I knew precisely what this thing was, and therefore what its weaknesses were.

I didn't have an Unholy Douchenozzle Detect-o-matic in my personal inventory, so I was left with the process of elimination. Once again, it came down to needing a priest. If I could rule out the more common demon of the Christian mythos, the whole affair would be over fairly quickly. It was worth a shot.

I locked up my books and hustled upstairs to find the nearest Catholic church. I paused as I spotted two missed calls. One from Julian, one from Abe. I chose to return Abe's call, which turned out to be an A/C unit on the blink. I gave him permission to call a professional to deal with it and jumped into my car. Julian could wait.

One thing about Baltimore, there was no shortage of Catholic churches. As the name might suggest, Maryland was one of the historic Catholic centers of North America. I drove past the closest one, however. It was too big. The Basilica would likely be a fantastic place to have high-minded conversations with some well-educated clergymen, but I wasn't keen on calling too much attention to our little problem. I settled instead for St. Aloysius, a cozy church tucked between the University and some of McHenry's new developments north of downtown.

I parked on the street and sat at the wheel, staring at the double doors at the front of the old stone building. I had no protocol for this. Did I need an appointment? Were walk-ins welcome? Did I just tap-dance inside and ask if a priest was on-call? What was the deal with the candles and the Holy Water? Hell with it. I figured Fortune favored the bold, and I didn't have time to screw around.

One of the doors was unlocked, and I stepped inside. The wall of energy into which I stepped nearly dropped me to my knees. It wasn't a shield so much as huge wad of resonant intent. There were tens of thousands of people in the city that feared the Devil, I was sure, and though I didn't personally subscribe to a specific belief in the Christian Satan, I knew I wasn't exactly on the welcome list. Still, I muscled through and managed my way into the nave, which was oddly circular. I had only seen movies of cathedrals in my youth, and expected something more rectilinear.

I spotted a young man rubbing furniture near the center platform, which I assumed to be the altar, and approached with a nod.

"Excuse me? I'm kind of lost. Well, I mean not literally, but I need to talk to a priest, and I don't know how to make that happen."

When the young man stood up to face me, I noticed the collar. He smiled and folded the wiping cloth, setting it on a table with a tiny bottle of oil soap.

"Then you came to the right place. Father Mark," he chimed as he held out a hand. I shook it, trying not to intentionally shield up. "How can I help you?"

"Do I need an appointment or something?"

"If it was Holy Week, maybe. But I have plenty of time on my hands today."

"I see that," I replied nodding to the oil soap. "Don't you have people who do that for you?"

"Sure, but I've always enjoyed a good polishing. Relaxes me. So, want to come to my office?"

I shrugged and followed him to a door leading out of the main nave. We ended up in a cozy if bland office with a short stack of bookcases behind a laminate desk. A large oil painting of some saint doing something saintly hung on the wall over the stacks of papers kept in neat columns. I never knew how much paperwork came with the priesthood.

"What's your name?" he asked before he actually managed to take a seat.

"Dorian Lake."

"How can I help you today, Mister Lake?"

"I have a friend who's having some trouble of a spiritual nature. I don't know if you're the one who can help her or not. But I thought I'd give it a shot. Worst you could say is no."

"Sounds seriously non-specific," he said with a grin. "What's the nature of her spiritual troubles?"

"She's being influenced, I think, by an outside force."

His eyes narrowed. I was already losing him.

"She's the daughter of my best friend. I don't know, maybe my only friend. More like family, really. I'm saying this so you get why I'm about to say this really ignorant sounding sentence out loud."

He nodded and waved me on with his fingers.

"Okay, so, what I basically need is an exorcism."

He nodded for several seconds before looking down to his desk and pulling a pad of paper in front of him. He clicked a pen and began making notes.

"Parents?"

"Yeah. Both."

"I mean, who are the parents? Are they lay members?"

Crap. Did they have rules about that kind of thing? "Uh, that would be a no."

"Believers?"

"They believe in plenty. Not necessarily your flavor of faith, maybe."

"A simple 'no' would work, Mister Lake. What has led you to believe she's being acted upon by some outside force? Describe her."

"I was called in after it began, so I'm not sure how it started. But she had been feeling sick. When I got there, she was someone else. Her eyes look darker. Maybe. No, that could just be my imagination. Sorry, I'm usually more skeptical than this." I really should have prepared for this better.

"But something makes you believe in this situation?"

"Well, yeah. She spoke to me about things she shouldn't know."

"Have the parents taken her to a medical professional?"

I paused and leaned back in my seat. For whatever reason, I had assumed that the Church would jump to a spiritual conclusion. I hadn't accounted for common sense. That was my fault.

"They have an appointment for her. Not until next week. Doctor's out shining his golf clubs or something."

"So the young woman isn't endangering herself or others?"

"I can't be sure. Mostly she's just talking filth."

Father Mark made several more notes before looking up at me with serious eyes. "Are you disposed to give me her name?"

"I'd rather not."

Instead of arguing, he simply nodded.

"I'm not trying to make a child protection case out of this, is mostly my thinking."

"You're obviously motivated for this child's well-being. I can't fault you for that. Can we both agree that we're interested in seeing this child safe and healthy?"

"We can."

"Then I'll be frank with you, Mister Lake. The mind is a complex and often terrifying apparatus. It's easily broken, even among children. When we see a young child in mental pain, it affects us. They are innocent, free of the corruption and complexity of adulthood. We have this universal understanding that a child is pure. When that assumption is shattered, it can very often seem sinister. Even Satanic."

"I think I see where you going with this," I sighed.

"Which isn't to marginalize your request, here. But what most people see as the work of the Devil is most often the work of a brain in need of healing. There are several routes to healing, many tools. Faith is one. Another, medicine. Therapy. Correcting the physical and spiritual since they are both connected."

"You're saying she needs a shrink."

"I'm saying that her parents seem to be of that thought already. But they haven't come to me, have they? You have. You were moved to step into a church, and I'm going to go out on a limb here and assume that's something you're not used to?"

I smiled and nodded once.

"You put yourself into an awkward situation because you wanted to help. I bet you're feeling pretty frightened for her. Maybe a little powerless?"

I tapped my fingers on the arm of my chair. "I wouldn't go that far."

"Then maybe you feel responsible?"

Damn, this guy was good. "Well, of course I'm responsible, that's why I'm here. Though I'm starting to see it was a mistake."

"I don't mean to make you feel ignored, but without the girl's parents here, there's only so much I can do for her. You, on the other hand, are in a position to blame yourself for her misfortunes, and I'm just wondering why that is?"

"Because the thing inside her is gunning for me. It's getting at me through her."

"And if a gunman took a person hostage and threatened to shoot her if you didn't hand over your wallet, you'd feel responsible for putting her in that position?"

I shifted in the seat and shook my head. "It's different."

"I'm sure it is because what's happening to this girl probably has nothing to do with you, and everything to do with her brain chemistry. Guilt, Mister Lake, kills hope. And when you kill hope, you open yourself up to despair. If you're going to be any help at all to your friends, you're going to need to shrug off this self-induced blame."

I nodded and took a deep cleansing breath. "There are other factors."

"There usually are, but in the end, do they really amount to you harming a child?"

"No."

"I'm glad to hear it." He set down his pen and leaned back in his chair, leveling earnest eyes on me. They were completely free of judgment, ready to shoot down any excuse I would have to feel sorry for myself. "I sense that your concern is motivated out of love. A desperate kind of love this world needs more of. I hope you see that I'm only trying to help you open that up to your friends. Be a comfort. Be an aid. Give them a fuller portion of this frantic need to heal."

"There were two others," I stated, folding my fingers in front of me.

"Others?"

"Two more suffering from possession. Both of them knew my name, knew particulars of my personal life. One of them was a complete stranger. The other was my girlfriend." I stood up and straightened myself. "I'm just saying this, so you don't think I'm insane."

"I never thought that."

"Well, then, you're probably crazier than me. Anyways, thanks for your time. I don't think you can help me. You were a long shot, in any case."

I extended my hand, and Father Mark shook it. I fished a business card out of my pocket and set it on his desk. "If you have any thoughts about this, feel free to call me."

He nodded noncommittally. I knew that business card was probably going to hit the trash can before the door closed behind me.

I left St. Aloysius in a dour mood. It would have been better if he had turned me out, called me insane, or tried to burn me at the stake. At least he could have scowled just once. Instead he was perfectly decent, concerned for everyone involved, and unforgivably realistic about it. Perhaps my entire problem was I was looking for real help. I was all but convinced this wasn't a Jesus-Mary-Joseph flavor of demon. Why bother with the consummate professionals who knew their asses from holes in the wrist? What I really needed was to run a ringer past the thing inside Elle's body and see if it offered any clues as to its identity or origin. What I really needed was a rank amateur.

CHAPTER SEVENTEEN

The Healing Waters Christian Tabernacle was one of those dizzying monstrosities along the beltway, a hulking church building with three two-story crosses on the lawn bathed in spotlights and a full color billboard screen with an animated logo and information as to their latest week-long excursion into doctrine. They had a daily spot on the local talk radio where the pastor of Healing Waters would dispense a politically seasoned platitude wrapped in a dubious scriptural quote, and conclude with the same slogan: "I'm not preachin', I'm just sayin'." His smug tone always made me switch stations, but today I needed him.

I had phoned ahead as I had the feeling this church was more a business than a social service, and figured they took appointments. I had a two-thirty with Pastor Wayne Scovill, and this time instead of playing it by ear, I had an entire pitch prepared.

Stepping into one of several double-doors into a vestibule larger than the mall's, I weeded through unmanned literature tables and found a wall sign indicating the Administrative Offices, just past the book store. Inside the office, I found a diminutive young woman with platinum blonde hair and a sharp business suit. She gave me a thin-lipped grin and cocked her head.

"Welcome to Healing Waters, hon. You got an appointment?"

"Yes. Dorian Lake for a two-thirty?"

She kicked away in her chair and rolled toward a back doorway to call for Scovill down the hall. In a few seconds, a gaunt man with sandy hair stepped toward me, hand outstretched.

"Hi, Mister Lake? Wayne Scovill. Won't you come on back?"

He wore a light gray suit with a corn-yellow tie. He had the bearing of a Southern gentleman, but his voice glistened with New Englander sharpness. I followed him into a spacious khaki-painted office brimming with sunlight and festooned with glass sculptures and world maps. Scovill settled into his plush wing-back swivel chair and spread his fingers out on his desk, grinning with a nervous energy that made my scalp itch.

"Thank you for seeing me," I offered in a practiced miserable tone. "I'm running out of options."

"Not at all. Linda said you're having some trouble with a friend of yours?"

"Uh, yeah. She's my best friend's daughter. Something's happening to her and, well, I don't know what I can do. I can't do anything. Just feels hopeless."

He leaned forward. "Nothing's hopeless, friend. We can do all things through He who gives us strength."

"I hope so, Pastor."

"What's she gotten into? What can you tell me?"

"Oh, she isn't into something. In fact, I beg your pardon for putting it this way, but something's gotten into her, I think."

He cocked his head. "Come again?"

"Okay, I need to start from the beginning."

I sighed with just enough histrionics to pull him in, and wound him through a white-washed version of what had happened to Elle. I focused on her innocence, and the sudden descent into madness, while glossing over our peculiar belief system and the fact that all of this was probably my fault. As I finished the tale, I rubbed the bridge of my nose and added, "Pastor, I think the Devil's inside that little girl, but I don't think anyone will believe that."

Scovill fidgeted in his seat, staring at me as he laid a hand on the side of his face. "I want you to know something, first off." He pointed at the map behind his desk. "I served in three missions to Africa in the last ten years. Once to Ghana, once to Mali, then Equatorial Guinea. On that first trip to Ghana I met a young man who wanted to make some extra cash as a porter for our trucks. Name was Kwame. Nice young kid. Well-spoken, eager to dress like us and talk like us. He thought the world of us, and we were just happy to have him tag along. He got sick the third week, just before we went to the airport, and we didn't see him again before we left. When I flew back to Mali two years later, I talked the Elders into a side trip back to Accra to see Kwame. And I found out he'd spent the last two years in hospitals, and had been nearly executed for witchcraft. He was taken with fits, especially when exposed to the Cross or a Bible. I bribed an orderly to let me see him alone." Scovill leaned forward, his eyes rimming red. "The look in his eyes, Mister Lake? I can tell you as one intelligent man to another, he was bound by demons. His eyes held this malice, this quality of hatred that shook me. I prayed with him. Laid on hands. And I heard him groan. Wheeze. It was perfect sadness. I remember that sound vividly. He was begging me for help."

He took a breath as he reached for a handkerchief inside his suit.

Scovill cleared his throat and added, "I believe you, Mister Lake, when you say the Devil's inside this child. I believe it's possible, anyway. And if that's the case, the worst case scenario, I want you to know that God is strong enough to deliver that girl!"

I had him.

Scovill invited some of the secretaries into the office, and we held hands as they prayed with me in a circle. They lapsed into babbling at times, squinting hard, and generally overloading their own chakras with unfocused energy. This wasn't new to me. It was a simple way for anyone to manufacture an ecstatic experience, the result of energy overpowering the third eye and crown to reproduce spiritual sensations. It was the opposite of the discipline Emil taught me. When working with intent, one had to keep one's energy completely checked, grounded, and focused.

We made an appointment that evening to meet at the Swains. There was no talk of money, donations, or compensation. Scovill seemed motivated by something deeper. Perhaps I misjudged yet another clergyman?

On my way out of the church, I called Edgar to fill him in. He sounded exhausted, so much so, it felt contagious. I only had a few hours to rest before I had to take my second trip to Frederick that day, so I made quick time to Amity and the comfort of my obscenely dark room.

Unfortunately, I found a town car waiting for me in front of my house. Two thick men in suits stood outside, one by my stoop and one by the car. When I pulled into the lane between buildings, one of the goons opened the rear passenger door, and out stepped the last person I expected to see at that moment.

Joey McHenry.

He took two steps up my walk, then paused, shoving his hands into his pockets. His hair was a little grayer than when we last met. That was the day he witnessed me taking down Osterhaus. That was my first Nether Curse, and it's what put me on McHenry's radar. The man was a wrecking ball in a Fioravanti, so I checked my usual attitude.

"McHenry?"

He squinted at me, then peered up at the façade of my two-story row house. With a slow nod he commented, "The Poe House. Nice."

"No shit, it's actually the Poe House? I thought that was a line the realtor fed me when I signed."

"It was." He sniffled and turned to his left to gesture down Amity. "The actual house he lived in was two blocks west. It burned down in the nineteen teens, and the owner just moved the address sign to this property. But you're not actually from Baltimore. You just live here, so you wouldn't know that."

What a dick.

"What do you want, McHenry?"

"Sixty-two oh one, three, five and seven, Fayette."

I smirked. "I'm reasonably familiar with those properties."

"You asked what I wanted. That's what I want."

"Ah yes," I chimed, lifting a thoughtful finger. "Manor at Carrollton. It's a brave new Baltimore, all of a sudden."

"It can be. Depends largely on whether the residents will embrace change."

"Change meaning they get squeezed out of their neighborhoods block by block until they can't afford to live in the city anymore?"

McHenry rolled his eyes. "No one lives in these buildings anymore, Lake. We're going to put that land to actual use."

"I have four tenant families who beg to differ."

"Which is why I'm here."

"Obviously."

I glared at McHenry for a long moment, forcing him to state the matter plainly. "Choose to believe this," he said, "or don't. But I understand you, Lake. Even though you're an arrogant, little snot hell-bent on being something greater than you actually are, I understand what puts the steel in your shorts."

"Stop it. You're giving me the vapors." So much for checking my attitude.

"I know this because you remind me a lot of my own son."

Being compared to a known rapist did nothing to improve my attitude.

He continued, "He feels everything. And he feels like he's entitled to everything. He likes the way people look at him, likes to feel important. But he isn't willing to put in the work to get there. He's happy to inherit his lifestyle, and he has zero appreciation for it."

I pushed my hand into my pocket to ball a fist. "You don't know a thing about my life, McHenry."

"I don't have to know your life story, Lake. I judge a tree by the fruit it produces, and you are positively crawling with the kind of lazy self-importance that makes me want to put your face through a plate glass window."

I held my breath. His nostrils were flaring, and he was exactly the kind of person who could put my face through a window. I cleared my throat and calmly countered, "Is that why you convinced the Druid Hill board to boot me out of the Club? Because I remind you of Joey Junior?"

He sneered. "There were so many reasons for the board to kick you out of the Club, I didn't have to convince them."

"And I'm sure the election had nothing to do with it."

"Correct. And don't you even give me that look! You just don't realize, Lake. That club has operated for over a hundred and thirty years. It was born in Reconstruction, survived Prohibition, the Great Depression, two World Wars, the Red Scare in the fifties, the Japanese speculators in the eighties, and the stock market crash a few years ago. You know how it survived? Because we leave our politics outside."

I snickered. "Hate to break this to you, McHenry, but more than half the members are politicians."

"But we do business in the Club. We don't steer the sails for the prevailing political winds, and we don't campaign inside the Club. You and your ankle-grabbing boyfriend were the ones who made an embarrassment of yourselves."

"... and we're done here," I stated, turning for the door.

"I came to make you an offer."

"Funny, because it sounds like you're just demonstrating your lack of class. I'm not selling you the properties."

"Before you draw your line in the sand, why not hear what I'm offering? You're not earning a lot of money from Bright. I know that. Not enough to maintain your standard of living. You can't raise rent on those tenants because they can't pay it. You're doing your little magic business, whatever that is. I certainly don't understand it."

"But you do believe in it," I ventured, peering over my shoulder.

He blinked at me and shut his mouth for one sweet second. I knew he believed in me. He'd been there when I cursed Osterhaus. He'd seen what I was capable of.

"It doesn't matter what I believe in. It isn't meeting your standard. Am I right? I like your car."

I blinked, and turned slowly to the Audi. "Thanks."

"Own it?"

"Yeah."

McHenry stared at it thoughtfully before continuing, "How many years does it have left, do you think? How long until you have to replace it? You have a nest egg socked back to buy a new model? Going to settle for pre-owned? Or are you going to have to step down a rung or two? How long were you going to be able to stay at Druid Hill, anyway? Dues are going up next year by ten kay. Did you know that? Are you sure I didn't do you a favor?"

"Your point?"

He nodded to the thug by my stoop. The thug approached with a thick manila envelope. He handed it to me and took several steps back, probably to keep me at a good shooting distance. I unwound the red string latching the envelope closed and pulled out a thick stack of papers with Sign Here stickers peeking from the edges.

"That's a handsome offer, Lake. Healthy enough for me to come here personally and talk some sense into you. Do I want that land? Yes, I do. Am I going to come out ahead on this deal? We both know I will. But what are you getting out of this?"

I inspected the first few pages and finally found his offer price.

There were a lot of zeroes.

He continued, "You can keep this shit row house if you like. The development stops at that corner. But with that offer, you could move into the Towers. The Ritz. You can tell Bright and Sullivan to have a nice campaign and finally get back to living your life. If you're clinging onto those properties out of some misplaced sense of duty to your tenants, then all you have to do is drive six blocks to the stadium, or eight blocks west to Shipley, and you're going find a lot of embarrassingly cheap properties. And so will they. Same bus lines. Same part of town. They're going to be inconvenienced, but they're renters, Lake. They know that. And they know you're a doormat."

"Why do you get to decide where they live?"

"I don't. The market does. The free market, Lake? The most powerful force on the entire globe? I'm nothing compared to the market, and neither are you. As long as you behave according to some kind of rational self-interest, then your choice is pretty clear. Maybe you're motivated out of spite. If so, then there's something else you need to recognize."

"What's that?"

"Sullivan's going to lose this election."

I chuckled. "You think so?"

"I've been doing this longer than you, son. I know a dead campaign when I see it. Magic or no, he's going to lose. Sooner is going to be the next Mayor of Baltimore. And when he is, how much difficulty do you think I'm going to have securing eminent domain over those properties?"

Definitely a dick.

"That's pretty corrupt, even for you."

"What's corruption got to do with it? The land is empty. The buildings are falling apart and breeding crime. How long until some cracked-out derelict sets fire to the whole block? Letting this land just sit here and fester is irresponsible. No, there won't be any obstacle to development come the Fall, and when it comes to that, you're going to get a fraction of what's in that envelope."

I gripped the stack of papers, but didn't give it back.

"Listen, McHenry, I have an appointment tonight. I have to get ready."

He nodded as his eyes pulled tight into an analytical squint. "I'll be on my way, then. You'll keep that offer in mind? It's good until the election."

"There's your car, and there's the road, McHenry."

He lingered for a moment, then turned on his heel, returning to his car.

I added, "I'll think about this." The words tasted bitter.

McHenry didn't look back. He didn't need to. He got to me, and we both knew it.

As I finally retired into my home, dropping McHenry's golden parachute onto my roll top desk, I spied the darquelle mounted over my mantel. The blade gleamed in the sunlight streaming through the blinds. The silver ran in a long curve, winding along the brick hearth. It reminded me of the soul I had lost.

But tonight, it wasn't my soul I had to worry about.

It was Elle's.

CHAPTER EIGHTEEN

Scovill waited for me outside the storefront of Swain's Antiques and Oddities. He had brought two women and a man with him, ostensibly his support staff for whatever he does to evict demons from children. We stood awkwardly in front of the locked double glass doors until Edgar finally appeared and let us in. He shook hands as the others entered in front of me. Edgar's eyes seemed heavier than usual. This was draining him.

Edgar led us upstairs where I found Wren hand-drying some dishes. She worked that dish towel with ferocity, her lips drawn tight.

Scovill offered her his hand, but she just stared at him. He pulled his hand back and cleared his throat. "Thank you both for allowing us this opportunity. Perhaps that's not the best way to phrase it. But it is an opportunity to do God's work."

Wren sucked in a breath and nodded.

Edgar smiled at Scovill. "Thanks for coming. We're, well, kind of lost here."

"We're all lost at some point. What we'll do tonight is to meet your daughter, and pray with her to seek guidance. This may require more than one session, depending on how deeply rooted the demon is."

"It's only been a couple days," Edgar grunted. "Don't think it's in too deep."

"It's not a matter of time with these creatures. It's a matter of the host. How close she is to God. How much purchase the demon has been given. But please know, there's no blame here. We're dealing with the Enemy. The Enemy hates all of God's children."

Wren sighed and tossed her towel over her shoulder. "She's this way." She stepped past Scovill and company, leading them down the hallway. She opened the door slowly, peering inside before opening it all the way. "Sorry, she's been trying to remove her clothes."

Scovill nodded once, betraying no embarrassment.

Wren waved them inside Elle's bedroom. I remained in the hallway next to Edgar as the four assembled in front of Elle's bed. She was lying stiff, her eyes still wild and insane, glaring up at the ceiling. Edgar and Wren had changed her soiled clothing, but the smell was still heavy in the room. One of the women put a hand up to her nose and grimaced.

Wren stood in front of me, watching as the four held hands and bowed their heads. Scovill mumbled his prayer, and all I heard was a frequent "Father God" and "name of Christ." Wren seemed satisfied Scovill and his people were in no immediate danger and turned to me, pulling me a few steps down the hall.

"Hey you," she sighed with a tired grin. "Where did you find these guys?"

"Off the freeway. They had a cardboard sign and a can of change. Thought they could use the work. Where do you think I found them?"

"I don't know, I guess I expected something more Catholic."

"I thought you said no priests? This guy isn't a priest."

"What is he, then?"

"Not sure."

"Do you think he has any ability at all?"

"I really don't know."

Her eyes hardened. "That's a lot of I-don't-knows to throw at my daughter, Dorian."

Edgar nosed in. "He wouldn't have brought them to us if he didn't think there was a chance."

"Actually," I admitted as I shifted my feet, "I don't expect this to work at all."

Wren winced, and then peered up at me. "Huh?"

"We're not going to make any progress until we identify this thing. An entity like this has to follow its own rules. We just have to figure out what rulebook it's using."

Wren nodded slowly before pulling Edgar gently away from the bedroom door. "Good luck."

I stepped back into Elle's doorway to check on their progress. The four were still engrossed in prayer, and continued for nearly half an hour before Scovill finally lifted his head and stretched his neck. He reached out for Elle's forehead and laid three fingertips gingerly across her brow.

"In the name of Christ, we call you, Demon. By the power of Christ, we command you. In His holy name, we bind you."

Elle's eyes narrowed, and she turned her head toward Scovill.

He continued, "We command you, Demon, identify yourself."

Elle's eyes shifted past Scovill, locking onto me. "Lake? Who is this simpleton you've brought me?"

Scovill nudged his entourage, and they began a babbling murmur of prayer in response.

"Demon! By the name of our Savior Jesus Christ, I command you!"

Elle snickered. "You met him, padre? Y'shwa? He was a hopeless Son of Solomon with a misplaced faith in the power of love. Look what love got him."

"By the name of Jesus—"

"You're not even pronouncing the name correctly." She looked back at me. "You're wasting our time."

I chimed in, "Our time?"

Elle blinked. This was already working.

I stepped up behind Scovill who was giving me a long glance over his shoulder. "Sorry, didn't mean to waste your time. If you have somewhere you need to be—"

"You won't get rid of me with a prayer and a pony."

Scovill stiffened, and I held up my hands.

Elle growled, "Giving up so soon?"

"No. In fact, I think I'll let these guys work on you a little longer."

"Pointless."

"Maybe. But my best case scenario is the power of Christ will actually compel you, and they'll give you the Holy heave-ho. Barring that, they might bore you to death. Either way, win-win for me."

I turned and stepped out of the room as the Healing Waters people stepped up their glossolalia, laying hands on her head and shoulders. For the next half-hour they kept it up, pouring their energy in a never-ending loop from their crown into their throat. I could tell it wasn't healthy, but it was their way. Elle just laid there, her eyes hard and stiff, but otherwise compliant. The Holy Spirit wasn't doing much to rattle the tiny cage that was her body. I hadn't expected it to, but a small part of me had wished these guys were the genuine article. They had a surprising dedication to their task, and I never once caught a whiff of judgment from them. I was beginning to drum up a plan to make a donation to their church on general principle, when Elle sat upright, pulling free from their touch. She jerked against the short lengths of jute ropes just long enough to allow her to change positions, but not actually stand.

She sighed a ragged hiss and spat into Scovill's face.

"You're not listening to me, Lake," she growled. "You know better."

"What do I know? Enlighten me?"

"You know what I am. Why waste time with these bell ringers?"

Scovill calmly wiped the spittle from the side of his nose and gestured for his people to step away.

"I know what you told me you are. Ever-dark muckity-muck, fishcakes baloney."

"I am the Lurker, the hedge-servant of Satariel's court, the possessor of the First Corruption. I don't require your respect, so I won't ask for it."

I shook my head and gave Scovill a nod. "You guys want to take a break? Get some water? We'll be here for a while."

Scovill took a deep, cleansing breath and gathered his people beside him.

Elle chuckled. "Light-headed, preacher?"

Scovill tried not to betray his exhaustion, but I saw his eyes flutter.

"Light-headed because you're pouring all of your essence into your Crowns. Poor discipline, isn't it, Lake? At this rate, they'll pass out before I even feel annoyed."

Scovill gave me a quick look, and Elle sucked in a breath before releasing a gleeful cackle.

"They don't know, do they?"

I tried to collect Scovill's people. "We'll look into getting some sandwiches or something."

"You didn't tell them what you are, did you? Oh, you dirty, little liar. Preacher? You think this man is God-fearing?"

Scovill lifted a hand and turned to Elle. "Be silent, in the name of Christ the Redeemer."

"I will not. Nor should you. You've been lied to. Did he even tell you this child's parents are witches? Do you think it was difficult for me to enter this vessel? She is unbaptized. An unbeliever."

I stepped in front of Scovill. "They aren't witches."

"Take a look, preacher. You'll find the pentagram hung on the wall. Just over the balcony door. The sign of the Devil himself. Yes, these are witches you've fallen in league with. I own this child as it was properly given to me. You should ask this child's father what he has locked up in the room downstairs. I wager you'd find the answer disturbing. And you, Lake. You are far worse. Preacher, do you want to know what he is? He is a Curse Merchant. He kills with magic."

Scovill pulled me aside. I shot Elle a look as we moved into the hallway.

He wiped his face with a handkerchief before sighing, "Is it true?"

"The Swains aren't witches."

"But are they believers?"

"They believe in the Divine. They didn't ask for this, nor should we give up on Elle just because that thing inside her is trying to shake your confidence."

"Did she say 'Curse Merchant'?"

I shrugged. "News to me."

The group filed back into the living area, and Edgar and I worked to make some roast beef sandwiches and tea. Wren fidgeted on the couch for a while before retiring to Elle's bedroom with a wet towel.

One of the women looked up and slowly put down her sandwich, tapping Scovill's shoulder. I followed her eyes and found one of Wren's pentacles. It was a nice one. Nickel, perhaps silver, mounted on a black velvet matte. Right over the door to the balcony, just as Elle had said.

Scovill cleared his throat and set aside his plate. "I feel like we're working at cross aims, Mister Lake."

"That's not what you think it is," I explained.

"Then what is it?"

Wren's voice shot across the room from the hallway. "It's a pentacle. It's a warding against unwanted energies. It represents the five elements and serves to bind evil intent and create a sealed environment for workings. It's not a goat's head. It doesn't represent Satan. And I'm not a witch, but I am Wiccan. My husband collects cursed objects and keeps them under lock and key so they don't fall into the wrong hands. My daughter doesn't really believe in any of it. She's basically an atheist, and I'm okay with that."

Scovill's people jostled in their seats.

I gave Wren a sharp glance, but she countered with her battle-axe of a jaw thrust out under her face. She was done.

"If you think my daughter somehow deserves this, then you're a small-minded fool. Now I've watched you pray and pray over her for an hour.

She doesn't look harmed by any of it, so I'm happy enough to simply ask you to leave."

Scovill looked over to me and back to Wren. "Ma'am, we will leave if you want us to leave. But I have nothing but the best intentions for your daughter, regardless of your religion and practice."

She took a deep breath and nodded. "I believe you. I'm really not trying to be a bitch, here. I just think you're wasting your time. Nothing good is going to come from this. So, please." She gestured for the stairway.

Scovill stood up and gathered the plates, handing them to Edgar. He straightened his jacket and gave Edgar a pat on the arm. As they filed toward the spiral staircase leading to the store below, I offered, "I'll see them out."

The summer sun was finally setting beyond the clustered spires of downtown Frederick, and the sweeps were darting from trees and gables overhead. Scovill stepped toward their minivan, crunching on the gravel drive as he looked over the scene.

"Nice town, isn't it?" he asked.

"It's quiet. Usually."

"This would have been smoother if you had told me everything."

"Trust me, Wayne. You don't want to know everything. But thanks for trying."

His eyes traced over my face before he finally offered me a single handshake.

After they pulled out of Edgar's alley and down the street, I stepped back inside to find Edgar waiting for me at the bottom of the staircase.

"Long day, huh?" I grumbled.

"Yeah. So, I don't want to be 'that guy,' you know. But that was a pretty big waste of time, don't you think?"

"On the contrary, I learned something today."

"You did?"

I heard Wren stepping down the wrought iron above Edgar.

"Like what?" she asked.

"Like, this thing is older than Jesus. That means it's pre-Christian."

Edgar shook his head. "It could have been lying."

"True, but in my years of practice I've learned a few things. One of those things is that a person can feign ignorance, but he really can't feign knowledge."

"I don't follow."

"It didn't bother making a distinction between a Witch and a Wiccan. We can probably rule out any European heritage there. Wicca, Stregha, Catholicism, hell even Manichaeism. None of that is going to help us."

Wren stepped down next to Edgar, wrapping a hand over his shoulder. "What will help us?"

"Did you hear what it said when it identified itself?"

"Something about Lurking?"

"That was crap. But the interesting thing? Satariel."

"What's that?"

"It was trying to rattle the Christians by name-dropping Satariel."

"Who's Satariel?"

"Old name for Satan. Too old. Pre-Christian. In fact, and I'm going to have to check this, but I think it's a reference to the Book of Enoch. Point being, this thing can't even get Satan right. It covered pretty well, but this isn't a sophisticated entity. It's almost anachronistic."

Edgar cocked his head and sniffled. "So, now what?"

Something buzzed in my brain, and I paced around that ratty green divan he could never sell while I tried to force the thought to land. "Something about Jesus."

Wren asked, "What about Jesus? It doesn't believe in Jesus."

"Said he was hopeless."

"Maybe a little unfair."

"No. Wait." It finally landed. "It called Jesus a Son of Solomon."

Edgar and Wren stared at me for a long moment.

"Solomon," I repeated. "I know how we're going to get this thing."

Edgar sucked in a breath and hopped forward. "Key of Solomon?"

"It's operating in a level that's post Second Temple Judaism, but pre-Christian."

"Goetia?"

"Goetia."

Edgar's eyes dropped and his face soured. "No."

"Yes."

"No, you're not."

"Edgar?"

"I don't want him in my house."

"He's the only Goetic on the Eastern Seaboard, and he happens to live in Baltimore."

"Fuck that, he's not coming here."

Wren jumped between me and Edgar, and nearly out of her own skin. "What the shit are you two talking about?"

I looked past Wren and into Edgar's eyes. "He's the only one."

"I can't have Goetia in this building. It's just fucking dark, man."

"I recognize that."

Wren pushed us apart and fluttered her hands in exasperation. "Someone needs to start educating me right now."

"Goetia," I explained. "The summoning, binding, and coercion of dark forces using a series of hermetic sigils and rituals said to be divined by King Solomon himself as part of his gifting of Wisdom."

"We're talking about the Old Testament?" she muttered.

"Kind of after that. It's a very specific hermetic practice."

"Can you do it?"

I coughed my best effort at a laugh. "Wren, Goetia is kind of like brain surgery. There's a hell of a lot to know, and a hell of a lot that can go wrong if you don't know what you're doing. You basically have to do Goetia full time or not at all. Besides, Goetia is Netherwork."

She scowled. "And here come your Presidium friends again." Her eyes worked circles on the floor. "But you said there's someone in Baltimore?"

Edgar grunted, "Not him."

Wren peered over at Edgar, then to me. "Who is this guy?"

I answered, "Frater Zeno. He has a temple of students he more or less keeps busy."

Edgar turned back to the staircase, mumbling, "Fuck. I really hate that guy."

Wren put both hands on my shoulders. "What's wrong with this Zeno?"

"He's arguably insane."

"Crazy? Like, believes in demons crazy? Or keeps his shit in jars crazy?"

"More like teaches Goetia by survival of the fittest crazy."

She sucked in a deep breath.

"He's the only Goetic the Presidium allows to operate on this side of the Mississippi, Wren."

"Why is that?"

"I have no idea. I suspect it's because he's the genuine article, and even the Presidium isn't willing to fuck with the forces he wields."

Edgar barked from upstairs, "Really hate that guy."

Wren looked up into my eyes, tears brimming in hers. "Can he get rid of this thing?"

"I thought you were banking on schizophrenia?"

Wren smirked. "I am, but a deal's a deal, right? Call this guy. Do it tonight. If it saves Elle, I'll put a saddle on the demon myself."

Chapter Nineteen

On my way home I found a voice mail on my phone that arrived when I was with Scovill's people. I recognized the number. Ches. It was five seconds of silence before her ragged voice muttered, "I'm okay, Dorian. Just thought you should know."

That put the day into perspective. No matter how huge an ass Zeno could be, at least I would have Ches' voice in my phone.

I made the call to Zeno. I had his lodge in my contacts book thanks to a specific favor I did for one of his students several years back. The phone rang six times before a nondescript voice mail message urged me in robotic tones to leave my message. I kept it short. Name and number, and some sense of urgency.

I hadn't hung up for a full minute before I received a call back. Son of a bitch was screening calls.

"Hello?"

"This is Frater Zeno."

"Good evening. I don't know if you remember me. I helped one of your students—"

"I remember you."

I didn't find that particularly comforting. "I have a situation you may be able to help me with."

"I believe we've already paid you."

"No, I mean, not as payment. I have a problem. I need your help."

"We don't do that," he blurted.

"Sorry?"

"Help. We don't help people."

"You don't help people?"

"Poor return on investment."

I paced a quick circle in the room. "I have the means to pay you."

It could have been paper rustling on his end, or he could have actively sighed into the phone. "We are comfortably funded. Thank you for your interest."

"Wait."

"Why?"

"Why? I mean, I helped you out once."

"And we paid you."

Son of a bitch. "Yes, but don't you have any sense of reciprocity?"

"Which was why we paid you."

"Not the point."

"Do you have a point?" he sniped.

I was seconds away from throwing my phone through the front window without opening it. "Zeno, there's an entity possessing a child. A friend of mine. Edgar Swain."

"I thought Edgar Swain was an adult."

"He is. It's his child." What an ass. "This thing is basically camping out inside her body, and I can't get it out."

"Call a priest."

"I tried that. I've ruled out European self-identities. And I'm reasonably convinced this thing is a Principality circa Second Temple period."

After a long silence, Zeno replied, "That would be unlikely. Principalities governed territorial stretches of the Levant. Finding one in an individual child would be a gross misuse of its power. Even with the encroachment of Christianity and Islam forfeiting many Principalities in the Tigris and Euphrates cradle, you're probably looking at a Legionnaire at the highest."

"Great. Well, I need it removed."

"Best of luck."

"Zeno? I'm not above begging. Okay, maybe I am, because I don't think it would help anyway. But you're probably the one person I can call who can get this done."

"That wouldn't surprise me."

"So what do I have to do to make this worth your while?"

Zeno left me with a long, torturous moment of silence before responding, "If I can't take the thing away, then I simply don't see any reason for involving myself."

"What do you mean?"

"The entity."

"Take it away?" I asked.

"I assume you plan to bind it for your own purposes."

"Are you kidding?"

He let slip a dry snicker. "I don't do that, either."

"Well look, Zeno. I have no interest in keeping this thing in a little jar on my shelf. If you want the fucker, you're welcome to it. As long as you can remove it without injuring the girl."

"Oh. You don't want it?"

"No."

"When can we meet?"

I rubbed the bridge of my nose. I was going to hit the Scotch after this call, I could tell.

I made arrangements to meet Zeno and his Goetic hit squad at the Swains the next day. I called Edgar to double-check the timing, which was a good thing since Eddie had outworn his host's welcome, and they needed to find a place to keep him while his sister was suffering through this.

After draining a lowball and collapsing on my bed for the night, I awoke to the sound of road construction. Summer in Baltimore. I spotted the fat envelope on my roll top desk as I made my way to the kitchen for some breakfast. The damn thing was still there, tempting me with an embarrassingly healthy offering price for those four row houses. McHenry was good for it, I knew that. He was nothing if not a shrewd professional. My tools were esoteric; his were financial. We were both practiced at our tools.

And he was right about my financial outlook. The charm-and-hex crowd wasn't as robust as it once was. I was leaning on Julian for my income, and that was about to dry up… one way or another.

I wanted to see Abe, listen to his voice, have him talk me out of this. I thought about him, Tyrel, and the other tenants as I struggled through a ham omelet. I would have to get used to making my own breakfasts.

After I powered down the eggs, I jumped into the car and made a quick run down the block to the properties. They were in good condition, Abe had seen to that. Between the two of us, we had restored much of the exteriors, patched old wood and painted. Some of the roofing was ragged, but that wasn't visible from the street. No, they were reasonably attractive and livable as opposed to the stark contrast across the street. That same clutch of shirtless men held court on the stoop across from Abe. I kept driving along Fayette, taking a visual inventory of the properties McHenry was purchasing in order to level for the new development. He wasn't entirely wrong about them. Most were derelicts, empty since the economic decline in the eighties. None of the original glass panes remained, even at the highest levels of what was once a brick-clad stamp factory. These shells of buildings were now home to squatters and probably a significant population of vermin. From a purely, viciously mercenary point of view, tearing these old buildings down brick-by-brick and building new would solve a host of problems.

But what would be solved, really? The homeless staying in these buildings would be relocated. The police would sweep the buildings; perhaps even bus the squatters to shelters. But they would scatter once again as would the rats and roaches that would scurry into the populated city blocks nearby. The real damage would be felt in the city taxes. With new mixed-use properties come higher property values. If McHenry found a way to proceed with his project without requiring my properties, I would see my taxes triple in the space of a year. I would have to sell, and then I would be stuck holding a handful of properties no one could figure a use for.

The real truth was McHenry had thrown me a life raft inside that envelope. Even if I had a long chat with Abe about this, I doubted he could find a more compelling argument than selling to McHenry. My stomach twisted as I thought about breaking the news to the tenants.

These were all my problems. At the moment I had to focus on the Swains' problem. Zeno would be the highest level of practitioner I could throw at the problem, and I had done my homework. Even if I hadn't nailed the exact period of origin, this thing would likely succumb to Zeno's bindings. Then this would all be over, and I could deal with McHenry.

After finding some mediocre coffee in a gas station on my way up I-70, I made it to the Swains with time to spare. Wren was babysitting some day trippers who were nosing through Edgar's collection of wall art. I meandered through the shop, trying to blend in until the others finished their rifling and took their exit.

Wren approached me with tired eyes. "They're on their way?"

I nodded. "They're probably going to need a space to set up a circle."

"Can't they do it in her room?"

"Probably not. These guys are hard core ceremonialists. Everything they do will require lots of planning and time. Everything in its place."

She wrinkled her nose. "I could never work like that. Magic is too organic for me."

"I never viewed it as magic. It's always been just another mechanic of the known universe."

"I'll get Edgar down here to help move some furniture."

"You're going to close for this, right?" I asked nodding to the front doors.

She gave me an eye-roll and went upstairs. Edgar descended in time for three young men to step into the shop, all lugging large briefcases. I recognized Zeno leading the other two in his khakis and a gray cardigan. In summer, he wore a cardigan. His glasses were large, square, and thick, causing his eyes to bulge a little more than they should have over his horse-like nose. His hair hung in a kind of stringy Fauntleroy, really selling the social awkwardness that sprayed off his body with the force of a fire hose. The other two didn't look a day over twenty. One of them had acne.

Zeno stepped right past Edgar and stopped in front of me, setting down a briefcase and offering me a hand to shake. I shook his clammy hand and tried to smile.

"Thanks for coming, Frater."

He sniffled and looked past my shoulder at the store. "Is this the space?"

"It can be. More room down here than upstairs."

He nodded and snapped his fingers. The other two dropped their cases and clicked them open. Edgar stepped around me and stood in front of Zeno, who gave him two seconds of his notice.

"You're Swain?"

"Yeah."

"Can you move that couch?"

Edgar gave me a *can you believe this guy* look, and I pulled him aside to help shift the green divan to the other side of the antiques before he actually socked Zeno in the nose. We cleared a few more pieces that looked delicate, and I urged Edgar to lock the doors and flip the Open sign to Closed. I unfolded two Asian screens and set them to shield the back of the store from the street.

Edgar gave me a pat on the shoulder. "It's Friday. Shouldn't be a lot of street business."

"Can't be too careful. Especially if it gets loud."

"We had a little trouble last night. She started screaming. Couldn't tell if it was the creature or Elle. Really hoping it wasn't Elle."

"I hate that this is happening to you, Edgar. You're the last person who deserves this."

"Deserve has nothing to do with it. Just get this thing out."

Zeno stepped toward us as the others began measuring the cleared space with a set of gilded tools. They made marks on the floor with chalk and sketched what looked like a large, squat compass. Zeno cleared his throat and stuffed his hands in his pockets.

"I should see the girl."

Edgar nodded. "She's upstairs."

He stepped aside as Edgar led us up the wrought-iron spiral into their living room. Wren stood outside Elle's door, arms folded. She gave Zeno a long, evaluating glance which he didn't seem to notice. He simply waited without a word until she stepped aside. Edgar pushed the door open, and Zeno took one quick peek inside.

A hiss spilled from inside the bedroom.

Zeno turned and gave us all a quizzical glance before motioning to me. "A word, Lake?"

I shrugged at Wren and Edgar as I moved to their outdoor balcony.

Zeno closed the sliding glass door behind us and turned to face the back alley.

"You know this is going to be very difficult."

"Wouldn't surprise me."

He cocked his head and gave me an impatient scowl. "Do you know why this will be difficult?"

"What say we skip the condescension and go straight to the part where you actually tell me?"

"You told me she was a girl, but she's really a girl."

"You were expecting what, exactly?"

"I mean, she's very young. Not even a teenager. How old is she?"

I guided him away from the patio door. "Thirteen."

"Do you see my point?"

"What's wrong with her being young?"

Zeno looked thoughtfully over the balcony rail. "How many possessions of small children have you seen in your life?"

"Sounds like a classic horror story to me."

He shook his head. "In your life, I said. In flesh and blood."

"Not really my usual scope of practice, Frater."

"It's damned rare. Children don't have any kind of sophistication. They haven't been complicated by higher thought. Now, this girl being thirteen, she's just starting to think about the Universe and what's out there. But it wasn't too long ago that she had no concerns outside of the immediate needs of the body and the psyche."

I mulled that over. "Children have natural psychic shielding, is what you're saying? I suppose I knew that."

"Anything that can penetrate a young child's innate disbelief has to be operating either out of sheer arrogance or outright ignorance."

"Well, this thing is trying to put the hook in me for some reason."

"Vendetta?" he ventured.

"More like a lion playing with its food."

"Lions don't play with their food. They just kill it quickly."

I rolled my eyes. "Okay, bad metaphor."

"Before we bottle this thing, have you put any thought into whether you wanted to interrogate it?"

"I've been trying. I get the sense it'll just throw more smartassery at me."

"No offense, but you haven't given it any credible threats."

"Fair enough."

"For example, would you want me to attempt to determine who sent it?"

I blinked. "What?"

"Its master. I figure if it's mentioning you by name, you'd probably want to know who sent it at your friends."

I froze and shook my head. "Wait. What makes you think anyone's behind this?"

"If it's a Goetic demon, then it wouldn't have done this on its own volition. There are hardly any left in Creation who haven't been captured and claimed and coerced at least on some level. Thousands of years at the hands of Mankind have effectively stripped them of their free will."

I backed away from the balcony railing. I had assumed the entire time that this thing was just another one of the shadows lurking in my peripheral vision, nosing into my life to mock me. Until that moment, it hadn't occurred to me that this thing was acting in the service of another.

"Human?"

"Probably. These things are powerful in their element, but weak in ours. Makes humans the most likely masters."

"Yes. I want to know who sent it. But don't tell the Swains."

He nodded. "I'll check on Chad and Mike."

Zeno slipped back into the Swains' home, leaving me on the balcony. I gripped the door handle with white knuckles, took a long breath, and followed.

Watching Chad and Mike, I couldn't help but snap into a ritual mindset. Their slow and deliberate attention to absolute detail was centering for me. They spent an hour charting one of the pentacles of Solomon on Edgar's floor in a combination of loose chalk, sand, and iron shavings. These were young guys, but they were well practiced. Each motion was coordinated with a measured amount of intent and energy. Perhaps it was Zeno's tutelage; perhaps it was virtue of the fact that these were the students who had survived his sink-or-swim methods. In either case, Zeno simply watched from the corner, offering no support or correction. I couldn't tell if it was because Chad and Mike were executing their sigil flawlessly, or if he knew they would be the ones devoured if they screwed up.

When they had concluded the scribe work and had walked the circle deosil with a censer thirteen times, they nodded to Zeno, who in turn faced me.

"We're ready. Who will bring her down?"

Wren answered, already climbing the staircase, "I will."

We listened in the shop beneath the living space. I heard raised voices and a commotion of footfalls on the floor as if there had been a brief struggle. A piece of furniture might have been overturned as a loud *thump* rattled the mirrors on the wall nearby. Zeno and I immediately took notice of the mirrors. He made a gesture to his pupils, who jumped for their cases and produced several black cloths, draping them over each reflective surface within sight of the sigil.

I wandered over to Zeno. "That could have been interesting."

"I'm more accustomed to a controlled environment."

"Tell me about it."

Footfalls and scrapes traced a line over our heads toward the staircase. Finally, we saw Wren leading Elle down the stairs by a jute rope cinched over her wrists. Her eyes found me immediately, wide, wild, and unnerving. She only broke eye contact in order to take her turn on the staircase. I was satisfied with that. The longer this thing was trying to put the hook in me, the less time it had to notice the pentacle on the floor.

Indeed, Wren had almost made it to the circle before Elle's eyes finally broke and spotted the chalk work on the floor. Her eyes widened even further, seemingly impossibly, and she grimaced.

"What is this ignorance, Lake? Another street preacher?" She turned to Zeno, and her eyes narrowed. "A studied man, perhaps?"

Zeno stared passively at Elle, betraying not the first emotion.

Elle spat in his direction. "You'll fail like the others, magician."

He waved Wren forward. She stepped gingerly onto the chalk work. Elle swiped her feet across the outside of the circle, spreading the carefully rendered scribing into a fine yellow smear.

Wren froze.

Edgar fidgeted on his bench by the reagent counter, but Zeno simply held up a hand. He walked a circle around the pentacle until he reached Elle.

"Oops," she chimed. "Did I ruin your little trap?"

Zeno removed his glasses and cleaned them on his cardigan. "No." He replaced his glasses and gave Elle a gentle shove in the small of her back, sending her stumbling into the middle of the sigil.

Wren hopped out of the circle, still holding the rope. Zeno waved at her, and she dropped it to the floor.

Elle stood still in the middle of the pentacle, holding out her hands as if to steady herself. Her eyes traced a wide circle around the glyphs on the floor, and she waited. After a few seconds, she straightened up and smirked.

"I remain unimpressed."

Zeno shrugged. "Come out, then."

Elle giggled and took a single step toward Zeno. Her leg stiffened, and she nearly fell flat onto her face. She thrust out her hands and landed palms-down onto the chalk. She waved them against the floor, smearing the delicate design further. But the more she struggled to erase the sigil, the more it seemed to bind her to the floor.

Elle released a primordial growl and began spitting against her hand, working the saliva and chalk into a lather that began coating her fingers.

Zeno turned to Edgar and took several leisurely paces to his side. "She will struggle a while. They always do."

Edgar's brows lifted a little. "I thought all the symbols had to be perfect?"

"They were, and that was enough."

I spotted Chad and Mike giving each other a discreet fist bump.

Zeno continued, "The outward appearance is only one part of the whole. Rendering the working in the physical, the mental, and ethereal requires focus and practice. But the end result is a trap that binds a creature that exists on all three planes of existence. It's simple theory."

I had to agree, but the absolute mastery of its execution had earned my respect.

Elle calmed after a bit and managed to pull herself up to her knees, rolling back onto her heels with her hands still firmly planted on the smeared floor boards.

"This is old magic," she wheezed.

I crouched down and looked her in the eye. "You had your chance to leave. I want you to realize that. Because this man won't be gentle."

"You arrogant, little shit," she growled. "We're going to pull your soul into tiny pieces for this."

"You know what you're going to do, you creepy, little bastard? A whole handful of nothing for a very long time. You know what this man is, right? He's a Son of Solomon. And as far as I can tell, he doesn't have any illusions regarding the power of love."

Zeno gave me a quizzical blink.

I shook my head. "Long story."

Elle pulled one hand from the floor and lifted a finger to point directly at me. "You amuse us."

"I'm happy to hear that, really. I was worried you didn't like me."

"The most amusing thing about you? You think you're winning."

"You don't get it. You're about to become this man's slave. He's going to stick your skinny ass into a bottle and put you on a shelf for as long as he wants."

"We're all slaves, Lake. We all serve a master."

"Do tell."

She grinned. The look put a chill into my stomach. She sucked in a breath and recited, "L'hatil, l'hitparek. L'tzam'tzem. L'harag."

The energy in the room shifted dramatically within the space of words. She repeated them, and I could feel a kind of vortex forming inside the building.

Zeno called out, "Chad!"

The young man reached into his bag and produced a roll of black gaffing tape. Chad tossed it over Elle's head to Zeno, who pulled out a length of tape and hurled himself into the pentacle. Sliding his knees around

Elle, he slapped the tape firmly over her mouth. She squirmed and tried to kick him away, but when her hands made contact with the floor, they fixed once again to the wood boards.

Zeno kept his hand over the tape, watching as Elle's eyes flickered with ferocity. Catching his breath, he turned to face the three of us.

"It's possible I've underestimated your problem."

"What was that?" Wren asked. "What was that chant?"

"Old charm of unmaking. Simple, but effective."

"You don't run into that a lot?" I asked.

"No. Kind of surprising." Zeno pulled himself to his feet, dusting the chalk from his khakis. "You know of many masters who give their servants the means to undo their bonds?"

"Uh, no," I fumbled. "Not really."

"Besides, it's not quite right. The Hebrew was tortured. And that particular charm predates the Second Temple period by, oh, several centuries at least. It resurfaced during the Golden Dawn when all the English mystics were plundering Egypt for relevance. Probably means it was a direct lift from old Egyptian mysticism."

"You're losing me quickly, Zeno."

He snapped his fingers and lunged toward Elle, examining her face through those thick glasses like a bug through a magnifying glass. "There was a brief period when Hebrew and Egyptian traditions blended into a syncretic practice. It remained a minority practice until the Babylonian captivity. That is very strange." He tapped Elle's forehead. "What are you?"

"Not a demon?" I asked.

Zeno replied, "Unknown."

"Can you remove it?"

"Unknown," he repeated.

I goaded, "Can we at least try?"

Zeno turned to me and put his hand over the tape sealing Elle's mouth. "This presents a certain difficulty in asking questions."

Wren shook her head. "So? Just get rid of it!"

Zeno kept his eye contact on me. I could feel Edgar and Wren staring at me.

I nodded. "Do it."

Zeno straightened up and stepped to his pupils. One of them, Mike, I believe, offered him a tiny glass perfume bottle. Zeno walked the perimeter of what remained of the pentacle and found a spot near our feet that was unmarred. A spiral. A widdershins spiral, counter-clockwise in order to draw in rather than to push out. He set the bottle in the direct center of the spiral and brushed us back with his fingers.

We gave him space, and he sprinkled the bottle with some salt from his pocket. The man kept salt in his pocket.

The three of them took positions aligning with a triangle hinted at by their sigil work, and they took a seat. After a long silent moment, they began a chant that lasted the better part of an hour. We withdrew to the front of the shop to let them do their work. Wren dropped onto that ugly green divan and covered her eyes with her hand.

"You hanging in there, Wren?" I asked.

"Just."

Edgar crouched beside her and cradled her head in his arms. They sat there on that couch mingling into one another, and I immediately felt uncomfortable. I was intruding on their space. Their home, their life. I turned back toward the rear of the shop and watched the Goetics chant. I found their world more familiar.

Elle twisted inside the sigil, and managed to meet my eyes. They were drawn, perhaps less wild. Perhaps even scared.

This was working. Remarkably, inexorably, this would be over soon, and the Swains would have their life back.

Elle's eyes closed, and she shook her head. When they opened again, they renewed their sharp quality. The fear was still there, but now it was mixed with defiance.

Chalk dust was thick in the air, and as the ritual continued Elle began smacking her legs against the floor. One of the pupils succumbed to a coughing fit, and when the cadence was interrupted, Zeno opened his eyes and clapped his hands.

"Stop," Zeno ordered.

The pupils slowly opened their eyes and stood up, stretching stiff muscles. Zeno ventured toward Elle and reached for the tape. Slowly he pulled it back as Elle glared at him. Her lips were red and swollen, but as he leaned in toward her, they pulled into a smile.

"This must be embarrassing for you," she whispered.

Zeno sighed and stood up, moving to the front of the shop.

I followed along after him. "Frater?"

"It's not coming out."

"What?"

Zeno shook his head cautiously. "I don't think it's even a demon."

"Well, we can keep going, right?"

He stuffed his hands in his pockets when he reached the Swains. "I apologize, but I don't think this is going to be effective. We've overlooked a possibility that appears to be more of a probability. Has this girl seen a mental health professional?"

"You think she's crazy?" I muttered in exasperation. "You?"

Wren shut her eyes and hung her head.

Edgar stood up and shepherded Zeno toward the front of the storefront for a private conversation.

I stood in front of Wren, hoping to be of some use to her. She looked up at me with red-rimmed eyes.

"I hate this, Dorian."

I nodded, and turned away before tears welled in my own eyes.

Zeno and Edgar returned from their whispers, Edgar with his hands rubbing the back of his head.

"Let's clean this up," he mumbled.

"Wait," I insisted. "Let's take a moment. Zeno, don't you think you're being a little dismissive here?"

"No," he stated.

"The pentacle clearly had an effect on her. We all saw that."

"Because she accepted that it would."

"You expect me to believe it was the power of suggestion?"

Zeno squinted at me. "Why are you being so dogmatic? It's the most reasonable explanation."

"She was chanting proto-Egyptian unmaking charms, Zeno. How do you explain that?"

He nodded to the Swains. "She has an alternative upbringing."

Wren offered, "We're not really hermeticists, though. I don't know where she would have picked that up."

"Edgar is," I pointed out.

He sucked in a breath to say something, but Wren cut him off.

"He couldn't handle anything like this. You could, probably."

The others slowly turned their faces to me.

Zeno asked, "Does she spend a lot of time with you, Lake?"

"Not a lot," I replied.

"Any unsupervised time at your home? With access to your books?"

I held up my hands. "I don't discuss the Life with Elle. She mostly just watches TV and bugs me."

"My point being, it isn't impossible that she's absorbed some knowledge."

"I'm not willing to accept that schizophrenia is the simplest explanation."

Wren sighed as she stood up. "We're taking her to the doctor Monday morning."

"Wren, you have to think about this," I blurted, holding out a hand to her.

"I have, Dorian. It's done. She's going."

"I have two more days. You gave me until Monday."

She turned to me and gave me a thin smile. "Can you tell me what your plan is?" After I floundered for a moment, she put a hand on my arm. "Thank you for trying, though."

Edgar stepped up and held her by her shoulders, giving me a sad shrug.

"Let's get her upstairs," he whispered.

They scooped up Elle, and Edgar carried her up the stairs. I caught a glimpse of Elle's face, exhausted, but still leering at me with a vicious air of triumph.

Zeno's pupils cleaned up the space with a handheld vacuum and a large magnet. Zeno even chipped in, wiping a slab of hematite over the floor once the chalk mess was cleared. As Chad and Mike packed up the kits, I leaned on the wall and waited for Zeno to pass me.

"Be straight with me, Zeno. Do you really think there isn't an entity inside that girl?"

He straightened his glasses and sniffled. "If there is, it's outside of my discipline. Which would surprise me."

"What could it be, then? Just work with me here. Assume it's not schizophrenia. What could possess a thirteen-year-old girl, would know about my personal details, and could unmake your Goetia?"

He thought it over, then shrugged. "Best explanation is she's a sick young girl and needs psychological help."

"So, you failed, and now you're back-pedaling," I stated. "Is that it?"

"Excuse me?"

I took a step closer to lower my voice. "You couldn't get it done, and now you're insisting it wasn't you, but her."

Zeno sniffled. "If you feel the need to goad me, Lake, then go right ahead. I have no need for your approval."

"Why are you so willing to give up on this?"

"Why are you unwilling to accept the obvious?" he countered.

"Because it's happened to two other women. I don't know of any kind of mental illness that jumps bodies."

"My advice? Let her parents deal with this. At any rate, I'm done here."

He turned to collect his students and take his leave.

"Zeno? I'm right about this."

"Then prove it. Do the work. Prove me wrong."

They left without further commotion, and I lingered in the shop for a while, waiting to hear back from Edgar or Wren. After ten minutes, I had to make a choice between leaving or barging into their living space again. It wasn't usually a decision I had to contemplate, but after the last couple days, I was left with the notion I wasn't much help to the Swains.

My phone interrupted my internal debate, and I stepped outside to take the call.

It was Julian.

"Dorian? Are you busy this afternoon?"

I had to summon the strength to even reply. "Not really."

"There's a big meeting here at the office. Kind of want you to sit in."

"Which office?"

"The Office," Julian underscored.

"As in—"

"The Mayor's office."

"Oh."

CHAPTER TWENTY

Sooner's face filled the pull-down screen at the other end of the conference room, and was quickly shunted to a split screen by an unflattering headshot of Joey McHenry. As dark music droned in the background, an announcer barked in a dramatic tone, "But Sooner doesn't want you to know who his single largest contributor is. Joey McHenry. A vote for Sooner is a vote for McHenry."

A few of the gathered organ-grinders bobbed their heads in amusement, particularly Toad Face who seemed especially self-congratulatory. Bright sat next to Sullivan at the end of the table, both twisted in their seats at awkward angles to watch the TV spot.

"Do you want a mayor, Baltimore? Or do you want a CEO?" The scene jump-cut to what someone in a production studio imagined a pink slip looked like with *Working Citizens of Baltimore* hand written across the top.

I spied a glimpse of Julian who visibly winced at that particular image.

Sullivan's face was solid, stony, inscrutable.

The TV spot wrapped with a flattering shot of Sullivan.

"Keep your jobs, Baltimore. Keep your homes. Re-elect David Sullivan."

The screen flickered to black and someone raised the lights in the room. Two or three of the organ grinders tried to start applause, but it was too crowded.

Julian announced, "Latest from Citizens United to Re-elect."

Toad Face cleared his throat. "It's time, Mayor. We've been ducking and weaving all week with Sooner attack ads."

Bright lifted his brow and scanned the other faces. "Everyone?"

Faces nodded one by one. The only one who seemed unconvinced was Sullivan.

"Dorian?" Julian called from across the room.

Eyes turned to me, and I tried my best to come up with a response that made me look as if I belonged there.

"It'll probably work."

"Probably?" Toad Face snorted.

Julian added, "You don't seem convinced."

I noticed Sullivan staring holes through me. His eyes were wide and expectant. He had the look of a man grasping for a life raft.

"Okay, no. Don't run it."

Toad smacked his hand on the table. "Here we go with this guy."

"You want my opinion?" I asked him, "Or do you just want everyone to throw you a princess party? People are sick of this. It's all they hear. It's all they think politicians know how to act."

"Every time one of Sooner's negatives runs, and we don't respond, we look weak. We have the high ground. He deployed first. We win."

Sullivan interrupted. "We don't win until we win." He turned to me. "I'm sorry, I'm horrible with names."

Julian said, "Dorian Lake. Grass roots in West Baltimore."

"Mister Lake, you feel the voters don't want negative campaigns. But they respond to them. Curtis has a point."

Ah. Toad Face had a name. I liked Toad Face better.

"I'm sure the people at large are jaded enough to think it's the only way to run an election, so Curtis is probably right."

"I know I'm right," he blustered.

I sighed and held up my hands. "You asked me a question, you have my answer. Run the ad, and you'll be everything all of the voters have come to expect from you."

The room fell silent for a moment. Julian in particular clenching up in his chair.

"I think what Dorian is trying to say," he offered, "is that there's still a way to play the high ground without rolling an attack ad."

Sullivan shifted to Julian and asked, "Is there?"

"I don't see how," he responded. "Curtis is right. We're taking a hit on Sooner's ads. Mostly because we have yet to refute his claims."

"Right. I'm a member of the Freemasons, so I must be participating in some shadow government," Sullivan scoffed.

"Are you?" I asked. "A Mason, I mean. Not the shadow government thing."

Sullivan grinned. "Knights of Columbus."

"Damn. I was kind of hoping you could put in a word for me."

This drew some chuckles from the room. Except for Toad Face. He worked at the conference table with his fingertips before jerking toward me red-faced.

"What are you doing, Mister Lake? You're grass roots. I've heard that twice now. But I haven't seen any numbers from Shipley Hill. Franklin-Mulberry. Hollins. Are you actually campaigning, or are you here to play Devil's advocate? I seriously want to know what you're doing for this campaign. Because if this man isn't a part of this team, then I don't feel like suffering his recriminations every time we talk strategy."

Julian held up a hand and drew in a breath. Probably to defend me. I didn't let him.

"I own properties on Fayette Street. Low income rentals. Which matters to you, all of you, because they're on the backside of the Carrollton block. You'll recognize that if you're keeping track of McHenry Construction's master plan for the downtown area. He's buying up the old stamp factory and all of the row houses lining the block to demolish and develop. He's made all the property owners offers."

I looked over to Julian, whose eyes were narrowing.

"Yeah. He made me an offer. He wants to buy my properties. It's a decision being made between two reasonably wealthy men. Well, one millionaire and one trust fund child."

More chuckles, though more subdued.

"Know who isn't a part of this conversation? The people living there. You know why? Most are supporting families at or below the poverty level. Probably leveraged on credit. Probably on assistance. I don't know their personal stories. I'm not that kind of landlord. But I have to tell you, I'd be profoundly stupid not to take McHenry's offer."

Eyes stared at me.

Especially Julian's.

I continued, "Mister Mayor? You want to know why these people are so jaded? They're losing their city block by block. You may agree with Curtis, you might not. But right now I have to think about how I'm going to tell my tenants they're going to have to find another place to live. And next to that, I'm sorry, but getting you re-elected feels kind of small."

I gathered my briefcase and turned for the door.

Curtis snickered. "Alright, anyway. Back to reality."

It was probably lack of sleep, lack of food, and almost certainly lack of whiskey that made me snap.

"Reality? What do you think reality is? Poll data?" I pointed directly at Sullivan "My God, you don't have a clue why this man is about to find another line of work, do you? These people don't want to leave, and it's not because they like where they live. It's because where they live stopped being home a long time ago." I turned to Sullivan. "The problem, Mister Mayor, is that people like me are the ones making these decisions. You want to make a difference? Put people like me out of work."

Sullivan stood up, and the entire room followed. I wanted to proceed with my dramatic exit, but I suddenly had three men standing in my way.

The Mayor leaned forward on the table, shaking his head.

"We're going to sit on this ad another week."

Curtis choked on a response, but had the presence of mind not to say anything.

Sullivan nodded to Julian before turning to take an exit through a side door.

Julian shoved his hands in his pockets. "Okay, that's the word people. Curtis? Your office in fifteen minutes. Dorian?"

I nodded to Julian as the others gathered their coats. Curtis, in particular, made sure not to put himself in a position to make eye contact as he slid past me into the front hall.

In the space of a couple minutes, I found myself alone with Julian, bracing for his wrath.

Instead, I got applause. Julian clapped a few times, his face bright with a smile.

"Dorian, you insufferable little prick, I think I'm going to kiss you."

"Buy me lunch, first."

"I wanted you here to see what you were doing for this campaign."

I cocked my head. "And what, exactly, am I doing?"

"Well, you're keeping Sully's karma nice and shiny for one."

"It's a living."

He nodded. "Seriously, though. Do you understand why I hired you in the first place?"

"I'm very sure you don't want me to answer that out loud in this building."

"I agreed with Curtis. I was ready to run the ads. I couldn't tell him it was a bad call."

I stared at Julian for a few seconds. I had always pegged him as a fundamental ideals man. I had no idea he came so close to compromise within these halls. "So I'm you're anti-Yes-Man?"

I gave Julian a baffled shrug.

"Well, you're welcome," I offered with a shrug.

"How are you doing? Things progressing with your new lady friend?"

"Jesus, Julian, I'm not eighty."

"Whatever."

"Hey, you remember Amy Mancuso?" I ventured.

His face darkened. "Not likely to forget her. Why?"

"That day, when you called me. Look, things are getting really screwed up in my head these days, and, well… you were there before I was. Tell me straight. Was what happened to Amy real?"

He drew in a deep breath. "It was real enough to call you."

"Something was really inside her. Right? I mean, you hinted there was something in her past with addiction and being mentally disturbed."

"Dorian, I can't tell you what was really happening with that woman. But I know enough to recognize a dark force when I see one."

"I need her address."

"Why?"

"I want to talk to her. One-on-one."

"And how is that a good idea?"

"Listen, this is personal. This thing, whatever it is, it's gunning for me. And my friends are suffering because of it. I need to talk to her. I need to figure out how this happened to her. See if I can't piece it together."

Julian's eyebrows pinched, and his jaw dropped slightly.

I realized why when I felt a tear running down my cheek.

The side door opened, and Sullivan stepped inside.

"Oh, I'm sorry."

Julian turned and smiled. "No sweat."

I tried to wipe my face as discreetly as possible.

Sullivan stepped around the table toward me. "Mind if I borrow Mister Lake, Julian?"

"Uh, no. That's fine. We're finished." He looked at me with a mix of alarm and amusement. "Dorian, I'll get that info to you by the end of the day."

Sullivan nodded to Julian and herded me to the door with a flat hand against my shoulder. We stepped into the front hall, and he set a brisk pace, his shoes clacking off the terrazzo floor.

"I wanted to thank you for your candor, Dorian. Sorry, I assume we're on a first name basis at this point."

"Sorry about that. That guy just really makes me want to punch him in the throat."

"Curtis is a handful, but he's also worked in campaign strategy for over eleven years. So, you know, you might want to cut him some slack."

Julian was right. I'd have to work on that snap judgment thing, one of these days. "I'll keep that in mind."

He paused by a large glass door with the word *Mayor* stenciled. He opened the door and gestured me inside. We marched past a receptionist. She was new. Last time I had set foot in this office, I wasn't prepared for a conversation with this man.

I still wasn't.

We walked into his office, and he gestured to a seat in front of his carved wood desk.

"Well, Curtis can say what he wants about you. I don't think you're the outsider he sees you to be. If you don't mind my saying, you seem to care."

"I try not to be completely intolerable when I can afford not to be."

He chuckled as he reached into his desk. "Where are you from, Dorian? Originally."

"New York City."

"Trust fund child? Your parents anyone I might know?"

I shook my head. "I'm the only Lake you have to worry about."

He produced a pamphlet from his drawer and slid it across the desk to me.

"Well, Dorian Lake, I want you to know that I heard you. About people losing their city? Property owners like you don't have a lot of options, and part of that is our fault. But really, the market drives these things. We can try to divert it with smart policy, but in the end, you can't stop the river from flowing."

I took the pamphlet, not really reading it.

"I know. It just feels like a living tragedy, is all."

"It really does, sometimes. Mind if I ask you what McHenry offered for your properties?"

"In all due respect, Mister Mayor," I answered, "that's really none of your business."

"Fair enough. So, you've decided to sell?"

"I can't figure out a way to say no just yet."

"Who are you going to sell to?"

I cocked my head. He wasn't a stupid man, but I wasn't quite getting the question.

"I think you know, sir."

"I know McHenry made an offer, but I'm asking who you're going to sell to." He tapped at the pamphlet. "My second year in office, we spearheaded a campaign with Representative Lachner." He pointed again to the pamphlet.

I looked down and read the large print on the cover. *PROPERTY OWNERSHIP ASSISTANCE ACT*.

Sullivan continued, "There are significant tax credits in place for rental owners who provide non-brokered sales to their tenants. Plus Federal assistance via the FHA. It was our pride and joy that second year. Problem is the people who benefit from this the most are the ones who are the least likely to have ever heard about it. That's been my curse since I took office."

"I know a thing or two about curses," I offered as I scanned over the pamphlet.

"So, anyway. You want me to put you out of a job? I did my part already, Mister Lake. Choice is yours what you do next." He stood up. "It was good chatting with you. Hope you stick around for the election."

I stood up and shook his hand.

By the time I left the building, I had an address in my pocket for Amy Mancuso, and a pamphlet outlining the details of selling my properties to my tenants.

What's more, I now possessed a small insight into what Julian saw in Sullivan. He was a good man. And he deserved to win this election.

I wished I could have given him my undivided attention, but I had a young girl to save first.

CHAPTER TWENTY-ONE

The sun had shifted to the dark, harsh tones of early summer evening when I reached Reisterstown Road. Amy Mancuso lived in a jumbled apartment complex crammed into the back corner of a mall parking lot. I sat in my car observing the apartments, trying to get a vibe off the place. I was dropping in completely unannounced, and though I was pure in my mission, there was always the off-chance that Amy had a Rottweiler or a coked-out boyfriend with a gun waiting for me in that apartment.

Besides, I didn't have a pitch rehearsed. I just needed to talk. I had always received more credit for my disarming charisma than I ever felt was warranted. Perhaps it would get me through this?

I mustered the courage to step out of my car and marched up the peeling metal stairs to Amy Mancuso's apartment. After a few knocks, I heard some shuffling. Someone was home at least.

When the door cracked open against the chain, I found one of Amy's eyes staring back at me.

"Yes?" she wheezed.

"Miss Mancuso? My name is Dorian Lake. I don't know if you remember me."

She squinted at me, then shook her head. "What do you want?"

"We met only briefly. Last week. You had an episode while canvasing for Mayor Sullivan."

Her eye went wide, and she shoved the door closed.

"Amy?" I called through the door. "It happened again. To someone else. A little girl."

She responded with a muffled "Go away!"

"I just want to talk about it. Try to help this girl."

I took the ensuing silence as a refusal.

"Amy? Listen to me. I know about the drugs."

My voice rang in the tiny breezeway connecting her front door acoustically to her neighbors.

The door cracked open once again. "Who are you?"

"I told you. My name is Dorian—"

"Are you going to tell Rolando?"

I steeled my face and took a gamble. "I don't want to."

Her eye fluttered, and she pushed the door closed. The chain scratched before the door opened full to me.

"Come in."

Her apartment was a snow globe of clutter, mostly dishes and plastic toddler toys. The smell of cheap incense lingered in the air, and I spotted a tiny brass try of ash on her mantel.

She waved me to her couch before dropping her weight into a ratty recliner, pulling a blanket over her lap. Her face was pallid, dark swaths wreathing her eyes. Her hair was pulled back into a pony tail, several fly-aways clouding around her forehead.

I took a seat on the couch, which sunk more than I was prepared for. I steadied myself, resting my hand on something cold and hard. It looked like one of those plastic blocks young children hammer through matching holes. I tossed it onto a small pile of toys at the end of the couch and cleared my throat.

"This won't take long."

She nodded, her mouth drawn in at the corners.

"That day, when you had your attack, I wondered if you could tell me a little bit about how it happened."

"Don't remember much."

I gave her a grin. "Well, let's give it a shot, maybe warm up your memory? How did it start?"

She shrugged and pulled her feet under her lap, tucking the blanket around her legs.

"Then, maybe you could back up into the day a little? You were volunteering for the Sullivan campaign."

"Yeah."

"How'd you start your day?"

She sighed and looked up to the ceiling. "They picked us up in a parking lot over by the Bargain Zone on Reisterstown. It was me and maybe three others. They took us in a minivan to the office, and gave us our materials. Yard signs, clipboards, papers. I didn't want to do the door-to-door stuff. I would have rather just hammer signs into lawns, but I was one of, like, two people there who spoke English. So they put me on door-to-door."

"By Loyola?"

"Yeah, I think so. Lots of expensive houses. Sure. That was it."

"Did you run into anyone strange or suspicious?"

"Nah. Mostly housewives with Botox. There were a couple of men at home."

I wondered if one of those men wasn't McHenry's mercenary. "Tell me about them."

"Uh, well, one was in a bathrobe. Kind of a creep. I dropped off the pamphlet and got the hell out of there."

"Who else?"

"There was this one guy in a suit. Looked like he was in a hurry. Nice car. I caught him walking out the front door. Got real pissy with me. Said Sullivan was a socialist or something."

"Did he give you anything? Touch you in any way?"

"No. Wouldn't even take the pamphlet. Just drove off."

"I see." I leaned back and tapped my chin as I stared at the fireplace. There were several pictures of Amy and a very young boy standing in a line. "Cute kid."

For the first time ever, I saw her smile. "He's rotten."

"Is he asleep or something?"

Her smile faded. "With Rolando."

I assumed Rolando was the child's father, and it wouldn't have helped my situation to ask her to confirm that. It was better if she assumed I knew more than I had a right to know.

"So let's move forward. At some point I think you had an encounter with a dog."

"Right. A little dog. Some toy poodle or one of those designer dogs. Little monster lost its mind on me. Went for my ankles. See, I'm usually pretty good with dogs. I'd have one, but Trey is allergic."

"What did you do?"

"I tried to run, but that bitch let go of the leash. Thing was on me."

"Which bitch?"

"Some upper class twat in a track suit. She was yelling at me. Just pissed me off that she was blaming me for her dog turning into a piranha."

"You hit the dog?"

"No. I got out of her yard, and it stopped."

I stared at Amy, and her face dropped a little. Her eyes searched out the design on the blanket on her lap.

"Your coordinator remembers it differently."

"Who?"

"The person who brought you back to the campaign office. She said you hit the dog."

"No. I kicked it. That's right. I did."

Her eyes moved up and down, searching for memory. I was pretty sure she wasn't making this up. "I don't blame you."

"A lot. I… I think I hurt it." Her eyes drew closed. "I didn't feel right. I was panicking."

"Did you feel like you were in control of your body?"

"Yeah. Maybe. It was my brain. Kind of foggy like when you're trying to think about something, but you can't because your thoughts get fuzzy? It was like that. I couldn't finish a thought. I was just kicking. And screaming. I couldn't figure out why I was screaming."

"Do you remember your coordinator picking you up?"

She shook her head. "I woke up, kind of, in the office. Ever wake up and not remember when you fell asleep? You were there, and Mister Bright. I remember feeling like I hated you. Like you were responsible for all of this. Then it went away. Like a dream after you wake up. Everything felt real, then it felt like a dream, then I couldn't remember it."

"Tell me more about this brain fog. Did you feel like something was inside your head making you kick that dog?"

"I guess. My head hurt. It was like blacking out."

"But you felt fine before then? It came on out of nowhere?"

She squinted and wiped a tear from the corner of her eye. "No, I was starting to feel sick. Like the flu or something, only quicker. Thought maybe it was food poisoning. Actually, it felt like withdrawal."

I leaned forward and folded my fingers together. I had to be delicate, here.

"Amy? Did you think it was withdrawal?"

"I didn't know what it was."

"Did you have a reason to suspect withdrawal?"

She shrugged.

"Amy, I'm asking you if you took drugs in the days beforehand."

Fresh tears streamed down her cheeks. "It was Rolando's weekend with Trey. He missed a month out of town. I didn't have any time."

I held up a hand to calm her down. "I'm just trying to figure out if this was something the heroin did, or if it was something different. Has anything like this happened to you before?"

She shook her head.

"Do you think it's possible that withdrawal symptoms caused this episode?"

"I don't know if it's possible or not. But nothing like that happened to me before. I didn't want to be there. Maybe it was those houses, all those prissy-ass rich bitches. That asshole with the suit. That whore with the dog. I just felt sick about it. I just didn't want to be there."

"Why were you, if you don't mind my asking?"

"Hmm?"

"You don't sound like you were very enthusiastic. Why were you volunteering for Sullivan in the first place?"

She tried to wipe the tears from her face, but new ones kept tracing tracks on her cheekbones. "It looked good to the judge. Volunteer work. Community work. Civic responsibility, whatever. I figured it wouldn't be worse than litter patrol."

"This was court ordered?"

"Kind of. Rolando's challenging for full custody." Her lips pulled back into a grimace and she sobbed. "I had to do something."

"I'm sorry."

"Rolando never used. So, he never understood. You know? He never understood why you can't just decide to stop. I tried. I really did. Went to the clinic a few times. Then one of the clinics did blood work, and they told me I was HIV positive."

I closed my eyes and tried not to look morose.

"That was the night he took Trey away. I've been fighting ever since. I can see Trey grow up. I can do that. I'm on medicines. That's the disease that I can manage. The other? The addiction? I'm trying. But it's just so much bigger than I am."

"Amy? I want you to listen to me. Try to breathe."

She wiped her face some more and tried to calm down enough to look me in the eyes. Her sobbing subsided, and she looked down. "If I lose Trey, I just don't see much point in even trying anymore."

"I'm not here to ruin your life. I'm not going to go to Rolando with any of this. Okay? In fact, I might be able to help you. I have a peculiar set of skills, and I've helped people fight addictions before. I'd like to help you, too. If you let me."

She didn't look up, didn't shake her head or nod. She didn't react at all.

I stood up and reached out to put a hand on her shoulder. "It's worth a shot, right? If it's that important."

"How?"

I curled my finger along her shoulder and wrapped a hair around my index finger. I slid it casually into my pocket. "Karma."

I left Amy sitting in her chair, perhaps a little more hopeful. If she was, she didn't let it show. Mostly I got what I needed from her when it came to information on this entity. What I needed was confirmation that this wasn't a drug hallucination. What's more, I knew she wasn't interested in turning this into a problem for Julian and the Mayor. Julian knew it, too. He must have had a similar conversation with her just after the attack.

It was confirmation, but not proof. Wren was convinced Elle was suffering from mental illness. Edgar looked like he was going along with Wren, but I had a feeling he was still open to my input. When it came to Edgar and Wren, though, he wasn't the one with the hand on the helm. Wren made the decisions with the kids, and in two days, Elle was likely to enter the System. Probably never to come back out.

If she lived that long. I had a dread suspicion that this thing inside Elle was using her as a source of energy, sucking the life out of her. It was possible that Elle's life was in danger if I couldn't extract this thing.

Hell, maybe I could borrow Julian's Taser. It seemed to work on Amy. Though I didn't think I could sell that to Wren.

I smirked to myself as I reached my car, imagining suggesting electricity as our next move when something smacked into the back of my head, throwing my face into the roof of the Audi. The world shifted and my shoulder hit asphalt. My vision blurred to black just as a pair of boots stepped into my field of vision.

The last thing I remembered was the sensation of being lifted, and a splitting headache.

CHAPTER TWENTY-TWO

The headache was still there when I came to. Black fabric hung loose in front of my face, but I was comfortable enough to breathe. Comfort in breathing didn't extend to sitting, as I was crammed between two people, my wrists tied together. By the motion and the tire noise, I could tell we were in a moving car. What felt like an hour could have been half that, but sitting with a black bag over your head not knowing if you're going to end up with a bullet in your skull by the end of the ride makes the minutes crawl by.

When the vehicle finally stopped, one of my bookends stepped outside and pulled me fairly gently by the wrist ties out of the car and across a space of gravel. Light jazz played in the background, and the smell of food drifted on cool night air underneath my hood. I stumbled over a threshold, and the music dulled, replaced by the clacking of my shoes across a wood floor. I was led up a wide flight of circular stairs and eventually the hood was removed.

A wide-jawed man in a suit inspected my face, then reached for my hair. He jerked my head forward, rolling it left to right. He released my hair with a grunt of approval before producing a pocket knife. I sucked in a breath as he triggered a spring, releasing a long, shiny curved blade. I stood stiff as he reached for my hands, slicing the plastic zip ties holding them.

"Wait here," he grunted as he stepped past me, closing a door to a posh sitting room lit only by a single lamp on a desk in the corner. I rubbed the back of my head and took in the room. Fine parquet flooring with two circular Persian rugs. A length of bookcases with leather-bound texts. A row of windows overlooking a wide, shallow river swelling past rocks.

Beyond the river stood a line of fine mansions, and just behind two of the gables I spotted the top of the Washington Monument.

I was in the hands of the Presidium.

I stepped to the windows and peered down to an outdoor garden soiree. Several ivory tents were illuminated by strings of white lights. A jazz trio played on a dais in the far corner beside a line of tables laden with appetizers and flutes of wine. People in evening gowns and tuxedos wandered in a kind of social Coriolis motion, laughing, chatting, and drinking.

Footsteps clacked up the stairs outside the room, and I turned in time to find the wide-jawed man opening the door for a sharp-dressed, silver-haired woman in a conservative gown carrying two flutes of champagne. The woman marched toward me with a genial grin and sharp eyes.

"Welcome, Mister Lake. I know Reginald, here, can be a bit heavy-handed, so I thought I'd offer you a palliative of sorts."

She handed me one of the flutes and stared at me with a calm deliberation that sucked the fight out of me. I had never heard of anyone who got black-bagged by the Presidium and lived to talk about it, and always wondered what happened to them. Even though it was likely I was about to find out, I took the champagne as a good sign.

"Couldn't hurt," I rasped, clearing my throat. I took a sip. Not bad.

"My name is Deborah Wexler. I suspect you know whom I represent."

My jaw stiffened in panic, though I managed to mumble, "I have a notion."

"I only have a few minutes before I have to return to my guests, so I'll have to make this brief. We have determined that your involvement with David Sullivan's campaign has become unacceptable. You are to dissociate yourself from Sullivan and Bright immediately."

The way she said that pissed me off, and the words "Just like that?" flew out of my mouth before I could stop them.

Wexler's brow popped up as if she were stunned that I responded with anything beyond a blubbering plea for my life.

"I'm sorry?" she asked with a bemused grin.

"Just like that, you people decide to curtail my rights? I'm not allowed to participate in the democratic process, is that it?"

"Mister Lake—"

"With all due respect, Ms. Wexler, the Presidium isn't the Constitution." Christ. Why wouldn't I shut up?

"Who do you think wrote the Constitution?" she snickered. "Besides, people like you and I don't have rights, Mister Lake. We have responsibilities. Ours is to this Nation, and if you cared anything about the democratic process, you'll recognize that it can only flourish when the people, their minds, and their fates are free from hermetic coercion."

"Then you'll be happy to know I haven't crafted a charm for Sullivan in months. The man's karma was spreading too thin, so I put it off."

"Do you really think we care about your petty charms? No, it's this cloud of chaos with which you clothe yourself. It's affecting a major election, and we have decided that is no longer an option for you."

"For the sake of argument, what say I refuse?"

Wexler laughed.

I prodded, "If you wanted to get rid of me, you would have done it long ago."

"Don't think that conversation hasn't taken place. More than once."

Shit. I knew I had rubbed the Presidium raw at times, but knowing they discussed my erasure chilled me. "Some of you must like me."

"Some within our group hold the assertion that you don't represent a credible threat. Considering you've executed a lethal Netherwork curse in public, resulting in a quarter million dollars in damages to Penn Station, some believe this assertion to be somewhat generous."

"That situation was complicated."

"Indeed, which is why we chose not to take action." She crossed to the windows, looking down to her party. "Your curse was elegant. Had you not executed it in person, one might have called it masterful. Recognizing that you were attempting to prevent the sale of American souls to a Levantine Cabal, we adopted a degree of circumspection." She turned and squinted at me. "Granted, despite your best efforts, you managed to deliver said souls directly into the hands of the Levantines."

"No one's perfect." I waited for another grin from Wexler.

Instead, I got received a stern lift of the brow. "There's fallible, and then there's dangerously credulous. In any event, the decision is made. I suggest you adhere to it."

"Okay, then," I countered. "If the Presidium is so invested in the Baltimore mayoral race, then perhaps it would be interested in the fact that Sullivan's opposition has hired a practitioner as well?"

Wexler stood silently, moving only to take a sip of champagne.

I added, "Or are you just throwing in for Sooner at this point?"

"I understand Sooner is backed by an industrial magnate. This hardly qualifies as a threat to American esoteric security."

"You'd think that, but ask my friends whose daughter is possessed by some vicious thing this hermetic hitman sicced on her."

She lowered her flute and frowned. So, this was news to her.

After the barest wave of ambivalence flickered across her face, she stiffened her lips and declared, "Mister Lake, our duties don't extend to protecting you from the consequences of your own actions. Now, I do have to return to my guests."

"Where's Brown?"

Wexler sneered, "Where he always is. Sitting in his pathetic little whore house on a hill. In case you're suffering from the delusion that Mister Brown is somehow your friend, you should reconsider your posture. Brown's influence only extends so far."

"I never doubted that."

"You know," Wexler continued in a softer tone, "if you could suspend your paranoia for a moment, you might see our purpose here. The Presidium was born out of the Enlightenment. Europe was emerging from a thousand years of religious war and the destruction of knowledge. It was a breeding ground for the Cabals to manipulate the Church, thrones, entire nations. Look what that produced. It may seem simple enough to reduce us to a kind of fascist umbrella, but the alternative could have been further ruin. Or the chaos you find on the West Coast."

I pounded the rest of the champagne. "Guess I'm just more worried about a little girl than world history."

Wexler lifted her brow. The corner of her mouth lifted slightly as she took my glass. "Reginald will see you back to his car."

She stepped out of the room as Reginald held the door for her. Once out of sight, Reginald produced the black hood again. I held up my hands and stood still as he cinched it over my chin and led me back down the stairs.

The long, silent ride back to Baltimore gave me plenty of time to think about my situation. I had smart decisions available me, and I had the decisions that I actually wanted to make. Mostly out of spite. It would be smart to take McHenry's offer, sell the properties, bank the cash, and simplify my life. It would be smart to call Julian, politely inform him I would no longer be involved in the campaign, and watch the election results in the Fall from my living room without worrying about the Presidium bushwhacking me in parking lots. It might have even been smart to let the Swains take Elle to the psychiatrist since every rational mind kept arriving at that same conclusion.

But McHenry wanted me to roll over. That was his goal here, not necessarily acquiring my properties. He was buying a victory with that offer. And I knew the families living in my properties. Okay, I didn't really know them that well, but I had put the effort into making their homes an enjoyable place to live.

The Presidium had no right to thumb me like that. They had the ability, sure. No one could argue that. But that didn't mean it was right. I wasn't affecting the campaign with my hermetic practice. If I turned Sullivan's ear, it was by the force of my argument. And Wexler dodged me when I mentioned McHenry had a practitioner on his payroll. I was getting squeezed, and I suspected the Presidium had some skin in this race.

And when it came to Elle, I simply couldn't accept this was schizophrenia. I had no proof, no sense of what this thing even was, and all of my efforts to remove it had failed horribly. But that didn't mean I was wrong. I just didn't have the solution yet.

Smart decisions versus right decisions. Why did it always seem to come down to that dichotomy?

Reginald released me at my car and sped away without a word. I eased into the Audi and sat at the wheel, questioning my next move. Which side of the coin would I choose? Smart? Right? It was exactly this kind of night when I used to head for the Club and forget everything for an hour or two. Alas, that was no longer an option. I could have tried the Blue Moon Diner, but it would just remind me of what could have been. I couldn't even really think about the Swain's house at that point without it conjuring the image of Elle's other-worldly stare and the smell of piss and puke in her room.

So I just went home and collapsed. I needed to clear my head. Making decisions while exhausted and brutalized rarely turned out well for me.

I woke up to my phone ringing. I hated early morning calls. No one ever called with good news before breakfast.

Checking the call, my stomach dropped.

"Hey, Edgar."

"Dorian?" His voice was yet more ragged and weak. "We have a problem."

"What happened?"

"Elle's gone."

CHAPTER TWENTY-THREE

"What do you mean gone?"

"Found her window busted out. She ran out in the middle of the night."

"Fuck. I mean, how? Wasn't she tied down?"

"Yeah, I just... look. I know Wren kind of shut things down, but I need your help, man."

"I'll be right over."

It was a good thing the Maryland State Troopers weren't clocking on I-70. I made record time making it to Frederick, and when I pulled up in front of the shop, I didn't see Wren's Jeep in the alley.

I stepped inside the shop and found Edgar looming in the back by the reagents counter.

"Edgar?"

"Thanks for coming, Dorian."

"I'm going to rent a room in Frederick pretty soon. How did this happen?"

He stepped around the counter and the rows of old wooden drawers lining the back wall to lead me up the stairs and down the hall to Elle's room. Her window, a tiny two foot by three foot thing in aluminum framing, had been busted out. Tremendous force had been exerted to bend the metal mullions outward. Tiny smears of blood lined the jagged metal remaining in the hole in the wall.

"Jesus, Edgar. You didn't hear this?"

"Wren says I snore."

"Yeah, but—"

"She says she could get murdered next to me and I'd never wake up."

It was the kind of remark we usually laughed about, but not today.

I spotted the jute ropes lying in neat circles on Elle's dresser.

"She managed her way out of your knots."

"No. I untied her."

"Really?"

"She's my daughter, man. And she was getting pretty tired. She didn't even eat last night. I didn't think it was going to be a problem."

I put a hand on his shoulder. "Of course you didn't. You're dense."

He sniffled and gave me half a smirk.

"Did you two call the police?"

"No way," he retorted, moving back out of the room. "She has rope burns on her wrists. She's wearing a night shirt covered in puke. You heard the way she's talking. We'd have a child protective services nightmare on our hands."

"Yeah, but is that more or less important than finding her at this point?"

Edgar blanched as the corner of his eye twitched. "I sent Wren out looking for her. Then I called you."

"What's up?"

"Follow me."

He led me back down the stairs to his reagents counter. He stopped by the large solid cedar door in the wall behind his counter and unwound a small length of gray wool yarn wrapped around the door knob. His magic lock. I was convinced there was nothing magic about it, but there was no convincing Edgar.

What lie behind that door, however, was nothing short of nightmarish magic. Edgar's collection. I had Emil's Library; Edgar had his collection of cursed objects. That was Edgar's real calling. He was a Collector, born into the business by way of his father who had started the entire shop as a front for the magical wares trade. Edgar had inherited the shop from his father, but had transformed it into more of a final resting place for cursed items than a marketplace.

"Edgar? What are you getting out of there?"

"We don't have time to deal with the cops, or Wren. Wait here." He disappeared into the room, clicking on a light that seemed to offer exactly zero illumination. After a couple minutes, he returned with a black shoe box in his hands. He set the box on the glass counter and reached underneath for a pair of rubber gloves.

I took a step forward and watched as he reached with gloved hands and removed the shoebox lid. Inside the box lay an exquisitely crafted gold wire spiral at the end of a long silver chain.

"What is that, a pendulum?" I asked.

"Yeah. Belonged to Gregori of Belarus."

"No shit? Isn't he the one they actually hanged inside a church?"

"Found it in a bazaar in Istanbul six years ago."

"You positively must take me with you on one of these trips."

Edgar pulled off one glove and reached into his pocket to produce a tiny tissue with a blossom of a dark red smear.

"Elle's?" I asked.

"Got it from the window."

"Edgar. This pendulum? Cursed, right? I mean, Gregori the Bastard was a notorious Netherworker."

"Yeah, I know. Buzzkill, right?"

"Point being if you use this—"

"I damn myself."

"I can't speak for you or Wren or your kids, Edgar, but I'd call that one steep God damn price to pay."

Edgar looked up at me wearily. "Don't care, man. I have to find her. I have to find her quick, before the cops do."

"I get that. I just…" I couldn't complete the thought. I didn't have kids. I had no idea what he was going through as father. As a practitioner, however, every ounce of my education was screaming to grab that shoebox and keep it away from Edgar's fingers. "Let me do it, then."

"What?"

"Me. I'll do it. I'm better at scrying than you, anyway."

"I'm not going to let you do that, man."

"Why not? I mean, I don't have a soul, do I?"

He blinked at me and opened his mouth to respond, but words never came.

"My soul's out there in the Nether somewhere with God knows how much of the Dark Choir searching for it. I might as well be useful to you while I'm in this condition."

"I can't ask you to do that."

"You didn't. I'm offering."

"No," he grunted, pulling the box away. "Too risky."

"Edgar, if you use that pendulum, it's a sure thing you'll taint your soul. With me, there's a chance it won't do shit."

"Might not work. If the thing uses the curse as its power source, you won't be able to make it work."

"That's a gamble we can afford to take. Come on, we're losing time."

Edgar tensed, and looked down at the pendulum. With a heavy sigh, he slid it back onto the counter in front of me.

"Alright," I sighed. "Never used a pendulum this old before. This should be interesting. Got a map of the city?"

Edgar nodded and trotted off for a few minutes. I spent the time centering myself, and observing the old gilded tool. It was gorgeous, a delicate double-helix of gold wire wrapping around what appeared to be a piece of tiger's eye. The orange striped stone seemed to shine with an unnatural luster. It was a well-loved tool.

Edgar returned with a gas station quality map of Frederick. I reached out for the pendulum, and he stopped me. "You sure about this, man?"

I answered by gripping the end of the silver chain and lifting it slowly from the box. There was definitely resident energy in that pendulum. Ants crawled up my fingers and along my wrist.

"Feels funky."

Edgar handed the bloody tissue to me, and I tipped the pendulum onto the blood. I focused my personal energy onto the pendulum, and the ants swam up my arm and into my heart chakra. I re-routed the ants up to my Third Eye, and waited for that release, that twang when the connection is made.

When the twang hit, it rang in my ears like a guitar string. I had never felt such a clear, obvious link with a scrying tool before. It was exhilarating.

"Okay. Ready."

Edgar unfolded the city map along the glass counter, and I gave the pendulum a simple sway of my wrist, sending it rotating deosil. The damned thing actually swung a figure eight in mid-air and reversed its direction to widdershins.

Edgar harumphed as it wound into tighter circles over the map. I felt a tug along the string and went with it. The connection was strong enough to physically pull my hand. And pull it did. East along the map, out of the downtown, past the aqueduct.

Off the map.

"The hell?" Edgar whispered.

The pendulum tapped onto the glass of the display case, and the tug stopped.

"She's not in the city. Not even in the county." I looked up at Edgar. "In for a penny. Got a state map?"

"I have to check the Jeep."

I winced.

"Oh. Right."

"Anything at all?"

Edgar searched around the back of his shop, then hopped out from behind the map, leaving me holding onto Gregori's pendulum, trying to maintain the connection. He returned with a notebook and a pencil. He sketched out a frankly horrible representation of the state of Maryland, put a star on Frederick, a large diamond toward the bottom middle with the letters "D.C.," and a square by the bay with the letters "BWI."

"That work?" he muttered.

"Let's find out."

I dropped the pendulum toward the notebook, and somehow, some way, the chain broke from the weight in my fingers. The gold spiral fell onto the pad, the tip sticking in the direct center of the W in BWI.

"Baltimore."

Edgar shook his head. "Don't that just figure?"

"How'd she get that far on foot?"

"Probably not on foot."

I went to pick up the pendulum, but Edgar scooped it with his rubber gloved hand into the shoebox. With wary eyes, he gestured for me to release the hand weight. It was strangely difficult letting that little hunk of silver drop into the box, but when it was gone, so were the ants.

"You okay?" he asked as he replaced the lid.

"I think so."

Edgar fished a hunk of hematite from his pocket and tossed it to me. I held it in my scrying hand, rubbing my fingers along its smooth surface to cleanse out the energy as if it were snake venom.

"Think she hitched a ride or something?" I asked, trying to sound normal.

"Maybe. Maybe she boosted someone's car."

"Does she even know how to drive?"

He shrugged. "If she drove a damn car, Dorian, then I'm going to call that evidence to your theory."

He was right. Unusual knowledge was a typical sign of possession, and she was racking up points in that category.

"Listen, we have to do this again. We need a Baltimore city map, hone in on where she is."

Edgar stepped away, clutching the box.

"Edgar? What good is it doing us to know she's in Baltimore? It's kind of a big city."

"I know."

"So you agree?"

"I don't disagree."

"Well?"

He stood solid.

I felt an urge to grab the box. He was being stupid. We needed to get the pendulum out of the box. It was necessary. The pendulum was suffocating in there.

A sharp burning pain lanced through my hand, and I dropped the hematite with a loud clack onto the glass counter. It was blazing hot!

Edgar looked down at the hematite with one brow lifted. I was dumping an amazing amount of energy into that poor little stone.

I took a deep breath and rubbed my hand on my shirt.

"I think we need to take a moment," I whispered.

We stood on opposite sides of the counter, just staring at the shoebox. The silence was broken by my phone ringing, and we both nearly jumped out of our skins. I moved to the front of the shop and checked the number.

My heart nearly stopped.

"Ches?"

Her voice, much stronger and more lucid than the last time I had heard it, replied, "Hey, Dorian."

"I... I'm glad you called."

"Figured."

"Wow. There's basically a million things I want to talk about, but if you can believe it this is basically the worst possible time."

"Dorian?"

"I really don't want to put you off, but I have this problem with the Swains—"

"Elle's here."

I stood silent, staring out the front windows.

Edgar stepped to my side, and I held up a hand for him to be still.

"Dorian? Did you hear me?"

"Where are you?"

"Your place."

I turned slowly to Edgar and chose my words carefully. "And Elle's there with you?"

Edgar's eyes grew wider than I had ever seen them, and the blood rushed out of his face.

"Yeah. I, uh… I think you need to come get her. She doesn't look too hot."

"Yes. I mean… stay there. Please. I'm coming to get her."

"I'm not going anywhere."

"Ches? Be careful. She isn't herself."

"Understood."

"Okay. I'll be there in forty."

I stared at my phone for several seconds before mustering the strength to hang up. I looked over to Edgar.

"I'm coming with you."

I nodded. He left a note for Wren, and we took off.

Chapter Twenty-Four

As I pulled into my alley, I spotted Ches sitting on my stoop. Elle was lying down behind her, resting her head on Ches' bag. Edgar was out of the car before it stopped. He dropped to his knees on my first step, laying a cautious hand on Elle's side.

Ches stood up and whispered something to Edgar before turning to me.

I met her halfway to the stoop, and froze in front of her, searching for anything to say that wouldn't sound insane.

"Hey," was the best I could come up with.

"Hey."

"What happened? How'd you find her?"

"Found her here," she replied, hanging her head a little. "I came by after my shift since I don't have class. I was hoping to find you at home. I don't know why I decided to walk over, to be honest. Guess she has a guardian angel or something."

"How is she?"

"Pretty bad. Confused. Scared."

"Wait, what?"

A tiny voice creaked from the bundle lying on my stoop. "Daddy?"

Edgar sucked in a breath and moaned, falling onto Elle.

"She's back?"

Ches nodded. "In and out."

"I should probably explain—"

"I know what's wrong with her. I recognized it. I mean, it was obvious to me when I saw her."

I stepped over to the stoop and crouched down. "Hey, kid."

Elle's brow creased, and she reached up for Edgar.

Edgar pulled her up into his lap and stroked her hair. "Found you."

"Where's Mom?"

"She's out looking for you."

Elle pulled her face away from Edgar long enough to look at me. "It's still here."

I balled a fist inside my pocket. "We're going to get it out of you. I promise."

Her eyes narrowed. "It's hungry."

"Let's get you something to eat."

I opened up my house and led everyone inside. Edgar carried Elle upstairs to my bathroom to clean her off. I fished out some rubbing alcohol and gauze for him to dress the wounds on her hands as he started the shower. I left them alone and marched slowly downstairs to face Ches.

She sat on the couch, gripping her knees.

"How's your head?" I asked.

"Got a lump. Not too bad. Listen, we never got to talk about this."

"I tried to call you."

"Yeah, I know. And I'm sorry. I wasn't ready until just now."

I sat next to her. "So, let's talk about it."

"This thing? It hates you."

"I'm getting that."

"Let me finish. It doesn't really hate you personally. It hates the idea of you. Like it doesn't really know who you are. It's just being told to hate you."

I leaned back and nodded. "I think this thing was sent by someone. Another practitioner hired by McHenry to win the election for Sooner."

She pulled away a few inches, her eyes narrow. "To do what? Kind of like what you're doing for the other guy?"

"Only this is aggressive. Bordering on evil."

"What do Elle and I have to do with an election?"

"Me. You both have to do with me. There was one more, a volunteer for the campaign. Same thing happened to her. All the same entity, all attacking women. Why only women?"

"So this guy's trying to take you out?"

"That's my theory."

"Dick move."

"Tell me about it."

She put a hand on mine. "Want to know why I really didn't call you back? I was scared, Dorian. Not about the creepy ass thing that took over my body. Not really about almost losing my job. But I was scared of you. I mean, I knew you had this magical life. You showed me that. And I guess I was convinced you were just living a fantasy. And I thought, okay. You're doing what you like and making it work for you. But then it got real. I mean, it was real to me. I started to believe you. And that just really freaked me out. If this thing that possessed me was real, then what else was real out there? You can make curses. What, is there a war going on out there between people like you? I lost sleep over it."

I leaned back and ran a hand over my face. "There's no war, Ches. It's just a handful of people who've done a lot of studying. We have secret knowledge. That's it."

"Well, I'm not used to thinking like that, and I was afraid of being around you."

"I can understand that."

She lifted a finger. "But then I got pissed. Because you know what? I'm not a person who scares easy. So I had to figure, fuck this. Okay. You're a wizard, or whatever. I got caught in the crossfire. I didn't die. I didn't lose my job. Only thing that almost happened was I could have lost you. Because I got scared? No. I'm not going to be that girl."

The butterflies were back in my chest. "You realize I'm about to hug you, right?"

"Shut up."

She threw an arm around my shoulders.

Edgar and Elle stepped down the stairs after a while, and Edgar set her at my kitchen table. I poured some cereal for her. Elle took the spoon and slowly, morosely, shoveled the cereal a piece at a time into her mouth. There was no joy there. Just exhaustion.

Edgar took a moment and stepped beside me. "Fuck man. She's tore up."

I took a peek at the bandages on Elle's forearms and hands. "Not surprised. Was she lucid?"

"Kind of. She stopped talking when I put the alcohol on the cuts. I don't know. "

"I want you to come talk to Ches for a second."

He watched Elle for a moment, then turned back into my front room.

Ches stood up, giving him a broad smile. "How is she?"

"Eating. Okay."

I asked Ches, "Could you describe to Edgar what happened to you? Specifically when you switched over and attacked me at the café?"

She gave me a long, guarded look, then nodded. "Uh, sure. I was just talking to him, you know. Then I got this weird feeling. Ever have your blood sugar drop and feel like you're tingling, ready to pass out?"

Edgar nodded.

"Yeah, like that. Then I started saying things I didn't want to say, then bang. I was on the ground and Dorian was getting his ass thrown out of the café."

I added, "You'd say for sure something was inside your head?"

"Definitely."

"Going to throw a personal question out there. Got any mental health problems in your family?"

Edgar elbowed me. "I get it, man. But I'm not the one you have to convince. And neither is Wren."

"I suppose that's true."

Ches added, "For the record, the answer was no."

"Yeah," Edgar mumbled, "with us the answer is yes."

"Sorry."

I explained, "Elle's going to see a doctor on Monday."

"A shrink?"

"I don't think that's the most sensitive term to use, but yeah."

My phone rang. I had a feeling I'd see Edgar's home number when I checked it. I handed the phone to Edgar who whisked it out the front door bellowing, "Yes, I have her… Dorian's…"

I found myself alone with Ches once more.

"Seriously," she chirped, "not crazy."

"Gotcha. Her mother's beyond her limit with this, though."

"Have you tried to get rid of it?"

"Twice. Both attempts ended badly. I feel like I could get some leverage on this thing if I could just identify what it is. Where it came from."

"You do realize that once she hits the health care system, you're going to lose your access to her?"

"The thought has crossed my mind."

"I want to help, Dorian. I just don't know how."

"When I figure that out, I'll let you know."

I paused to listen for the conversation outside, and realized how quiet it had become in the kitchen. I trotted over to the doorway and found nothing but Elle's cereal bowl and spoon on the table. As I rushed into the kitchen, I jumped as Elle called from the sink next to me.

"Dorian?"

I froze. "Elle?"

"What's going on? Where's Mom?"

"Elle, put the knife down."

She cocked her head and looked down to the chef's knife trembling in her hand. With a gasp she set it gingerly on the countertop.

Ches stepped in and put a hand on my arm.

"Be cool," she whispered to me as she inched toward Elle. "Hey, you feeling better?"

Elle gave her a cautious glance and nodded.

"We're going to get you home to your mom. She's on the phone right now."

"When is this going to be over?" she asked.

Elle looked over her shoulder to me.

"We got the right man on this, Elle. Don't worry."

Edgar returned from his phone conversation with a sense of urgency, so we decided to leave immediately. Edgar herded Elle into the car and gave Ches an earnest thank-you. I stood in front of Ches, trying to figure out if I should go for the hug or a peck on the cheek, or maybe jazz hands.

She saved me the trouble by squeezing my arm and saying, "Call me tonight."

Elle was quiet all the trip back to Frederick. She seemed to fall asleep, but it was impossible to tell. When her eyes were open, they looked barely aware.

Edgar finally broke the silence when Elle had closed her eyes for a while.

"Ches really seemed to calm her down."

"Yeah. They get along."

"I don't know what you have to do, Dorian, but you gotta keep that one."

"Well, that's the plan."

"At least you have a plan."

"Wasn't easy, believe me. Getting the plan, that is." After about a mile, I changed the subject. "Have you told Eddie yet?"

"No."

"Are you?"

He didn't answer.

"We have to work on Wren, you know."

"That ain't easy. She's got her head going one way, and when she does, she doesn't change it."

"Is she pissed at me?"

"No, man. She's just taking charge. You know."

"What about you?"

"I'm okay with that. She knows what she's doing."

"I meant are you pissed at me?"

I gave Edgar a quick glance. He was grinding his jaw.

"I'll take that as a maybe."

"I'm not pissed at you, Dorian. I'm just tired."

"You know, Edgar, you're allowed to have an opinion in this. If you don't think Elle should go to the doctor, you should tell Wren."

He shrugged, and we passed the rest of the trip in silence.

We returned to Frederick, and I parked behind Wren's Jeep. Elle was asleep or something like it when we arrived. Edgar pulled her gently from the back seat and carried her in as I held open the door. Wren was waiting in the front of the shop, hands on her hips. When she spotted Elle, her face melted a little, and she rushed forward, scooping her out of Edgar's arms and bolting up the staircase with her cradled tight.

Edgar turned to me and shrugged. I followed his eyes as they centered on something behind me.

"Oh, bad timing," he grunted.

I turned and found Del Carmody stepping into the front doors. He pulled off his hat and ran his hand over the fuzz covering the bald center of his scalp. With a dry grin, he announced, "Edgar Swain and Dorian Lake, as I live and breathe!"

Edgar paced a tight circle, his hands on the back of his neck.

"Hey, Del," he sighed.

"Warm fuckin' greeting, mate. Looks like you've been dragged behind a bull elephant." Carmody turned to me. "Always a distinct pleasure, Mister Lake."

"What do you need, Carmody?"

"Well excuse the living hell out of me! I was just popping in for some ingredients."

Edgar nodded and trod quickly to the rear of the shop.

"You gents suffering from a case of the Black Saturdays?" he muttered to me.

"Been a long week in general. I suggest we make this quick."

"Not a problem. I'll keep it sharpish. Only looking for a few grams of yarrow and some consecrated water. Orthodox if you have it. And this," he added handing a slip of paper to Edgar.

Edgar reviewed the note, then lifted his brows over his glasses. "I don't exactly keep this sort of thing in the shop."

"What, sanitary codes?" Carmody quipped.

"We're an hour north of the Presidium, you jackass. You think I'm going to carry something like this here?"

"But you can get it, right?"

Edgar sighed. "It'll take time. And it ain't cheap."

"Time? How much time?"

"Couple weeks."

Carmody's face soured, and he paced a tight circle before returning two quick nods. "Right. Fine. Put in the order. I'll pay whatever. I'll take the rest now if you have it."

Edgar pulled one of the spice drawers from his side cabinet and set it on the counter next to his old knife scale. As he measured the yarrow blossoms into a brown envelope, Carmody produced a flask from his pants pocket and offered me a sip, which I declined. He sucked a few gulps of some kind of peaty hooch and nodded to the door to Edgar's collection.

"To be a fly on the wall in that room, eh?"

"I'd be happier on this side of the door, to be honest."

"Swain," he called out. "What's your gathered value in that room?"

"Never appraised it. The market's kind of flat."

"Rough estimate, then. For shits and giggles. Two, three hundred?"

Edgar looked up at the ceiling for a second, and answered, "More like five-two."

"And you're still living in this old dump?"

Edgar glared at Carmody before reaching for a black-painted mason jar beneath the counter and a small plastic vial.

"No offense, mate. Just wonder when you're going to actually start selling again."

"When I find something I feel I can sell."

"Bollocks. You have buyers up and down the Seaboard. I know. They keep prodding the piss out of me to light a fire under your arse. 'When's he going to sell?' they keep bleating. I tell them 'He's in the game, he's just got kids is all.' Which is as good an excuse as any, I suppose."

Edgar wrapped up his packaging and shoved the merchandise into a brown paper bag.

"What's the damage?"

"Twelve even."

"Dollars?"

"No, lira. Yes, dollars."

"And the other thing?"

"We'll talk price when I get a supplier."

Carmody shrugged and dropped a ten and two ones onto the counter and scooped up his package. "Thank you, sir. Saints preserve your health." He turned to me and grinned. "And you. I wanted to tell you, I've been putting the ear to the stones. I may well have some leads for you and your problem."

"Good to hear. Keep me posted."

"Right. And you keep that little care package I gave you in safe keeping. It's not that I don't enjoy hiding up the Presidium's knickers, I just feel a little cagey is all."

"Don't worry about that."

He nodded and stepped back to the front door and took his exit.

Wren stepped out into the shop from the staircase, watching as Carmody turned up the street on foot. "So, who was that?"

I answered, "A giant pill of personality. How's Elle?"

She looked past me at Edgar. "She's lying down. What did she say?"

Edgar rounded his counter and stood beside me. "She was herself for a while. Tired. Real tired. She said it's still inside her, but it was getting weaker."

"Hungry," I corrected.

Wren finally turned to me and sighed. "Thank you for finding her."

"Actually, it was Ches who found her. Spotted her sitting on my stoop."

"Well, thank her for me next time you see her."

"I will." I lingered as Wren folded her arms. "So…"

"Let me piece this together," she declared, tossing a finger at Edgar. "You sent me out to scour the streets of Frederick, then immediately called Dorian."

Edgar tucked his chin to his chest and paced a circle.

Wren continued, "Then the two of you pulled out a cursed artifact to find her on your own. I'm not being unfair, right? That's how it went down?"

I leaned toward Edgar and whispered, "You told her about the Gregori pendulum?"

He shrugged.

I held up a hand to Wren. "I didn't let him touch it. I swear."

She nodded politely, her lips tight against her teeth. "Thanks for that. I realize that Edgar needs someone to keep him from accidentally damning himself. That's why you sent me away, right? This was your first option."

Edgar mumbled, "We didn't have time."

Wren stepped up to him and leaned in. "What, now?"

"We didn't have time to just drive around," he repeated at full volume. "And yeah, I called Dorian. Why is this a problem?"

Wren took a step back and shook her head. "Calling Dorian wasn't the problem, Edgar. Cutting me out of the decision? That's the problem." She unfolded, then refolded her arms as she built up steam. "What, you thought I was just going to get in the way?"

"You made up your mind about Elle."

"That doesn't mean I wouldn't want to find her, Edgar! I'm going nuts out there, inching up and down the streets, praying a cop finds her and praying they won't. Then I find out she's safe and sound with everyone else way the fuck across state. How do you think that felt?"

"I wasn't trying to cut you out. I mean, I did. But I wasn't trying to be a dick."

She glared at Edgar for a long moment, then threw up her hands. "Here to Baltimore is a long way to walk. How'd she even get there?"

I answered, "She could have hitched, or stole a car."

"She can't drive."

"She also doesn't know proto-Egyptian unmaking charms," I added. "This thing is giving her unnatural knowledge. Knowing how to drive isn't a stretch, really."

Wren blinked. "Still think this is a demon or something?"

"The evidence is stacking up. Just my opinion."

"Okay," she sighed. "So what the hell was it doing at your front door?"

"Good question. It seems to have weakened, though. Weak enough for Elle to come through."

Edgar offered, "Maybe Dorian was right all along? This thing really is gunning for Dorian, and went to find him."

Wren shook her head. "It's not Dorian this thing is crawling inside of."

"No," I replied. "It's only attacking women. Why is that, I wonder?"

Wren and Edgar shared a look.

"If only I knew what this damn thing was, I could get some traction."

Edgar stepped forward. "I can nose around, call people. See if anyone recognizes this."

Wren released a single dry laugh. "I think this is Dorian's thing, Edgar."

"What does that mean?" he coughed.

"He's the expert. I mean, don't get me wrong. I love you. But Dorian has a lot more experience than—"

"You know what?" he blustered. "I have plenty of experience. Swains have been in the Life for generations, Wren. I've been running with practitioners, vodouns, witches, and all kinds of assholes my whole life. I'm not just some idiot you married."

Wren pursed her lips and shook her head. "I never said you were an idiot."

"Okay, then. Maybe take my word on it every once in a while. Maybe? Trust I have an opinion? Respect that opinion and don't constantly try to talk me out of it?"

She looked to me then back to Edgar. "What do you want from me? I'm just trying, here."

He paced a little.

"Edgar?" she muttered. "You think I don't respect you?"

He shrugged.

Wren whispered, "Stop being stupid. I know your opinion matters. And I'm sorry if I made you feel like it didn't."

"I'm just scared."

"Me too."

As tears welled up in their eyes, I felt incredibly out of place. All I wanted to do was to run away and crawl into a bar somewhere. I held up a polite hand and stepped toward the front door. I picked up my phone and held it to my head, mouthing the words "call me" at Edgar. He nodded as he turned to face Wren.

Stepping outside, I looked up and down Carroll Street. I didn't want to go far; I had a feeling they'd want to work out a new plan once they hashed this out. I took a stroll into town and spotted a cozy Irish pub down the block. I dove into the dark, air conditioned interior and bellied up to the bar to order a whiskey. The bartender poured me three full fingers and left me gracefully alone to drink it.

This had been brewing for years. Edgar had always been a capable hermeticist in his own right, but had eschewed the actual practice after marrying Wren. When the kids came, he really did shut down his collecting trade. He started to view the objects in his storage room more like loaded weapons than merchandise to sell. I really wanted to chime into the conversation inside the shop, but for once I appreciated the fact that I was not an actual member of that family.

As I worked my way into the whiskey, I sat and contemplated the situation. Elle said the thing was hungry. If I was correct in assuming this thing was consuming Elle's soul, then she had less time than I had hoped. It didn't respond to Goetia or traditional Judeo-Christian mystical practices. It was weakening, but it was dragging Elle with it. Whatever power source it used, it was depleting it at an alarming rate. What would happen when it ran out?

And why wasn't it just leaving Elle? If it was starving to death, what kept it inside her? Was Zeno correct about it being trapped by the child's innate psychic defenses? And why was it limited to attacking women?

And there remained the possibility that Wren was right, and I was wrong. What if it was all a huge cascade of coincidence, and I was somehow, directly or indirectly, projecting myself onto someone else's mental illness?

As I settled into a circular mode of contemplation, my phone rang, jarring me out of my reverie. I wasn't really in the mood for a conversation. Less so since I didn't recognize the number.

"Hello?"

"May I speak with Dorian Lake please?"

"Speaking."

"Oh, hello Mister Lake. This is Father Mark from St. Aloysius. You came in the other day to speak with me."

Holy shit. I had forgotten about him. "Oh, right. How are you?"

"Doing well. I wanted to follow up on your friend. The girl?"

"Funny you should call, I'm with her now."

"How is she doing?"

"Worse, to be frank."

"I'm sorry to hear that. Have the parents taken her to a doctor, by any chance?"

"They have an appointment on Monday."

"I see. With luck she'll find some relief."

"No offense, but I'm not holding my breath." I regretted the tone instantly. "Sorry. It's been a long couple days."

"I understand. You're clearly upset over this."

"I am. And other things. Not to bore you, but I have job problems, I guess you could say."

Father Mark chuckled softly. "I can definitely understand that!"

"So, anyway. Thanks for checking in. It was good of you."

"I don't know if it's good or just reasonable. I try to keep my mission on this Earth in mind, but sometimes I just want to know if people are okay."

The Father and I had that in common, to be sure. "Must be nice having a clear cut mission to work with."

"Perhaps. I wouldn't know."

"Well, you literally have a rule book to go by."

"Mister Lake, every man's walk with God is a peculiar agony. It's personal and complicated. If I take peace in my life, it's from the knowledge that there's someone greater than I who actually does understand it."

"Well, I'm splitting my time between esoteric practice and politics, so I doubt there's a force in the Cosmos that actually understands any of it."

"Sounds like a real struggle."

"You have no idea. I feel like I can't focus on one without screwing the other."

He laughed again. "Now you sound like a man of the cloth."

"How so?"

"From the Gospel of Matthew. No man can serve two masters. He will either hate the one and love the other, or be devoted to one and despise the other. Granted, Christ was talking about money, but I think He had a greater sense of how we can get pulled in too many directions."

I leaned back on my stool and took a breath.

No man can serve two masters. But that's what this thing was trying to do, wasn't it? Serving a master. Zeno was right about that. This thing had a master.

What if it wasn't just obeying a master? What if it was created to obey? Created to serve?

It occurred to me...

This thing could have been created. And it wasn't centuries old.

"Mister Lake?"

"Father? You are an absolute genius."

"Oh. Well, I—"

"Seriously. Father Mark. I could kiss you."

He chuckled, "I'm glad I could help, then."

"You have. You really have. I'm really sorry, though. I have to let you go."

"God bless, Mister Lake."

"Yeah. Back at you."

I hung up and pounded the last of the whiskey. I slapped a tensky onto the bar and ran out onto the street, sprinting until I hugged the corner of Carroll Street. My lungs burned, but I sucked in as much humid summer air as I could and bolted across the street, slid between the Jeep and the Audi, and barreled into the shop door.

Edgar and Wren sat on that horrible green couch. Their faces snapped to me as I galloped into the shop, trying to catch my breath.

"I… I know what it is."

Edgar stood up. "Huh?"

"The thing inside Elle. I know what it is. Makes perfect sense."

It was Wren's turn to stand up. "What?"

Edgar offered a hand to steady me, but I just bent over and worked to get my breathing under control.

When I finally pulled in a steady breath, I straightened up and coughed.

"It works on every level. Remember what Zeno told us? This thing was either acting out of ignorance or arrogance? Well, I think it was a little of both. My God, it even explains why it knew a basic, but obscure Egyptian charm."

"What, Dorian?" Wren demanded. "What is it?"

I took one last deep breath and looked Edgar in the eye. "It's a servitor."

CHAPTER TWENTY-FIVE

"What's a servitor?" Wren asked.

"Thoughtform, projected from a practitioner, and given a power source to make it autonomous. Usually it's a shard of the practitioner's soul. My God, it's been staring at me this whole time."

Edgar walked a circle. "Whoa."

"Right?"

I explained, "This thing is limited in its knowledge. The knowledge of its creator. But it's not independent. It's limited. It's working off a playbook it was given, and now it's trapped inside Elle, without orders."

Edgar snapped his fingers. "And it's a soul-powered thoughtform, right? Prayer won't dislodge it. Neither would the Key of Solomon. Neither modality is geared to manipulate human soul energy. But there's a problem. Servitors can't possess people."

"Says who?"

"I've never heard of it happening before."

I shrugged. "Think about it, though. If it was possible to send a servitor into another person, it would be another soul-powered entity residing within a body. Hell, the owner's soul would mask the alien presence. That's why my pendulum didn't pick up anything."

"But who would do this?" Wren demanded. "Why us?"

"It wasn't you this thing was after. I keep telling you, it hit two other people first. That campaign worker, then Ches. It's being sent out to people who would get close to me."

"I thought the other person was a stranger?" Edgar chided.

"He knew Bright would call me in. Son of a bitch!"

"Who? Who made this thing?" Wren asked pulling close.

"This hermetic hitman McHenry called in. I've seen him a couple times, I think. Standing outside my house."

Edgar sniffled. "What did he look like?"

"I… don't know. It was impossible to see his face. Kind of fuzzy. I think he was using a glammer."

"When did it start? The first time, I mean?"

"The day you met me at Lexington Market." I winced. "The day you introduced me to Carmody."

Edgar frowned. "Ah, man. No way. He isn't into soul magic."

"Really? Because I have a particularly scary soul merchant over on the West Coast who wants Carmody put into a curse locker something fierce. I wonder why that is? Maybe because this isn't the first time he pulled a trick like this?"

Wren put a hand to her forehead. "For the love of Goddess, someone please tell me who Carmody is."

I muttered, "That man who was just here earlier."

Her eyes lit on fire. "He was here?"

"Yeah. Probably checking in on this thing."

Edgar shook his head. "Why would he risk that? Doesn't make sense."

"No. It does. Because of what Zeno said. Elle was younger than he expected her to be. Maybe he didn't even know better than to send a servitor into a child. Arrogance and ignorance. But he's a practitioner, right? Remember that unmaking charm Elle was chanting? That's basic hermetic theory. Probably didn't even get it right. Zeno said the Hebrew was tortured. But it was enough to undo his Goetia."

Wren put a hand on both our arms. "So the question is, what can get rid of a servitor?"

I stared at Edgar, who just stared back at me.

"I'm not really sure."

Wren rolled her eyes. "Back to the beginning, then?"

"Well, we know who sent it. We get him involved in extracting it."

Edgar countered, "If we're right about this."

"Yeah. If we're right. If we're wrong, and we accuse Carmody, he'll disappear. Which poses a problem for…"

"For what?"

Holy shit. "I might have a solution."

Wren hopped up into my face. "What's the solution?"

"I'll have to make a call."

Edgar squinted. "Quinn Gillette?"

"There's an exchange of services on the table."

Wren gripped my shirt. "You have a phone, right? So call."

I held up a hand and took a step back. This was big. It was scary big. Gillette made me an offer. She'd reacquire my soul if I did her that one task. And it wasn't a small task. But if I did manage to curse Carmody, likely the one who caused this entire calamity to begin with, it probably wouldn't matter to Gillette if she saved my soul or Elle's. She was, after all, practiced in the creation and removal of servitors. Hell, at that point, she was the only name that came to mind when it came to this kind of soul magic.

"Dorian?" Wren droned. "Magic phone call?"

"We have to be really damn sure about this, guys."

"What's to discuss? We're sure."

I shook my head. "I can probably get Gillette to remove it. But it's going to mean I have to curse someone else. Like, a for real Nether Curse."

Edgar grumbled, "Like you did to Osterhaus?"

"Yeah. Basically exactly like Osterhaus."

"So you have to kill someone," Edgar clarified.

I nodded.

Wren cocked her head. "Do it."

"Wren."

Edgar stepped in front of her. "Hang on. We don't know who he has to curse. What if it's someone else's daughter? You okay with that?"

Wren set her jaw. "Who? Who do you have to curse, Dorian? Do you know?"

I nodded again.

"Then who is it? I think we have a right to know."

I answered, "Carmody."

Edgar turned to me, then slapped the side of his thigh. "He was just here. That was our chance to get a piece of him."

I winced at Edgar's sudden shift in caution. "Carmody's small-time, but he isn't that careless."

"Don't you need his blood or something? For a curse, you have to have that physical component."

"This is true, and I already have it."

Edgar's brow lifted. "You do?"

"A vial of his blood."

"Where did you get a vial of his blood?"

"He gave it to me."

Edgar chuckled, then frowned. "Carmody just gave you a vial of his blood? Why would anyone in the Life give someone a vial of their own blood?"

"Collateral," I explained. "At least that was his angle. Obviously it's not his."

Wren peered at me from behind Edgar. "So either he's stupid or he's an asshole?"

"Maybe a little of both," I answered. "I swear dabblers will be the death of me."

Wren asked, "He honestly gave you fake blood?"

Edgar waved his finger. "Who said it was fake blood? Maybe we should be asking whose blood it is?"

He had a point. I had spent more time assuming the blood wasn't Carmody's, but I hadn't questioned whom he was handing over for me to curse.

"I have no idea."

Edgar added, "Do you still have any of that blood mojo you got from Osterhaus?"

"No. That burned away with the contract."

Wren leaned against the spiral stairs. "Dorian, is this man worth cursing?"

"He isn't well-liked. But he looked like the better party in a particularly messy West Coast intrigue I'm wading through." I looked to Edgar. "You ever hear anything about Carmody using soul magic?"

Edgar shook his head. "No. He's mostly just an information broker."

"What about glammers?"

"Can't tell. I don't really know a lot about him. He knows more about me, really."

"Well, that fills me with all kinds of fuzzy. At least I know he needed a primer text on curses, so he can't be that thoroughly schooled."

"Dorian, if this is the guy, then I'm down to curse his ass." He turned to Wren and put an arm around her. "We'll do it if we have to."

"Not going to happen."

"Look, you put it out there for us already. You can't keep doing this without expecting it to bite you, man."

I waved him off. "Hey. This is for Elle."

Edgar's eyes moistened, and he quickly ran a finger under his nose. "So, how can we know for sure?"

"Good question. My guess, we have to do it the old fashioned way. Hit the books, do our homework. At least now we know what we're looking up."

Edgar glanced at Wren and shrugged. "Can you call Gillette, get more info?"

"I can try, but she's... I don't know. Grumpy. What we really need is someone who knows both Carmody and Gillette."

Edgar shrugged and held onto Wren.

That's when it occurred to me.

I sucked in a breath.

"Damn it."

Edgar followed my expression. "No way."

"How much you want to bet he knows both of them?"

"Probably, but he came into my house once. I don't feel like dealing with him again, man."

"Edgar, Zeno's the best connected man on the East Coast outside of the Presidium. How could it hurt just to call him?"

"You can call him, then."

"Deal. Also, I'll check Emil's Library. I found a book last week about servitors. Might help."

"What should we be doing?" asked Wren.

"Best thing you can do is keep Elle safe. Wouldn't hurt if you hold off on the doctor come Monday."

I could tell by her pinched expression she was struggling with it. After a deep sigh, she nodded.

Good, that was one less thing.

I peeked in on Elle before I left. I watched her from her bedroom door as she lay on her bed, staring at the ceiling. She slowly turned her head to me and muttered something incomprehensible.

"You really are trapped inside that girl, aren't you?"

Elle's eyes hardened.

"Not really your fault. Your master either knew and didn't warn you, or wasn't fully aware of the danger." I took a step inside the room. "And I know you don't really hate me. At least, you don't have any reason to hate me. It's just the way you were created. You know, it kind of helps to know you're just a sliver of someone's soul wrapped inside a thought. You're man-made; you're not part of the Dark Choir. You don't have a clue where my soul is, and never did."

She pulled back dry lips and replied, "I suppose that gives you hope."

"Not really, but it does give me a little satisfaction."

She went back to staring at the ceiling, and I left the thing alone to dwell on its fate. It was slowly devouring Elle from the inside out, and even though Wren had relented on the deadline she had imposed on me, the truth was that I still had a countdown which I couldn't avoid, and didn't know how much time was left on the bomb.

I drove back to Baltimore, now thoroughly sick of the scenery on that particular stretch of I-70. Finally alone at home, I took a seat at my roll top desk and relaxed for a moment. I found my hand resting on McHenry's envelope. Despite everything in my being desperate to shove that offer directly up McHenry's ass, I still felt the raw and savage tug of the money he was prepared to throw at me. I'm a pretty decent guy, I like to think. But that was a lot of money and a lot of headache I could forestall.

Still, McHenry hired this hitman. I had to secure proof it was Carmody, but ultimately the chain of responsibility stopped with McHenry. I mused at my meeting with Carmody in which he "let slip" the existence of a practitioner working Sooner's camp. That was precisely the kind of half-intelligent play I expected from the man. Still, Carmody had made a lot of headway with only a minimum of effort. He wasn't particularly good at lying, but he had a knack for making friends. Chums, he might have said. One might even say he was charmed. A man like Carmody survived by slipping between the railroad tracks, not by standing in front of the train. He had to have some angle. I just couldn't figure it out.

With those thoughts rattling through my brain, I called Frater Zeno.

The phone rang its requisite rings, and rolled to voice mail. I was running short of patience with Zeno, so I left a curt message.

"It's Dorian Lake. Call me now."

He was good for it.

My phone rang in a minute, and I answered, "Zeno?"

"Your phone etiquette leaves something to be desired."

"I need information."

"Don't we all?" he grumbled.

"What can you tell me about Del Carmody and Quinn Gillette?"

After a pause, Zeno replied, "More than we have time for."

"Can you make some time, then?"

"I seem to recall not wanting to ever speak to you again after our last meeting. Why am I even talking to you?"

"I can pay you."

"Again, not really an enticement."

"I know why you failed, Zeno. That alone must be worth at least ten minutes."

Another pause. "If I failed, it was because I wasn't given full possession of the facts."

"No shit. Look, there's still an entity to bottle up, if you can use it. And I still want it out of that girl."

"Fine, Lake. Carmody is a charm broker from Leicester, relocated to the states in the mid-eighties."

"Is he any good?"

"Not particularly."

"What about soul magic?"

"Sorry?"

"Is he a known practitioner of soul magic?"

"Not to my knowledge. Gillette, on the other hand, is what I would call an authority of soul magic. And I don't use the word 'authority' with any kind of informality."

"I knew that much. But do you know why Gillette is hell-bent on mounting Carmody's head over her fireplace?"

Zeno chuckled. "It would be easier to find a reason for Gillette not to be."

"How'd it start?"

"I'm not informed on the particulars. West Coast magic tends to bore me with its needlessly human drama. Carmody had some kind of close call with a poorly anchored hex and decided to move away from active practice. So, he cultivated his puerile interest in gossip into a career in information brokerage. He and Gillette played in the same sandbox for several years before Carmody managed to stumble into a turf war between Gillette and the Seattle people. Carmody got paid, lives were lost, and Gillette knew whom to blame."

"His information got people killed?"

"When I said turf war, I meant it."

"So Carmody hauls ass to the East Coast figuring Gillette won't chase him so close to the Presidium?"

"That follows."

"And now it looks like Carmody's trying to get back into the Practice, trades me Gillette for a book of curses, and here we are. Only he's grossly misjudging the Presidium's patience for penny-ante Netherwork. Jesus, at least Osterhaus was discreet."

"Does that satisfy your need for information?"

"Almost. In your opinion, would Carmody have the means or the skill to create a servitor?"

Zeno responded with a very long pause.

"Zeno?"

"Of course. Human powered thoughtform. My traps weren't crafted to attract or retain a human soul, regardless of how small."

"You're welcome."

"Lake, if someone sent a servitor into that girl's body, that girl is probably doomed."

"Why do you say that?"

"Servitors are short-lived creatures by nature. Even a soul shard loses its potency as a source of power over time. I can't say I've ever heard of a servitor possessing a human. That would be bold as a servitor would likely consume most of its original soul shard attempting the crossover."

"So it would have to feed on the new host's energy?"

"And so on and so forth. This creature may not have been warned about the quagmire of a child's psyche. If it's trapped, it will starve unless it finds a new energy source. Which means it'll start eating her soul to survive. This isn't just a physical condition, Lake. If that girl dies at the hand of this construct, any hope she has for a meaningful afterlife will die with her."

I rubbed my eyes.

"Any idea how I'd yank it out before it comes to that?"

"Sorry. I work in demons, not humans. I couldn't use the thing, regardless. It's a tangled mélange of hostile energies at this point, probably unaware of its own nature. That kind of chaos is more than even I'm willing to work with."

"Understood. Thank you, Frater."

"Lake?"

"Yeah?"

"Don't call me again."

He hung up.

Carmody probably wasn't my man. Oh, he was definitely playing me against Gillette, that much was clear. But I wasn't convinced Carmody had the ability to create a servitor. Which left me with a very real and pressing conundrum. I had an unidentified practitioner out there responsible for the imminent demise of Elle Swain's soul.

And I had no clue how I was going to find him.

CHAPTER TWENTY-SIX

I spent two hours in my working space downstairs boning up on thoughtforms, courtesy of Asok the Sharqui. The information was patchy. I was basically aware of thoughtform theory. That much wasn't Netherwork. One generally worked with thoughtforms for Ego Magics, attempts to re-write one's personal psychological makeup. This was particularly useful in treating personal psychological issues like eating disorders, addictions, and social anxiety disorders. I mused on whether Ches would be interested in any of this information.

When it came to powering a thoughtform with a soul shard, that dropped the entire practice squarely into the sphere of Netherwork. It was a forbidden act of creation, playing God with a thought. Servitors were unpredictable, chaotic, and often destructive. The only saving grace was that they were most often very short-lived. Zeno was right on that account.

But I found nothing about a servitor possessing a human body. What I did find, however, was that a servitor presented itself as a version of the one who crafted it. That meant it possessed a portion of its creator's knowledge, personality, and even its gender. My thoughts strayed back to one nagging question.

Why was this thing only possessing women? Perhaps it could only possess women?

That would make its creator a woman. Which made Gillette a suspect. She was the only person I knew who was familiar with how servitors were made, how they break, and how to dispatch them when they wander off reservation. Could Gillette have been the one to create the servitor?

No, that wouldn't make sense. She was too far removed from the East

Coast and its peculiar esoteric dramas to want to be involved. More pertinently, she was a master of soul magics, and had already proven she knew how to locate and liberate a servitor when it strayed. She wouldn't have gotten a thoughtform stuck inside a child. Not unless she wanted the child to die, in which case I was convinced she knew several cleaner methods toward that end. No, she wasn't McHenry's hitman, but she could end up being Elle's savior, if not mine.

I dialed Gillette's number and remained standing, pacing into and out of my kitchen.

"Yes?" she answered with that familiar gruff tone.

"Gillette? It's Dorian Lake."

"Who?"

"Dorian Lake? Of Baltimore? The one you want to curse Del Carmody?"

"Oh right," she grumbled. "You. What do you want? Is it done?"

"Not yet."

"Then you can call me when it is."

"Wait," I grunted before she could hang up. "I've decided to do it."

"You want me to throw you a parade, or something?"

"I want to negotiate a change in your service. In exchange for cursing Carmody."

"I thought this was all ironed out, Lake."

I had to be careful. Old school Netherworkers weren't fond of contract negotiation. "It was. But I want something else, now."

"No additions. The deal is struck."

"Not an addition, Gillette. A substitution."

After a pause, she responded, "Go on."

"There's a friend of mine out here in Baltimore. Someone crafted a servitor and sent it to possess a human body. The thing's been hopscotching through bodies, and now it's trapped inside a thirteen-year-old."

Gillette made a noise that could have either been disgust or amusement. Probably both at the same time.

"Is this what you people do for fun on the East Coast?"

"You see the problem, then?"

"I see several. None of which are mine."

"Here's my substitution. If I curse Carmody, instead of finding and securing my soul, I want you to remove this servitor from this girl."

"That's it?"

"Can you do it?"

"Yes. If she were here, that is."

"What do you mean?"

"Do you really think I'm going to fly out there and do this little task for you? There's no way the Presidium would even let me leave the airport before they bagged me and tossed me into the Potomac with a few dozen pounds of lead tied around my throat."

"I don't think I can move her. She's in bad shape."

"Sucks to be her, then."

"Gillette! This is my friend. Actually, she's more like family. You understand that? I know you've lost people who were close to you. I know that's pushed you to hunt down Carmody like this. Do you even get why I'm asking you to do this for me?"

"I understand, Lake. I just don't care."

I took a deep breath and tried to get my blood pressure to drop. "Look. This is a simple exchange. Instead of my soul, which is out there somewhere, this is a Frankenstein thoughtform bottled up exactly where you'll know where it is. If the Presidium wasn't an issue here, would you agree to the change?"

"If you can manage a way to get her out here to Portland, then yes. I'll agree to that."

"What if I can guarantee your safety here?"

"Against the Presidium? There's no such thing."

"You seem to do okay."

"No deal."

I took a split second to reevaluate my options. "I have connections. People I can call."

"I've never known the Presidium to keep their word."

"Then I'll push harder. I'll make them agree."

"How, exactly?"

"Leverage. It all comes down to leverage."

Gillette mulled it over for a while, then answered, "I have an associate in Gresham. Her name is Judith Wilcom. If the Presidium delivers a sealed letter of guarantee to her, I'll book my flight."

"Um, okay."

"But that had better not happen before Carmody is cursed."

"Out of curiosity, how will a letter of guarantee change your mind if the

Presidium always lies?"

"Judith is an expert sigilist. When someone gives her a written word, she can sanctify it as a *verum inviolata*."

"Meaning?"

"She will turn that into the spoken Word of God. The Presidium will understand what I'm asking, and I guarantee they won't agree to this."

"Let me worry about that. I'll be in touch."

I hung up and laid my phone down on the desk next to McHenry's envelope. I had Gillette on board to extract the servitor from Elle's body before it consumed her soul. All I had to do now was find a way to get some of Carmody's real blood, and find a way to convince myself to curse a man who was probably innocent. How could I do that? Osterhaus was one thing. He was utterly despicable. Carmody might not have been McHenry's hitman. He was slippery, sure, but I didn't suspect that he was clever enough to pull my strings to this degree. Anything was possible; I had certainly misjudged people before.

What it really came down to was family. Carmody was the one who had pulled me into this entanglement in the first place. Perhaps he had karma due in arrears. But Elle? She was family, and that was enough.

I reached for my phone and made a few calls.

The first was to Carmody. I fished out his business card and dialed his number.

"Who's this then?" he asked directly.

"It's Dorian Lake."

"Twice in one day? I feel like a celebrity."

"Good for you."

"How can I be of service?"

Here came the bluff. "Actually, I need your knowledge. You know the Library of mine you're hell-bent on plundering?"

"That I do."

"Emil left me a kind of index. All handwritten. A kind of list of the texts he's collected and from whom."

"I'll wager that's a hell of a list."

"I have a few holes here and there. Missing texts from his index. I suspect they were loaned out or otherwise pilfered. You can imagine how important it would be to me to find those texts."

"And you figure I know how to sniff out the odd truffle, so to speak?"

"Something like that." He was silent for a moment, to which I added, "I figured it'd be worth it to you just to lay eyes on this list of names."

"It is something of a tease."

"Look, if you're not interested, no harm no foul. Just thought since we'd be working together, this might, I don't know… be a team building exercise or something."

He hummed to himself, then responded, "I read you, Lake. I'm a bit occupied at the moment, however."

"How's tomorrow look?"

"I can make time. What say Silver Lane Diner in Catonsville? Around and about noontime?"

"I'm writing it down now. Thanks, Del."

He hung up without response. It was done.

I moved on to my next priority… Ches.

"Hey there," she answered.

"Hope you're having a better day than I am."

"I've had worse. How's Elle?"

"Tired. Possessed. Probably scared."

"If it makes you feel better, I wasn't aware of anything when it had taken me over."

It did make me feel better, to a point. "Yeah, but it didn't pitch a tent inside your skull for days."

"She seemed to come through today. I took that as a good sign."

"I don't know. I kind of wish she hadn't. I wanted her just to wake up from all this."

Ches lingered on that for a moment. "Are you okay?"

"Hmm?"

"You sound a little lost."

"Maybe a little, but I might have a plan."

"Do tell."

An intense longing to see Ches at that moment burned in my chest. "Look, I know I already saw you once today, but are you busy tonight? I could tell you all about my clever plan over dinner or something."

After a second's pause too long, she replied, "Actually, I kind of have plans."

My stomach dropped. "Oh."

"It's not a big deal. You shouldn't be worried or anything."

"Why would I be worried?"

"Nothing. Forget I said that."

"You have a date?"

Another second's pause. "A guy from my class asked me out yesterday."

I swallowed the lead weight in my throat that was threatening to jump out of my mouth and bludgeon me to death. "Hey, no problem. I should probably get ready for a ritual tonight, anyway. Besides, we're not actually... I meant, we're not exclusive. We're not even dating. Or, what?" I broke down into a nervous laugh. "What are we, exactly?"

"Let's start again tomorrow. Reboot the whole thing. What do you say?"

I nodded, then rubbed the bridge of my nose when I realized she couldn't see me. "Morning coffee sound good?"

"I don't think you're allowed back at the café, to be honest."

"Then swing by on your way in."

"It'll be early."

"That's okay," I blurted. "I'm probably not going to sleep tonight."

"Alright. Cool. I'll see you in the morning, then."

Piece by piece, my life was stitching back together.

And I had a plan for Carmody. All I had to do was make one more phone call, and spend the rest of the night rifling through Emil's Library for an appropriate curse, preferably one that didn't require cadaverous reagents. It would be cold, draining work. Just touching those books made my skin crawl.

But as I dug through my research, a stray idea flew into my head. I made one more phone call, then fished Amy's hair from my pocket. I spent the night on a very specific working. Very soon, and it would all be over.

CHAPTER TWENTY-SEVEN

The front door called with three quick knocks. I emerged from the basement with gauze on my forearm and a vicious case of the blinks. When I opened the door, I found Ches smiling back at me in her café apron. She dangled an expensive-looking bag of coffee in front of me.

"Hope you didn't get the coffee going already," she chimed. "Got this at the organic market."

"Looks incredible."

She nodded over her shoulder. "Oh, mind if I park my car in your drive? Won't get towed or anything?"

I eyed her old blue Chrysler parked behind my Audi. She was far enough away from the street. "What, no bus?"

"I wanted to stop by the market for the coffee."

I nodded her inside and shook my head. "You have a car and you take MTA every day?"

"Screw you, gas is expensive."

"Especially in that thing."

"Try driving here from Florida."

"Pass."

I searched my cabinets for my old French press, and tossed some bread into the toaster.

By the time the coffee was poured and I had spread some honey over my toast, I found Ches grinning at me.

"You look like a zombie."

I nodded. "I wish the most complicated thing I had to deal with today was how many brains to eat."

"You'll figure this out. I know it."

I stared at my shoes. Everyone kept saying that, for some reason. "You have more confidence than I do."

"I'll lend you some of mine, then."

She reached out and put her hand on mine.

"Thanks. I need it."

"I was just thinking about what you do. The magic stuff."

"The scary stuff?"

"I told you I won't let it scare me anymore, right? Well, I'm going to put this out there, and feel free to tell me butt out. But what if you brought me in?"

"Brought you in?"

"Your work. Teach me a thing or two?"

I rolled my head and tried to grin. "Okay, trying to find a pleasant way to tell you to forget it."

"I'm serious. I think part of your problem is that you do this alone. You don't have any backup. If these things are so dangerous, maybe you could use an extra pair of hands to carry the load."

"I thought you didn't believe in this stuff?"

"I have a bump on my head that's making a believer out of me. What do you think? Is all of this something you feel like you could share with another person?"

I stared at Ches for a while, thinking it over. The last time I shared this Life was with Emil. That was over ten years ago. I had a routine, a way of working my career. None of that felt like something I could share.

But how much of that was keeping me from really connecting with someone?

"It's not like candle-making, Ches. It takes years of study. Just straight study."

"I'm a professional student, Dorian. Studying is all I do."

"Dead languages, correspondences, constant meditation and energy awareness."

"I'll show you my psych text if you like. You're not going to scare me away from boring reading that easily."

I pulled my hand away. "I've never taught anyone before. I frankly don't know if I can."

"Alright. Just do me a favor, then. Don't dismiss this. Think it over."

"I wasn't dismissing it. I'm just communicating, here."

She nodded. "I know. But you're a snap judgment kind of guy. I'm going to have to break you of that, one of these days."

I had already put that on my to-do list, but it made me grin to hear her say it. "Alright. I'll think it over."

She stood up and gathered her purse.

"For the record, if you say no, I won't be mad."

I reached over and grabbed her hand, holding it tight for a moment.

"I gotta get to work," she whispered.

I walked her to the door. She kissed my cheek and gave me a wave just before she hopped into her car. I watched her drive down the block and take the last turn.

Ches had just given me something huge to think about. I shut the door and returned to my work space.

In my downtime last night, I had located a curse which would work with the materials I had available to me. It would be relatively simple. The hardest part was securing fresh blood. There could be no substitutes. But best of all, I didn't need Carmody to be there to fire the curse. It could be done at my leisure.

Leisure. What was that like?

By noon, I had made one important phone call and put myself together enough to drive to Catonsville. I was familiar with the area; I kept my first work space after moving to Baltimore in a mini-storage not far from the Silver Lane Diner. That was back when I forced myself to separate what I thought was my private life from the professional. And now I had someone asking to join me in both.

The diner wasn't terribly busy, which I considered to be a saving grace. I spotted an appropriate booth by the windows and took a seat. Carmody was late, but he did arrive. He shuffled to my booth and took a seat across from me, pulling off his hat and giving me a wink.

"Afternoon, then."

"Hi."

"I hope you don't mind, but I feel like I'm starving to death, so I'm going to order something." He waved his hand furiously, flagging down a waitress. He ordered a short stack of pancakes and a side of sausage, then cracked his knuckles. "So, shall we get down to it?"

I looked him over. His eyes moved in short, nervous motions.

"Out of curiosity, have you made any progress?" I asked.

"Well, I haven't seen the list yet, mate."

"About my soul."

"Oh, that. I do know a vodoun in New Orleans whom I've been meaning to ask for you. He's a handful, grant you, and he sometimes checks out in the middle of a sentence, but he's a hell of a medium and maybe he can put out some feelers. Best shot, at this point."

I cocked a brow at him. "Sounds thin."

"Well, you dance with he who brung you."

"Indeed, you do." I let the words sit on the table between us.

Carmody leaned forward. "So, you've decided to do it, then?"

"Do what?"

"Curse me."

The bastard was perceptive. "What tipped you off?"

"I told you before. You have a shit poker face, mate." He leaned back and pulled his hands off the table, shaking his head. "I simply cannot catch a break in this life, you know that? So what is this? One last chance for me to talk you out of it?"

"This isn't just about my soul, anymore."

"What are you going on about?"

"There's a servitor that's been hounding me ever since the day I met you. Now it's trapped inside Edgar's daughter, and if I can't remove it, she's going to die. Her soul along with it."

Carmody squirmed in his seat. "Servitors are Gillette's domain. Not mine. If you're casting accusations about, then you should start with her."

"Is that actually blood in that vial you gave me? Just curious."

He chuckled. "Couldn't sell you, eh?"

"Whose is it?"

"Truth be known, I have no idea whose blood it is. I know a guy who knows a guy in life insurance. Gets me vials from time to time when he needs something."

"So you just tossed a random person under the bus in case I decided to go through with it?"

"Better them than me." He reached into his pocket. When I flinched at the motion, he jerked his hand out holding a wallet. "Easy." He dropped a twenty onto the table and slid out of the booth. "No offense, but I'm removing myself before you get any cheeky notions about my actual blood."

"Funny you should mention that."

I made a gesture with my finger.

The woman in the booth behind Carmody reached around him and jabbed his hand with a disposable specimen needle.

Carmody reeled away from her and pushed back toward the window, gripping his hand.

"The fuck is this?" he stammered.

I looked up at the woman. "Thank you, Amy."

Amy capped the needle with a tiny, plastic cap and slipped it into my hand. I reached into my pocket and produced a small jewelry box containing the charm I had spent the night crafting for her.

She took the box and opened it, her eyes wide. "So, I just wear this at night?"

"That's right."

"And that's it?"

"It'll help you with the need," I explained. "The rest is really up to you."

Amy reached out and put a heavy hand on my arm. "Thank you."

Carmody watched as she hustled away, then gave me a grave look. "Seems I misjudged you."

I pocketed the capped needle and sighed. "Probably doesn't matter so much, at this point, but at least I'm trying to balance my karma."

Carmody stared at me for a long time, and I let him. I simply didn't have anything more to say to him.

His food arrived, and once the waitress finished setting out the plates, he slid slowly from the booth. His face washed in a mixture of emotions, and ultimately he turned and walked out of the diner without another word to me.

And that was one obstacle out of the way.

The harder obstacle was yet to come.

CHAPTER TWENTY-EIGHT

Sundays were business days at the Druid Hill Club. And by God did I have business to tend to. I parked my car in front of the doors and took my key with me, shoving past Ramon. I pushed open the double doors and paused just enough to let my eyes adjust. Kim stared at me from the coat check wide-eyed.

"Uh…"

I ignored her and hustled down the entry hall. By the time I had reached the Great Room, two thick gentlemen in suits bounded down the side stairs. They spotted me and reached for me with meaty hands. I ducked them both, running deeper into the room. Eyes turned toward me. But none of that mattered. I kept moving, searching all of the faces inside the Club.

One of the meat hands clamped around my arm, and I turned to take a swing at him. My fist made contact with ribs, and though I was sure it wasn't anything like a solid hit, it was enough to force him to let me go.

Another pair of hands landed on my back, shoving me down into one of the nearby chairs. I spun around to find Giancarlo towering over me.

"Dorian, what the hell are you doing over here?"

"Where's Brown?"

"I want you out of here. I'll carry you if I have to."

"Mister Brown. I know you know who he is."

Giancarlo nodded to the meat hands, who reached down and pulled me to my feet, securing me by my arms. "You're making a big mistake here, Dorian."

A gravelly voice spilled over Giancarlo's shoulder as Big Ben tapped that shoulder with a baseball bat. "So let him."

Giancarlo swiveled around to Ben, whose face was redder than usual.

"You kidding me with this, Ben?"

"Let the boy go. You know who he is. You know why there's a problem."

I tensed as Ben tightened his grip. For a second, he looked like he was about to go full thug on Giancarlo.

"Just doing my job, Ben. The owners say he goes, so he goes."

"I'm sure he will," Ben added with a tap of the bat. "When he's done."

Giancarlo waved off the meat hands, and I stood on my own power.

"Thanks, Ben," I muttered, straightening my shirt.

Giancarlo smiled at Ben. "You even know how to use that thing, Ben?"

Ben smirked. "I used to play in the Minors. Right after Korea."

"No shit?" Giancarlo stepped away and put a hand behind his two thugs. "We'll be by the door. Brown's upstairs, Dorian. You got fifteen minutes. Get your business done, then you're out of here."

After they skulked off, I turned to Ben and offered him my hand. He shook it with a tired smile.

"Thanks, Ben. Thought I was going to get further than I did."

He nodded and returned to the bar, tucking the bat under his arm.

I had never been upstairs at the Club before. That space was for VIPs and owners. Even the working girls used rooms downstairs. I felt like Bellerophon climbing that staircase, and for all I knew, Mr. Brown was about to send a gadfly right up my ass. As I rounded the top flight, I found a simple hall of doorways leading to a picture window near the rear of the building. I peered into each open door, finding only empty offices, most of which appeared to have gone unused for decades. I nearly passed Brown's office, as he was sitting still in a dark room. I backed up a couple steps and stepped into the doorway.

"Good afternoon, Mister Lake," Brown cooed as he looked up from his tablet. "Ever the glutton for drama I see."

"This would have been less dramatic if McHenry hadn't booted me from the Club in the first place."

"I'm not sure I care, to be honest with you."

"Fair enough."

"Come to chastise me over Wexler's heavy-handed diplomacy?"

"No. I need something from you."

Brown set his tablet aside and folded his hands on the table. "Intriguing. What is this boon you require?"

"Are you familiar with a Judith Wilcom in Gresham, Oregon?"

He thought it over before nodding slowly. "Sigilist, I believe? Often associated with Quinn Gillette's cadre."

"Gillette is about to fly into BWI, possibly tomorrow. I need the Presidium to send a written guarantee of Gillette's safety to Wilcom for her to, I don't know, notarize or something."

Brown stared at me without a flicker of acknowledgment.

I continued, "And I need it done today."

"Not a week ago Gillette killed one of our listeners."

"The word you're trying to avoid is 'spy.' Don't preach to me about casualties of war, Brown."

"Do you have any idea what you're asking? This sigilist will reduce any written guarantee into a binding hex on the entire Presidium."

"*Verum invoilata*. All I'm asking for is a guarantee of safety. No one can move against Gillette while she's in Baltimore. That's the deal."

"That's the deal?" he repeated. "Well, I'll keep this brief then. I refuse."

"No, you won't."

"I'll bite, Lake. What feeble threat are you prepared to level against the Presidium that I'm sure you expect will have me shivering in accommodating fear?"

"No threats." I reached slowly into my pocket and pulled out a photograph of myself, Eddie, and Elle taken back at the beginning of baseball season. I slapped it down on Brown's desk and tapped the photo with my finger. "I'm appealing to your basic sense of humanity. McHenry hired a hack to make my life miserable. I tried to warn Wexler about it, but she seemed oddly blasé. I figured she's just one person in the Presidium. You're quite another. The girl's thirteen years old, and right now she's having her spiritual essence drained from her body by a servitor this amateur sent into her body."

Brown's eyes narrowed.

"She might have days left. Her parents are going insane. And they're good people. They're the kind of people you want representing the Craft in this country. They believe in Good. They play by the rules. And if the Presidium actually gives a shit about the good people of this country like they say they do, then they're going to let the one person I've found who can remove this servitor fly in without grief."

Brown looked down at the photo, then back up to me. "This is personal?"

"As personal as it gets. So, I've got about ten minutes before Giancarlo comes up here with a gun. I need an answer. You going to let this girl get eaten alive, or are you going to allow me this one-day cease fire?"

He shoved the photo forward to me. "If I arrange this guarantee for you, would you say this would affect your decision to continue campaigning for Sullivan?"

"Wexler drove that point home already."

"Did she? My experience watching you, Mister Lake, is you tend to accept authority about as well as you accept cheap Scotch. I told Wexler you wouldn't react well to being threatened. But if you agree to it of your own volition, not coercion, I would feel more confident in your word."

"Fine. If it gets this done, you have my word. No more Sullivan. I'm out."

Brown reached into his desk and produced a sheet of paper with the Presidium's Eye of Providence embossed in gold print. He wrote the letter long-hand, signed it, and stamped a seal in wax over his signature. He offered it to me to review. It was kosher, a one-day agreement that the Presidium would not take any action or allow any action to befall Gillette that would result in her inconvenience.

I nodded and handed the letter back to Brown.

"I'll have a courier pick this up within the hour. Gillette should have it by morning."

I stood with my arms at my sides, unsure of what to do next.

"And we do have an agreement, don't we?"

I nodded.

"I'll inform the others. This should make our lives considerably simpler, Mister Lake. And we may return to business as usual."

I turned and stepped out of his office.

Brown called after me, "It's not too late, you know."

"Too late for what?" I asked without turning back.

"Your talents are considerable. Your resourcefulness, your perseverance. You tend to side with us more often than not. It's not too late to consider joining us. There's much you could offer."

This was the second time the Presidium floated that pitch past me. Though, it was slimier coming from Brown.

I smiled at Brown and replied, "You'd think that, wouldn't you?"

"It's worth considering."

"Sorry, Brown. But I do have standards, and you people are just... cheap Scotch."

I made it down the steps before Giancarlo came storming up. Rather, he was waiting patiently by the front doors. He even held the door open for me, though he didn't say goodbye. As I got into my car and drove back down the gravel path, I caught a glimpse of the white-bricked building in my rearview mirror, and I just knew this would be the last time I'd ever see the place. What surprised me more than anything was how little I felt as I drove away. This Club wasn't just done with me.

I was done with it.

So I had the Presidium's guarantee. Carmody's blood. All I needed was for everything to fall together smoothly, and maybe there was a chance to save Elle after all.

I did have one last call to make, though.

I tried three times on the way home to reach Julian, but his phone continued to roll into voice mail. I got a dreadful feeling as I drove back down the Jones Falls Expressway. I needed to warn him not to contact me, and find a way to word it so I didn't invoke the Presidium's wrath any further than I had already. It was bad enough I basically marched directly into one of their offices and made demands. It would be quite another if they realized that my payment for Gillette's services was to perform an unsanctioned Nether Curse on an innocent man.

When I got home, I poured myself the last of my Talisker, sat on my couch, and for the first time in over a week, actually bothered to turn on my television. It wasn't long before I realized why Julian wasn't picking up his phone.

A news reporter stood in front of City Hall as the banner beneath her name proclaimed *Breaking News* and *Sex Scandal in City Hall*. I turned up the volume and leaned forward as the reporter droned on.

"—for the past three years. His name has been withheld out of respect for his family, but our sources confirm that the victim was under the age of eighteen when he began an ongoing sexual relationship with Deputy Mayor Bright."

CHAPTER TWENTY-NINE

"Please tell me it's bullshit."

"Of course it is."

"Then you can fight this."

"That's not the point, Dorian. I can't let this hang around Sully's neck. The damage is already done. It could only get worse."

I paced with my phone in my front room, trying to sort my thoughts. "Look, this is obviously McHenry. It's slander. It's criminal. You can use this against him. Maybe finally have a smoking gun we can put him away with."

"There's no smoking gun," Julian explained, barking into his cell phone over a din of voices in the background. "I made calls. If it's McHenry, then he covered his tracks."

"Of course he did. We just have to dig deeper."

Julian sighed. "Well, that's what I have you for, right?"

My stomach balled into a knot. "Uh, well. About that."

"What now?"

"Julian? I've made a deal with some powerful people today."

"Look, things are a little insane right now. Can we talk about this later?"

"We can't talk after this phone call."

After a space of background noise, Julian coughed, "Huh?"

"I have to get out of politics. Off your payroll."

"Dorian?"

"It's something I have to do."

"McHenry?"

"No. This is bigger. Look, it's up to you to make sure Sullivan stays in that building. You can't resign over this."

"It's done, Dorian."

"Oh, please don't tell me—"

"What do you think I was going to do? I can't help him anymore. I've become a liability."

"They can't get away with this. They can't ruin your life with lies like this."

"I'll be fine, Dorian. This only has to stick long enough to win Sooner the election. Then I bet this will all magically disappear, and we'll all go about our lives, or whatever resembles our lives when this is over." He sighed. "I guess we couldn't win this one, huh?"

I chewed on my lip. "Look, uh, Julian. After the fall, when you're in your new resemble-life, call me up then. We'll get a drink."

"Maybe talk about old times, something like that?"

"Something like that."

He held his phone aside to make a few comments to someone in his room, then muttered to me, "I have to go. But I just wanted to say thank you, Dorian."

"Don't think I did much, Julian."

"You did. We did. I'll see you."

After he hung up, I was left with the distinct impression I wouldn't ever see him again.

And just like that, McHenry had won the election. Rather, Sooner would win in a few months. But the final nail had been driven. McHenry's grip over Baltimore would be final, and there was no telling how long it would take to remove him. I thought about McHenry for a long time that evening. I considered running out for more Scotch, but something about leaving my house at that moment just felt terrifying to me. I needed something to be solid, constant. I needed something to be the way it was.

But there was no one to call. I couldn't call Edgar without having something definitive for him, and I wouldn't get that until tomorrow morning. I couldn't belly up to Big Ben's bar and spend some time receiving my share of abuse from him. And as weak as I was that night, I couldn't call Ches. It wouldn't have helped.

So I sat in my house with nothing to do with myself beyond stewing over the way McHenry had just screwed Julian's entire life. My anger built and redoubled, and I found myself pacing. At some point I spotted the envelope on my desk, still sitting there, still waiting for my signature. There was a time not too many hours ago it seemed to be a set conclusion that I would sign those documents and sell my properties directly to McHenry. It made sense at the time. It made all the sense. But now? Fuck him. I was willing to hold onto those properties out of sheer vicious spite. It was the most I could do; it was perhaps the only route available to me.

I snatched the envelope from the desk and hucked it into the waste basket under my window. My nervous energy remained unabated, however, and I continued to pace. I made a pass through the house trying to tidy up, though I hadn't been around enough in the last couple days to really make a mess. By the time I had rinsed and hand-dried all of my glassware, I was already re-thinking trashing McHenry's offer. The lure of the money was potent. My brain tangled with possibilities and options that money could open up for me. I wouldn't simply catch up on my bills. I could build on something new.

I looked back down at the envelope in the trash. With a quick teeth-clench, I reached in and pulled it back out. When I slipped it back onto my desk, the paperwork slid out a little, taunting me. I thumbed the first few pages free of the envelope and snapped them in front of my face.

An intelligent man would put these papers in front of an attorney's nose, or at the very least an accountant. I couldn't imagine what it would be like to be McHenry's attorney. My eyes rose to the letterhead, curious who was washing McHenry's financial blood off their hands.

Grey and Lisle.

By God, that son of a bitch had Grey and Lisle on retainer.

I took a seat, and let the thought simmer for a moment. When the plan finally landed, I reached for the brochure Sullivan had given me, and my phone.

And I called Ari Leibnitz.

"Hello?"

"Ari? It's Dorian Lake."

"Hmm? Oh. Oh! Hello, Mister Lake."

"How are things in the office?"

He muffled his voice a little. "Much improved, thanks to you."

"That's good to hear. Listen, I have a matter I need some professional advice on."

"I don't know how much use I'd be in your line of work."

"No, no. This is a matter of dollars and sense, and real estate."

"Ah. Well, our office hours are Monday through Friday—"

"I want to deal with you, Ari. We've done business, and I trust you."

"I take it this is a sensitive matter of real estate?"

"You could say that."

"Well, Mister Lake, I'm unsure if we clearly stipulated whether any further professional dealings would be owed to your services rendered."

"Don't worry, I'll pay you. We're both professionals. Professionals get paid. Can we meet tomorrow?"

"Lunch time is the best time for you?"

"Let's make it early," I countered. "I'm expecting a busy day tomorrow."

"Can you meet me in my office at nine a.m.?"

"Done."

I hung up with a sense of forward motion. This offer would come in handy after all, just not in the way McHenry had intended.

I took some time to step out of my house and walk down to the café. It was closed, now well past lunch. The patio chairs were turned up on the tables, and the windows inside were dark. I kept walking, making it to the MLK. The first waves of cool evening air drifted off of the harbor, and I kept walking. People passed me on the street, not noticing me, not really caring. I was a shadow, completely innocuous. I dropped a fiver in a panhandler's bucket, and managed to catch a woman engrossed in texting before she stepped into traffic. The deeper I plunged into the heart of the city, the more I felt like my feet were calling the steps.

I looked up around me, and realized I was passing beneath the University of Maryland Baltimore campus. This was Ches' turf, her destination after work. It was remarkable how we even found one another. It was mostly by virtue of my location. Had the bus line dropped her off two blocks away, she may have taken a job in some Cuban deli or a packaging plant. Instead, she found the bus stop two blocks from my house, so she took a job at my café. Well, it used to be my café. It was just a place now.

Both McHenry and Curtis the Toad Face were correct about one thing. I was still an outsider in this city. Part of me felt smug owning those properties. They granted me a sense of ownership, not only of the real estate, but of the city. But the truth was I had lived here for a decade, and never walked anywhere. I only ever drove. I only wanted to be somewhere; I never wanted to go there. I had hidden in the Club, retreated to the Swains' in Frederick, bunkered down in self-storages and basements to perform my craft. For all of my secret knowledge, I lacked a meaningful understanding of Baltimore itself. As I walked into downtown, I regretted that ignorance profoundly.

Ten or so blocks into my sojourn, I hooked a right and paused beneath the Belvedere Hotel. My stomach dropped when I realized where I was. Not seven months ago, I had witnessed a suicide here. A man had jumped in front of a bus. He was a desperate man who had sold his soul, and couldn't see any point in continuing this life. Just beyond this hateful patch of asphalt lay a dark alley, threading down the shadow of the Belvedere. I stepped slowly down this alley, sidestepping a few dumpsters, checking for potential muggers behind each. When I finally stopped, I stood at the top of a flight of stairs leading down to a basement door.

This had been Osterhaus's office. For years this had been the destination for people out of luck and out of options, willing to sell their soul for two years' comfort. I had ended that, and not well. Osterhaus was dead, and the souls he had collected were now in the hands of foreign mystics. I remained the last man standing, sans one soul. The "For Lease" sign screwed to the door gave me at least a flutter of satisfaction, but ultimately the affair was a failure.

And here I stood, on the precipice once again, wondering if I would fail. This time there was so much more at stake.

The shadows in the alley were scurrying into my periphery. I stepped back out onto Light Street, and looked up and down the avenue. I spotted a bar two doors down. Rich red carpentry adorned the front with leaded glass windows. It exuded Old World charm, and that simply called to me. I had spent enough time in old London pubs during my time studying under Emil. This was precisely what I needed.

I stepped inside the bar, which was largely empty. The elderly gentleman behind the bar gave me a tired nod, and I elected to sit right up front. Out of habit, I checked the taps in case this place had something approximating a decent English bitter. Alas, I found little more than the usual bland American lagers, so I ordered a Scotch.

The old man poured me two fingers of rail Scotch, and I tried to be cordial as he set it in front of me.

I gave him a nod as I pointed to the ornate woodcarvings adorning his backbar. "Gorgeous place you have here."

He shrugged. "Like it?"

"I do. Nice, dark. Comfortable."

"You'd be the only one."

"Business slow?"

He pulled a stool from under the bar and settled his frame onto it. "Slow for five years, since they fixed the harbor."

"Shame. If I worked downtown I'd probably be here every afternoon."

"Want to buy it?"

I smiled and took a sip. When he kept staring at me, I realized he was serious. "Buy it?"

"Been on the market for years. No one's biting."

"Tempting, but I'm not really the management type."

He smiled and folded his hands.

I muscled through the cheap Scotch as I turned on the stool. The line of booths along the side wall made for cozy little conversation pits. The row of leaded glass windows sent prismatic light glittering along the manicured ceiling tiles. The whole place smelled of wood soap and leather.

I ordered another, this time specifying a reasonable single malt. A couple businessmen stepped into the bar and grabbed one of the booths. They hunkered down over a couple beers and pulled out some paperwork to argue about. They must have been regulars, as the old man just brought them their drinks without their asking. I imagined what the energy of the place would have felt like with a dozen more regulars colluding over beer and whiskey.

I wasn't seriously considering this.

Really.

The sun began to set, and I took my leave of the place just as the old man lit a few tabletop candles for guests who would probably never arrive. The pall of resignation hung on his shoulders, sad and lonely as he went through the motions. Either the Scotch or the look on his face as I stepped out of the bar dropped drowsiness on me like a warm blanket.

I walked back home beneath the streetlights and illuminated signs of the city, hustling quicker past the unlit blocks. When I reached the MLK, the sun had long set behind Shipley Hill, though a splash of orange in the sky remained as stars made their appearances. I took in the view for one brief moment of peace before my phone rang.

"Hello?"

"What do think, mate?"

"Carmody?"

"How's our schedule lookin'? Am I on the block yet, or do I have some time to win you over?"

"Look, I don't have a lot of options here."

"Oh, right. You're the one who wasn't given any options. I almost forgot."

"I know you don't have the skills to fix my problem, and I don't have time for you to find a solution."

"Yes, very nice. Shall we ask your friend, the deputy mayor, what he thinks about my skills?"

I blinked through the question before it dawned on me. "That was you?"

"Behold the power of information, chum. Information is my trade, and you backed me into a corner. I had to push back."

I shook my head in bafflement. "You ruined an entire mayor's race for this?"

"Yeah, fuckin' right I did! It's my life on the line, isn't it?"

"You have dirt on everybody, why him? Why not me?"

"Because, you daft little terrier, I'm trying to save my life, not end it. I hit you, you hit me. Bang. Gone. See, here, I have your attention."

"That, you do," I snarled.

"And it doesn't end with your government friend. You said it best. I've got dirt on every bloody body. Whose life do I have to ruin next? Or can we call a halt to all of this?"

"There's dirt, and then there's slander."

"Oh, I don't deal in falsehoods, mate. They're dime-a-dozen. The only real value is in the bonafide, genuine choice cuts."

I lowered my phone and stared out over the highway at the last full rays of daylight. I'm not one to judge one's lifestyle choices, but Julian had lied to me.

I picked up the phone slowly to my face and stated, "Just remember. You started this."

"Lake?"

"Goodbye, Carmody."

"Lake. Lake!"

I hung up and crossed the highway with the light.

CHAPTER THIRTY

I found a café not far from Light Street the next morning, and took a leisurely breakfast there of a bagel and quite a serviceable cappuccino. It was close enough to walk to Grey & Lisle, and left me with enough time to arrive early. I signed in at the front desk, took the elevator to the ninth floor, and signed in at yet another desk. Most of the offices behind the receptionist were dark. Sunday was clearly not a popular day to work in this office. Yet there came Ari, upright and confident. It was quite a switch from the last time I laid eyes on him.

"Good morning, Dorian."

"Ari."

He led me to his office, which was somewhat cozy and crammed with file boxes, but at least it wasn't a cubicle. He pulled aside several stacks of papers to make room for me.

"So, what is it I can help you with?"

I set McHenry's envelope on his desk and leaned back in my chair. "I own some rental properties, and I'm looking to sell them to my tenants."

"I see. Your lease terms?"

"Month to month, mostly. The one still on contract is up at the end of the month."

"You intend to give thirty days' notice?"

"Yes, if needed."

"It's required by law."

I leaned forward in my chair, trying not to bump my knee into his desk. "If they want to close, then they can move faster?"

"Naturally, but you'll have to be careful not to imply any haste in their decision."

"That's not my intent."

"Very well. What are the properties?"

I pulled some extra plot documents I had stuffed into McHenry's envelope. I had purchased the properties for a steal back when I first moved to Baltimore. The entire area was slated for a major renewal at the time, and I was banking the property values would rise sharply. Then the urban renewal project hopped across the expressway, and my side of the street ended up with nothing. Ironic, now that I had a fat offer on the properties, and I was trying to sell them off quick.

Leibnitz reviewed my parcel info and nodded knowingly.

I set down the pamphlet Sullivan had given me and slid it forward. "There's an assistance program available. My tenants aren't exactly upper income. I'm hoping to steer them to a participating bank, get them a zero down mortgage."

He took the pamphlet and smiled. "I wish every landowner was as courteous as you. I'm sure we can find several banks who offer a product that would work. However, by what you say and from what I glean from these street addresses, there may be an issue with the program."

"What issue?"

"Fair market value for these properties might not be what you're hoping for, and you're not allowed to exceed market value if your tenants are going to be eligible."

I chuckled. "I don't think that will be a problem."

"Well, our first order of business will be to ascertain the market value—"

"Got that covered." I pulled McHenry's paperwork out of the envelope and handed it to Leibnitz. He adjusted his glasses and reviewed the first few pages. I could tell when he hit the offer amount. His eyebrows lifted quickly toward the top of his head.

"I... I don't understand."

"I'm refusing this offer."

He looked up at me in bewilderment. "How?"

"Fair question." I tapped the first page again. "Double-check the buyer."

He flipped to the front page, and dropped the paperwork on his desk. He pushed away in his chair, wheeling several inches on squeaky casters.

"Now you're starting to see why I came in on a Sunday?"

"This offer would make you a millionaire."

"I recognize that."

"Well, what are you looking to sell for?"

"Far less. Probably an order of magnitude."

"Mister Lake, this... this is simply insane. I'll grant you, there may be some altruistic motive at play here, but you're literally throwing away millions of dollars."

"No, Ari. What I'm doing is rogering McHenry. You know who the man is, and so maybe you'll understand it takes a small fortune in brass balls to put the screws to that guy." I collected myself and changed the beat. "By the way, how's Jacobs?"

"Hmm?"

"You know who I mean."

He looked over his shoulder to the door uncomfortably, then leaned back close to his desk. "On unpaid leave, pending an internal audit."

"Karma found him."

"That was the idea."

"Tell me something. You weren't personally invested in Jacobs. Right? You just recognized that some sons of bitches simply need a swift kick in the jimmies."

He smirked. "McHenry is your Jacobs?"

"Basically."

"I'd hate to find myself at the other end of your hexes, Mister Lake."

"With any luck, I won't have to hex him. A man like that doesn't respond to Cosmic dictates. The only language he understands is written in dollars and cents, and I intend to force some of those dollars and cents into the hands of the people who actually live in those properties."

Leibnitz considered me for a long moment before picking up the papers and reviewing them in detail. We stayed in his office for two more hours, hashing out forms and procedures. I left Grey & Lisle with a shopping list of errands, twice the paperwork than I arrived with, and perhaps most importantly Jacobs' phone number.

I checked my phone for messages. Nothing yet from Gillette. Anything could get in the way of the Presidium courier. Weather. Traffic. Flight delays. An uncooperative sigilist in Gresham. I was a bit optimistic in hoping to hear from the West Coast that early in the day, but it didn't stop me from getting frustrated.

Most of my financing errands would have to wait until Monday, but the entire project felt too hot to keep tucked under my arm. The tenants had been kept in the dark too long regarding the fate of their homes. I pulled my phone and dialed Abe's number.

"Yessir?"

"Abe? Dorian."

"Ah, good mornin'!"

"Yes it is, isn't it? Listen, I need to call a meeting of all the tenants. How many do you think are home?"

"Well, I suspect the Hayeses are in church right about now, but the Dumonts usually spend the day at home. And I can hear Lakeisha's radio already this mornin'."

"Good. Do me a favor and spread the word. I'm going to come by your place around noon with some important news. Keep an eye out for the Hayes."

"Yessir."

There. The fix was in. I needed them to know. And I needed to get this out of my mouth before I changed my mind and took McHenry's money. My spite was strong, but it had limits.

I tried not to compulsively check my phone for missed calls, without much success. When noon approached, I gathered as much of the information as Leibnitz had photocopied for me, and drove to the properties. I spotted Lakeisha camped out on the curb, looking down the street in my direction. Abe and some older woman, who I assumed was his current sublet, were waiting on his porch. I parked in the middle of the block and nodded up to Abe, gesturing for him and his companion to join me out in the postage stamp lawns each of the properties claimed inside hurricane fences.

Abe trotted past me and gave me a smile. "I'll get the others."

Lakeisha turned on her heel and before Abe could even round his own fence bellowed, "Yo, Tyrel! Jo-Jo! Lake's here!"

Her voice echoed off a couple alleys down the block.

Abe paused and watched as the Dumonts and the Hayes filed out of their front doors, the Hayes still in their Sunday best. Jo-Jo looked dapper in his seersucker white while his aging wife appeared to have stuffed herself into a dress she fit in when she was in high school. When everyone had gathered near the corner of the Dumonts' fence, I walked the street and passed out Ari's paperwork.

"Hello, everyone. You've heard by now about this Carrollton Manor project that's going up. A couple of you asked me if I planned to sell the properties. I had zero interest in selling these properties, until yesterday."

The Hayes murmured on to another, and I could see Tyrel clench his jaw.

"Jo-Jo and Dee, you're both still on lease until the end of July. The rest of you are month-to-month. So, the choice is up to me whether I want to sell. And I've decided to sell."

Lakeisha cocked her hip at me. "Oh now!"

I held up a hand. "But I'm not going to sell to the developers. These houses are your homes. All of you have lived here longer than I've been in Baltimore. Abe, I inherited you from the previous owner."

He nodded wearily.

"I can't be the one to put you out of your own homes. I'm just not ready to do that, no matter how much money they toss in my lap."

Tyrel unfolded his arms and paced a half-circle. "We ain't got time for this shit. What are you going to do?"

The others murmured agreement.

"I want to sell these properties to you all."

After a moment's silence, Tyrel snickered at me.

Abe leaned across the fence. "Now, Mister Lake, we can't afford nothing like that. You know that, don't you?"

"Take a look at the papers I handed out. There's a way to do this. I got together with a professional, and he walked me through the procedure. There's a program from the government that allows a bank to offer you a mortgage loan with zero down payment as long as I sell the property direct to you."

Tyrel shook his head with a smirk. "Still can't afford no payments, man."

"You can, because you're already paying it. To me. I worked out a sales price for each of your properties that, with the current market interest rate and the higher taxes, will amortize into a monthly payment equal to what you're paying in rent."

Lakeisha peered at me. "You're saying I can own this place and pay the same that I'm payin' now?"

"That's right."

"Shit, where's your pen? I'll sign now."

I laughed out loud and nodded. "Thanks, but we have to get a bank involved first. Actually, you do. I've done everything I can. In your hands is the information a bank will need from you to offer you a loan according to the program. Not every bank is required to play along, so if you get any static, just move down the street to the next bank. And keep going until you find one that will. I'd do that for you, but turns out it isn't legal. Also in your paperwork is the correct dollar amount to offer me for the property. I'm selling as owner, so I don't need a realtor."

They stood there staring at me. Lakeisha was smiling, as was Abe. The others seemed thoroughly baffled by this turn of events.

"Any questions?"

Tyrel turned and made it halfway to his porch before spinning around and pacing back to the fence. "What're you doin', man? What's this about? I mean, people just don't do this."

"I'm not trying to screw you, Tyrel. Truth be known, and you all should hear this, when and if this all goes down as planned, you'll be the last holdouts on this block against the Manor project. I wouldn't be surprised if the developer doesn't come to each of you with a fresh offer. I can tell you, they're desperate for this real estate. But the choice is yours at that point. Stay. Sell. If you stay, you'll be in control of your destiny. If you sell, you'll probably be able to move to a pretty good neighborhood. And I don't mean you'll rent in a good neighborhood… you'll buy. Anyway, come see me if you have questions."

Abe walked forward and shook my hand before returning to his house without a word. The rest milled around for a while before retiring to their residences. The Hayes were the last to take their leave as they stood on the front lawn looking over the paperwork. When I was finally alone, I gave the stoop across the street a double-check before returning to my car, and drove back home.

I was giddy. Just saying that out loud felt final, though it was anything but. There was a lot of work my tenants had to navigate before this happened, and a lot could go wrong. But I had done what I could, and most importantly, it was the right decision, if not the smart decision.

When it came to that dichotomy, I seemed to have made my choice.

The phone rang several hours later, and I had forgotten that I was supposed to be obsessively checking it. The call was from Gillette.

"Did you get it?" I asked.

"Judith received a hand-delivered letter from the Presidium this morning, and she has sealed the letter as *verum inviolata*."

"So, you're satisfied?"

"You confronted the Presidium. That takes balls, Lake, so I'm going to give you the benefit of doubt."

"When can you fly out?"

"By your tone I assume the sooner the better?"

"You tell me. This girl has had a servitor chewing away at her soul for the better part of four days, now."

She sighed. "Let me tell you something, Lake. If you ever find the man responsible for this, I do hope you find the justification to release the more hellish of your darkest workings on his slapdash ass."

I white-knuckled the steering wheel. "I'll figure that out later. Right now I just want it out."

"Good. You're focused. And I can't guarantee satisfaction. Only execution."

"I understand."

"I'm looking at a red eye right now, should put me at BWI at seven-ten in the morning."

I did the math in my head before responding, "Perfect. I'll pick you up myself."

"One thing."

"There always is."

"Don't forget your part. I want to see Carmody's curse in effect, or I do nothing."

"I can't promise you'll see the effect. Curses are organic creatures. Maybe it'll be immediate, maybe it'll take days. Weeks. I'm not in control of timing. What I can offer you is to witness the ritual."

She sniffled. "I'm surprised you would allow that."

"This is important. I need you to be satisfied, but like you I can only guarantee execution."

"Fair enough. You perform the curse, I witness. Then I extract this servitor and destroy it."

"Can you contain it?"

"What?"

"Bottle it? Trap it, Goetia style?"

"What could you ever want with a Frankenstein mess like that?"

"I owe someone consideration for services rendered. If it's a problem—"

She grumbled, "It can be done. I don't really care what you do with it."

"Fine. I'll see you in the morning."

I hung up and checked the clock. It was five in the afternoon. Fourteen hours until I had to pick up Gillette. Another hour to bring her back to my work space and execute the curse. I had the ritual planned and reagents collected. However, I hadn't prepared for the logistics of the day. I couldn't cart Gillette around from Baltimore to Frederick. I sensed the Presidium was simply itching to find some way to circumvent their bound agreement, and I didn't want to give them any opportunities do so. And recognizing the Presidium didn't specify that Gillette would be safe outside of Baltimore, I decided that the extraction had to take place in my work space. It made more sense that way. I had better wardings than Edgar, and I could easily transition from the curse to the extraction in one fell swoop, and get Gillette back to the airport before even God would notice.

However, that meant transporting Elle to Baltimore, and convincing Wren this entire scheme wasn't completely balls-out insane.

I dialed the Swains and ran through my pitch in my head.

"Hello?"

"Edgar? It's Dorian."

"Got good news?"

"Yes, I do. Gillette is flying in tomorrow morning. She's agreed to remove the thing."

Edgar released a tremendous sigh. "Yeah, that's good news alright."

"So, I don't want her moving around too much. I want to bring Elle here."

"You want to do it there?"

"Right."

"Hmm."

"Think you can talk Wren into that?"

"Well, there's a problem."

Of course there was.

CHAPTER THIRTY-ONE

I stood in Swain's Antiques and Oddities, hands in my pockets, staring at Eddie who sat nervously on the old green couch downstairs, clutching his electronic game.

"How sick is she?" he asked.

"Pretty sick."

His eyes were wide, and he tucked in his bottom jaw the way he did when he was worried or in trouble.

"Did she throw up?"

It pained me to hear that. Ah, the mind of a child where throwing up was the worst possible thing that could happen to you.

"A couple times, yeah."

"Did she get medicine?"

"Eddie, it's not something medicine can help. But we've got a special doctor coming in tomorrow morning who's going to make her better. Okay?"

He nodded, though his expression seemed unconvinced.

I looked up at the spiral stairs for either Edgar or Wren to make an appearance. They had asked me to keep Eddie distracted while they cleaned up Elle's room. I could still hear scuffling upstairs, so I took a seat next to Eddie. I noticed his game wasn't even on.

"Not playing your game?"

He shook his head solemnly.

"Did you have fun at your friend's house?"

He shrugged.

This was going well.

After a series of deep sighs from his little chest, I tickled the back of his neck. When that didn't work, I flicked his ear until he smiled. That was my opening. I went for the ribs with both hands, and he doubled over giggling, kicking back at me. One of his feet landed on my knee, and I pulled my legs up behind me.

By the time Wren appeared at the top of the stairs, the two of us were practically upside down on the couch looking back at her. I straightened up and tried to recover my dignity.

Wren stepped slowly down the stairs and put her hand on the back of Eddie's head.

"Okay, big guy. Want to see her?"

She led the two of us back upstairs, through the living room, and into the hallway. Edgar emerged from Elle's bedroom, tossing a cleaning rag over his shoulder. He gave Eddie a nod, and the boy stepped into his sister's doorway.

His expression never changed. His eyes never moved. He just stood there, arms at his side.

A thin voice called from inside the bedroom. "Hey, jerkface."

"Hey," Eddie whispered.

"Where you been?"

"Jack's."

"He let you play on his trampoline?"

Eddie nodded.

"Good."

"Are you going to get better?"

Elle didn't answer.

I held a breath as Eddie entered the bedroom. I stepped behind him, peering in around the door to watch. Elle lay under her comforter. Her face was pale and drawn. I spotted a wooden wafer hanging on a length of yarn around her neck. Probably a health charm.

She reached out from under her blanket for Eddie, who stepped slowly to his sister.

"You will," Eddie mumbled. "Dorian's fixing it."

I stepped away from the door. I didn't want Elle to spot me. The last thing Eddie needed at that moment was for the thing inside of her to get stirred up. Plus, I wasn't fixing anything. I made a phone call, and that's about all I did. This thing was beyond my capacity, and I hated that the Swains seemed to think I was some kind of hero.

Edgar watched me from the front of the hall. I gave him a cock of my head. "Nice charm, there."

He grinned and shrugged.

I prodded, "Enochian?"

"With a little neodruid. Wren helped."

"I'm glad you're not in Baltimore. You two would put me out of business."

Edgar kept an eye on the kids while I moved back into the front of their loft. I found Wren in the kitchen, holding out a glass of what I assumed was pink lemonade. I took it and sucked back a long sip.

"What happened?" I asked.

"The people he was staying with had a family emergency. He didn't have anywhere else to go."

"We almost made it. One more day and this could have been all over."

Wren guided me to a chair. "Edgar told me about this woman you're flying in. I'm not crazy happy about this."

I nodded slowly. "Neither am I. But she's the best we can find. And I mean, she's the best anyone can find."

Wren looked me in the eyes. "She's a murderer."

"In the sense that a soldier in a war can be called a murderer."

"She's not a soldier. She's a thug."

I held up my hands. "Still, there's a war between her people and the Presidium. They disappear people all the time. She's just returning force with what force was given."

"And now we're caught in the crossfire."

"Looks that way," I grumbled.

Wren put a hand on my arm. "Dorian? Are you really okay with cursing this Carmody guy?"

"You have to ask?"

"If the Presidium finds out about it, chances are you'll get disappeared too."

"But Elle would be okay. That's all that matters. She's family."

Wren stepped around the back of my chair before throwing both arms around my shoulders.

"So are you." As she pulled away, I caught her wiping a single tear from her cheek. "So, you want to do it in your ritual space, Edgar says?"

"That's right. The less Gillette moves the better."

"I don't want Eddie involved."

"Agreed. Is there no one else he can stay with?"

She shook her head. "We're running out of friends. And with all this, I don't feel like leaving him with a stranger."

I took a step back and snapped my fingers. "Yeah. That's right."

"What?"

"I might have a solution."

I hopped out onto their balcony and pulled my phone to make a call.

"Hello?"

"Ches? It's Dorian."

"Hey."

I pulled in a breath. "Listen, you told me you wanted to help me out with Elle?"

Her voice rose a register. "Yes, definitely!"

"I might have this figured out, but I need your help."

"What's the plan?"

"Mostly I need you to babysit."

Long pause. "You're kidding."

"Really not."

"You want me to babysit Elle?"

"Her brother. Their parents and I are about to bring her to Baltimore, and none of us want him to be exposed to this."

"Back up a bit. What are you going to do? I mean, how are you going to fix Elle?"

"Long story. I'll fill you in when it's done. In the meantime we really, really need someone to watch Eddie for the next, oh, eighteen hours."

"Eighteen... Dorian, I said I wanted to help—"

"Awesome. They're in Frederick, by the way. It's about an hour west."

She shuffled her phone with a lot of ruffling. "You realize I have class in the morning, right? Can you bring Eddie here to Baltimore?"

I hadn't thought of that, but as I gave it a second's consideration I realized that I didn't want either Eddie or Ches in the same city as Gillette. There was just too much that could go wrong, especially with Carmody on the warpath.

"It's basically a hundred times safer out here in Frederick." Her silence didn't give me lots of encouragement. "Ches? This is end game. Last thing we have to do. It's all over after this."

"What aren't you telling me?"

"What do you mean?"

Her voice dropped a little. "Why are you brooming me out of Baltimore?"

"Am I that obvious?"

She muttered, "I told you I'm a pro at sniffing out bullshit."

"Okay, truth is I don't want you in Baltimore. I basically have two practitioners at war with each other, and I'm choosing sides. I don't want you in the trenches."

"Well, thank you for leveling with me. And the answer is yes. I'll help."

Muscles I didn't know were tensed released across my back. "You're a life-saver."

"I'll pack some things and get there as soon as I can. What's the address?"

I gave Ches some basic directions and stepped back inside. Wren sat at the table next to Eddie. I gave the boy a smile. "How're you doing, buddy?"

"I'm okay."

"You are, aren't you?"

Wren asked, "Well? What's going on?"

"I called Ches. She'll watch Eddie here overnight."

Wren closed her eyes and nodded with a sigh. "Okay."

"We should pack some things."

"Edgar's already on it."

"That much faith in me?"

Wren smirked. "What's family for?" She stood up and ruffled my hair. "Well, you're not like a brother or anything. More like the asshole cousin who keeps calling in the middle of the night for bail money."

"I'll take it."

She disappeared into the back, leaving me with Eddie.

He stared at me for a while before asking, "Is she your girlfriend?"

"Who, Ches?"

"Yeah."

"That's right. You met her once."

"She's the spy?"

"Barista. She just makes coffee. Also, she's a psychologist, so don't try to pull anything over on her, or she'll tell your Mom."

The Swains put together a bag for Elle, and Edgar finally reappeared lugging it in tow.

"You set?" I asked.

He shrugged. "I guess so. Ches is coming?"

"You okay with that?"

"She's cool. Glad she's talking to you again."

"Listen, there's something that you might need to know about."

"What now?"

"You remember Julian Bright?"

"Yeah."

"He's just been publically stoned for a relationship with a minor. He's resigned his office, and probably won't be able to work in politics again."

Edgar winced. "Fuck."

"Right?"

"That sucks, but what does that have to do with us?"

"Carmody."

"What about him?"

"Who do you think leaked the story to the news?"

Edgar squinted and jutted out his jaw. "He's swinging back at you?"

"Preemptive. A warning shot."

"Think he's got something on us?"

"I'd be prepared for it. Until the curse takes hold, however it takes hold, he's going to be a threat."

Edgar stared at the floor, then paced a tight circle. "Okay. We'll be ready for him."

I found myself wandering down to the store, watching Carroll Street for Ches. At the hour mark, my phone buzzed in my pocket. I figured Ches had gotten lost and was nudging me for directions.

I was wrong.

It was a text from Carmody, a single word. *RECONSIDER?*

Before I could even ignore the comment and shove the phone back into my pocket, it buzzed one more time. This time Carmody had sent me a photo. It was just a single photo.

It was the act of a desperate man, but it succeeded in knocking the wind out of me.

CHAPTER THIRTY-TWO

My knees weakened, and I grabbed the door frame to keep from hitting the floor. The phone shook in my hand. No, it was my hand that was shaking.

I stuffed the phone into my pocket to keep from dropping it, but managed to get my legs again. I paced. Keeping my feet moving helped to keep the vertigo of cascading thoughts from physically knocking me over. My brain spun with calculation, deduction, contemplation. My heart raced. I balled up fists. Before I could turn another corner to pace, I kicked at an old coat rack, sending it teetering across the shop floor.

Edgar poked his head down the stairs at me, but I held up a hand with enough force to warn him off. He disappeared back upstairs, and I managed to snap out of my cycle of anger and alarm. I had no idea how to deal with this latest salvo from Carmody. None.

Tires crunched up the alley beside the store, and I bolted for the door. I spotted the back end of Ches's crappy, old blue Chrysler sliding between buildings, and released a long slow breath between my teeth. I trotted around the corner and found her stepping out of her car. She turned and gave me a bashful grin.

"Hey," she chirped.

"Hey."

"Sorry it took so long to get here. Missed my exit, and couldn't figure out how to turn around."

"Yeah," I grumbled.

She cocked her head at me. "You okay?"

"Sure."

"You look pale."

I stretched my neck and took another deep breath. "No, I'm fine. This has just been one hell of a month."

"Everyone inside?"

"Yeah, but I wanted to catch you before we go in."

"What's up?"

I cleared my throat and tried to shake the nerves out of my arms. "I really suck at this, so I'm probably going to ramble. Bear with me."

She frowned and leaned against her car.

"Okay, so, I feel like I owe you an apology."

"For what?"

I held up my hand. "Just let me go with this, or I'm going to screw it up. I feel like you've given me a couple second chances already, and maybe it's because I've been making assumptions about you. Maybe it's my past, maybe my upbringing. I'm not sure, really. But I haven't given you enough credit. I assumed you couldn't handle the Life, and that's my fault."

Her frown melted into a thoughtful melancholy.

"It's possible I've misjudged you for as long as I've known you. That makes me feel like shit because I could have saved us both a lot of suffering if I had just taken time to know you instead assuming I already knew."

"This all sounds really sweet, Dorian, but I really don't follow you."

"Yeah, I suppose not. I have this bad habit of taking the blame for other people's dickbaggery. I mean, look at Elle. Some rank amateur stuck this thing inside her, and they didn't have any clue what that would do to her or the servitor."

Ches blinked at the word, and leaned back. "The what?"

"Servitor. Cognizant thoughtform."

"You think that's what this is?"

"I know it is. And I blamed myself for the longest time because it was clearly sent to screw with me. I'm not entirely sure why, or why the person McHenry hired to fuck with me didn't have the basic sense God gave an eggplant. Because if they did, they would have known children have a basic fundamental psychic shielding that makes them living soul traps. They would have known this thing would begin to starve to death inside that girl, and it would have to consume the host's soul to survive. They would have known they were effectively murdering a thirteen-year-old girl, but they were too incredibly, unforgivably stupid to put that together. Either that, or they were so thunderously arrogant they thought they could fix this before it turned into my personal crusade. Before I got creative. And when I get creative? I get scary."

She took a step back. "Why… why are you telling me this?"

"Because I'm curious, and I want to know. Was it arrogance or ignorance, Ches?"

"What?"

"I'm betting on ignorance because as cool as you played me this entire time, I don't think for a second you're capable of murder."

Her eyes narrowed.

I pulled my phone from my pocket and flipped to the photo Carmody sent me just minutes ago… a photo of Ches receiving an envelope from McHenry. It looked like they were on a boat, probably on the Bay. A discreet meeting. A payoff.

Services rendered.

She shook her head and took another step away.

"Francesca? Is that even your name?"

"Yes."

Bile burned in my esophagus. "Well, at least there's that."

She sighed and slapped her leg. "That fucking scumbag." She worked her jaw, grinding her teeth as she stared into the distance. "For the record," she added, "it was ignorance."

I turned and walked a few paces to keep from blowing my top. I paused behind her Chrysler. The old blue Chrysler. I had seen it once before.

"It was you. At the campaign office. You were there watching us."

She turned and nodded curtly.

I squinted at her license plate.

"Oregon tags?" I looked up at Ches. "You're not even from Florida."

Her eyes were heavy. With a ragged breath, she answered, "I went to Disneyworld, once."

"Don't!" I held a finger up and paced around her car, putting it between us.

Her voice drifted from across her hood. "I didn't have a lot of choice."

"That's crap."

"It's true. Yes, I lied to you. But I had to." Ches unfolded her arms and turned to lean against the fender. "That wasn't supposed to happen. You're right. I didn't know this stupid thing would get trapped inside Elle."

"Why did you even send it to her? What did she ever do to you?"

"It was supposed to be in and out like the other one. That was actually how it was supposed to happen. Short. Sudden. Then back out again. Just enough to rattle you. That was the job, keep you distracted. He wanted you out of the campaign."

I growled, "McHenry."

She nodded. "That was the plan."

"Instead, you performed a working without full possession of the facts. And now Elle is paying for it."

"I told you I wanted to help." She looked over to me, her eyes weary. "And I meant that. I tried pulling it back out. It just can't leave. It's changed, anyway. I've lost my energetic affinity. I think it's mutated. Wound too tightly around her mainline."

"The night Elle got out. She wasn't coming to my house. She was coming to you."

"I tried. I really did. All I did was weaken it."

I shook my head. "Where did you study soul magic, anyway?"

"Where do you think?"

I thought about it. "Oregon. Quinn Gillette?" Oh, fuck me. "You were her student?"

Ches' face soured. "I was until Carmody screwed us all."

"What happened?"

"Quinn was brokering borders with the Dead Ch'ans, dividing up the Willamette Valley, so we could stop the open fighting."

I held up a hand. "I'm already lost, here."

"I'm not surprised. No offense, Dorian, but you really have no idea what it's like outside of the Presidium's sphere of control. Out there, where every working has consequences, no matter how elementary. Where you can't even buy reagents without permission from four cabals. Where you keep wardings sewn into your clothes in case some vodoun decides to take offense over something your lodge-mate did years ago. The Presidium has a good thing going here, which was why Carmody dragged me out here."

"What did Carmody do?"

"He sold the Ch'ans a list of our addresses. People like Quinn and her seconds were safe. People like me? Not so much. They came after us. Our families. After the third 'accident,' we realized what was happening, but all I could do was beg Quinn to intervene. By then, she was hip-deep in a war with the Ch'ans, and my brother and his family had a curse carved into their door."

My shoulders wilted. I took a seat on her hood, back-to-back with Ches as she continued.

"I knew a few unmaking spells."

"Proto-Egyptian?"

"Uh, yeah. How did you—"

"Go on."

"I tried to unwind the Ch'an curse, but it was too strong. I saved their lives, but not their marriage. I moved my brother to a safe house, but without an address, he couldn't fight for custody of his kids. I had to make a deal with the Ch'ans to keep him safe."

"Let me guess. Carmody brokered the deal?"

"When Quinn found out, we were both screwed. Coming to the East Coast was Carmody's idea. We'd be safe from Quinn, and as long as we kept our heads down, we wouldn't have to worry about the Presidium." She sighed. "But he got restless. Started nosing around the practitioner community from Atlanta to New York, looking for work. He couldn't do any business without crossing the line into Netherwork. It seems there's only one Curse Merchant on the East Coast, and he doesn't take on many clients."

I looked over my shoulder, but held my tongue.

"Yes, I know it's you."

I turned away.

She continued, "Then my brother sent me an email. He was broke and couldn't pay the lawyer. I mean, I got him into this. He didn't ask for any of it, and here he was about to lose his kids."

"So you went to Carmody."

"He got me together with McHenry. By the time I sent the money to my brother, I realized McHenry was just as scary as Quinn. There wasn't anything I could do."

I sighed and pushed off of the car, walking around to face Ches.

"Is your brother still in danger?"

"No. He's safe from the Ch'ans and Quinn. It's not her style to go after innocents."

"What about you? You're in school under your real name. You don't think Gillette will find you here?"

She took a deep breath and looked up at the side of the Swain's building. "I'm sure she could if she really tried. I suppose I'm banking on it being too much trouble for her. I'm small potatoes."

Clearing my throat, I offered, "She's way more pissed at Carmody. I can tell you that much."

Ches nodded. "That's not surprising. He's a genuine pile of shit." She looked over at me. "Dorian, you can believe me or not. But I had no idea this would happen to your friends. To Elle. I didn't mean to hurt anyone."

"I do believe you, as a matter of fact. But as scary as Gillette is, as scary as McHenry is… do you have any idea what the Presidium would do to you if they knew you had created a servitor and sicced it on innocent people?"

She scowled and looked back down to her lap.

I took a step forward. "And that's not the worst of it." I pointed up to the side of the building. "There's a mother in there who is probably the most frightening force of nature I've ever encountered. If she ever finds out you're responsible for this, you'd better find a god to pray to."

"If?"

I shook my head and leaned against the car beside her.

"What the hell was with you jumping me at the café?"

She started and stopped the same sentence a few times before finally saying, "I needed distance."

"I'm listening."

"We kept talking. And you invited me over. And then you asked me out, and then you got kicked out of that horrible Club. I was happy for you, but you were crushed." She let slip a single laugh. "You're so much more likable when you're not trying to be."

We stayed there in silence for a while before she asked, "Are you going to tell them? About me?"

I chewed on my lip for a minute, pondering the question.

"The way I see it," I answered, "that won't help anyone. Look, Carmody can still go to the Presidium with this, and you'll end up with a black bag over your face. And no one will ever hear from you again. Carmody has to go away. For good. And happily, that was more or less my plan to begin with."

"I want to be there."

"You can't."

She hopped off the car and faced me with a frown. "Why not? This is still my thoughtform. I still have some affinity with it. Together, maybe we can—"

"Gillette's coming."

She closed her mouth and took a step back.

I continued, "She's going to remove it. So the best thing you can do is stay here in Frederick and just keep Eddie safe while she cleans up your mess."

"And then?"

"And then we'll see."

She nodded, then peered up at me. "I actually thought you'd be more pissed off than this."

I had to think about that for a second. "I am, in fact, pissed off. But you're right about something. I don't know what it's like out there. I don't know what it was like to live like that, and I have no idea what it's like to be you. So right now, we're going to go up there and help the Swains pack up. Then you're going to be a charming, nurturing, and as perfect a companion for Eddie as is physically possible. Nothing… absolutely nothing… is going to happen to Eddie. Are we on the same page here?"

Ches nodded slowly.

"I'm trusting you with him, Ches."

"I understand."

She extended her hand.

I shook it, adding, "I'm not sure I do."

I turned and led her around the corner and into the shop. The bags were packed, and all that remained was to situate Ches and Eddie, and to feel out the best method for coaxing Elle into a car and down the freeway.

The time came for Edgar to guide Elle out of her room. She looked alarmingly thin like she had been starved for a month. Her sunken eyes twisted up at my face, and they set with as much edge as Elle's body could muster. But there was no taunting or invective. No posturing. Just anger and slow death.

I heard a voice gasp "Oh, my God" over my shoulder. I turned to find Ches covering her mouth, her eyes red-rimmed.

Elle's eyes transferred to Ches, and her lips pulled back to reveal a hard sneer. It knew where to assign blame. Ches had created the thing and sent it to its death. And now it stared its creator in the face, neither one capable of solving the problem.

Wren put an arm around Ches. "Thank you for coming."

Ches turned away from Wren and nodded quietly.

Elle sucked in a rasping breath, probably preparing to release some kind of indictment in bile against Ches. But I stepped in front of her and lifted a finger. Elle's sneer melted into a frown.

"Tomorrow morning, you'll be free."

Both Elle and the servitor seemed to understand.

CHAPTER THIRTY-THREE

The trip was fairly uneventful. Edgar followed me in the Jeep while Wren held Elle in my back seat. I caught glimpses of the two of them in my rearview mirror, squinting against the sun setting behind us. Wren looked tired, reaching over to rub the wooden charm around Elle's neck to keep its energy up. Elle, on the other hand, kept staring with those glassy eyes directly back at me. When we reached my house, I helped guide Elle up the stoop and into the front room.

"Where should we put her?" Wren asked as Edgar closed and locked the front door.

"We'll do the ritual downstairs, but for now let's just keep her comfortable." I pointed at my futon, and they settled her onto the cushion while I fetched one of the pillows from my bed and the yarn afghan Aunt Viv mailed me six years ago. I put on a pot of coffee while Wren hummed some kind of lullaby to Elle. Edgar joined me in the kitchen and poured us all some thick, bracing mugs of coffee.

The evening was quiet, being a Sunday night. No one was on the street, and there were no ball games to break the peace. At times the only sound in the house was the whistling of my air conditioner vents as Edgar, Wren, and I sat in the front room staring at each other. In time, both of them nodded off, despite the coffee's best efforts. And I was left alone.

With Elle.

"You're going to fail," the servitor hissed through Elle's dried lips.

"No, I'm not."

"This vessel is doomed. Her soul is only a stain, now."

"I'd worry about yourself."

"Why do you force yourself onto your own fate?"

I checked the Swains. They looked like they were catching up on a week's sleep, and probably were.

"It's a living."

"It's folly."

"I'm good at it."

"Why can you not accept your fate?"

"Because I didn't choose it."

"Naturally."

"I don't have a lot of faith in forces I don't control. If you don't understand that, then I'm sorry."

"You find misery in your craft because you know it's a sham."

"I get that a psychology major crafted you in her image, but I really could go without the head shrinking."

"Nothing you do creates anything but a zero sum. On your death, you will look on your life, and you will realize you had no power."

I leaned forward and lifted my voice just above a whisper. "Look. As much as I accept the supernatural, you are quite simply an abomination. The fumbling failure of a novice. A screw up. You tell me nothing in my life is more than breaking even? Well, you can go to Hell. I choose the life I live. And I'm done with you."

I leaned back and closed my eyes.

Elle's breathing dropped into a light snore after a while, and I was finally alone with my thoughts.

I finished the coffee pot in time for my phone to warn me of my schedule. I stirred Edgar awake with a nudge of my shoe. He groaned, pulled off his spectacles to rub his eyes, then hoisted himself up to join me in the kitchen.

"I have to go get Gillette."

"You need me to come with?"

"No. Don't want to surprise her. And I need you here with Wren in case Elle gets cagey."

"Tell me straight, Dorian. Can she get it done?"

"I think so. She seems to think so, at least. It's our best shot."

"Okay, then."

I left the Swains reclining in my front room and drove south of the city to the airport. The airport itself was flooded with people in business suits preparing for their day's travel. I grabbed a bench on the public side of the security gates and kept a close eye on the arrivals board. A plane from Chicago was scheduled to arrive at seven-ten. That would have to be Gillette's.

I caught eyes peering away from me here and there. Innocuous men and women in bland suits. The Presidium was keeping a close eye on this arrival, even though they had pledged Gillette's safety. Not only had they pledged not to move against her, they had vouchsafed her safety while under the terms of the letter.

I finally spotted Gillette stomping through the gate, still wearing her trench coat. I stood up and gave her a nod. She marched up to me and paused, waiting for me to say something.

"Welcome to Maryland."

"So, where are we doing this?"

I escorted Gillette to the parking garage. We shared an elevator ride with a stranger whom I assumed was one of the Presidium's enforcers. When we cleared the parking garage and were finally alone on the freeway, I asked, "Is there anything you need for the extraction? Reagents? Tools?"

"I don't use tools."

"How does that work?"

She didn't answer. Apparently, this wasn't meant to be a learning exercise.

"I have the family at my work space already. If it's alright with you, I'd like to get started immediately."

"I'll require some time to prepare my consciousness."

"Um, okay. How much time?"

"Depends on how long it takes the drugs to kick in."

"Drugs?"

"Nothing illegal, relax. Souls aren't physical elements that can be portioned, divided, and disposed of. More like forces to be channeled. The only effective way to manipulate soul energy is in creating an affinity with their essence. This takes decades of mind alteration to be useful."

"Noted. So, minutes? Hours?"

She rolled her eyes. "A couple hours."

"That should work."

"After your curse."

"I'll perform the curse when you're good and altered, thank you. I want zero down time."

"Why are you so squeamish about this?"

"Why aren't you?"

She snickered. "Have you met Carmody?"

We arrived back at the house without incident. I escorted Gillette through the front door, where she paused as she laid eyes on the Swains. She gave Wren and Edgar only the merest of acknowledgments, but when she spotted Elle her face drew long. Her eyes lifted to mine, filling with as human an expression as I had seen from the woman. Gillette put a hand on Elle's head and swallowed hard.

"I should get started," she muttered, turning to me. "Where is your ritual space?"

I led her to the steel door to my basement work space. She paused to inspect the energy of my wardings, seemingly satisfied as she plodded down the stairs. I had arranged as much space as I could downstairs, moving my reagents to a corner cabinet and finally relocating the more harmless of my craft theory books back upstairs. I had even taken the precaution of locking the cabinet with Emil's Library in case Gillette got light fingers. Gillette walked a single circle around my work table and sighed.

"Cozy."

"It's home."

"It'll be adequate." She reached into her trench coat and produced a tiny black pouch, which she unzipped to reveal two syringes and a vial of liquid.

"They let you on the plane with that?" I quipped.

"Travel kit for diabetics."

She pulled off her trench coat, revealing a sleeveless shirt and surprisingly muscular arms. She folded her coat and handed it to me distractedly.

I took her coat. "Need anything? A chair?"

"No. Just time."

She stared at me until I realized I had been dismissed.

I ascended the stairs and dropped her coat onto a chair in the kitchen. Edgar and Wren looked on nervously as I poured myself some orange juice and took a seat.

Wren blurted, "Well?"

"She has to get ready."

"For what?"

"The extraction. What else? Said it would take a couple hours."

Wren wilted slightly and returned to the couch.

By eight-thirty we were all bobbing in and out of the room, walking off nervous energy. When my phone rang I nearly jumped out of my skin. It was Ches.

"Something wrong?" I answered.

"Just a warning. Child Protective Services stopped by."

"Oh, shit."

"I did what I could. They weren't happy Elle wasn't here, but I don't think they're calling in the sheriff just yet."

"This was Carmody. What did you tell them?"

"I told them everyone was at Hershey Park."

"Seriously?"

"Yeah. Best I could do with, like, no warning. Eddie backed me up, too. Said he was afraid of heights. He's a pretty good kid."

"Yes, he is. Okay. Give me a call if cops arrive."

"Have you started yet?"

"No." I lowered my voice. "Gillette's here. Apparently she has to chase the dragon before we can start."

"Anyone ever tell you that you have a really strange way of talking?"

"Never once. Gotta go."

I broke the news to the Swains, who seemed to take it in stride. Like me, they were far more focused on the actual immediate goal. Carmody had to have called that in yesterday; it would have taken CPS a day to respond. I wondered how many more surprises Carmody had lined up for me.

My foyer clock struck nine o'clock, and I fought the urge to check on Gillette. The last thing I needed to do was to start this whole process over. Edgar offered to get doughnuts, but when we all agreed he just stood at the door, unable to actually leave. I couldn't blame him.

Finally, somewhere between nine and nine-thirty, I heard a voice call from downstairs. I pulled open the steel door, and Gillette repeated, "It is time."

I turned to the Swains, both on their feet, and gave them a slow blink.

"Last chance to talk me out of this, guys."

Edgar looked to Wren, who just lifted her chin an inch.

It was decided.

I stepped through my kitchen and opened the side alley door to pluck a glass mason jar from the outside window with its week's worth of collected rain water. A stray seed pod from the trash tree in my neighbor's front landscape floated along the surface, as did a couple mosquito nymphs. They were welcome additions to this ritual. Mosquitos were dreadful creatures that never asked permission to drain the life from their prey. They were a fine component for invasive magic.

I pulled the door closed behind me as I marched down the stairs. Gillette sat in the corner, propping her back up against the concrete block wall. Her eyes moved in quick, sudden jerks. Her energy was disorganized, spearing out into the room without focus or shape. I re-centered myself and stepped through the cloud of energy hosing out of Gillette's chakras to pull a canvas box from underneath my work table.

One by one I set the reagents and tools onto the table. One burial shroud, vacuumed. Spider silk. A quarter ounce of twelve karat gold. My old iron smelting pot and a slug of coal powder. A liquid ounce of tar. One quill. And finally the tiny specimen of blood that Amy had drawn from Carmody. Laid before me were the ingredients for a Nether Curse, a twisting of the natural laws intended to bring the doom or downfall of another against their will and the will of the Cosmos. This act carried with it a penalty by way of the insulted Cosmos, typically in the form of damnation. Damnation itself was a subjective term, but in the case of educated practitioners, it meant selling your soul to whatever power had the interest and ability to execute your Curse across the Veil.

However, I was not in possession of a soul at the moment, so I felt very little otherworldly compulsion as I lit the charcoal slug to heat up my cauldron. When the iron was hot, I dropped in the gold which melted immediately. I spread out the burial cloth across my work table, pinning it at the intersecting nodes of the Golden Spiral engraved on the table's surface. From this point on, I had to sharpen my focus to a razor's edge. No other intent could enter into my mind. No extraneous thoughts, no emotions. This was the true Hermetic Art. Self-mastery.

I dipped the quill into the molten gold and started scribing the curse onto the cloth. The gold flowed unevenly along the course linen weave, but I broadened the length and height of my script to accommodate. I walked a circle around the table, scribing the verbiage of the curse in a widdershins spiral. I had chosen an old Brythonic dialect to scribe the curse, due in part to Carmody's seeming roots to the British Isles, but also by virtue of old Celtic magic and its indirect paths to calamity. It was as lazy as it was vicious, which suited Carmody nicely.

The greatest pull on my concentration was Gillette, still sitting in her in-between state of inebriation and intensity. I felt her eyes on me, boring through me as I concluded the scribing. My fingers cramped when I dropped the quill back underneath the table. I wondered for a moment how much time I had consumed in the process, but quickly pushed it aside. Time always seemed relative in the ritual space.

Next came the tar. I poured it into the cauldron over the leftover gold, stirring it with a stainless steel rod. A tiny nautilus of gold laced into the black tar as the odor filled the work space. I charged the tar with my intent. I ruminated on Carmody, picturing his face, hearing his voice with its tight-lipped inflection, feeling the anger that rose when I thought about Julian and the wreck of his meteoric career. It was a fight to keep that emotion pure, free of diversions into guilt and betrayal. The problem with Nether Curses was that they had to draw strength from emotion. Most Netherworkers fell prey to their own emotions, often stitching their own karma into the very curse they were firing. I couldn't afford that, even assuming I would find my soul again someday.

The tar fully charged, I pulled the cauldron from its stand by its handle and tipped the iron bowl with the steel rod. A delicate trickle of black landed on top of my gold script. I walked a slow circle once again, covering the script in hate-charged tar. I struggled to keep the flow steady and even as footsteps from the guests above gnawed at my attention.

Focus. Focus was paramount.

Once the black spiral was complete, I set aside the cauldron and reached for the final, most vital reagent. Carmody's blood. I dropped the tube from the blood test kit into the mason jar and gave it a gentle swish. In the space of a minute, the rainwater blurred into a light red. It wouldn't take much of this diluted blood to charge the curse, but I wanted to rehydrate as much of the blood as I could just to be sure. I didn't want to come back to this table for the same curse.

More footsteps clambered upstairs, and I heard a furniture leg screech against the hardwood floor. The Swains knew better than this. One stray alien thought crossed my mind, threatening to derail the entire working. What if Elle was causing trouble?

The panic center of my brain kicked around dire possibilities. Was she having a seizure? Was the servitor making a final attempt to escape? Two decades worth of rigorous training under a particularly surly Spaniard unraveled as I listened to the scuffling upstairs.

But it was the shriek that really pulled me out of the moment.

CHAPTER THIRTY-FOUR

I set the jar of blood-water down on the center of the shroud and took a step to the stairs.

"Everyone okay up there?"

The shuffling paused, and I was answered with a blurt I couldn't make out through the door. It was likely to completely offset the intent I had already laced into the curse, but I couldn't let this continue upstairs. I still had the blood, and if I had to, I could dig up more gold from my mother's old jewelry chest.

I fished a hunk of hematite from my stone shelf and grounded out the remaining charge from my hands and turned for the door.

I froze, however, when I heard the latch engage and the door slide against its massive hinges.

"Hello?" I called around the corner of the stairs.

"Suppose you couldn't hear me through this bleeding vault door of yours," Carmody's voice dribbled down the stairs.

Gillette's wandering eyes centered on me for a brief moment.

"Carmody?" I responded.

"I require your attention presently. Best haul your bollocks up here before someone gets hurt."

Gillette's mouth drew back into a sneer.

I held up a finger to my lips, then gestured with wide palms for her to stay put.

"Lake? I am not taking the piss here. Upstairs, now."

Edgar's voice called down with a tremolo, "He has a gun."

Fuck.

I held up my hands, took in a breath, and started up the stairs. When I crested the steel door's threshold, I spotted Carmody standing in my front room, his back to the windows. He gripped Wren by the hair on the back of her head, arm straight out. His other hand had a revolver trained at the center of her back. Edgar stood by the futon, his hands up by his face, his body shielding Elle.

"And there he is," Carmody proclaimed. "Had me worried. Thought he was going to let you bite a bullet, love."

"Carmody, you can't be serious with this," I said.

"Can't I?"

"A gun?"

"Oh, that offends you, does it? Here you are in your basement with a fully loaded curse cocked and ready to fire."

"Don't do this, Carmody. You're asking for trouble here that even you can't weasel out of."

"Then let's be brief, shall we? You salt my blood, and we'll call it even."

I bit my lip. He was dead serious about this. I didn't have any leverage on Carmody. All I had was an arrangement with Gillette. Carmody had a gun. At that moment, the gun was more compelling. Still, if I salted his blood, I'd ruin its efficacy, and I wouldn't be able to even start over with the curse.

"Listen to me. You drew me into this conflict between you and Gillette. You could have stayed out of the Life, left well enough alone. But you had to get greedy, didn't you?"

"A man has certain material needs, mate."

"You really thought you could start up Netherworking this close to D.C.?"

"It's a gamble. Safer than Portland, at any rate. Unfortunately for me, Swain here doesn't carry human skin in his shop, so fuck me sideways."

"That's a lot of lives you're ruining over a gamble."

"Oh, cry me to sleep. Now if you don't mind dispensing with the chit chat, I'd very much like to see you salt my blood and be on my way." He tightened his grip on Wren's hair. "Or are you such a soulless piece of shit you don't mind watching your friends get their skulls ventilated?"

Edgar flinched.

I held a hand out to Edgar, trying to interrupt his impulse to jump the man.

"Murder, Carmody. Actual hands-on murder isn't like a curse, and you know it. A curse is coincidence in the eyes of the law. A gun? That's something that'll get the FBI crawling so far up your ass you'll be shitting Quantico blue for the rest of your life in federal prison."

"Then let's not force me into that uncomfortable predicament, shall we? You're not the one who wants me. I know it. You know it. It's Gillette who wants me, and when I'm long gone, she'll find some other poor bastard for you to dash to pieces in her name."

"I don't have time. She doesn't have time," I added pointing to Elle.

"Right. Very sorry about that, but that wasn't my doing."

"Perhaps not directly. But you're the one who put the hermetic merc into McHenry's hands."

"And she's the one you should be cursing, mate. Isn't she the one who created this particular little nightmare scenario?"

"We all share a little blame on that account. But right this very second adding to the suffering isn't going to—"

A shadow loomed in the leaded glass pane of my front door, and a heavy knock rang through the house.

Carmody's eyes narrowed, and he pushed the gun into Wren's back, causing her to yelp.

Edgar looked to me in panic.

"Who's that, then?" Carmody growled.

"No idea."

"Everyone shut your yap until it goes away."

Another knock, and a low, thunderous voice called through the door, "Yo, Mister Lake! You home?"

I recognized the voice. Tyrel.

"It's a tenant," I whispered.

Carmody rolled his eyes and leaned back to look through the front window.

"Right. Get rid of him." He added as I stepped toward the foyer, "I don't have to warn you about kinky business, right?"

I nodded and cracked open the door to the chain.

Tyrel stood on the stoop in a snappy shirt and slacks, his head freshly shaven.

"Hey, Mister Lake."

"Tyrel?"

He waved a stack of papers in front of me. "You said to come to you if we had questions. I'm on my way to the bank, and I have questions. You got a minute?"

I squinted and took a deep breath. "Actually, I have some friends over."

"Oh. Sorry."

"No, it's okay. Just old friends who stop by, you know. Like your neighbors across the street."

Tyrel's eyes narrowed, and he glanced over to my front windows.

I continued, "I'd be happy to chat later, though."

Tyrel clenched his jaw and gave me a prodding look.

I moved my eyes deliberately to the side of the house.

"Thanks for understanding."

Tyrel nodded. "Uh, oh. Yeah. Not a problem, Mister Lake."

"I'll see you soon?"

"Sure thing. Have a good time with your friends."

Tyrel trotted back to the street, turning casually toward my alley.

I closed the door slowly and neatly, and turned to Carmody.

"Done."

"And you're stalling, mate. The blood. Now."

I lifted my hands. "Alright, alright. You win, dammit. I'll do it."

"That's a smart chap."

I marched to the basement stairs and added over my shoulder, "I can trust you not to get gun-stupid while I'm downstairs?"

"Despite my course appearance, Lake, I am actually a perfect gentleman when you get to know me."

"Right."

I descended the stairs, and found Gillette hovering by the bottom step. I gestured for her to step aside, but she wouldn't budge.

"He doesn't know you're here," I whispered into her ear as I squeezed past her.

"You lose that blood, I won't lift a finger for that girl," she whispered back.

"Yeah, well right now I'm more worried about bullets than servitors."

"Your call."

I gripped the mason jar of rose liquid and turned back for the stairs. "I know."

Gillette moved aside.

I climbed back upstairs slowly, trying not to spill a drop of the liquid. Carmody's eyes lit up as I arrived in sight. His posture stiffened, however, as I turned to the hall.

"Where are you going, then?"

"Salt's in the kitchen, Einstein."

I gestured with my head, and Carmody tightened his grip on Wren's hair even further. She released a sputtering exhale.

"You," he barked at Edgar, "stay in front of me."

Edgar looked over his shoulder at Elle, who was lying on the couch, eyes closed, seemingly oblivious. I hoped she was asleep. Finally he wilted and moved in front of Wren, his hands still held up to his ears.

I turned to the kitchen and paused. The door to the alley was ajar.

I let Edgar catch up with me. This was my gamble. Edgar had to keep it cool. There was no way to communicate with him, no time to warn him. I just had to leave up to the Cosmos.

Three steps into the kitchen, I spotted Tyrel in my periphery, but didn't move my head. I set the jar on the table and moved to a cabinet across the kitchen from Tyrel.

Edgar stepped behind me, turning his shoulders to watch me, and doing so turning his back to Tyrel.

I fished a canister of kosher salt from the top shelf of my pantry cabinet and paused. Carmody wasn't inside the kitchen. He and Wren were parked in the doorway. I moved back to the table and put my back to Carmody, blocking his line of sight with the blood water.

I chanced a peek to Edgar, who stared at me with panicked bewilderment. With as modest a shift of my eyes as I could manage, I looked behind him at Tyrel, then back to Edgar.

Edgar's posture stiffened, and he shuffled several feet to the side.

I exhaled, and picked up the box of salt, being sure to keep it close in front of me. Carmody would have to enter the kitchen to watch.

Pausing for a moment, I listened for movement. Nothing.

I took a chance and poured a handful of salt onto the table, allowing some to spill to the side.

A shuffling of feet behind me let me know he was agitated.

"Here, Lake. What did I say about kinky business?"

"What?"

"I want to see it."

"Then come see it. Christ."

Wren grunted, and feet stepped forward.

I heard a thin yelp from Wren, and turned just in time to see Carmody's gun hand slip into view of the kitchen. Wren's eyes were planted on Tyrel, now just inches from the two of them.

I turned with a handful of salt, gripping Carmody's blood with my other hand.

"Here, Carmody. You don't trust me?" I dropped the salt into the jar. The weak energy signature in the diluted blood flickered into an electric saline death. "There. You win."

Tyrel's arm dropped down on Carmody's gun hand, and he slammed his shoulders into Carmody's ribs.

Wren twisted in Carmody's grip, shrieking as she wrenched her hair free.

Tyrel and Carmody careened across the kitchen, smashing into a door jamb on their way to the floor. I backed away and watched as the gun emerged from the two-man pile with two sets of hands gripping it. Tyrel had slipped the meat of his thumb over the hammer, though he grunted as Carmody lifted his knee repeatedly into his side.

Edgar slid past my legs and clamped his fingers over the revolver chamber. He wrestled with the gun with a series of quick jerks, but couldn't pry it from Carmody's hand. He shook his head with enough violence to send his spectacles flying across the floor, and with a ferocious baring of teeth, bit down hard onto Carmody's wrist.

Carmody yelped, and finally the gun released. Edgar pulled away and rolled back into the refrigerator, the gun in his hands.

Tyrel pulled his sledgehammer hands around to Carmody and gave him two quick jabs, sending his head back onto the kitchen tile with loud claps. Carmody went limp, and after looming over him for a minute, Tyrel stood up, panting.

I put a hand on Tyrel's shoulder. "Thanks, T. You're getting a God damn fruit basket for Christmas."

He gave me a satisfied nod.

I checked Edgar, still cradling the gun like a live grenade. He was trembling, refusing to look up from the floor. It was going to take a moment before he'd return to us, I imagined.

And Wren? She stood near the kitchen table, oddly stiff. She stared down at Carmody with intensity. It wasn't until she lunged forward that I spotted the chef's knife in her hand. I flung myself across the table and reached for her arm as she slashed down at Carmody's face. I jerked her arm back, and the knife stopped just short of his nose. Tyrel reached in and helped me hold Wren, who was growling like an animal.

"Get off me!" she snarled. "I'm gonna kill him!"

"Wren, no. This isn't your way."

"He did this! He has to pay!"

"He will," I whispered. "But you can't kill someone. Not anyone. The price is just too high, Wren."

She loosened in our grip, and Tyrel let her go. I fished the knife out of her hand and handed it over to Tyrel. Tears streamed down her face as she grimaced.

"Why, Dorian? Why can't we ever win?"

"We will." I guided Wren to her feet and looked down at Carmody's unconscious frame.

Tyrel shifted uncomfortably nearby. I saw where this was going, and Tyrel needed to leave before he became an accessory to something.

"T?" I muttered. "Not to sound ungrateful or anything, but you might want to bounce."

He nodded and gave me a solid slap on the shoulder before slipping out the kitchen door.

Wren looked up at me in perfect grief. "What about Elle?"

Edgar mumbled, "Get more blood. We can still do the Curse."

I looked over to Edgar, now fumbling across the floor for his glasses.

"I don't need it anymore," I answered, then turned to the front room. "Isn't that right, Quinn?"

Gillette stood in the kitchen doorway, surveying the scene spread before her. Her eyes hovered in jerking motions, but her face was focused tight on Carmody's frame on the floor.

She replied, "Are you changing our arrangement again?"

"Yes, I am. You take the servitor out of Elle, and we hand Carmody over to you."

She crouched down and stared at Carmody's face.

"Come on, Gillette. This is what you really wanted. You were settling for a curse, but given the choice, wouldn't you rather take him home with you? Get really creative?"

Gillette looked Carmody over, then stood back up. "Agreed."

I reached down to give Wren a hand. She dried her face on her sleeve and took my hand. Then, with a sudden, fierce motion she pulled her foot up and smashed it across Carmody's jaw.

"There," she panted. "I feel better."

Edgar helped me fasten Carmody's wrists and ankles with some plastic zip-ties I kept in a drawer, and tied him to one of the kitchen chairs. Carmody was secured, and the outsiders were out the door. I was left with the Swains and Gillette.

And one servitor about to become homeless.

CHAPTER THIRTY-FIVE

I led everyone down into the work room, Edgar carrying Elle in his arms. I spread them out around the tight space, ensuring Gillette had enough room to do her work. I cleared the curse materials from the table and helped Edgar sit Elle on its surface. It wasn't large enough for her to lie down, so I stood behind her and held her shoulders steady as she bobbed and swayed. Edgar lifted the charm from around her neck, and returned to Wren's side, holding her hand.

Gillette gave everyone a solid hand gesture to stay where they were, which was utterly unnecessary. I kept my focus tight as she turned to Elle. She was pliant in my hands; I could guide her forward or backward as Gillette made several waves of her hand to the sides of Elle's face. Gillette's energy snaked out of her body, rushing across the work table in waves. If I didn't know better, I'd suspect it was the typical energy pattern of an untrained novice who hadn't learned yet how to center properly. But as the energy pushed and pulled into and out of Elle's body, I recognized the gentle pressure it was putting at the base of her mainline.

A subtly cyclonic motion formed in the room, pulling up at the center of Elle's crown chakra. This was slow, deliberate work, and I respected it. Emil had drilled into my brain the value of slow pressure when it came to sharp-edged magics. And as I observed and palpated Gillette's procedure, I recognized that this was a working for which I was utterly unqualified. It was no wonder Ches had utterly ruined this thing simply by creating it.

The ebb and flow of the extraction energy was nearly mesmerizing. My grip on Elle's shoulders loosened, and she twisted on the table and swung a foot at Gillette. The servitor was indeed awake and aware, and the gravity of the moment had settled on whatever passed for its mind. Gillette parried the kick with preternatural ease as if she had read the shift in energy before the kick was thrown. I re-secured my grip on Elle's shoulders, receiving a pointed glare from Gillette.

A rumbling gurgle bubbled up from Elle's throat as the energy in the room tightened. Tiny fingers slashed out against my arms, but I held them fast. The gurgle blossomed into a scream. I gave the Swains a warning look. To their credit, they were holding their ground.

Gillette reached out and planted her palm on Elle's forehead, her face adopting a menacing glare.

"The trap?" she grunted.

"Hmm?"

"You wanted this thing?"

"It's time?"

"Quickly."

I nodded Edgar over to take Elle in his hands while I withdrew to the bottom of my worktable. I had an old perfume bottle handy, a trinket I'd picked up on one of my travels. I had never actually planned on trapping a soul in the damned thing. It was just one of those things practitioners owned. And yet here I was, ready to drop a living servitor directly into the tiny blown glass vial.

"Anything I need to do with this?" I asked Gillette, brandishing the bottle near my face.

"Is it consecrated?"

I wiggled the bottle again.

"You're kidding, right?"

"Never mind. It was just a thought."

Gillette sighed. "Do you have any quicksilver? Sandalwood?"

"Sandalwood I got. Mercury is toxic, so no go on that one. Look, if it's an issue, just kill the thing."

"No, no," she growled. "You wanted it, we can do this. I can hold it for now." Gillette looked over her shoulder at my racks of reagents, now stacked one on top of another to make room for the guests. "Clear the glass with frankincense."

I jumped to the rack and ran a finger along the clear mason jars until I found the tiny nuggets of resin I was looking for.

"Got it." I fished out a single tiny crumb of frankincense and dropped it into the bottle, following that with some grapeseed oil. I spun the oil along the interior of the bottle, the nugget of resin swirling it top to bottom. I could feel the Veil thickening around the glass. Satisfied it was thoroughly cleared of latent energies and now fortified against spiritual permeability, I emptied the oil and the resin into the leftover slag inside my cauldron.

"Now what?"

"Thinking," Gillette mumbled.

Elle kicked again, landing a solid strike to the inside of Gillette's thigh. She exhaled hard, and cleared her throat.

"Rosemary," Edgar offered.

"Rosemary?" I echoed.

"Strong protection reagent," he explained. "Creates a barrier along the interior of the Veil. Plus it acts as a memory inducer thereby creating a cycling memory state for the entity—"

"—which keeps it docile while in storage. Jesus, it's so simple, it's brilliant."

Gillette grunted, "So, now would be good."

I fished out a couple rosemary needles from another jar and dropped them into the bottle. The oil wasn't thick enough to swirl. In fact, it only served to stick the needles to the side of the bottle. I fished them around the best I could, and as I reached for more grapeseed oil Gillette sighed.

"Good enough. Bring it here."

I handed the vial to Gillette, who took it in her free hand. Her other hand maintained its hold on Elle's forehead.

Elle's eyes swished left to right, and when they found me, they pulled up in the middle. It was panic. I couldn't tell whose… Elle's or the servitor's.

Gillette huffed three times in a row, and her energy rushed out of her crown chakra, cascading over Elle's body. With a clench of her fist over Elle's bangs, the energy shifted, almost crystallizing over Elle's body.

"*Exu-de*," she chanted in a near-baritone. "*Exu-de. Exu-de.*"

Elle's body spasmed. Choking noises filled the room, and her hands flew up to her throat.

"Hold her!" Gillette bellowed.

I reached for one arm, and Edgar gripped the opposite from behind.

Gillette continued her mantra as Elle's face contorted into a mask of desperation. Elle's throat throbbed, likely from her gagging and gasping, though it wasn't hard to imagine something writhing up through her windpipe.

"Her lips are turning blue," Wren cried from the corner.

"Almost over," Gillette stated. "*Exu-de! Exu-de!*"

Elle's spine stiffened, then wrenched backward, pulling her head away from Gillette's hand. Her eyes blinked rapidly behind her, searching Edgar for some kind of intervention. Her mouth drew open, gaping as hot breaths lashed out into the air. Gillette held the vial above her mouth.

With one final shift, releasing the hardened energy into something blazing hot like molten lava, Gillette shouted, "*Kata tropho!*"

I nearly blacked out from the incantation. It was as if the gravity in the room shifted to the ceiling and back again. Something sprayed against my face. It could have been spittle, possibly blood if we were very unlucky. Elle's hand went limp in mine, and her body fell back onto Edgar, sending us both sprawling behind the work table to keep her from dropping to the floor.

The single bulb light hanging in the work space flickered, settling back to a steady glow as I caught my balance.

I blinked up at Gillette, clearing my head in time to watch her cap the perfume bottle. She stretched her neck, and finally centered herself as her energy snapped back into her body like a regiment of well-drilled soldiers. The woman was a master, and I was utterly glad I hadn't managed to make an enemy out of her during this process.

She held out the bottle, and I stood up to take it gingerly in my fingers. She stared at me with hard intent, her eyes probing me, thoughts cascading behind her pupils.

"Our business is complete," Gillette finally said.

I stared at the bottle. It didn't look any different than before. It was still the same stupid glass trinket as before. I couldn't feel the first sign of energy within it. Of course, no decent soul trap would leak energy. Such a deceptive little thing.

I looked over to Elle, sprawled over Edgar's torso. He cradled her carefully, bending his knees at an awkward angle to keep her from twisting uncomfortably. Wren rushed forward to help him, pulling her legs away from the table. The two of them lifted her off the table entirely, settling her on the ground between them.

"Baby?" Wren whispered, stroking the side of her face.

I saw her chest moving. She was breathing. More importantly, her eyes shifted behind their lids. This was a good sign. She wasn't just breathing, she was dreaming.

"I think it worked," I offered, setting the vial down carefully in the center of the table.

"It did," Gillette corrected. "Wasn't easy. This girl is a labyrinth."

Edgar gave me a weary smile and looked to Gillette. "Thank you. You have no idea what this means to us."

She nodded, then pulled me aside. "Listen, Lake. I know you're used to Presidium double-talk, and assuming that everyone's lying to you. But there is a world where we professionals treat one another with respect. You just have to escape this artificial world the Presidium has created to realize it."

"Thanks, but I've heard how screwed up the outside world is. I don't think I'm ready for that."

She leaned in and whispered, "I know it was Baker. I recognized her energy."

I stiffened.

Gillette continued, "I'm tired of this. I can pledge her safety on one condition."

I whispered, "What condition?"

"You continue her training. I watched your curse working. Looks like you retained Desiderio's education well enough. You keep her from doing anything like this ever again, and I'll suspend my judgment."

I took a deep breath, then nodded.

She considered me for a moment, then sniffled. "I'll collect Carmody."

Gillette stepped around me for the stairs. As she took the first step onto the stairs, the light flickered again. She froze.

As did I.

Edgar whispered, "What was that?"

I looked over to Gillette, who turned slowly to me, her eyes wide.

"Lake?"

"Yeah?"

"Check that bottle."

I turned to my work table. The vial sat still in the direct center of my Golden Spiral. I waved my palm over the bottle, palpating the energy.

The light flickered again.

More importantly, tiny needles of white-hot energy lanced into my skin.

"Oh, shit."

Gillette rushed back into the room, and the two of us twisted away as the tiny vial of glass shattered on the table.

I brushed the glass off my arms, checking for blood.

"You okay?" I asked Gillette.

She looked up and down, turning around, his eyes scanning the entire space.

"It's out," she whispered. "What did you do?"

"What do you mean it's out?"

"The bottle didn't hold, obviously."

"I said kill the thing if this was a problem!"

"Where's your frankincense?"

I marched over to the shelf and grabbed the mason jar, jingling it in front of Gillette.

Edgar brushed past my shoulder and snatched the bottle from my hand. "Dorian?"

"Yeah?"

"That's myrrh."

I double-checked the bottle. And my stomach dropped.

I'd studied the hermetic arts since I was eighteen years old. I was taken under Emil Desiderio's wing and instructed over the period of ten long, laborious years. He took no shortcuts. At times, I wanted to punch him in the face. The better years of my youth were spent not in dating, getting drunk and screwing, but in studying dead languages and memorizing correspondences within sacred geometries.

And surely somewhere along those years I learned the difference between frankincense, a powerful Veil-strengthening warding resin, and myrrh, another tree resin that served to blur the boundaries between the spiritual world and the mundane.

"Oh, fuck me."

The light flickered aggressively, sending long shadows into the space. The temperature dropped rapidly.

"It's drawing energy from the room," I whispered. "Damn it. Everyone, upstairs. Now!"

Gillette and I gathered the Swains and almost literally shoved them up the flight of stairs. I was the last one to the steel door, and as I turned to close it behind me, I could have sworn for a moment that I caught two yellow eyes glaring at me from the darkened room below. It sent the hairs on my arms on end.

I closed the door and pushed against it with my back, catching my breath.

"Okay," I muttered. "That was my bad."

Gillette paced an impatient circle. "I did say frankincense, didn't I?"

"Yes."

"Of all the reagents you could have mistaken for frankincense—"

"I know, Gillette. Thank you, though."

The door was still and solid behind my back. Nothing of spiritual merit would be penetrating that door, and though the surrounding structure of the building was made of hermetically weaker material, the power of doors and corridors translated onto the other side of the Veil. Yet despite the comfort that door offered, I knew something horrible was in the basement.

And I couldn't let it just stay down there.

I looked over to the Swains, gathering Elle onto the futon. "Guys? Stay here."

I marched across the front room and reached for the silver blade mounted over my mantel.

Gillette gave me a quizzical glance. "You're going back down there?"

I held the darquelle up to my face. "This thing has been a pain in my ass long enough. There's no way I'm just going to let it squat in my fucking basement."

"You realize it's consuming all of the latent energy built up in that room?"

I thought about Emil's Library, and had to put faith that he had worked some significant natural wardings into the cabinet itself. If something incorporeal had managed to tap into the content of those texts, this thing could turn into a living nightmare in a big damn hurry.

"Sooner I deal with it, the better."

A tremble vibrated the floorboards, and Wren snapped her head up.

"What was that?"

We all jumped as some kind of scratching crash erupted from the basement.

"That had better not be what I think it is," I grumbled as I rushed into my kitchen and fished a flashlight out of the junk drawer. If that thing had gotten into Emil's Library, this was about to turn into an even bigger nightmare.

Gillette leaned against the kitchen door frame, hands in her pockets. "Good luck."

So much for Gillette's cooperation. "Thanks."

I turned to the steel door and centered myself.

One of us was going down.

I opened the door slowly, peering down into the darkness, gripped my flashlight and darquelle, and stepped into the shadows.

Chapter Thirty-Six

The light at the bottom of the stairs flickered back to life. A pall of dust wafted into view, clouding my line of sight into the work space as I descended the steps one-by-one. The air smelled of mold and gypsum, charged with a sharp twang of ozone. I waved at the dust in futility as I followed the wall to the Library cabinet. I ran a hand along the top and front. The doors were closed, and the wood felt unmolested. This thing hadn't made a move for the texts. Good.

Something skittered in the distance, too far away to reasonably be within the same room. I waited for a moment, darquelle held out in front of me as the dust cleared. The bulb overhead streamed beams into the space, and soon a dark patch in the room presented itself. I advanced, energy centered, knife held tight. As more dust settled, I realized I wasn't looking at a hellish thoughtform mutant, but a hole in my wall. I blinked against the remaining dust and inspected the damage. A single thickness of sheetrock and a frame wall separated my work space from an entire coal cellar I hadn't realized existed. I had always assumed the basement was smaller than it ought to have been, but I never had the wherewithal to look into whether there was more to the basement than the work space. Now I knew.

I peered into the darkness beyond the hole. It was deep. The basement was as wide as the entire house, I figured, which left lots of room for this thing to lurk. Room without any light. I switched on my flashlight and scanned it back and forth. I found a nearby rock wall, most likely a footing for my fireplace, and a series of old steamer pipes that probably hadn't been used for a half-century.

More skittering caught my attention, and I slowly embraced the uncomfortable fact that I was going to have to chase this damn thing in this pitch black coal cellar. Lovely.

I took my first two steps into the dark space, still partially illuminated by the bulb shining behind the hole in the wall, and steadied my footing as I inched through the drywall debris. The temperature dropped sharply the deeper I advanced. I wasn't sure if that was a function of the coolness of the basement or the servitor sucking in more energy to power itself. The thing was removed from a soul source, now. It was going to starve itself back down to a thoughtform state if it didn't find a new source to feed upon. Which was why I was bothering to hunt the thing down myself. Given time and opportunity, it would latch onto someone else, and I couldn't vouch for the wardings on a cellar I hadn't known existed.

A length of wood groaned to my right, and I shined the flashlight quickly to the side. Dust trickled from the joists, most likely unseated by my guests upstairs.

The skittering resumed, this time clacking against the stone floor rapidly toward me. I spun and slashed out with my darquelle. A sickening wheeze filled my hearing, and a subtle fog washed across my face.

I slashed again, but my blade only sliced through the fetid air.

The wheeze dropped into a growl.

White-hot trails of lancing pain sliced down my back. I yelped and stepped forward, shoulder-blades convulsing backward against the heat. I coughed and rolled my shoulders, trying to work through the pain as quickly as I could while getting my blade back in front of me.

A pair of yellow eyes glared at me for a split-second in the gloom before my flashlight shone on top of it. The eyes vanished, and nothing more than floor joists and a thick support post appeared in the beam.

The pain throbbed as something wet trickled down the small of my back. This thing had drawn blood. Amazing. It was a thought. A simple thought. And now it had enough power to open my skin.

I heard the skittering again, this time moving in a wide arc from right to left. The damn thing was circling me like a predator. I kept the silver blade centered on the noise and decided to go on the offensive. I plunged forward, swinging the blade into the air. There were no shrieks or wheezing. I hit nothing.

The air to the left of my elbow chilled rapidly, and I ducked down on reflex. A wash of cold air and a growl flooded my ears. I rolled against the wounds on my back and slashed up above me. This time I connected. The servitor released a moan, almost baleful.

Almost feminine.

This thing was a manifestation of Ches's thoughts. Before it became twisted by hate and starvation, it had been part of her very mind. And now it was a blend of Ches and Elle. It was difficult to imagine those two people stitched together into a being of hate and revenge, but here it was, lurking in the darkness with me. Wounded.

Killing this thing became suddenly painful to me. But that was my thoughtform. Love of those two people. Granted, my love for Ches had diminished. No, it had vanished.

Or had it?

I took in as much of my surroundings as the flashlight would allow. No windows. No doors. No natural exits. The only exit was the hole this thing made in the wall. That, granted, was a feat. And it probably burned up most of its remaining soul energy to do that much. It was trying to escape, though, and probably couldn't navigate through the wardings on the steel door frame. Creatures of energy, living and unliving, tended to follow architecture. Especially old architecture. There's something about the planning and building and living in a house that imprints hard and fast boundaries on the other side of the Veil. Which was probably why such beings preferred forests and swamps and anything but cities.

I backed swiftly to the hole in the wall. This was its only exit. Sure, given enough time, it may find a way out. Perhaps the plumbing leading up into the walls or down into the sewer. Perhaps some innocuous rat hole leading to the street. But it would take as much time to find as it would me. At least, that was my theory.

I reached up behind my shirt and smeared my finger across one of the gashed in my skin. It stung like hell, but it gave me a potent warding reagent, and one which I didn't have to charge. Reaching behind me, I painted four solar crosses on what I decided would be the four corners of the hole the servitor knocked through the sheetrock. It was quick and dirty, but the warding snapped into life with verve. This fly-by-wire magic wouldn't last long. Hopefully I wouldn't need it to.

"There!" I shouted into the darkness. "You're trapped in here with me, now."

I paused to listen for any more skittering, wheezing, or even a response.

"You're buried underground. You getting that yet?" Still no response. I had to try and rattle this thing to find it. "The first homo sapiens had this figured out. You trap a soul underground, it can't escape to haunt the living. And that's what waits for you here. Slow death and decay."

Something fell in the corner of the cellar. I moved the flashlight to see, and found an old tin can rolling on its side.

"You've long outlived your purpose. Even your creator wants you dead."

Skittering shot across the space directly in front of me, and I stabbed forward with my darquelle, hitting nothing.

"You don't like that, do you? What's the point in creating life if it's meant to die? We all have an appointed time, and if we attempt to extend that time, the Cosmos responds with unspeakable cruelty. I've seen it happen."

The energy in the basement shifted. It was sudden and dizzying. I wasn't sure what it indicated, but I braced for something to happen.

Yellow eyes blinked open several yards in front of me. I shined the flashlight in their direction. Instead of simply vanishing, a full-figured silhouette remained in its light, detailing a humanoid shape against the ragged brick and mortar wall of the cellar. The silhouette didn't approach as much as it grew larger against the brick. I brandished the darquelle nonetheless.

"Are you ready?" I muttered to the dark figure.

The yellow eyes blinked away.

Skittering.

Pain.

Fresh slashes across my chest and right arm sent pain flashing through my chest. This felt deep. Internal.

Like a heart attack.

I swished through the air with the blade, but the pain grew unbearable. I lost my breath. My chest heaved, trying to suck in any kind of oxygen. The floor slammed against my knees, but the only thing that cut through the panic of suffocating was the mind-shattering pain inside my ribcage.

The flashlight beam dulled into darkness. It couldn't have been the battery. I was blacking out. The remaining shadows scurried. The frenzy had begun. The damned shadows had been waiting for this moment for several months, now. They were ready for me to perish, and then escort me to whatever Hell awaited me.

Part of me was prepared. I had spent so much energy hunting down my soul. It was draining. It had robbed me of every good thing in my life. My career was in ruin. I lost my last chance at wealth. My friends had all suffered as a consequence of my actions or inactions. I was so damn tired.

The pain dulled, and on a deep level I understood I was dying.

Well, I had tried.

My vision blurred into the final darkness, and I sucked in one breath.

And saw Emil Desiderio.

He was hunched over his desk in our flat in London, hand-copying some stupid text he had loaned from a smelly Baltic fellow in the East End. This was his usual Saturday night thing. Copying. Translating. Doing anything but living a life that, by God, I was entitled to live. Ten years we had lived in this moldy flat, couched between a charming Pakistani family with an unbearably noisy toddler, and a twenty-something from Kent who liked to play punk music in the middle of the night.

Our flat was a maze of books, scrolls, cabinets, jars of reagents, and bric-a-brac from Emil's travels. I had long since explored the interesting items in his collection. All that remained was more work.

And I was sick of it.

He was particularly engrossed in this one particular translation. I caught a glimpse of the original text. Looked like Cyrillic. Whatever. The last important magic that came from Russia was wiped out by the Golden Horde. The Huns had well and truly driven magic west of the Caucasus, and all that remained were minds eager to explore every practical element of life. Ah, the Russian perspective. It was refreshing, really, but useless to a man like Emil.

So whatever had held his attention so thoroughly had to be historical, and thus of no use to me. I decided to take this opportunity to slip out. This was getting to be my regular thing. Weekends avoiding Emil, ditching and spending an evening at the Carpenters Arms with Genie and her friends. I had been working up the nerve to ask Genie out for weeks, but Emil's demanding schedule had made that nearly impossible. Still, she always managed to find me at the Arms, probably because she figured I would always find a way to sneak out on a Saturday night. That had to mean something.

"You're done with the Diometrides, then?" Emil grumbled as I tried to turn the door knob. Busted.

"Yeah."

"Care to present it for inspection?"

I sighed and stomped over to my desk. I had, in fact, completed my translation of the Diometrides text earlier that day. I hadn't double-checked it, though. That could take a good week. At that very moment, I didn't care. I snatched my composition book and tossed it onto Emil's desk.

He lifted his hand, keeping his quill from smearing onto his page, and turned slowly to glare at me with those bushy gray eyebrows. His eyes were deep, constantly ringed in dark circles as if he applied makeup each day to sell the whole world-weary look.

"You're angry," he cooed. "What is this?"

"The Diometrides."

"No. This attitude. This recent distaste for the studies you requested of me."

"Emil. I'm tired. I'm thirsty. Frankly, I'm bored."

He turned away. "You're allowing the demands of the flesh to cloud your focus."

"Too right, I am!"

"Then you will succumb to the flesh. This is what is left for you, Dorian. You have chosen to awaken to a reality that has no respect for the flesh." He turned back to me, his eyes oddly drawn and soft. "You cannot choose to return to ignorance."

"I just need a bitter, Emil. I did my work. I did the translation. I even cataloged that stupid box of crystals that Joe from Australia brought you. I need to blow off some steam."

"It is important to realize you are young now. When you are old enough to feel the weight of this other Life we have chosen, then you will realize the simple things are no longer available to you."

He reached up and gripped my hand. I jumped. He never moved this quickly.

"I have given you the key to a Cosmic endeavor, Dorian. Open the door. Step through the passage that leads to gnosis."

I pulled away, trying not to completely freak.

"Emil? You're hitting the vodka early tonight, aren't you?"

His eyes fell, and he shook his head, turning back to his text, though his quill didn't move.

I stood behind him. He was being completely weird. I mean, weirder than usual. I was ready for a tongue-lashing, some sermon about my responsibilities. But instead he gave me a half-drunk diatribe on gnosis.

The beer sounded real good at that moment. I stepped out of the flat and hustled down the street to the Arms. Genie and her usual crew were already there. They had bought me a pint. God, their faith in me was eerie! That night I had three pints, and I managed to get Genie's phone number. The beer gave me the courage to ask her out. Her beer gave her the grace to say yes.

It was going to be the best night of my life.

Then I returned to the flat and found Emil. He was lying on his bed. His arms and legs had been hacked away from his body. His face lay to the side, calm and accepting. Whoever had done this to him had his cooperation. He seemed ready to die, and my stomach dropped when I realized that he knew this was coming. That diatribe he gave me was to be his last words to me. And I practically ignored him.

Those words had been forgotten.

Until that moment as my flesh perished.

Another breath.

The pain rushed through my chest again.

This flesh. This agonized flesh. The heart could stop, and I may die. I may not even have a soul, but something of my mind remained. And that mind had broken free in that one fleeting second from this shadow world into which it was born.

I opened my eyes and took in the room. It was no longer dark. At least, it was perceivable. The walls were made of living shadows, all sharp-toothed, all reaching for me. These were imps, blasted, hateful little creatures of death no more potent on this realm than a swarm of hornets.

As my body crumpled away under the pain, my mind hummed with thoughts aflame.

I thought of Emil. I asked myself how he would have judged me at this moment.

That was easy enough. He would sniff at these simple creatures. They were nothing a basic Banishing Cross couldn't repel.

The Banishing Cross.

How utterly simple. It was the first lesson Emil had taught me, even before we had left New York for London. It was the cornerstone of all hermetical workings, at least for any novice. As one became naturally attuned to one's personal energy, the Banishing Cross became unnecessary.

But I had never visited this realm of existence. I had never crossed the Veil. And my heart was still pumping.

I centered my mainline and released a pure white light in the form of a cross, emanating from my heart chakra. I situated myself in the center of this cross, then fired the third axis out from my heart chakra. All lines of white light extended out as far as I could perceive the Cosmos, and at once I was anchored, an immutable fixed point in my personal universe.

The light intensified and awaited the banishing ritual. Some used the Sephiroth of Qabbala. Some invoked archangels. Emil had trained me in those early days to choose my personal angels, the forces of Good in my life that possessed the strongest meaning. In those early days, I had chosen my parents, Aunt Viv, and Emil as my banishing angels.

But this was a new life. I had new angels.

One by one I called them, firing them against the imps clouding me.

Edgar.

Wren.

Julian.

Ben.

The light burned away the shadows. One by one, the imps wilted, fled, dissolved.

Leaving only one shadow glaring at me with yellow eyes, wreathed in the white light of my burning intent.

I forced myself to my feet, gripping the darquelle with my palm against the hilt.

"And this one is for Elle."

I thrust forward, stabbing directly into the heart of the servitor.

White-hot energy spilled across my arms, against my chest, and out into the Cosmos along with a final baleful moan.

My face hit the floor.

Dust filled my nose.

The light dropped into immediate darkness.

My flashlight lay several feet away, shining at a few innocuous bricks.

Someone called my name. It was Edgar. Yes. Edgar.

I pushed against the filthy stone floor, wincing at the slashes in my back. I took several deep breaths, coughing out dust. But otherwise, my chest felt fine. No arrhythmia. No tightness.

My back, on the other hand, still hurt like hell.

"Dorian? You okay?"

I coughed again and tried to speak.

"Yeah," I croaked. "More or less."

A flicker of silver reflected the flashlight beam as I rolled to my feet. I snatched my darquelle and considered it in the low light.

Footsteps bounded down the stairs to the room behind me.

"Hey, man." It was Edgar's voice. "Holy shit!"

"I'm in here."

"What's back here?"

I turned to find Edgar peering through the hole in the sheetrock.

"Apparently I have a coal cellar."

"What about the thing?"

I paused and re-centered myself. The energy in the dank space was utterly terrestrial. Nothing was in flux. Nothing was drawing energy. I looked down to the darquelle and noted its disposition. When a ritual blade is first "blooded," it takes on a kind of life of its own. A kind of sinister cognizance that only seasoned Netherworkers can stomach. It wasn't easy to describe the fullness of character the blade exuded at that moment, but the best single word I could conjure was "sated."

"It's gone."

"For good?"

"Yeah. For good."

Edgar stepped into the darkness, putting a hand on my shoulder.

"You did it."

"I had help."

I dusted off my pants and picked up my flashlight. As the two of us returned to the artificial light of the work space and rounded my table toward the stairs, I paused by the cabinet housing Emil's Library. Placing a hand on top of the dark wood, I released a single simple thank you out into the Cosmos. If there was any kind of meaningful existence for Emil, if the Dark Choir hadn't utterly consumed his soul by this point, I hoped he had the means to sense that one thin point of light I had sent out into the hereafter.

When I reached the top of the stairs, there was no sign of Gillette or Carmody.

I turned to Edgar. "Where's Gillette?"

"She called a cab. Stuffed Carmody in it like some drunk asshole."

"Didn't even say goodbye. Figures."

"If it's worth anything, she did ask me to tell you never to call her again."

"So, the usual then?" I looked over Edgar's shoulder. "How's Elle?"

"See for yourself."

I stepped into the front room, and found Wren holding Elle's head in her lap, stroking her hair as Elle stared up at the ceiling. Those eyes shifted to me as I stood in front of them, and one thin, but glorious smile spread across her face.

"Hey, Dorian," she wheezed.

"Hey, kiddo. How are you feeling?"

"Hungry. Got any cereal?"

I have never been happier in my life to pour a bowl of Captain Crunch.

CHAPTER THIRTY-SEVEN

"So, how's your replacement handling the campaign?"

Julian's brows lifted in disapproval as he took a sip of his martini. "She's doing her best."

"Doesn't sound promising."

"She has to cut her teeth on my dropped work load just in time to find a new job, so I'd say she's coping better than expected."

"Oh, have some faith," I snickered as I did my level best to get the old man's attention behind the bar. He finally noticed me and nearly snapped back to life as he labored over pouring a whiskey. "I think he's going to die of old age before I get my Scotch."

Julian leaned back and shook his head. "How did you find this place, anyway?"

"It's not the Club, but it's cozy. Reminds me of a pub I used to frequent in London. Except, you know, there were actual people there."

Julian looked around the dark interior of the old pub at the foot of the Belvedere and smiled. "It's peaceful, anyway. I'll give you that." His face drew long as he folded his hands nervously in front of him.

"What's next for you?" I ventured.

"I was going to take a couple weeks in the Hamptons, but I'm already getting cagey. They'll have to put me on medication if I don't find something to do with myself."

"Any leads jobwise?"

He grimaced. "I'm not actually free to pursue anything at the moment. Ongoing investigation."

"You're lawyered up, I assume."

"I'll be fine."

The old man set a fresh lowball on the table in front of me, and I gripped it tightly, mustering the will to ask the question.

"So. This kid."

"You're asking me this question, aren't you?"

"The individual who leaked this had to assume the allegation was genuine."

"Just political mudslinging. Doesn't have to be actual mud. The public just has to think it's dirty."

I wasn't eager to detail my involvement with Carmody's actions. It wouldn't have helped.

"I'm not trying to butt into your personal business, Julian. You know that. I'm just trying to support you, for what that's worth."

He withdrew for a moment in his chair. Something clicked in his brain as he unfolded himself and leaned toward the table.

"I was nineteen. He was sixteen. We met at the Dayton Academy. We were kids, and we weren't smart enough to know what we wanted. We were just feeling our way through the emotions we had, and we didn't exactly have a lot of people we could talk to about it. I graduated and went to Georgetown, but that was still only a couple hours' drive away. My mistake was in not realizing the relationship needed to end, not because I had turned this magical number that made the relationship inappropriate. No, it needed to end because I was finding myself, he was going to find himself, and we were just chaining ourselves together out of fear of heartbreak. If I could go back and change how that happened, I would. In a second. That's my regret. We could have done so much more with that year than we did." He took a long sip of gin. "He ended up at Stanford, anyway. Haven't spoken to him since."

Julian sat straight, his chin up. Though his eyes were heavy and pinched, he didn't seem the slightest bit broken by the memory.

"I think we all have people we should have cut loose before it was too late," I offered.

"Do you?"

"You remember Carmen, right?"

"Oh. Right." He chuckled awkwardly. "What about now? You have someone new, right?"

"That got complicated."

Julian lifted his brow and nodded wearily.

That was something I hadn't made a plan for yet. Ches was still in Baltimore. We maintained our veneer of affection for the Swains when the business with Carmody was over. I hadn't told Ches about Gillette's ultimatum. The proper time never came to mention it. Besides. I deserved a small vacation from all of this.

The door opened, and a massive figure stepped inside, eclipsing the sunlight from the street as he moved into the bar.

"There he is," I quipped as I stood up and held out a hand.

Big Ben shook my hand and slapped my shoulder, nearly knocking me over. He was wore a polo shirt and jeans. I had never seen him out of white shirtsleeves before. The image was jarring.

"How you been, Dorian boy?" he sputtered.

"Busy as hell. Did you bring it?"

Ben reached under his arm and produced my bottle of Glenrothes.

I smiled and turned to the table. "You remember Julian Bright?"

He nodded and reached to shake Julian's hand. "Of course I do! Sorry to hear about your job."

Julian smiled and waved off the comment. "I'm fine." He gave me a lift of his brow. "Is this a meeting? Did I miss a memo?"

"Didn't send one, but yeah." I gestured for Ben to take a seat at our table. "Way I see it, each one of us finds himself at a crossroads here."

"I don't follow," Julian muttered.

"Well, Ben's hung up his towel after, what, twenty years at the Club?"

"More like eighteen," he corrected.

Julian frowned. "Retirement?"

Ben cocked his head, a chin roll puffing out as he grinned. "Forced retirement. I got a little hands-on with the Club staff."

"That was my fault," I added.

"So I was courteously asked to beat the bricks. Ain't that a kick in the ass?"

"I'm sorry to hear that," Julian offered, still giving me a dubious look. "You were a real asset to that place."

"I couldn't agree more," I said. "And I feel that wasting an asset like Ben would simply be criminal."

"What's your angle, Dorian?"

I held up my hands and gestured at the walls surrounding us. "This joint has been on the market for years."

Ben's eyes lit up, and he twisted in his chair as much as his girth would allow him.

Julian smirked and tapped his fingers on the table. "You want to buy a bar, Dorian? That's reaching, even for you."

"No, hear me out. I'm about to lose all of my properties, and my charms and hexes aren't the money-makers they used to be. My rental income was keeping me in the black, and I'm about to lose that. I figure I can't make enough from the property sale to live off, so I need a new enterprise."

"I hate to break this to you, Dorian," Julian said, "but if this place has been on the market for years, as you say, there might be a reason."

"It's not location, I'll tell you that. We're three blocks from the Inner Harbor, three blocks from Lexington Market, two blocks from City Hall. We're literally surrounded by offices and pedestrian traffic is strong."

"It's stronger on Charles."

"Not the point. The only thing keeping this place from taking off is poor management." I added, tossing my thumb over my shoulder, "And I don't think Grandpa Moses over there is exactly ready to shake things up."

Ben nodded. "Just enough room for a neighborhood bar. You don't want too much space. You want shoulders rubbing together."

"Right."

Julian laid a hand on the table and smiled. "Well, alright then. Best of luck with it, Dorian."

"Hold up. You're not off the hook, here."

"Didn't realize I was on a hook to begin with."

"Like I said, I don't have the liquid assets to invest in this place, especially after making sizable donations to a couple of churches."

Julian and Ben both gave me a look.

"It's complicated. Anyway, when the properties move in the next couple weeks, then I'll have probably half the asking price. Even if I negotiate down, it's a stretch."

Julian grumbled, "You're looking at me, Dorian. I'm not crazy about the way you're looking at me."

"You know Ben. You know he can manage this place. We'll get some servers who are younger, maybe another manager for nights and weekends."

Ben's head bobbed. "Thank you."

"Look, Julian. I could finance it, but I don't want to. Truth is, I think this is right for you."

"I'm a political strategist, Dorian. Not an entrepreneur."

"Which is why it works. Take another look at where we are. Who do you see walking up and down that sidewalk right now?"

He glanced over my shoulder at the businessmen and women yattering away on cell phones.

"These are the same people you've been working with. You know you can't work for Sullivan anymore, but that doesn't mean all of your contacts just vanished on you. You can still be relevant. The tavern is the original forum for discourse and conspiracy. If anything it'll free you up to open channels you couldn't risk before. And what's better, you get to have a private life."

Julian looked back and forth between Ben and me. "You realize nine out of ten hospitality startups in this city fail in their first year?"

"We get to cheat."

"How?"

"Well, I happen to know someone who can make charms and hexes. And we have Ben. Druid Hill meant something to me for the longest time. But you know what? I've outgrown it, now. And so have you. We both love to feel important. Well, now instead of fitting in, let's create the space, so that other people come to us."

Julian smiled. "I'll give you this, Dorian. This was the last thing I was expecting today. So you'll forgive me if I have to take a day or two before rejecting you out of hand?"

I smiled. "At least two days. Then you can reject me out of hand."

Julian nodded.

"Good. Let's go talk to Grandpa Moses. I popped in here yesterday and got his numbers. See? I do my homework."

"Fine, fine."

We stood up, and as soon as we moved for the bar, my phone rang.

"Crap. I need to take this," I explained. "Go ahead and start without me. Ask questions. Convince yourself this is a good idea."

I moved to the front windows where reception was better and answered my phone.

"Is this Dorian Lake?"

"Yes it is, Mister Jacobs. Thank you for returning my call."

"What do you need, Mister Lake?"

"I understand you have extra free time on your hands these days."

A long pause. "What do you want?"

"I have information for you, Mister Jacobs. Information regarding your recent spate of bad luck."

"I don't have time for this."

"You've been hexed, Jacobs. Trouble sleeping? Even worse trouble down below? Sound familiar? Listen, you can choose to blow me off, or you can listen to me and learn how to lift this hex. The choice is yours."

After an even longer pause, he answered, "What does that even mean?"

"It means you can get your life back. Your job. Your good name. Well, as good as it ever was. I mean, there's a reason the Cosmos has been giving you a good beating. You've been naughty."

"Who are you, Mister Lake? What is this about?"

"I'm the one who hexed you, Jacobs. And there's a way out. All I need from you is a little information."

"What kind of information?"

"I understand your firm represents a certain Joey McHenry, Sr.?"

CHAPTER THIRTY-EIGHT

McHenry shot me a smug grin as he stepped into the flimsy paneled construction trailer parked beside the recently demolished stamp factory on the far end of the Carrollton Manor site. A neatly dressed young woman accompanied him, lugging a fat valise. She set the case on the table and immediately began pulling out documents. Meanwhile, McHenry had taken position across the table from me.

I stood up and offered him a hand. To his credit, he shook it.

"Mister Lake."

I nodded, and we both took a seat. His assistant was already sliding papers in front of us. This was a well-oiled machine.

"And how have you been?" he added, pulling a pen from his jacket.

"Keeping busy, you know."

"That I do."

I bobbed my head at the assistant. "Mind if he and I speak privately?"

McHenry looked up at me and blinked. After a quick moment of consideration, he nodded to her. She hovered over her papers with an annoyed scowl, and finally left us alone in the trailer.

"So," McHenry began with a pluck of joviality, "you're about to become a very wealthy man. How does that feel?"

"I'd feel happier if I could get a decent single-malt for less than eighty dollars."

"Your perspective may change on that point very shortly."

I pulled out a thick brown clasped envelope. It was the same envelope McHenry had presented to me several weeks ago. "I doubt that, but I appreciate the sentiment."

"Tell me something, as I'm curious. What precisely changed your mind?"

"About?"

"Selling."

"I suppose I just decided to get over myself and do the right thing."

He chuckled. "That's good to hear. I'll have to admit something to you, Mister Lake. I've always admired your tenacity. Your dogged, sometimes insufferable vanity. I like that. I value that."

"What, vanity?"

"Absolutely. Here's a secret I'd like to tell you. It's a nugget of business wisdom I learned a long time ago, and if I had learned it earlier, I'd be a far more successful man."

I shrugged. "Go ahead."

"They say humility is a virtue. Well, my secret it this. Humility is for the weak and the worthless. There's no benefit to convincing yourself you don't matter. You believe that, then you'll never rise above."

"Interesting. I suppose not everyone is interested in rising above, though."

"This is true. Thankfully people like you and me have higher ambitions."

"Such as City Hall?"

He smiled and shrugged. "Politics isn't so different from construction. Both take planning and patience."

I pulled out the documents from the envelope and gave McHenry a grin. "I can't sell you my properties, McHenry."

His face froze, then he chuckled. "What's that now?"

"I've sold them to other interested parties."

"You've sold?"

"The interested parties being the tenants."

His grin finally melted. "You sold your properties to your tenants? Are you insane?"

"An argument could be made."

"How could they even—"

"Special program courtesy of Mayor Sullivan. Oh, and Congress. But it was his initiative, meant to keep this exact transaction from screwing people out of their homes."

McHenry sneered, then gathered up the papers in front of us, balling some of them up and shoving them back into his assistant's valise.

"For a moment," he grunted, "I thought you had finally snapped out of it. You just threw away a fortune."

"Why are you acting so pissed? I saved you money by doing this."

He paused and sighed. "We're done here."

McHenry grabbed the valise and turned for the door.

"We're not, actually. And you're going to want to sit down." He pretended not to hear me, so I added, "Five hundred and sixty-six thousand dollars' worth of unpaid taxes, Joey?"

He froze.

"Well, unpaid because you dodged them. There's a good way to do that, and then there's the way you actually did it, which, it turns out, is pretty damn illegal."

McHenry turned slowly to me, murder alive all over his face.

I gestured for the chair. "Sit. Let's talk."

He glared at me for a minute, then finally set the valise down and took a seat. This time it was my turn to pass papers over to McHenry.

"Improperly reported market values on properties, Joey? You're looking at Federal time for that."

His eyes skimmed over the documents Jacobs had copied for me. "Where did you get this?"

"From someone who needed a booster shot to their karma."

I gave him a few minutes to review the documents to be sure I wasn't bluffing him. When he leaned back in his chair and rubbed his eyes, I recognized that he knew I wasn't.

"What is this going to cost me?"

"Believe it or not, I don't want your money. I don't want to have to declare it on my W-2, and failing to do that would be wrong."

"You little prick! You think you're going to muscle me with some bullshit accounting? Do you have any idea what Hell I can make your life?"

"I'm actually very familiar with the Hell you can make my life, McHenry. But I don't think you fully understand the Hell I can visit on your head. Remember what I am."

McHenry smirked. "Two can play that game."

"You're referring to Miss Baker?"

His smirk vanished.

"You think you did your research, don't you? You think Del Carmody was the kind of person who looks to rise above? You trusted he would put you together with someone who could keep me occupied? Francesca Baker was a novice. In the end, she came to me to fix what she had broken. Want to know where Carmody is right now? If he isn't dead already, he's in the hands of people who will make him pray for death. So, you say vanity is a virtue? I'm the last one standing, McHenry. Maybe you should try a little humility for a change?"

His face paled. "What do you want?"

"You're going to pull your endorsement of Sooner. We only have a few weeks left until the election, but I suspect that without your support and your machine, Sullivan is going to kick Sooner's ass from here to Dundalk."

McHenry shook his head. "That's it?"

"It's enough."

He stared at the table. "Done."

I stood up and tossed the empty envelope onto the stack of papers in front of McHenry. "You can keep those copies for your personal records."

"That's twice in one conversation you refused my money, Lake."

"I suppose that's true."

"Don't you care?"

"A man once told me if I make the desires of the flesh my focus, then I'll succumb to them. I'm trying to focus on the things that are a little more permanent."

McHenry stared at me, and I realized there was simply nothing left to say. I took my leave of the trailer and stepped carefully past the bricks strewn across the muddy landscape that used to be a city block of Baltimore. When I reached the curb, I found a long black limo sitting across the street. A large man exited the driver's door and crossed to my sidewalk.

It was Reginald, Wexler's thug.

I stopped mid-step and watched as the rear window rolled down revealing Wexler's tight grin. Reginald stood at my elbow, and instead of causing a scene, I decided to approach the limo.

"Meeting with McHenry, Lake?" Wexler purred.

"Tying up old business."

"You were warned, Lake. You were warned not to involve yourself with this election."

"And I haven't lifted a finger to campaign for Sullivan."

"There's campaigning, and then there's campaigning."

I shook my head. "I didn't use magic."

"Is that a fact?"

"If this man was stupid enough to let someone like me stumble over his cowboy accounting, then he deserves what he gets."

"Now, Mister Lake, we both know you didn't precisely 'stumble upon' anything. More accurately, you used a hex to leverage a key individual into unseating this information. So, let's be honest. You did use magic to interfere with this election."

"I suppose that depends on how you look at it."

She laughed and looked forward thoughtfully. "This affair with Quinn Gillette has concluded?"

"It has."

"I need not tell you how awkward the *verum inviolata* was for my associates. A great deal of inconvenience, all around."

"I suppose I should thank you people for not finding a way to side-step it."

Wexler's brows lifted in amusement. "There were ample opportunities."

"So why did you play ball, then?"

"It was suggested that you were poised to eliminate a particularly noisome entity, and in doing so would show your quality to our organization."

"Gillette did the heavy lifting."

"That's not how I understand it."

I nodded. It was profoundly unsettling to receive a compliment from the Presidium, no matter how back-handed.

"At any rate," Wexler continued, "it would behoove you not to attempt such manipulations in the future. They may not be viewed with quite the same indulgence."

"Understood."

Wexler rolled up her window, and Reginald gave me a curt nod before disappearing back into the limo. The car pulled away, leaving me on the side of the street looking over the demolished city block.

I pulled my phone and dialed a number.

"Hello?"

"Hey, Ches. It's Dorian."

"Hey." After a long pause, she added, "How's Elle?"

"Better. Listen, I have something I need to tell you."

"Here it comes," she mumbled.

"Here what comes?"

She exhaled into the phone. "The whole 'we never talked about our emotions' speech that you've probably rehearsed for a week now. I only say that because I've been rehearsing, too."

A grin crept onto my face. "Oh, really?"

"How long is yours? I got mine down to a minute-twenty."

I chuckled. "Actually, I wanted to talk about Gillette."

Long silence. I had her attention.

"You're safe, Ches. And your family."

"Okay?"

"She's willing to forgive. Maybe not forget. But there's a condition."

"Oh, God," she sighed. "Alright, what's her pound of flesh?"

"You wanted to learn from me? Well, that's good because I'm now responsible for keeping your nose clean."

Ches laughed, then cleared her throat. "Wait, you're serious."

"It was Gillette's condition. I continue your training in the Craft. Hey, the way I see it, you have a little knowledge, and you know, dangerous thing and all that."

"Yeah, that's become painfully clear."

"I had a good teacher. Well, he wasn't a good man, but he was an excellent teacher. Strict. Hard-ass. Thorough. He didn't let me cut corners. He never let me stumble into a dangerous working. I suppose I never really appreciated how important the basics were until recently."

She released a sigh of relief. "Thank you."

"Don't thank me yet. I'm just as hard-nosed as Emil."

"I can sniff out bullshit, remember?"

"Oh, right. I'll be in touch. I have to get some kind of plan together, make a list of books you're going to need. I probably have most of them here. And there's a lot more we have to discuss if we do this. Expectations I'll have. Tools you'll need to acquire. And we'll definitely have to get you working on your Banishing Cross."

"Can't wait!"

I hung up and walked up the street to Amity.

CHAPTER THIRTY-NINE

"That's it?"

"What were you expecting?"

"I don't know. Something less bullshitty."

"The guy gave me paperwork."

I crouched down and surveyed the skull in the glass case Edgar had set onto my work table. It looked for all purposes just like a human skull, but with an elongated jaw.

And of course, the fangs.

"How does someone certify a vampire skull?"

"The guy bought it from a Collector in Khartoum. It's supposed to have been encased sometime around Napoleon. The identity is unknown, but he said it's Egyptian." He leaned in to me. "Showed me a slide of tissue from the cheekbone. The tissue was still living."

"You do realize that's a baboon skull or something?"

"Why do you have to ruin my moment?"

"I just hate to see someone pull one over on you, is all."

"So you're saying you don't believe in vampires?"

"That's exactly what I'm saying." I wandered back around the work table to inspect the masking tape holding a sheet of plastic over the hole knocked into my wall. In flusher times, I would have called Tatapoulis to come open it up and finish out the rest of the cellar, but that would have to wait until the bar turned an actual profit.

Edgar grumbled, "Well, I'm keeping it anyway. I don't care what you say."

"Go right ahead, Edgar. It's your thing. If you want, I can mount it over the bar after we finish the lacquer."

"You guys decide on a name yet?"

"Julian wants to go with Light Street Tavern. I said that was too generic, but he insists that generic is the way to go downtown if you want to draw the business set."

"What did you want to go with?"

"I don't know. I'm kind of leaning on Julian for the marketing side of things."

"So what are you doing for this whole thing, exactly? I mean, I'm not trying to sound like a dick, but are you doing anything over there?"

"Yes, I'm doing stuff."

"What?"

"Stuff."

"Okay."

"Hey, wood enchantments are draining enough. You try charging a bar full of paneling and see how much time you have for market analysis."

He held up his hands and chuckled. "Sorry, man. Just asking."

"Well, your daughter is about to get into the petit verdot, so maybe we ought to move this upstairs."

Edgar craned his neck back to the stairs. "Elle? Don't!"

Elle's voice stammered from the open door at the top of the stairs. "Oh my God, Dad!"

Edgar smirked at me. "That's creepy, by the way."

"What can I tell you? I have a very close relationship with the hooch in my house."

He leaned against the wall and crossed his arms, smiling to himself. "I don't know if I ever said thank you."

"You did. Like, a dozen times already. But you're welcome."

"What's the word on you and Ches?"

"Nothing new. Things are still kind of weird."

"You two seemed to work. I hate to hear that."

I waved him off. I wasn't eager to discuss Ches with him at the moment.

"So," he muttered as he shoved his hands into his pockets, "it's too bad you couldn't catch the guy who made that servitor thing."

I looked up at Edgar. His eyes watched me over his spectacles. My blood chilled slightly. He was using his serious voice. He never used his serious voice.

"I suppose that's true."

"Yeah, man. Too bad. Because Wren probably would have wanted to know he wasn't still out there."

"I don't think she has to worry about that."

"You said it was woman who made this thing, though. Right? It had to be a woman that made it."

I considered Edgar for a second. "How long have you known?"

"About as long as you. Came to check on you that day when you two were talking behind the house. Overheard you shouting at her. Kind of hard not to."

"Why didn't you say anything?"

He shrugged. "You tell me. I'm still trying to figure it out."

"Maybe because she made an honest mistake?"

He raised an eyebrow.

"Okay, maybe not so honest. But she was under pressure."

Edgar unfolded his arms, ran a hand over his hair, and moved to collect his case.

"I'm sorry," I offered.

"Wren doesn't know," he muttered. "We should probably keep it that way."

I watched as Edgar gathered his bogus vampire skull and hustled up the stairs. After a moment collecting myself, I followed. Elle and Eddie were in the kitchen trying to roll dough over the old pizza stone I forgot I owned.

"I don't know guys," I quipped. "Looks kind of under-done to me."

Eddie stuck his tongue out at me.

The kids continued to wrestle with their pizza as I snatched the bottle of wine teetering precariously close to Elle's grasp and brought it back into the front room to refresh Wren's glass. She gave me a tired smile and returned her attention to the television.

"How's it looking?" I asked, settling myself on the arm of the futon.

"Sullivan, so far. He's kicking the shit out of Sooner."

I watched the local coverage of the election for a minute, taking in cleansing breaths. McHenry had held to his agreement, and Sooner's media presence dwindled to jack shit. By the last debate, Sullivan was skewering Sooner on every conceivable issue, especially since he no longer had McHenry's money to hire debate coaches. It didn't hurt that Sooner effectively admitted his campaign was bankrupt a week prior to the election.

"Feeling good?" Wren asked over her shoulder.

"I feel good for Baltimore."

"But what about you?" she prodded, laying a hand on my knee.

I gave her hand a squeeze. "Trying to focus on something more permanent."

Edgar shoulder-checked me as he dropped himself next to Wren. "Wuss."

After an hour watching the midterms' coverage, the Swains called it an early evening to get the kids home on a school night. I sent them off with a wave from my stoop and closed the door behind me.

And at last, I was alone in my home.

The television continued to flicker with election coverage, but I put it on mute. The silence in the house was deafening. For the first time in a month, I really sat down and thought about what nearly happened, how close we had come to disaster.

How close I had come to a real relationship.

I took a long, cleansing breath and paced in the room. Lingering on this wasn't helpful. Instead, I focused on Sullivan's face on the television. He was winning. The good guy was winning. And despite every effort from the powers that be, a cheeky, little bastard on Amity Street helped make that happen.

The thought coasted me through the wave of depression threatening to overtake my brain. I paused by my window to look out onto the street. The lights from downtown reflected off the low clouds hanging over the city. Soon, one of those lights would be my bar. I wasn't just buying into the people of Baltimore anymore. I was buying into the very heart of the city. Finally, I was going to be a part of the city, and there was no getting rid of me, now.

Before I could close the blinds, a motion across the street caught my eye.

A blurry silhouette stepped to the side beneath a street light.

It was the shadow man.

I jerked myself away from the window, hiding behind the wall.

I had forgotten about him. When I last saw him, I had assumed he was McHenry's hitman operating under some powerful glammer. But that wasn't Ches standing across the street.

I fumbled for the darquelle on the wall beside me and peered back out the window. The shadow man was still there, and for the most fleeting of moments, I thought I caught a glimpse of his face through the glammer.

It was his eyes that I saw. Crystal blue and penetrating. There was no way I should have seen those eyes through that glammer.

He wanted me to see them.

With a marked casual disregard for my notice, the shadow man tipped his hat to me and walked down the street.

I stood frozen for a good while, still gripping my darquelle, staring out my window.

Well, shit. This was going to be interesting.

ACKNOWLEDGMENTS

I'd like to thank the miracle-workers at Curiosity Quills for taking a chance and transforming the Dark Choir novels into reality.

I'd also like to acknowledge the unceasing labors of my beta-readers and critique partners, who in turn keep me writing... and keep me honest.

Lastly, I want to thank my wife, Courtney, for incalculable hours of patience, support, and conspiracy.

About The Author

J.P. Sloan is a speculative fiction author, primarily of urban fantasy, horror and several shades between. His writing explores the strangeness in that which is familiar, at times stretching the limits of the human experience, or only hinting at the monsters lurking under your bed.

A Louisiana native, Sloan relocated to the vineyards and cow pastures of Central Maryland after Hurricane Katrina, where he lives with his wife and son. During the day he commutes to the city of Baltimore, a setting which inspires much of his writing.

In his spare time, Sloan enjoys wine-making and homebrewing, and is a National-ranked beer judge."

THANK YOU FOR READING

© 2015 **J.P. Sloan**
http://jp-sloan.com

Please visit http://curiosityquills.com/reader-survey to share your reading experience with the author of this book!

The Department of Magic, by Rod Kierkegaard, Jr.

Magic is nothing like it seems in children's books. It's dark and bloody and sexual—and requires its own semi-mythical branch of the US Federal Government to safeguard citizens against ever present supernatural threats.

Join Jasmine Farah and Rocco di Angelo—a pair of wet-behind-the-ears recruits of The Department of Magic—on a nightmare gallop through a world of ghosts, spooks, vampires, and demons, and the minions of South American and Voodoo god shell-bent on destroying all humanity in the year 2012.

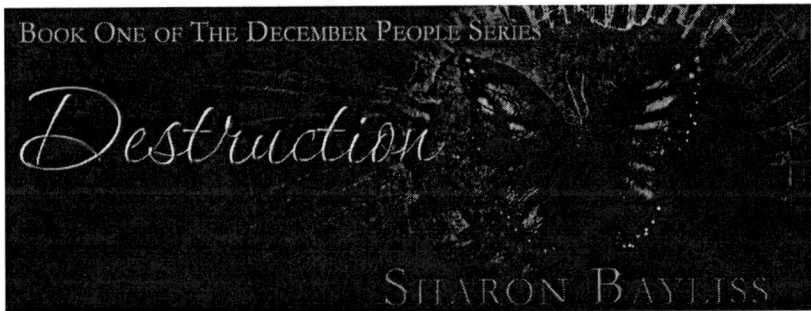

Destruction, by Sharon Bayliss

When David's two lost children are finally found, he learns they suffered years of unthinkable abuse. The children claim to be dark wizards, and David believes they use this fantasy to cope with their trauma. Until, David's wife admits a secret of her own—she is a dark wizard too, as is David, and all of their children.

Now, David must parent two hurting children from a dark world he doesn't understand and keep his family from falling apart. All while dealing with the realization that everyone he loves, including himself, may be evil.

Sweet Dreams are Made of Teeth, by Richard Roberts
How does a nightmare hunt? He tracks your dreams into the Light, and chases them into the Dark. How does a nightmare love? With passion and obsession and lust and amazement. How does a nightmare grow up? With pain and grief and doubt and kindness and learning and dedication and courage. First Fang hunted, now he loves, and soon he'll have to grow up.

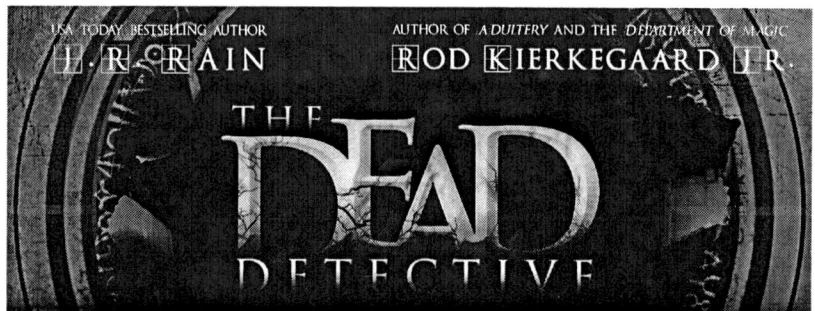

The Dead Detective, by J.R. Rain & Rod Kierkegaard, Jr.
Medical-school-dropout police detective Richelle Dadd is… well, dead. But that won't stop her from trying to hold on to her house in a divorce battle with a bitter husband. Or keep her from digging into her own murder, to discover who put the bullet into her heart. And it certainly won't stand in the way of finding out the reason she's been reanimated as a zombie assassin, no longer in control of her life.

Richelle will face off against Gypsy shamans, double-crossing ghosts, a partner she can't trust, and her own undead nature in a journey into the depths of the occult world and out the other side without losing her sense of humor—or humanity—along the way.

It's a good thing her deductive skills - and her aim - are still up to par.

CPSIA information can be obtained
at www.ICGtesting.com
Printed in the USA
LVOW11s1834150318
569996LV00001B/142/P